I0667305

Lola Unmasked
Part 1
S.K. Presley

Copyright © 2024 Independently published by S.K. Presley

2nd Edition

All rights reserved.

Lola Unmasked I by S.K. Presley is intended for a 18+ mature audience

No portion of this book may be reproduced in any form without written permission from the publisher or author, except as permitted by U.S. copyright law.

No part of this publication was created using Artificial Intelligence (AI). Furthermore, it is expressly prohibited to use any material from this publication, in whole or in part, for the purpose of training artificial intelligence systems or models, without the explicit consent of the copyright holder, and except for the use of brief quotations and mentions in book reviews. Any unauthorized use of this material may result in legal action. **I also request that you do not feed my work through AI systems for <u>any reason whatsoever.</u>**

This is a work of fiction. Names, characters, incidents, and places are the product of the author's imagination, and used fictitiously. Any resemblance to actual persons, living or dead, business establishments, events, or locales is entirely coincidental.

Cover Design: RJ Creatives

Editor Traci Bullman

CONTENTS

S.K PRESLEY

Hello Friends,

First, this humble indie author wants to give you a warm *thank you* for choosing my book. A book that is one of millions in the market that you could have picked to spend your time reading. I hope I don't disappoint.

Having said that, I do want to inform you that this is a series, and feel I need to give you a little heads up so you can decide how far you want to go with this. I know that there's a million labels, trigger warnings, tropes, etc... and while authors do their best to make sure that we cross all our T's and dot all our I's, it's almost impossible to do everything perfectly, though I try.

Hudson and Lola's story is quite dark and through them, we delve into just about every facet of human emotions throughout the course of almost two years spanning three books.

We push boundaries in this series, and the subject matter gets darker and darker as we go. I took the time to do research to make this book as accurate as possible, pulling from prior professional experience in the mental health field, as well as from various individuals I know who have gone through this exact thing. It is my hope that through this book others will find a place of solace and perhaps even healing from their trauma.

At the very least, I wish you a few hours of escapism, should you so need it.

I have said that for every couple's story I tell, I would do my best to give them justice. And so far, I feel like Hudson and Lola are right up there with Olivia and Colin from The Billionaire's Assurance duet.

Through Hudson and Lola, we discover a woman who is stuck in a domestic violence situation with two children who feels all hope is lost, until she of course, meets her hero. Someone perfect for _**her.**_

I hope you love them as much as I do.

Yours,

S.K. Presley

Trigger Warning

If you suspect that someone you know, or a child is being abused or is a victim of domestic violence, please reach out to your country and or States' child abuse and DV hotline.

Resources
USA Child Abuse:

1.800.4.A.CHILD http://www.childhelpusa.org/

USA Domestic Violence:

1-800-799-7233

FMC Inner dialogue of feeling "dead"

Dub-con-proceed into chapter 8, and 12 with caution.

Intense Sex Scenes

Dirty talk

Stalking

Knife Play

Offensive language by book character

Verbal description of child abuse/ and allusion to child starvation perpetrated by the father

If you like to buck while you're being fucked, this one's for you.

Hudson's ready to play.

Enjoy.

Prologue
Hudson

"See! Just look at you! This is why you need a woman, Hud! For fucking shit like this. *It's ridiculous.*"

I sigh and glance at my best friend, Clayton, who is folding his arms as he leans back against the wood plank of the horse stall we are occupying.

Well, we *were* occupying. He's still in there, *I'm* not.

Clayton's peering at me over the top of the stall wall. *I* am now a few feet over in the utility area. Tying a torn rag around my forearm from where I'd just cut a slash into my skin while fucking around trying to clean the shoe of my steed, Champ.

"I'm not just going to settle for *any* woman, Clayton. You know this already."

Using my teeth to tighten the knot, I grimace at the feel of the rag tugging on my skin. Grunting, I turn, throwing the tool I was using on Champ at Clay with a smirk.

"Yeah, well, *you need one.*" Clayton shoots back too humorlessly for my tastes.

His tone betrays his worry to me, he doesn't like me being alone like I am. Even though he's alone too.

When I point that out to him, he scoffs and waves me away. "It's not the same thing at all," he responds when we have these conversations. "You're a different type of breed than I am."

He's not incorrect either.

"Here, since you know every fucking thing, go on ahead and finish the job for me while I muck out Beauty's stall." I grit out, reaching over to grab the pitchfork I need.

I stomp over to Beauty, hearing the beginning of a storm in the distance, causing my third horse Nay Nay to bay loudly. The lightning and sound of thunder is getting closer, prompting me to hurry.

Cliché, I know, to name the black mare 'Beauty.' But you know what? Fuck cliché's. You only live once, so you should do what makes you happy even if other people don't understand it.

At least, that's what I tell myself.

I am oh so proud to say that I've lived *hard*. I've built a successful business from scratch worth around a billion dollars, give or take. It's the most successful construction company in the nearest few hundred miles and thanks to the tough-as-nails work ethic my mother instilled in me, I've made something of myself like I always wanted.

Some might call me a workaholic, but honestly, *I* say they just don't understand what it takes to be successful.

I have spent *years* honing my skills, ensuring that I hire the best of the best for my job sites. It's why my company has such an amazing reputation. That and the fact that I don't let shit slide. I run my company with an iron fist and that's how it should be. I won't accept half ass work, or people who slack.

If you want to succeed then you need to be the best and to put it frankly...I am the best in this business.

So people trust my business, my reputation, and my workers. And so far I've found that if you don't want too much, and treat people decently, you can live a good life.

I make good money regardless thanks to not being greedy. And I've finally reached a point where I can have the things I want as well as the things I need.

Which was a few horses, and to name one Beauty.

She was quite expensive too. So, I told Clayton one time that If I wanted to name her 'Money,' that's my business. But I wanted to name her 'Beauty', so that's what I fucking did. And Clayton can go fuck himself speaking on my non-existent love life. It's not as if he has one either so he's no better.

Maybe that's the problem, if he had a love life, then Clay would stay the hell out of mine. Nosy ass.

I can't be ungrateful though. He *is* here on a Wednesday night helping me with the horses, cleaning the stalls, and giving me company.

"Man I don't know everything, but I do know that your hair is starting to get a little silver in it." Clayton shoots me a look as I finish my job and then throw some hay into the stall. I give Beauty a pat and murmur in her ear.

"One would think Clayton has a hard on for me, as close as he's looking." I say in a teasing tone, throwing my friend a wry glance as I make my way out of the stall.

"Fuck you, man. You wish you had this cock," Clayton scoffs, making his way out of the stall and meandering over to the utility room.

He tosses the tool onto the wooden work table and proceeds to open up the fridge in the corner and grab a beer. I screw my face up in annoyance, hang the pitchfork up in its spot on the wall, and pick the tool back up, putting it in its rightful place.

I do not like my property or home out of order. I couldn't run my business if I didn't stay organized. 'Cleanliness is next to Godliness' and all of that, and I'm not ashamed to say I like the smell of a kitchen when you walk in and can tell it's been freshly bleached, along with the hot humid smell of the dishwasher going.

Call me neurotic, I don't care, at least my shit stays clean.

"I got a cock of my own. Want to see it? Bet it's bigger." I rib back, seeing his shit eating grin.

"Naw, don't even play like that my man. Unless that's the real reason you haven't been with anyone in over a year. If so, just say it. Live in your truth, I'll support you." He tosses me a beer, forcing me to catch it midair. If it broke here in the stables it would have garnered him an automatic ass whopping.

I throw him an annoyed glance. "Bro, is it possible for you to leave me the fuck alone?"

I crack open the beer via the beer bottle opener mounted on the wall that says *Hudson's place,* and take a hearty sip. Seeing the pail on the floor that catches the tops getting full, I pick that up and take it to dump it in the recycling, just as the rain begins to pound down on the barn.

Clayton beats me to the door, and I lean over, turning on the radio to a classical station for my horses to listen to during the night.

Yeah... they got it like that. I treat them well, sue me.

"So what's for dinner?" Clayton bumps my shoulder in a brotherly fashion as we make our way to the steps of the wrap-around porch of the sprawling two story home. A mansion that cost way more money than I ever thought I'd see in a lifetime, much less be able to drop on one asset.

"How's deer burger sound?" I sigh a long suffering sigh, but secretly, I'm glad he's not leaving yet.

Thunderstorms are meant for long hours of fucking in front of a fireplace on a bear skin rug. Since I don't have anyone to do that with,

I'll have to settle for regular good company, which Clayton is great at providing.

We make our way into the house and I listen to him tell me all the annoying and just outright obnoxious things his siblings have gotten into.

And maybe it's my age. Turning forty did something to me this year, it seems.

I feel a pang that I have no family of my own to tell him wild stories about in return. I can only share news of my parents, who live across the country in a souped up mini-mansion, living their dream life. And *maybe* an occasional story about an employee here or there.

But as the big boss, no one really comes to me with anything and for the first time it hits me like a ton of bricks, making me reconsider if I'm really living my dream life after all.

I don't know, because I'm starting to feel more lonely than I've ever felt before. Regular vanilla sex has never interested me, which is the real reason why I don't have a woman. I have a what society considers to be a sick kink that many women don't go for, and unfortunately it's hurt my love life a lot to have a nastier, more forbidden preference in my sex life.

And because I just can't see myself engaging in this kind of lifestyle, living out this kink with a woman who I'm not serious with, well, I stay single. It's just better this way.

So yeah, I'm terribly lonely.

And when I'm lonely, I start thinking about shit that isn't right.

I

H. MONTGOMERY
HUDSON

"MA'AM, IT'S JUST QUALITY assurance." I sigh, folding my arms I avert my face, looking out past the woman who's been tasked with dealing with me for this part of the project.

This client, a local technology conglomerate, hired my company to build their skyscraper. But when I explained that we needed to make sure we cover all bases such as test the ground soil, look up old weather patterns in this area etc... *before* we break ground, all hell broke loose over a *deadline*.

I fight to not roll my eyes.

Fuck lady. Why hire the best if you're just going to be a pain in the ass about it?

Pinning the tall, blonde woman with a no nonsense stare, I narrow my eyes. "I will not start this project until a geotechnical evaluation and analysis is done and in my hands for me to review. *A correct one.*" I emphasize.

I'm beyond irritated and ready to go. This woman has been poking and prodding at me for well over an hour. While it's never bothered me before to have a difficult client, I usually feel better about it because I deal with the difficult clients to their face.

This one had sent someone else to do their dirty work, and I can't respect that.

"Tell your boss that until these things are done, and I see the reports for myself, I will not start breaking ground. I don't care about a deadline. *Your people know where we live.* Our state is notorious for landslides," I state factually...for the hundredth time.

"My client is from-"

"I don't care, honestly." I interrupt. "To build such a massive undertaking, and cutting corners while you're at it, is not only certifiably *insane*, but it puts the businesses who help bring this to completion at risk. And *I'll be damned* if I get sued because this thing topples over due to your boss choosing to be negligent. Do what the rest of us do, and not worry about making a profit until your business is above the red line." I growl this last part, further irritated and almost ready to break the contract between our companies.

I give her a polite nod and turn, making my way over the harsh terrain heading to my truck, leaving my right hand foreman Tyler to see her out of the property. I'm done. I got a long drive home and need some coffee to help decompress after this bullshit of a day.

Seeing my truck just ahead on the grassy field, the tension in my shoulders begins to fade slightly. A massive sleek black Raptor with light blue lights, it was a splurge for me. I could have gone more luxurious. But I like trucks, so I went ahead and let myself get the kind I wanted since I was a kid.

Climbing into the drivers seat I take a second to roll down the windows.

Though it's late August, September fall is firmly upon us, and the air is getting crisper as it trickles in from the North. It brings with it a tinge of loneliness for me, I always get like this during this time of the year when it starts getting cold. It makes the drives longer, especially when crossing the bridge into Bainbridge Island, Washington.

The place that's been my home the last eighteen years.

Nights like tonight, I pretend I'm driving home to a woman who is busy cooking us a nice meal for dinner. I imagine she's got the lights on to give me a warm welcoming glow to see as I roll up my long driveway. She'd see me driving up... maybe open the front door letting the cold air in the house just to hear me complain about it.

Stand there on the porch looking pretty with an apron on, preferably with a stain or two from dinner on it, welcoming me in.

She'd try to ask me about my day but I'd haul her up against me and walk her into the house, silencing her with a hot kiss because I want to feel her more than I'd want to talk about my day. Maybe fuck her against the door before we can even close it.

No matter how much I pretend, I can never imagine what she looks like. She's an elusive little thing. Maybe that's why it's so hard to find her. I don't know what I'm looking for.

Pulling off the grass and onto the blacktop I set my course home. I squint against the harsh rays of the setting sun and slide on my sunglasses, a cheap pair as I always end up breaking them. Casualties of the job.

I take my time, hitting the few buttons on my phone to pull up my parent's number. Calling them over the car's bluetooth system I wait longer than I usually do for other people to answer the phone. They are getting older, after all, approaching mid sixties, and require a bit more patience. Since I'd forced them to finally get a cell phone, they lay it down all over the place and tend to forget it.

It takes seven rings before they answer. Ironic, as it's my lucky number. It took seven years of hard diligent work to see my first million dollar check, my house address is all sevens, and now, my bank account stays in the sevens constantly. My savings accounts are a different story, however.

"Well hello there! How's my millionaire doing today?" My pop's easy going southern voice makes me smile.

"Now pops, no need for all that." I say with a little sarcasm. Wanting some coffee, I quickly put an added stop into my gps following the directions through the traffic in a neighboring town. "I'm okay, just had to let this new development know my standards before I begin work. You know how it is."

Pops chuckles, making me smile broader, because this is his and my little game. He in fact really does not know how it is, but he enjoys hearing about it, and I love my weekly updates with my parents.

My father was the principal of a high school my entire life. Never knew what money was like because what little we had, he made sure we used it to travel. My parents took me everywhere they could afford to give me a taste of the world. Wanting to expand my horizons, and broaden my worldview.

When I decided I wanted to start my own business, he and my mom took out a second mortgage on their home to put me through school.

We thankfully have a great relationship, and because of how much they invested in me, I make sure they are completely taken care of in their old age. It's sad that they wouldn't move and be closer to me, but I get it.

They use the same excuses every time I attempt to coax them into moving closer. It's always the same...*maybe when you have kids,* or, *we're still young,* or, my personal favorite - *our friends are still alive, we cant leave them.* So, I funnel them a sickening amount of money so they can truly enjoy their golden years to the fullest extent.

I don't have anyone to spend the money on, other than my hobbies.

The day I deposited five million dollars into their account, buying them a gorgeous house in their preferred residential community, was the first time in twenty years I'd seen my father cry.

I swear, I'll never forget that feeling. Nothing's been able to top it as of yet.

I continue my conversation with them, seeing how their week has been, speaking with my mother a little. Her voice is starting to sound thinner, making me sad, because I know all she's ever wanted was grandchildren, and she never asked for much from me. I take a deep breath of the chilly evening air and hang up with them, finding a parking spot down a quaint road with lots of little shops.

Little twinkle lights crisscross the street attached to flickering lanterns, giving the entire street and its glass-paned exposed businesses a romantic glow in the setting sun.

It's nights like tonight I wish I had a woman on my arm. One who would pull me into shop after shop. I'd pretend to be annoyed, but really I'd just be waiting to get her home and into bed. I can see me and the imaginary woman now. I'd hover close, trying to hurry her up, she'd respond by going even slower. Purposefully teasing me just so I can give it to her harder when we get home.

Desperate for coffee at this point, I hightail it to the nearest coffee shop, and commence to paying way too much money for an eight ounce cup of joe. Taking a sip I wince. It's overpriced *and* gross. How the fuck are you going to charge eight dollars for a cup of yuck?

This should be an arrestable offense, honestly.

I groan, hating that I'm either going to have to drink this to make it through my drive, or throw it away.

My phone pings, momentarily distracting me. It's the text from my neighbor's teenage daughter, Haley. When I work late out of the city I pay her a little allowance and she comes on her four wheeler through the trees between mine and her parents property to feed my horses and brush them. I'm thankful for her help.

Hey Hud, I took care of the horses for you, see? I even gave them a little treat.-Haley

She sends me a picture of Champ, Nay Nay, and Beauty. I smile at the sight of their spoiled selves in their stall with carrots in their food bowl, munching away. She's holding a thumbs up, smiling broadly. The bands in her braces are pink today, making me grin at the bold color.

I'd never tell anyone but I'm a sucker for slightly imperfect teeth, and seeing everyone trying to constantly fix their smile, or shoving ridiculous veneers in their mouth makes me shake my head.

I'd never tell Haley that though.

God knows I wouldn't want to give the girl a complex. The world already has enough ridiculous pressure on girls and women, who am I to add to it and make it worse.

Putting my phone in my pocket I spy my truck and go to cross the street, unlocking it, cursing as a kid on a bicycle flies by and almost knocks into me. In my haste to back up, I turn, seeing a woman in the window of a shop. The sight of her cements my feet to the asphalt, rendering me incapable of movement.

My eyes flit to see everything I can through the broad words painted on the window, partially hiding my view.

She's in the orange glow of the little shop, standing halfway up on a rolling ladder, placing a book onto a shelf. Desperate to see more, I squint my eyes as I stand still in the middle of the street. The breeze flickers my deep brown hair and my jacket, seeping through and cooling me off.

Her head turns just slightly affording me a partial view of her profile.

She has deep tan skin, betraying an exotic heritage, and slightly thick eyebrows. Nothing like the thin, perfectly arched brows women sport today. Hers are full, fanned out, and frame her face beautifully. Her hair is pulled in a high thick bun, and I can *just* see the side of her mouth before she moves, denying me the sight as she steps off the ladder and away from the window.

"Dammit." I groan.

Curiously, I hurry across the street, throwing my hand up in a wave as a car had come up and was honking at me. Taking my keys out of my pocket I hit the button to lock my truck, striding down the sidewalk towards the store before I know what's hit me.

I don't read. Not like that anyways.

Approaching the store, I pause to read the store name. Lolita's Books and Tea Shop.

Spotting the store hours and glancing at my watch quickly, I see the store closes in ten minutes. I smile, thinking it's quaint, and push my way into the half glass and half wood door. The minute I step in, I'm blanketed in a comforting cloud of nostalgia that feels intertwined with a hint of Christmas morning.

It's cozy.

I inhale a deep breath of the warm, spicy air. It smells like chai tea, vanilla, and books. I blink, taking in my surroundings, observing there's no one in the bookstore except for two twin boys in the front by the window.

My eyes peruse, seeing it's not too large of a shop.

Books line walls that are painted in a moody color from floor to ceiling, and there are a few chest tall shelves that form aisles that are more a maze designed to make you lost. On top of the shelves sit a mixture of plants, crystals, more books stacked on top of each other, multicolored vases and other odds and ends that fit perfectly in the ambiance of the store.

In the front, by the huge picture window are cushy chairs flanked by small round tables adorned with tiffany lamps of varying sizes. Two twin boys sit side by side, reading quietly.

They have the exact same hair style: floppy, curly, thick, black hair, slightly coarse. They have light gray eyes and thick black lashes, and their coloring is a rich tan, like they could have went sunbathing just this morning. They're young. Look to be about seven, or eight. And from my stance, they seem terribly well behaved.

I come a little closer, seeing they have light freckles on their faces. One looks to be reading homework, the other one has his entire body situated in an overstuffed chair reading an actual book. A lamp glows between them giving the area a soft, warm, comforting glow.

Immediately feeling all the tension from the day melt away I release it on a long exhale. Loosening my shoulders.

"Hello." I greet them politely

The one reading a book looks up and gives me a serious once over before gracing me with a smile. The other doesn't move, he simply says hello back. I see the rolling ladder behind them, but no brown haired woman. My eyes continue to roam. In the back is the register, with a small area for drinks.

I see an espresso machine, *hallelujah*, a tea machine, and a door that's cracked open a few inches that leads to a back room.

As I walk to the counter, I hear a humming coming from the back. Intrigued, I tilt my head slightly, trying to see through the crack in the door. I see the tiniest flash of her gray boatneck sweater, and her brown hair up in a bun, but that's it. She keeps moving around, doing something back there.

"Mami!" One of the twin boys hurries past me and behind the counter, opening the door further to show me a stock room, and her moving around inside. "There's a man at the counter!"

Frustratingly, I still only see just a sliver of her person but I see she's curvy, with bigger breasts, round fleshy hips, and her stomach's not too fleshy but plump still. But it's her thighs, encased in dark blue jeans that hug every curve. The tight denim shows me her thighs are deliciously curvy, and I spend a second envisioning them wrapped around my waist.

I wonder how fast she can run. Will her thighs and tits slow her down?

Then another thought hits me. I don't want her to run, I want to shove her to her knees and make her crawl for me. Riveted, I continue to eat her up with my eyes.

Sweet Jesus. My mouth waters. It's not fair for a woman to look this good. It's just not. My heart begins to pound, and I hear her reply to him softly in Spanish, causing my eyes to narrow slightly in displeasure with myself because I am not bilingual. That is one skill I never could amass, sadly. But I think I'm about to have to.

She comes out, just as I hear the bell ring behind me distracting me momentarily. My head turns to see who it is just as the other twin at the front speaks.

"Dad!" he shouts.

Standing up, he flings himself into the tall, stocky male with the face that looks... well... *mean.* If I'm being honest.

He looks like an asshole.

He's Latino, with dark tan skin, wavy black hair. Deep brown eyes boast a pair of bushy eyebrows that are set in a harsh brow bone that slightly juts out, giving him an almost permanent pissed off look. He's tall. Though not quite as tall as me, probably two or three inches shorter, and his body does not match his head.

He takes off his jacket, forcing me to recant my prior observation of his body type. You'd think he'd be stocky but no, he's on the leaner side. His leather jacket does much to make him look bulker.

I watch longer, not caring if it's impolite, as he pushes, literally *pushes* the little boy firmly from him before he can even wrap his thin arms around him. I catch the disappointed look on the boy's face before the man places his hand on his shoulder and gives him what I can only describe as the claw. I frown.

It's fucking *weird*.

"How was your day at school?" I hear the man ask.

His voice is gritty, with no kindness or affection in it. Turning my head, I hear the other twin come out of the storage room. He doesn't rush the way his twin did. As a matter of fact, he walks steadily back to his seat and doesn't even spare the man a glance. Just grabs his papers, puts them in a backpack, grabs his brother's book and his backpack, before turning and handing it to him quietly.

He doesn't even bother to say 'hi', which in itself is quite odd.

The whole fucking interaction is unnatural, and reeks of issues. And if it makes *me* uncomfortable, how the hell do those boys feel? The woman? And what's worse, is the father says nothing to *him* either.

Enraptured by this spectacle, I lean my hips into the counter patiently, waiting, and watching this whole scenario play out. The woman walks past me quickly with a lunchbox in each hand.

I stiffen as I catch a whiff of her perfume, causing my dick to stir. God she smells delicious.

"*Lolita!*" The man calls out.

The tone in his voice makes my eyes narrow and causes me to curl my lip in disdain of this mean looking fucker.

I really do not care for the way he says her name. It makes me want to cut out his tongue so he can't speak.

"Excuse me for one moment, I am so sorry to keep you waiting." She all but breathes the words at me, because she surely hasn't looked at me, before she's halfway through the store headed towards her family.

My chest deflates, seeing she's involved with this asshole of a guy. Seeing as I don't have a shot at asking her on a date, I settle in, finish my disgusting coffee, and observe.

She bends to give the boys a kiss on the cheek accompanied by a big squeeze for each of them individually, and shoves their lunch boxes in their backpack.

"Can you please make sure they wear the clothes I sent with them?" Lola says to the man.

He's staring at her with an interesting expression; it's almost like he doesn't like her, but he's fascinated at the same time. The sight makes the hair on the back of my neck stand up, the look in his eyes is strange...the way his eyeballs don't move is fucked up.

As she finishes her instructions, he bends forward to kiss her cheek making me clench my jaw.

However, in a move that surprises me, she turns her face and backs up out of his reach. Through the reflection in the window of the shop, I see her place a tight, polite smile on her face before bending down to kiss each of the boys on the forehead before stepping back and folding her arms.

Good girl, I think to myself with a carefully hidden smile. *I'm back in business.*

Her lips in the reflection look luscious, plump.

The man goes out the shop door first, and the boy who didn't greet his father, turns back to throw himself into her arms. It's almost as if he was waiting for his dad to leave to show any sign of weakness. Lolita bends, hugging him back for a long minute and my chest tightens as I can hear him sniffle.

I feel bad for him, because there's obviously something going on here that's not quite right.

I finally look away, feeling like I'm witnessing something truly private, and disturbing. If I'm to be honest.

Granting them a moment of privacy, I turn back towards the register. I toss my empty cup into the bin behind the register, spreading my fingertips on the counter, and glance at the handwritten chalk menu on the wall. I peruse the contents slowly, giving Lolita the time she obviously needs, as her boys and their father have already left and she still hasn't made it back here.

Observing the pretty cursive slant, I briefly wonder if it's her handwriting I'm looking at.

"Again- I'm so sorry."

I turn, hearing her come up behind me and give her a polite smile. Her voice is slightly accented, low and breathless as she hurries back behind the counter. Finally, I get my first true full look at her, and it's *amazing.*

"Have you had enough time to look over the menu? Do you know what you want?" She continues, looking flustered.

But *I'm* more flustered, ironically.

My eyes are greedy. I can't help it, there's so much to look at. They train themselves on the exposed skin of her collarbone and the tops of her shoulders first.

Though I'm a breast man through and through, I'm oddly pleased that I can't see her cleavage. Just the smooth expanse of her collarbone and her shoulders. It feels like she wore this boatneck sweater just for me. Usually when you see a woman, the top of her shoulders aren't ever bare as she has a bra on, or is covered by a shirt or something.

So this feels *seriously* intimate, like I'm seeing something I shouldn't be, and I really, *really* enjoy this.

The fact that her breasts are heavy, and I know they aren't being held up by anything other than a strapless bra, has got my dick seriously aching.

I can't stop staring. She is all *woman.*

Her collarbones are delicate, and a thin gold necklace nestles itself right between them. My gaze slowly rises over an even more exquisite jawline that just begs a man to rub his lips on it. And her ears. *Fucking hell.* She's got the prettiest detached lobes, decorated with these interesting looking dangling geometrical brass earrings that highlight how elegant the curve of her neck is.

A neck that has a singular blue vein roping it's way across her throat. My hand can span her throat easily and my fingers flex as I envision myself doing just that.

Swallowing hard, I feel my own throat tighten viscously at the sight of how vulnerable her features are.

Goddamn. She has a *beautiful* heart-shaped face, full pink lips, and the prettiest almond-shaped gray eyes I've ever seen in my life. They're light gray, almost devoid of color strangely enough. Made even lighter by the thickest, longest black lashes. She's got true does eyes, so beautiful that I'm scared if she blinks too hard, I'm going to nut on myself because...*holy fuck*...I can get lost in them, and never want to make my way back.

I wonder what her lashes feel like brushing against my cheeks. Because I've just *got* to be able to kiss her at some point. Her lips are too inviting to not be kissed often.

I'm aware I've been silent too long but I *need* this. Need a minute to get a handle on myself while I take the time to study her.

Her nose has a small bump in the bridge, and I find myself so freaking thankful she hasn't gotten a nose job to get rid of it. There's a tiny smattering of light brown freckles on her nose, and a beauty mark at the very top arch of her eyebrow.

She's got wispy bangs with side pieces that frame her face which I think is adorable, considering most women today tend to do the long, straight thing with the middle part. Though there's nothing wrong with that, everyone's starting to look the same.

"*Yes.* What's your name?" I ask, even though I know. I just want to hear it from her lips.

Her lips curve into a smile, and I notice with pleasure one side tips slightly higher than the other. Whew God I am in trouble with a capital T.

"Me llamo Lola. Y tu, ?Como te llamas?"

Her soft voice washes over me, slicking over the synapses in my brain and I harden, just like that. I take a step into the counter, slowly, so it'll hide the evidence of just how badly I want her, giving her a smile of my own. Common sense tells me that she asked me my name.

"*Lola,*" I drag her name out, tasting it on my tongue. It's flavor is sweet. "My name's Hudson. I don't speak Spanish by the way so I can't understand it, but it's a pleasure to meet you."

"Oh, I'm sorry Hudson, I tend to forget myself sometimes." Her eyes brighten and she laughs, the sound husky and full bodied.

Lola's lips pull back into a smile, showing me slightly crooked canines. Canines that protrude out from the rest of her teeth just the *tiniest* bit. I'm ashamed a very small rumble escapes my chest, however, I keep my eyes tight on hers. Her teeth are fucking gorgeous.

Goddamn it, I'm fucked.

She has me absolutely mesmerized, yet I'm aware I'm still staring. I can't bring myself to stop. But her next words bring my eyes back thoroughly to hers.

My brows pinch together. "I thought I heard that man call you Lolita. Do you not want me to use your full name...." I trail off, tilting my head and pinning her with an inquisitive look.

"Oh!" She wets her lips, adopting a rather uncomfortable look. "Just *Lola* please, I don't go by Lolita."

"Hm..." I let it go, thinking it has something to do with that man.

"So *Hudson*, huh? Well there's a name you don't hear everyday. How unique."

I lock my throat down, holding back another grunt. *Fucking hell.* Clearing my throat with difficulty I hold my hand out and am pleased when she accepts it. Her skin is incredibly smooth. So I'm yet again lost thinking about that as she takes my hand in hers very softly at first, but then surprises me by locking her hand down on mine in a rather hard grip.

Our eyes lock hard as something indescribable passes between us right before she pulls back, turning to gesture to the menu.

My head tilts. I know a warning when I'm presented with one. And this little missy just let me know, though she may look soft, she's aware she's alone in a bookstore with, well, *me.* And everything I look like.

Which to her is probably a lot.

I fight to keep my eyes from narrowing in displeasure at the blatant display of masculinity. I get she doesn't know me, and theoretically she's entitled to give me or anyone she damn well chooses a warning, but this woman doesn't feel like *just anyone* to me. So I don't want to be just anyone to *her.*

Fuck, that beauty mark above her eyebrow makes me want to inspect every inch of her body for more. I have never been this enraptured by a woman before and the instinct to turn her inside out throws me a little off balance in a way I can't say I care for, if I'm being completely honest.

I wonder if she's got a beauty mark hidden in her pussy somewhere. My throat tightens as I imagine her taste. I want my mouth down there, in between her fleshy thighs, making her wail my name.

"So.." Lola say's slowly, letting me know that she's catching on to all this staring I'm doing. "Do you want a coffee... or maybe a tea? I'm assuming you aren't here to buy a book otherwise you'd have one by now."

Lola's words bring me back from my musing. She licks her lips, turning to pick up an interesting coffee cup shaped like a cow. Uncaring that she's aware I'm blatantly ogling her at this point, I watch riveted as she takes a deep drink. She does this little amusing thing where she swishes the liquid around in her mouth before she swallows it.

I bite my cheek hard to keep from chuckling at her, not wanting to accidentally hurt her feelings, but that quirk of hers is adorable. As is her voice. I never thought of myself as someone who's a sucker for an accent. My right-hand man, Tyler, is Latino, so I thought I was immune to these kinds of things, but I guess not.

Or maybe it's just *her* I'm seemingly not immune to?

"Can I have a couple minutes to look at the menu?" I ask, testing her, seeing if she'll let me stay after hours. Is she sweet and kind, or a rigid, unwavering bitch?

Or am *I* the dickhead making shit harder for her when that piece of shit, whoever that man is to her, just walked away with her boys, and they obviously have some family issues, and I'm keeping her here?

I wonder if she cries after these interactions with him. The thought makes me disturbed. Over a stranger. My lips tighten, not sure what's going on with me.

She nods. "Sure, while you do that, I'm going to put the closed sign up. Be right back."

I already know what I want, but what I'm doing now is scoping the place for cameras. I turn as she rounds the counter, watching her walk. She has a interestingly distinctive walk that's sexy and feminine. She'd kill my ass with that walk if she were wearing heels so I'm thankful she's not. My eyes raise, spying the cameras quickly in every corner of the room and in the middle of the ceiling. I feel relieved and irritated at the same time. What a juxtaposition.

She flips the sign, hurrying back quickly.

"I'll take a coffee."

She smiles, showing me that crooked canine again. "So you caffeinate at night before bed? Boy, your body must love you for that." She giggles, turning to the paper coffee cups. "How do you drink it?"

"Think I want it black tonight. I have to cross the bridge into Bainbridge Island."

"Oh yeah? That's a pretty drive. I've been on it once. So do you live there?" She says, making me arch my eyebrow. "It's about an hour from here right?" Her hand instinctively reaches for creamer before she pulls back with a little apologetic smile. "Sorry, it's been a long day. Hey, speaking of, do you want *two* cups just in case? These cups are kind of...small. So, I try to not charge too much you know..."

Lola fills my coffee cup an puts the lid on, gesturing to the little black straws to the side.

"I do live there, and that'd be nice. Thank you."

She turns to quickly make me another cup of coffee, which is incredibly thoughtful. "Nice. Well, for being so patient, you can have the coffee on the house. My treat." She also treats me to a breathtaking smile, forcing me to melt just a little more for her. I dig into my wallet and pull out a one hundred dollar bill, fold it so she can't tell it's one hundred dollars, and unceremoniously shove it into her tip jar.

"Thank you." I say politely, I go to turn, sure she needs to have a moment after the boys leaving and all. "And oh," I turn back slightly, giving her a grin. "Lola's a beautiful name. Stay safe."

With that, I walk out the door without another word because, honestly, I need a moment myself as well. Lola has turned me inside out, and doesn't even know. Those thoughts are back again, and I'm seriously considering if I need to call a shrink.

I'm fucked.

2
THE AWAKENING
LOLA

"LOLA'S A BEAUTIFUL NAME."

Relieved, I busy myself nodding at this handsome, well put together man who frankly looks intimidating. I'm glad all he wanted was some late night coffee, because if he asked me out I have no clue how that would have gone down. I'm flustered. The way he was staring at me, as if he wanted to leap over the counter and gobble me up, has my emotions all over the place.

Wrapping my arms around myself I tighten down hard as I attempt to keep it together myself.

How is it possible to feel so much at once? Maybe it's because I've been dead so long on the inside. It's been a long time since I've felt a man's gaze caress me the way Hudson's just did. And I had to stand there and endure it while my body slowly came to life.

My own eyes do their own thing, seeing thick brown hair on his head that I bet feels so good to sink your fingers into. He sports a beard that looks well maintained and encases a jaw that I promise I'm going to be seeing in my dreams. The man's bone structure is top notch, even his cheek and brow bones.

He's fucking Adonis.

He's got the most striking eyes I've ever seen. They are a *pure* green, no blemishes to be found.

By his build, I can tell he's a hard worker, which is sadly my weakness. I am a sucker for a man who can be outside and sweating all day. When he first came in, I saw that his dark brown steel-toed boots are scruffy, and have some dirt on the bottom. His jeans are older too, dark blue, slightly fading in some spots, like they might be his favorite pair.

He has this thick belt on and I am struck. Like truly struck at how *thick* this man is.

His torso is wide, his thighs are thick, his feet are big. His *hands* are big. With muscular thick wrists boasting a simple watch with a leather band that's worn.

I know it's fucked up, but for a moment I find myself nursing a pang of jealously towards his watch. Wishing it was *me* he could look at all day instead. I bite my lip and take a deep steadying breath.

You've been without sex for too long girl, being jealous over a watch. What the hell is wrong with you? I chastise myself.

But I can't stop staring.

Hudson's got what looks to be a thin smattering of crisp dark hair that peek out from the neckline of his long sleeved plaid shirt. It's unbuttoned, sitting on top of a deep gray t-shirt. His sunglasses are hooked into the neckline, drawing my attention down and making my mouth water at how broad this man's chest is.

I haven't seen a chest like this in a minute, and it takes me back a bit at how lustful I'm feeling.

It causes me to straighten my spine uncomfortably tight, with the unfamiliar feeling swamping my senses. Try as I might, I can't look away. He's just so *manly*. I've never felt muscles like that beneath my fingers before; Dominic's body type never allowed him to bulk up.

I swallow thickly, offering for him to have the coffee for free. I'm scared that if he goes to hand me money and our fingers brush again, I might just melt into a puddle on the floor. And considering I'm fighting like hell to keep my tears to myself until he's gone, I can't afford to touch him.

I can't afford to give the coffee away for free either, honestly, but it is what it is at this point. We all gotta make concessions somewhere.

I watch Hudson leave my shop before heading into the storage area, so there won't be any chance of him or anyone else peeking through the glass window and seeing me at the counter dealing with too many emotions that roll through me.

Finally alone, I gasp. The adrenaline of putting on a show for Hudson abates, and the earlier feelings of despair takes a front seat. A deep shuddering breath leaves me, along with a hot tear trailing down my cheek. Upset, I allow myself to break down crying into my hands.

I cannot believe I have to give my kids to that asshole. *What the fuck were you thinking, Lolita!*

To be honest, I don't even know why I still ask this question eight years later. My brother "Skee" asks it enough for the both of us, and it doesn't help to remind myself I fucked up in a major way when I was just eighteen years old. Having had the twins by nineteen.

I only fell victim to Dominic because I was lonely, having been grieving the deaths of my parents by myself.

My brother was gone, too busy making it big in Hollywood to care about his little sister anymore. And I was trying to figure out what to do with myself after my mom's sudden death. She passed just four months after my father died of cancer in a freak car accident. Leaving me my dad's life insurance money, her life insurance money, and the house.

I'd found out later that Skee had paid the house off for them, so mom didn't have to worry about that on top of being a full-time caregiver.

Skee gave me his half of everything, from our inheritance to life insurance, and then some. I enrolled in school, seeing my options were wide open, but then, like a dumb ass I just had to go and get pregnant by Satan's younger brother.

Our extended family decided that since Skee wouldn't be their doormat and give them money just because he made it big, they would try and latch on to me. And I had to unfortunately and methodically cut off every one of the money hungry fools I could. We both did. It hurt that they would abandon our mother while she wore herself out for two years taking care of my father, who had cancer.

No one helped when we needed support the most.

Skee sent our mother money to help with hospital bills, but he couldn't come and be physically present. No, his career was taking off in a major way. So major, that when he invited me to go to his first movie premier and I went, I got to see firsthand the sick stuff that a lot of our revered celebrities get into.

I wanted no parts of it.

That weekend I decided never ever fucking again would I come around those "celebrities," and lose my soul to that lifestyle.

I'm proud of him, though; he could get by better as a man. Hollywood just wants too much sick stuff from women. So, I found myself eighteen, an orphan, taking care of myself in this big house with too much money.

Though I was responsible, I unfortunately latched on to someone who wasn't. I take a second to wipe my eyes and try to compose myself.

Putting my thoughts away I exit the storage room and go to the tip jar, reaching in for the money Hudson put in there. He really didn't have to. What is with people? Can't take a free cup of coffee when it's given?

I pull my hand back and unfold the note to put it in my purse. My eyes widen. Not seeing a one dollar bill like I'd thought, but a one *hundred* dollar bill.

My eyes flick to the store window as if he might be standing there, staring at me. I relax, seeing nothing.

I hurry through the store, not liking the dark. I really should pay an electrician to install a light at the front as well so I don't have to keep turning it off in the dark and then hurrying through the store like the devil himself is at my feet. But I can't justify that money for an electrician right now. I can't afford it.

Making my way through the door and outside, I turn and lock it with a harsh exhale. My heart is pounding from my imaginary chase reminding me of the book I'm reading and how the main character lived in a haunted house and liked being stalked.

But hey, at least she got good sex at the end of the day. I just get to go home to an empty house on Wednesday nights, and every other weekend. It's lonely those days without the boys.

Dominic only agreed to the divorce if we split custody. Otherwise, he promised to drag me to court until the kids turn eighteen, and I couldn't imagine the lawyer and court fees or the trauma the kids would be subjected to. I'm beginning to get worried, as I'm getting to the point where my money is running out.

I only have about twenty grand in my savings account, and I'm doing everything I can to stretch every dollar.

The store only makes so much, and Skee has been having to supplement the rent for it so I can keep it. If I lose my store, my boys are as good as gone.

I drive home in silence, not even wanting to listen to my streaming music. I'm lost in thought about my boys. Wondering what they're doing.

I pick up my phone to call and tell them goodnight, and just like I expect, Dominic doesn't answer. I sigh, pulling up my text app, sending an 'I love you' and a 'goodnight mi amor' to their watches I bought them last year. When Dominic decided to stop answering the phone and letting me say goodnight to them on "his time."

"You wanted a divorce, then deal with it!" He yelled at me one time on the phone. "I don't call the kids when you've got them, do I?"

To which I replied, "No! Because all you do is use them as pawns to get money from my brother."

Tucker came home the next day saying he was hungry.

When I asked why, he said his dad doesn't feed them all the time and that sometimes he forgets. I really think it was because he was punishing the kids because I retaliated, calling him out on his behavior. So now, I pack them a lunch box for every time they go to their dads. I fill it with sandwiches, fruits, juice boxes, and little notes telling them I love them.

Tatum's lunch box comes back full. But Tucker's is always empty, and he's always hungry.

When I question them, the boys trade a look and tighten their lips. I'd really love to know what's going on. But when I ask them, I get crickets. And I can't help what they won't tell me about. I've even taken them to a play therapist, and *she* couldn't even get them to talk. The second and third therapist couldn't either.

I'm at my wits end. Something's obviously going on; Tucker is becoming slowly more and more reserved, and for some reason, Dominic keeps asking for more money. It took only one time for him to hit me, and now I give him everything in my tip jar and extra because I'm terrified he'll hit the boys when I'm not around. So, I do my best to keep the peace.

He swears to me he won't hit the boys, but if I don't cooperate, I see that changing. I'm so stuck. I can't afford to be drug into court for the next ten years. I won't be able to afford to keep the shop if I try to fight for them because lawyer fees are so expensive.

Like... I just literally don't know what I did in a past life but it must have been something bad. Because out of the six billion people on the face of the earth, *why* did my first life lesson in love have to be *Satan's brother?*

I pull into my place in the garage and then exit my vehicle, walking to the mailbox at the end of the drive. Just like clockwork at seven thirty-five, Frank, my neighbor, peeks through his green curtains, and then the next minute he's coming out onto his front porch.

Frank and his late wife, God rest her soul, helped me out so much when my mom died.

Frank has been keeping an eye on me and the boys ever since. And If I deviate from schedule too much, he's blowing up my phone to ask me what's going on. One time, I detoured and went to see a movie when I didn't have the boys and he called me eight times in a row. Wouldn't stop until I stepped out of the theater and answered it.

He made me promise to stop by after I got home to make sure I was okay in person.

Everyone, and I mean *everyone* should have a neighbor like Frank. He's always watching. He even picks the kids up for me during the week so I don't have to shut the shop down for an hour and lose customers. Frank's amazing, and I let him know it. I get my hands on every history book I can find just for him as my own way of saying thank you.

But don't get me wrong, the man can be an asshole.

"Lolita! How're you doing?"

I smile. Every day it's the same question, and every day it's the same answer. "I'm okay Frank. How was dinner tonight?"

"Ohhh it was good. I had some leftover hog head cheese. You want some? I can make you a sandwich real quick?"

I inwardly gag because what the *hell* is hog head cheese?

"Noooo." I sing, waving my hand. "I already had a huge dinner," I lie. "But thank you... maybe next time?"

Frank eyes me, almost like he's trying to catch me in a lie. "When are you making that lasagna again?"

"Next week I think."

"Okay, will you-"

Waving my hand I scoff, grinning at him. "You don't even have to ask anymore Frank, you know I'll make you one too."

"Okay, thank you." I turn to head back up the driveway. "Hey Lola!" I turn back, surprised by him still talking. I thought we were done.

"Yeah Frank?"

"Are you an LGBTZ?"

But he says it as if it's a word, doesn't say each individual letter so I have no clue what the hell he's talking about.

I frown. *"A what,* Frank?"

"You know, a *pansexual?"*

I almost die fucking laughing; I'm bent over very unladylike, screaming with laughter, and tears are streaming down my face. I can't even talk for a moment I'm so overcome.

"Frank!" I gasp. God bless his old ass heart, he tries so hard to keep up with the new lingo. "Do you even know what a pansexual is?"

"Yeah, it means you don't love nobody. I want to know why you don't love nobody Lola! I never see a man come to your house. Just that fucking buzzard."

What the hell?

I snort because he's mentioning Dominic. And I decide I like 'fucking buzzard' a whole lot more than 'Satan's brother' except, I can't go around calling people 'fucking buzzards'. It's just not right.

What might fly for Frank's old ass, won't fly for mine, unfortunately.

Wiping a tear away, I shake my head at him. "Frank I think the term you're looking for is *asexual*. And it's because you men are not-"

"No!" Frank interrupts me with a bark that makes my eyebrows raise. "Now don't start with me! It's not *'you men'.* " He pins me with a hard stare that makes my toes curl and my soul shift inside my body. I feel straight chastised. "It's *ya'lls* generation of men. There was nothing wrong with mine. We did what we were supposed to do by our women. I don't know what is wrong with these young people today; they're not men, and I don't even feel comfortable calling them that."

"Okay well Frank, will *you* marry me, then?" I bat my eyelashes and fake propose to the only man on this side of the universe I would ever ask to marry me.

He gets a scowl on his face. *"No!"* He says it so sharply that I go back to frowning. "The last young Latina beauty I was with back in nineteen seventy-two almost killed me. No, thank you." And with that he goes in the house and shuts the door.

I giggle, making my way into the house.

Turning, I eye my yard in a fit of OCD. It's looking okay, but the side of my house is starting to get built up. So because I don't want to go into that lonely house by myself, I dump my bag on the front porch and hightail it to the garage, grabbing a pressure washer.

I know it's nighttime, but with Frank watching over me, I feel no fear out here like this in the dark.

Listening to a spicy audiobook through my car pods, I spend the next hour cleaning the side of my house. By the time I'm done, I have enough material to finish this week's blog for my bookshop.

Happy, I put my tools away and go into the house.

I cross into the foyer, heading for the stairs leading to the top of the house to the left. I hang my jacket on the rack, keeping my purse with me, taking the stairs two at a time.

One time years ago, I read that women should always keep their purses with them; that way, if they ever have to leave in a hurry, they have all their identifying information on them in case they have to run for whatever reason. House catches on fire? You just grab it and go. Some shits going down? Just reach over and leave. You don't have to hunt for your car keys, nothing.

I started this practice and never looked back. You will never see me without my purse near me. Especially at night.

Desperate for a shower, I hightail it upstairs and put it in its spot on the chair next to my bed before throwing myself into a warm shower. It's truly the highlight of my day. That and having a small glass of wine before bed. It's like the *only* adult thing I let myself enjoy. The rest of it is all kids.

The movies we watch, our fun days out... I save it all for them.

It's what they deserve, and I love them so much that I'll do anything for them.

Amazingly, they tend to let me take my showers in peace, which is nice. But tonight, I don't have to worry about that. My thoughts take a left turn, wondering how they are doing. If he's yelling at them. Did he take them to his grandma's and are they sitting off in a corner being ignored? Is Tucker eating out of his lunchbox right now?

I force my thoughts away and they go to Hudson.

Jesus, I've never seen a man so fine before. My hands roam over my body, slicking the soap off as the water sprays down, and I turn, wetting my hair and rinsing the conditioner out. I lift my breasts, making sure I get under the heavy globes thoroughly.

The trade off of having big breasts.

I replay him walking into my shop. The way his jeans hug his thick thighs just right, and his hips. *My Godddd.* You ever see a man with wide hips and a torso? You just know your legs are going to hurt from how wide you have to spread them when he's on top.

My pussy tingles and I lower my hand down and brush over my clit, thinking about Hudson.

I moan, thinking about the way he said my name in that growly voice of his. My excitement gets the better of me, and my other hand goes to my breast to squeeze my nipple. I jerk as the sensation shoots through my body, causing me to flinch on a gasp.

My fingers fall away fast, I'm always too sensitive there. I can't make myself play with them too long because it's so overwhelming. So I focus on my clit, and as usual, the water runs cold before I orgasm holding myself up with a hand against the shower wall.

I've always been this way.

Back when Dominic and I were still having sex, he used to be frustrated with me. Then made me go to the doctor because he thought there was something wrong with me. There's nothing wrong with me, I just don't come fast.

I agree with him, though, that it's irritating.

I spend a few minutes brushing out my hair before I put on a mid-thigh-length robe and then head downstairs. Padding over the hardwood floor to the back of the house, I ignore the picture of Dominic and I hanging on the wall in the hallway and walk into the kitchen to make a simple sandwich.

I throw a glance outside, happy I have the only house on the block where the other neighbor's houses can't see into mine and my back-yard faces the woods. So I can afford to walk around in a robe, and hell, right now, if I really wanted to, I could walk around naked.

But it's too late, I have my robe on.

Next time, I promise myself. I grin at the thought of lounging around my house in the nude and open my double-door stainless steel refrigerator, a Christmas gift from my brother. He replaced all my appliances last year. I make the world's messiest sandwich, complete with chips and a small glass of wine, before hightailing it back upstairs.

I peel off my robe and fall into bed with my laptop, sandwich and wine to settle in and finish up my blog.

Between my orgasm, my smut book, the hot shower and wine, I write my filthiest blog yet about the cat and mouse duo that currently has the book world on its head.

Exhausted, I fall asleep with my laptop open on the other side of the bed and don't move or wake up until nine the next morning. Just how I like it.

3

SOMETHING SINISTER

HUDSON

LOLA HAS SOMEHOW CLAWED her way into my very being and made her way home. She's all I can think about. I haven't felt this way about a woman since I don't know how long, and it's as discombobulating as it is thrilling and refreshing.

So obviously, because I can't get this woman out of my fucking head, I walk into the bookshop about five minutes until closing time, seeing Lola behind the counter sweeping.

It's Wednesday, Lola's twins aren't here, and in a stroke of luck, there are no other patrons. I take a deep breath, inhaling the comforting scent of spice and vanilla, letting it settle me. I'm slightly more tense than usual, having been worried the entire hour drive here that I wasn't going to make it in time to see her.

I groan quietly as I feel the tension melt away at Lola's first look at me. She glances up just as the bell to the door rings and puts the broom and dustpan away, giving me a smile as I saunter to the register with a smile of my own for her.

"Well hello again, *Hudson.*"

God dammit, why does she say my name like that? The woman couldn't let me make it all the way into the store before she makes my dick harden? God help her if I am ever able to get my hands on her.

It's going to be a rough night, I'll tell you that.

"What can I do for you?" Lola wipes her hands on a dry towel and places it under the register.

The way her voice says my name sends chills down my spine. It's raspy, and I'm assaulted with sudden visions of what it would be like to hear her moan my name while I fuck her sweet, curvy body. Can her voice go raspier...lower? Or is she a high moaner? A whimperer?

I need to know, almost like I need my next breath of air.

With my previous sexual partners, I preferred them to be quiet. But with this one, no. I'd love for her to strain her vocal cords, screaming for me.

I flash her a smile in an attempt to keep myself in the present. But unfortunately for me in my mind's eye, I'm on top of her naked body, snatching her knees up and back while I slam my fat dick inside of her... and I can *almost* hear it. She's a raspy, whimpering mess for me. Biting down on her bottom lip just right with that crooked, prominent canine that I want sinking into *my* flesh, not hers.

So I start thinking about what I can do to make her bite me.

"Depends," I say, placing my fingertips on the counter. I wet my lips briefly and see her eyes flicker, catching the movement. "Did you happen to already throw out the coffee? I'm in dire need of a cup, and yours is the best in this area."

My voice is deeper than usual, hoarse with desire because I want this woman unlike anything I've wanted before.

Lola's eyes widen, and I smile inwardly at seeing just how much the compliment pleases her.

"Oh... yeah... I'm sorry. I did just now actually." She purses her lips before her face brightens back up. "But I can make another pot for you. It's no problem."

I feel relieved. "You don't have anywhere to go?" I inquire, trying to feel her out. See what she does with herself.

"Nah," Lola gives me a husky laugh, making my chest warm. "What about you? Hard day at work? Surely you want to get home so you can put your feet up. What do you do?"

"I work in construction." This seems to peak her interest as her eyes do another quick assessment of my person.

"Oh nice. Well, then you're probably *reeaalllyyy* needing the caffeine." She says with a laugh that makes her eyes sparkle, and I find myself so drawn to her, her energy.

I smile at her. "So what about you? Nowhere to be?"

She gives me a laugh that sets my blood on fire, and then she turns to the coffee maker.

"I'm a single mom, I have no life. On Wednesdays and the weekends, when my boys are with their dad, I stay here a little late and catch up on reading. I have a little blog through my shop's website where I make biweekly book recommendations."

"Oh yeah?" I'm so curious. A reader, shop owner, and blogger? Sounds like she's got a life to me. She's fascinating. "What's the book for this half of the month?"

I tilt my head as Lola works with her back to me, letting my eyes get their fill of her curves. Her hair is up again in its bun and I find myself really wanting to know how long or short it is. She's in another pair of blue jeans, these ones black, and a white, thin turtleneck sweater that cups her breasts so nicely. My fingers twitch, itching to touch them.

She's got this matte, rust-colored lipstick on today. Her eyelashes and eyeliner are dark, visible through her bangs. I love the way she does her makeup.

I can see just a little more of her beauty mark above that left eyebrow, which lets me know she just got her brows done, and I'm so fucking pleased she keeps them thicker. My eyes flicker to her ears seeing she's got another pair of geometric, chunky earrings on that dangle, and damn, if she's not the sexiest thing I've seen in a hot minute...

My fingers flex, wanting to know what her hair feels like. Does she like her hair pulled during sex?

"Oh, it's right there on the counter! See?" She says as she hits the button for the coffee maker.

The steam billows before the brown liquid starts to splash slowly in the pot, filling the air with the strong smell of coffee. My eyes lower to the book in question, seeing a skull on the cover.

"You sit here in the shop alone and read a scary book?" I ask.

My eyes peruse it curiously.

She's stuck a little bookmark at the end, letting me know she's almost through with it. I tilt my head, noticing so many little tabs of different colors stuck all throughout the pages. I pull it to me and open it up, flipping through a few of them. As I'm not really a reader, I don't see the fascination.

She turns to me, giggling. "Trust me, when you go through a nasty divorce, some bullshit between the pages of a book doesn't hit the same way, if you get what I mean."

I give her a slow smile, happy she's not married to that piece of shit. "Well, I've never had a divorce before, *but* I get what you mean."

"Well, that's nice." She looks me up and down curiously. Her eyes lock on the ring finger of my left hand, which is bare. "What's your wife's name?"

The fact she believes I have a wife even though I'm not wearing a ring shows me just how savvy she is. She doesn't seem to miss much or assume that just because she can't visibly see something doesn't mean it's not there.

I chuckle, getting ready to answer her, but right before I do, the door to the shop opens. The clock says it's seven on the dot, closing time. I turn, seeing a man come in, bringing a sack of food, and the smell that hits my nose is mouthwatering.

"Thank you Ryan!" Lola calls out, looking relieved.

She's got the biggest smile I've ever seen on a person's face, full of joy, showing all her teeth, and it's so cool to witness her abandonment. I hope it's over the food and not Ryan, because that would suck. The thought is enough to kill my chubby, and I work incredibly hard to tamp down these unwanted feelings of jealousy.

Ryan walks up to the counter and gives me a once over.

"Hey man." He greets me, and I say hello in return, watching him place the food on the counter.

Lola rummages in her pockets and pulls out a crisp twenty dollar bill and a crumpled five. Noticing a delicate gold bracelet on her left wrist, and a chunky bangle on her right arm, I make a mental note she likes jewelry.

"Keep the change." She winks at him, and Ryan takes the money looking thankful.

"Hey, I put an extra couple of scoops in there for you. You don't take enough care of yourself on Wednesdays, Lola." The man tsks and begins to back away with his thumbs up.

Lola twists her lips and scrunches her nose playfully at him. I don't like that. I want him gone *now*.

"Thanks Ryan. Hey, want a cup of coffee?"

I bite the inside of my cheek hard. *No Lola, I'm here so pay attention to me and let's get this fucker gone.*

I clear my throat, trying to express my displeasure.

"No, I won't be able to go to sleep tonight, silly girl." He backs his way out of the store and disappears without a goodbye right as the coffee pot chimes, signaling the coffee is made. Thank God.

I turn back to Lola and eye her, then the food. "I don't have a wife." I state simply, resuming our conversation but not elaborating.

She gives me an approving nod and a half laugh. "Oh, well *good for you then*. Marriage *sucks*, stay single. You want it black again or would you like some sugar tonight?"

My eyebrows almost fly off my face and I give her a disbelieving chuckle. "Not all marriages suck. My parents marriage doesn't and they've been together for four decades. *Black* tonight, please."

Lola makes my coffee silently and then hands it to me. "Well, good for you, and them." She repeats with a slightly sad smile, making me want to know more about her.

"Do you think I can buy a book real quick, or am I keeping you too late?" I eye her food again, really wanting a bite.

"Oh," She's shocked. "A book? Did you see one you liked?"

"Yes." I give her a smile and point to the copy of the book in between us on the counter. "That one."

Lola glances down at her book and frowns. "This one is *my* copy. It's got all my little tabs in it. See?" She holds it up and turns it, showing me what I already know. She lets it hit rather hard on the counter when she puts it back down, making me smile again.

"Oh, I see," My eyes meet hers once more, seeing her looking at me with a rather vulnerable expression on her face. "What I'm curious about is what you find so fascinating about it that you needed to mark it with a hundred little tabs. Must be some book because that seems quite time consuming."

Lola lets out a laugh and her face flushes bright red, catching me slightly off guard. She catches herself and quiets, seeing me eyeing her silently with a little grin of my own.

"What's so funny?" I ask.

"Well, I just never pegged you for a *dark romance* reader." Lola giggles, and her eyes sparkle in a way that I know I'll see them in my dreams later.

"What's dark romance?" I push her food towards her. "Go ahead and eat. I have a feeling whatever you're going to say is going to be good and I don't want to leave without that book." My eyes flick to her, and I treat her to that grin I know make all the women weak. Except the only one I want weak is *this* particular woman, so at this point, I can no longer grace everyone else with this smile.

It's all for her now.

Lola shoots me a somewhat shocked look and she takes the container out of the bag, opening up the top to show steaming, dark-fried rice with chunks of chicken, spring onion, and egg.

"Sorry, I'm starving and well," she looks at the clock. "I haven't eaten today and we are after closing time, sooo... do you mind?"

"I don't mind at all." I encourage her.

I look down at the delicious-looking chicken fried rice, and my mouth waters, reminding me I haven't eaten since ten this morning myself. Lola catches my look.

"Do you want some?" Lola asks hesitantly.

My eyes raise back to hers and something interesting passes between us. "You'll share?"

"Yes, of course I will." She gives me another smile and turns, taking a plastic spoon, and hands it to me. "Unless you're too chicken to eat from the same container?"

"Chicken?" I scoff, feeling that tingle raise up my arm as our fingers brush. "You have no idea who you're dealing with. I love Chinese food. Second to Italian." I laugh and scoop up a spoonful of rice and we stand there, taking a bite together. I groan as the flavor hits my tongue. "Holy shit, *this is amazing. This is different isn't it?"*

I've never tasted rice like this before. It's rich with a deep flavor.

"I know right? It's St. Louis style. Ryan makes it just for me." She takes another bite and her head tilts back, moaning quietly. Making my eyes narrow as the sound travels straight to my aching dick.

I grunt softly, eating another bite. My chest warms, finding this incredibly intimate, sharing a meal with this beautiful stranger.

"So about the book. May I buy it from you?"

Her head lowers back down, and she gives me an incredulous look. Her eyebrows furrow, and she rolls her lips.

"*I mean...*" She makes a little scoffing noise. "You're going to see the stuff I think about it. It's kind of... *intimate* don't you think? And this isn't just *any* book. Do you even know what dark romance *is?*"

I pointedly eye our meal.

"More intimate than eating out of the same carton of food?" To prove my point, I knock my spoon into hers playfully, taking the rice off her spoon and putting it onto mine. I chuckle as I put it in my mouth. "And besides that, I think common sense tells me that it's like a romance, but more intense?"

Her eyes narrow and her face flushes even more. "I cannot have you knowing what I like about this book, *Hudson.*" She's a feisty one and I eat it up right along with this delicious rice.

"*Why not?* Are you scared?" The question hangs in the air between us. I keep my eyes steady on her, unrelenting, and I enjoy her eyes dilating.

We're full on flirting, and I love it.

"*Nooo.*" She says this slowly, and I know something's up with why she isn't relenting.

"I'll pay you one thousand dollars for it." And right then, by the disappointed look on her face, I know I fucked up. I made the wrong move. I try and pivot. "But I'd much rather pay a penny for your thoughts."

Her face relaxes and she licks her lips. I make a mental note that money seems to be a sore spot with her. I'm not sure why, but I'm damn sure going to find out.

"Or, I could wait until your blog comes out. But to be honest," And I'm being really really honest here. "I'd rather read it straight from your source. Or you could just tell me?"

We take another bite, and as she chews, she assesses me curiously. I see her eyes rake down my body, taking in my features, my arms, my brown hair. I know I look good, but I try not to draw attention to myself. I dress understated so as not to be so loud with my wealth. My dick throbs under her slow gaze down my body, and I swallow hard. My groan *and* my food.

I mentally pencil in a trip to St. Louis because this rice is amazing.

"What about this book is so fascinating to you?"

She stares at me for a second. I see the thoughts flash through her eyes but can't read them.

"*I think*, and I don't believe I'm just speaking for myself here. I think what's so fascinating is the...*plausible* consensual non-consent of it all. And not just the non-consensual sex-"

Hearing her say the word *sex* has me catching a growl in my throat.

"The man *stalks* her, and it's her response to him. There's a pivotal scene in just the first book that has the readers divided. It's caused quite the ruckus in the book reading world."

I eat some more, keeping my expression neutral. Lola doesn't realize just how close to home she's hit for me.

"Non-consent. Like rape? That's what's in this book?" I tap my finger on it quizzically, trying to understand it, and her. I decide if she doesn't let me buy the book, I'll steal it somehow.

Her demeanor changes, she becomes stiffer, more on guard. The fact that she's in her shop after hours alone, sharing a container of St. Louis-style fried rice with a man she's only met twice, has finally sunk in. This counter between us is a flimsy thing; I could vault it in a heartbeat if I truly wanted to.

So why am I here with her, like this.

"W-well technically it's *consensual* non-consent." Her eyes are wide as she regards me. "But it's actually not...I don't think. I don't know, their dynamic is confusing in the beginning."

She flushes so red, I'm almost worried she's going to pass out.

I ask myself why. Might this be *her* kink? Everyone has one, and this makes me more excited than before because if I'm right, then it seems her kink might be aligning with mine.

Those thoughts start up again. Fuck. I blink, trying to make myself come back to the present and concentrate because she's still talking.

"Well, you'll have to read it. You know how beauty is in the eye of the beholder?"

I nod, taking another bite. Between the two of us, we made a decent dent in this rice, and I just know that when I get home, between the drive, the coffee, and the food, I'm going to get the best night of sleep I've had in a long time.

"Well, the book is really in the eye of the reader. What resonates with *me* might not resonate with you. I'll let you have the book, at the cost of the book. No point in paying a thousand dollars, I'm sure my thoughts aren't worth quite that much." She says with a little huff of laughter.

But she's wrong. Her thoughts are now priceless to me. I ignore her self-degradation because I'm not interested in fueling it and I gesture to the tabs.

"What do the different colors signify?" I glance over the tabs curiously.

"Well, pink is romantic, white is what I'd like to research more, black is what I think is awful, gray is what I believe I might be into and well..." her ears turn bright red. "The red is the interesting spicy stuff. I like to pick a scene or two to highlight and talk about in my blog. Women love discussing this kind of stuff."

"Spicy stuff, huh?" I eye her. "Like sex scenes? Written porn?"

Her eyes leave mine as she scoops more food onto her spoon. "Uh-huh."

Chuckling, I put my fingers on her book, beginning to slide it to me. Almost salivating, because I can't fucking wait to know what she thinks. But before I get it to my side of the counter, she pulls the book back, opens it and tears a red tab off.

"Hey!" I exclaim, snatching the book back rather harshly.

Her eyes widen, but I can't find it within me to care. I lean forward to her, placing my fingers alongside hers and take the tab she tore off and place it back where I saw it.

Electricity zings between us as our skin meets for the first time today, and from her lips parting, and the look on her face, I know I'm not the only one that feels it.

"That's cheating." I admonish, tucking the book under my arm, I toss my spoon in the trash can behind her before fishing a fifty-dollar bill out of my pocket and hand it to her. "For the book." I place it in her hand and I turn to leave. "Bye Lola." I call over my shoulder, pushing my way through the front door with my coffee in one hand and her book underneath my arm.

I sit for a while until I see her settle into a chair through the coffee shop window, she's reading a new book. The Lovely Bones. My eyes narrow because I know that book.

It's *not* a romance. Or even a dark romance.

It's something much darker. And I wonder, what is it about Lola that is drawn to the sinister side of things?

I sit in my truck idling, watching her for a bit. She reads for an hour, plucking a tab off and sticking it in every other page. These tabs are all blue and black and white. Her method fascinates me, and I see the different colors of the book I successfully got from her.

Running my fingers over the red, black, white, pink, and gray tabs. I'm a reader now.

I smile, seeing her get up and turn her store lights off, making her way out of the store and to a white, modest Hyundai SUV with a pink bear hanging from the rearview mirror. She didn't notice me, and I thank God for that because I'm about to start following her curvy little ass. Find out who she is and what makes her tick.

I need to know the secrets behind this mask she wears.

I follow Lola twenty minutes away to a quaint neighborhood with very nice stone houses and see her turn into a nice two story, dark blue and stone house that's at the end of the cul-de-sac. She pulls into the garage and then leaves the door open, walking out of the garage and hitting the button on the pad to lower the door.

She spends a moment taking her trash bins and rolling them to the curb, taking her sweet time.

She looks like she's enjoying the night air.

A neighbor, an older man with silver hair, comes out their front door and calls out to her. She stands in the middle of her front yard, smiling, and speaks with the man for a second. As they talk she rocks on her feet, as if she can't sit still.

They finish up their conversation and the man waves at her before going back inside his house. But I can see him sit just inside the curtains at the window, watching over her.

Lola meanders over to the mailbox and takes a small package out, tucking it under her arm. She takes a second to stand there under the orange glow of the streetlamp and flips through the rest of her mail. She tears a few pieces up, walks to her recycling bin, and tosses it in before walking slowly to her front steps. But then right when I think she's going to walk to the front door, she stops and throws her bag down onto the porch.

Heading back to the garage.

I take a deep sip of my coffee and slink down in my seat a little, stretching out my legs. Lola opens the garage door and I see her head to the side that she isn't parked at. She digs in a little cabinet and pulls on a pair of gloves, grabs a leaf disposable bag and a rake, and heads back to the front.

What are you doing baby? I think to myself as I take another sip of my coffee.

The neighbors curtains rustle just a tad, letting me know he's watching her too. Sure enough he comes back out and calls to her, but she just turns and smiles at him brightly, waving him away.

I spend the next hour watching her rake her front and side yards. Filling eight bags of leaves before stopping. She slowly drags them to the curb, looking thoroughly worn out, before she puts everything back in her garage neatly. Closing the door before letting herself in the front door.

Light after light turns on in the home and stays on.

From my vantage point in the street, I see a light flick on in what I assume is the upstairs side back bedroom window. The lights downstairs remain glowing. My eyes search her front for any sign of home security signs but I don't see anything. I keep looking, I see no cameras, nothing. She doesn't even have floodlights, just the flickering gas lights that flank her garage and front door.

The older man next door seems to be her only source of true security.

Her house is immaculate, there's not even build up on the areas of the house that does have siding. And now that I think about it, her car is clean too.

I stay another twenty minutes just contemplating on this woman before I start my truck and pull off into the night, making my hour journey home.

The next day I finally hear from the tech job that they secured the reports for the services they needed for us to break ground and it's all systems go.

I spend the day overseeing what employees need to be doing what, and just making sure that everything is good there before I head to the job site and finally meet the asshole client who should have been present at the first meeting.

I don't like him. But he did what I requested so we're off to get the money.

I have a hearty lunch and finish my day, finding myself working late again and on the road to Lola's. All I can think about is this damn book. I got home too late last night thanks to playing Sherlock Holmes, and had to check on my horses before I went inside and went to bed.

I get there about fifteen minutes early this time and I hold my hand up in greeting, seeing she's got a line of about two people she's taking care of. The twin boys are sitting in the same chairs as before, so I decide to go up to them to say hi.

Just like last time, the other one looks up and greets me in the face, the other one keeps his head down in his homework but says hi.

I look back to the register.

Lola eyes me as she takes the last customers order, pointing silently to a cup of coffee nearby on the counter letting me know she's already taken care of me. Grateful, I beeline over and grab it, shoving another one hundred dollar bill in the tip jar. She throws me a knowing glance and a feisty eyeroll, finishes cashing out the customer, and they leave. Leaving just us and her boys in the store.

"Lola," I smile, leaning a hip against the counter. "How are you?"

Lola giggles. 'Hudson, hi. I'm sorry to tell you that not much has changed since last night I'm afraid. I haven't won the lottery or anything. Hence *why I'm still here."*

You might win the lottery baby, if you keep it up. I think.

My eyes roam her body slowly, and I feel a muscle jump in my cheek at how tightly my dick hardens at just the look of her.

I chuckle at her.

"Tatum, can you turn the sign around so we can get ready to go?" She calls out.

The twin who always looks up to greet me gets up and walks the few feet to the front door, turning the sign around before walking back to his seat and sitting down.

"Tucker," she calls, craning her head to look past my shoulder. "Are you done with your math homework sweetie or do you need help?"

The boy finally looks up and over. "No, I got it mami."

She furrows her brow, looking worried, and I don't like that for her.

Lola's eyes slide back to me and tilt my head back at her, giving her a little wink. She blushes, making my skin feel hot and my heart skip a beat. Lola licks her lips, looking a little unsure. As she reaches for the broom, I briefly contemplate her nervousness around me as she begins to sweep the little tiled area back there, eyeing my book tucked under my arm.

I came here thinking I might read, but I'm still not sure of her schedule with the boys.

"So, I don't mean to be too forward, however, I'd love to come and sit with you and read one night when you're closing down." I just give it to her straight. I'm not much of a bullshitter, and if I want something I'm pretty direct with it. Her eyes widen in surprise.

"*Oh,* well tonight I have the boys, but this is their weekend with their dad. So tomorrow they'll be picked up, and I'll be here at seven pm as usual. If you'd like to come?"

Fuck yeah I'd like to come Lola. All over your tits and your pussy, as a matter of fact. I clear my throat. *One step at a time, Hudson.* I chastise myself.

"What about Saturday?"

She giggles. "Seven."

I smile. "Sunday?"

She glances up at me with an amused look on her face. "*Are we having a readathon?*"

"Well, we gotta get to these red tabs, don't we?"

Lola turns fire engine red, making my aching dick hurt even more. Jesus, I can't believe it's been almost a year and a half since I got my dick wet last.

"Sunday is my day off." She whispers so low I can barely hear it, and the fact that I'm turning her on just as bad as I am, well...she should be thanking God those boys are right behind me.

"Great. That sounds great." I smile at her, making her blush deepen. "Will you meet me for dinner Sunday night?"

Lola looks at me with raised eyebrows. She pauses, dumping the trash into a hidden trash can slowly. So slow I can tell she's using the time to concoct a response that I know I'm not going to like. I wait her out patiently, seeing her eyes flick to her boys before a sad look crosses her face.

"I don't think that's a good idea, Hudson. I'm sorry. I'm really flattered you asked, though."

I tilt my head. "Because of their father?" I say it softly so the boys can't overhear. She stares at me a beat too long, her light gray eyes blink slowly before flickering away. "You don't need to worry about him." I lean my palms onto the counter and get just a bit closer. "Let me take you somewhere nice. It'd be my pleasure to treat you to a night out."

"Mami, we're *hungry.*" The boys complaining reaches the back of the store.

I catch her eye again, fighting desperation. "Dinner Sunday? I just need a yes, Lola."

She twists her lips as the boys start yelling in earnest now for her attention. She wrings her hands together and shifts on her feet, clearly feeling cornered. *"Fine,"* she grumbles, heading around the counter and snatching her jacket off the little rack by the door.

I follow her over, leaning down into her ear as I pass behind her.

"I'll see you tomorrow. It's red tab weekend." I give her a little chuckle as she stiffens and then I straighten up. "Bye boys. Be good for your momma." I call out as I push out the door reluctantly.

Climbing in my truck, I sit quietly, waiting to see them out. They pour out of the coffee shop in a mass of boy limbs and backpacks. She has a boy on either arm tugging on her, and she struggles to lock the door with them pawing all over her. The wholesome sight makes me grin.

Lola's got a bright smile and she's laughing as she stumbles while they pull her hard to her SUV. She opens up the back door by the curb and stands there patiently while they get in one after the other, and she waits a minute, probably to make sure they get their seatbelt on before she climbs in the driver's seat and pulls off.

I pull out right behind her, texting Haley to please feed and water the horses. I Venmo her three hundred dollars to do it the next three nights as well, and she sends me a shocked emoji and a thank you.

She's so humble, despite her parents literally being multimillion-aires. They got themselves a good daughter, and I can only hope that if I am ever blessed with children of my own that they turn out just like her.

She accepts every dollar I offer her with such grace and humility.

Lola stops to get gas and as she spends a second filling up her car. And proving my point that she's a neat freak, just like how I like them-a tad crazy with a touch of OCD- she also takes the time to wipe the windows down with the squeegee tool before helping the boys out and walking into the gas station.

Her lights beep, indicating her car is locked, and they walk into the store for a few minutes before coming back out. The boys have a root beer in each hand and a bag of chips, yet she carries nothing.

My eyes roam, it doesn't look like she's got anything for herself.

I wait until she pulls off and follow closely behind, seeing we are on the way to her neighborhood. She pulls into the garage, checks the mail, and chats with the older male neighbor next door before heading inside after the boys through the front. They go into the home through the front and then disappear.

I shake my head, and exit my truck, needing to see more.

The trick to getting away with something is to act cool, like you belong there. So, I walk the sidewalk leisurely before making my way in between her house and the house that isn't the male neighbors, and I walk straight through the backyard and into the wooded area behind the homes.

I settle against an oak tree and watch.

The woman's got no curtains or window treatments. Probably feels a false sense of security, seeing that unless you're hiding in the woods like I am, you can't see into the home. But I *am* hiding in the woods, so I see everything. She's standing at the kitchen sink, in front of a recessed window which houses a couple jade plants and an aloe vera. Along with a little cute watering can shaped like an elephant.

She's talking to the boys who are settling at the table with a plate and one of the twins is placing a jug of juice on the table.

Lola disappears for a few seconds before reappearing with a pan of lasagna and places it on a wood cutting board in the middle of the table. They're talking, and she laughs at something one of the boys says as she's cutting into the food and plating their plates first.

She pauses for a minute and blinks at the table before turning and disappearing again, appearing by the refrigerator. She reaches inside to grab a bowl that has saran wrap, nabs three bowls out of the cabinet, and heads back to the table. Placing everything down carefully, she scoops out the salad to the boys utter horror. Based off the look on their faces. They start visibly complaining before she sighs, holds up her hands, and gives them a mom look.

The two of them share a glance before she arches an eyebrow and flicks them both a teasing look. Lola suddenly mouths something, and I can just *barely* read her lips say "big and strong" before she holds up her arm and flexes it. Giving her bicep a little kiss. She holds the other one up and repeats the movement, making me smile.

The boys get up in excitement and start flexing too, and I honestly can't believe what I'm seeing. They're jumping around the kitchen, yelling about being strong and flexing.

And no one has visible muscles amongst the three of them.

I bite my cheek, holding back a laugh and then suddenly she turns, distracted. She goes to the front, out of my eyesight, and I watch as the boys begin to tear into their salad, even without their mother there. So they're respectful. That's a good thing.

Suddenly their heads swivel, and Lola appears in my line of sight again, but this time when she comes back, *Dominic* is behind her.

I bristle. *Fuck.*

A hot flash of annoyance and jealousy hit me hard, making my muscles lock down tightly.

Fuck. Fuck. Fuck. I'm seething. *What the hell is going on?*

One of the twins gets up and goes to give him a hug but this time, when Lola is looking, he lets him actually hug him. The other twin doesn't even look up to greet him. He finishes his salad quietly, a completely different person than the happy go lucky boy who was just goofing off with his twin and his mom.

I watch, while they eat dinner. Noticing the mood completely sours upon the arrival of Dominic. It's a palpable thing, so strong I can feel their pain all the way to this tree I'm leaning against. Lola is trying to keep a happy face on, but hers is different too. Pretty soon, they finish eating, and the boys leave to run upstairs.

Lights begin flickering on and off haphazardly, presumably them getting ready for bed because it's late.

Dominic and Lola disappear upstairs as well and I see the boys bedroom lights go off shortly later. Another light turns on in the house upstairs. My heart skips a beat and I look down at the ground, feeling something happening with my chest.

Disappointment fills me and replaces the anger, making me put a hand to my nape and squeeze hard. I haven't felt like this in a minute.

I imagine them fucking, and my lips tighten and pull back at the thought of her spreading her legs for this asshole. My eyes narrow imagining him tasting her. But it doesn't make sense because she wouldn't let him kiss her the other day. So I don't get it.

But then a second later I see them appear back in the kitchen. Just the two of them. And my being fills with bone shattering relief.

She leans against the counter in my direct eyesight and the expression on her face is not good.

They begin to argue, and her arms stay tightly folded to her body as he begins to dominate the conversation. I witness her shaking her head, making herself smaller and smaller, and then suddenly her arms fly outward and she shouts at him so loud a vein sticks out in her forehead and her eyes flash. I can make out she's saying *"enough."*

And what happens next is *enough* to make my blood boil.

Dominic reaches out and slaps her straight in the mouth, hard. Her head turns and she holds a hand up to her face.

I fist my hands in anger, taking a step forward to the yard before forcing myself to exercise some common sense and stop. Because I'm not supposed to be here. She'll *never* give me a chance if she knew I was stalking her. As I work to calm my heart rate down, I watch as she brings a hand up to wipe at her cheek before nodding.

I take a deep steadying breath. Willing some common sense in alongside the anger consuming me.

We're not going to talk about how that made me feel so we're just going to *do*.

To keep from going to prison tonight, I push off the tree and head to the front, seeing a gray vehicle there that is parked in her driveway and begin taking pictures. I get license plates, make and model, VIN number, inside of the car, and tire make. Everything I can get.

When I'm satisfied, I go to walk back to the side of the house and hear the front door open. I watch from the shadows as Dominic walks out of the front, not even bothering to close the front door and he's counting a wad of cash. Twenties and fifties, and two hundred dollar bills.

I just know without a doubt, those are the two one hundred dollar bills I left in her tip jar.

Goddamn, how on Earth is it even possible to be this pissed? It can't be healthy.

I make my way to the tree back in the shadows and my eyes roam, seeing her standing there in the same spot leaning against the counter. Her head is bowed, and she's sobbing into one hand. Holding the other one to her stomach with the other.

Everything in me strains to go to her.

Lola cries for a few minutes before pushing her hips off the counter and begins to clean. She starts with the table, gathering up the dishes, packaging up the food. She wipes down the table, does the dishes, giving her aloe some water from the elephant can. She sweeps, mundane stuff.

And I don't know what the fuck is going on, but the fact that she's cleaning like this while actively crying really fucks with my psyche more than I thought humanely possible. I stand there a little stunned at her tenacity and tilt my head as she begins to mop.

Leaning harder against the tree, ignoring the bark scraping my clothes, I once again contemplate her for what feels like the thousandth time. She's confounding me completely. I don't understand her situation, just like I also don't understand how she's not dead tired.

After working in the yard for an hour and a half last night, all day at the store, then everything she's done tonight. This is her schedule? Then to be *hit*.

My face twitches, that's how displeased I am.

Nope. It's just not going to work for me. None of it. None of it's going to work.

From the top on down it's all going to change.

I pull out my phone and send Clayton the pictures of Dominic's car, telling him to run it. Then I pull up my lawn care company and contact them, leaving a voicemail and setting up lawn service for Lola for the rest of the year and through the next year to include snow shoveling service for this winter.

I'm in the middle of asking Clayton to run a background check on her, and to hack into her accounts to see what kind of money she's working with when I see the patio door slide open and she's suddenly out on the back porch.

She takes a deep breath and sits at the glass patio table, carefully placing a bottle of wine and a glass down in front of her. And I debate just how bad it would be if I show my hand too soon and step out of the darkness and reveal myself. But if I couldn't step out to interrupt their argument, then I damn sure won't reveal myself to her like *this*.

She pours a very small glass of white wine and before she can even take a sip, her face contorts with pain. She lets out a sob, then another one before she lowers her forehead to her arm and begins to cry again quietly. Her shoulders heave with emotion, and she just lays there for about ten minutes straight crying her heart out.

My own heartstrings tug for her. However, in the midst of my musing, I can't help but think that she seems to do everything in long increments of time.

Really gives it her all, every task.

Lola sits back up and wipes her eyes with the sleeve of her jacket, gives herself a little shake, and I just think she's so *beautiful*. She finishes her wine, and goes back inside. Locking the door and turning off the lights in the house except for one side light in the foyer, and the light over the stove.

I do the same thing, leave the little light on over the stove. It's homey feeling.

She places the bottle of wine back in the refrigerator and heads upstairs.

I see the bedroom light turn off before a soft golden glow replaces it, letting me know she has the lamp on. My eyes widen, seeing her face appear in the window, again with no curtains, working to crack it about a fourth of the way. From my angle looking up, I see the top of her head briefly as she walks past the glass pane into what I presume is the bathroom.

Another window there cracks open and for the next couple minutes I'm teased with little sights of movement before steam begins billowing out into the crisp fall air. My eyes narrow because I know she's in there naked. Taking a shower.

Unfortunately, I'm too busy thinking about the slap Dominic gave her and how exactly I'm going to handle that to get hard. It's frustrating because this would have been perfect, had he not shown up.

But he did, and so he needs to be dealt with.

I'm debating leaving to head home because she takes long ass showers, when suddenly I see the top of her head again and the bathroom light click off. The soft glow of the lamp goes off as well. There's a few minutes of silence and then I turn to leave. I'm heading to the back of the house to make the short journey back to my truck when I hear it.

A little buzzing noise.

I freeze midstep, and for some fucked up reason my nostrils flare, as if I expect to smell her arousal all the way in the back yard. I stand deathly still, scared to move before glancing at my watch, wondering how long my torture is going to be.

It's exactly forty nine minutes.

She pleasures herself for forty nine torturous fucking minutes straight before I hear a frustrated whimper, and then the toy cuts off. That in itself drives me absolutely nuts because now I'm wondering...

Could she not orgasm because of the slap? Or does she take a long time to cum? Did the slap turn her on and that's why she felt the need to and she couldn't *because* of the slap? It didn't look like it, but you never know.

To say my mind is racing is an understatement. But she didn't orgasm for some reason, and if I were a fucked up person I'd find a way to scale her house, climb through her window and demand she tell me.

I give her window one lingering last look before I take my nosy ass to my vehicle and drive off. Making the trip in silence, because I have *a lot* to think about.

4

Pink Tab Dates

Hudson

I sleep like a rock, knowing I'm going to see her the next day, and I make my work day one at the office. I'm not here too much, spending a lot of my time out in the field surveying my various jobs. Keeping my employees on their toes.

I love popping up on them, keeps them sharp. But today, I kick my feet back and start this damn book with all the tabs, because I see there's a little ways to go before we get to the first red tab.

And I desperately want to get to *those* tabs when I'm with her.

But let me tell you, this book is something the fuck *else*. And the spots that Lola thinks are romantic, well, excite me. To say the least. Because it's looking like Ms. Ma'am's desires are parallel to my own. If this book is any indication.

My eyes flicker up from the pages, wondering about this shit I've seen so far with Dominic. He's clearly an abuser, and Lola clearly does not like him. But again, looking at this book, something about a domineering man seems to turn her on. And then I begin thinking about her little solo session last night.

What the *hell* took so long for her to fucking orgasm?

Stowing my thoughts away, I want to do something to put a smile on her face. So at noon I send her some lunch, and three dozen long stemmed white roses. I pay a grip for a real crystal vase before I dog ear her book and continue throughout my work day, because I'm not a slacker even when it seems like it. At five in the evening I get a text from Clay.

> Hey, I ran that plate. It's registered to a man named Dominic Patrick. His insurance is ex pired.-Clay

My eyebrows fly up. He drives the kids around in that car I presume. I'll pay attention today when I get there.

I grab my wallet and my keys and leave slightly earlier than I have been. I don't usually hang around as late as I've been lately because I get in early. But since I've been busy spending my nights trying to get into Lola's good graces, and now subsequently stalking her, I've been staying later.

It doesn't make sense to go home then backtrack when her shop's on my way to the house.

I stop quickly at an ATM and pull out five hundred dollars and busy myself for a minute learning how to fold them into origami roses, managing to make it actually look like the one in the tutorial video. Proud of myself, I shove them into my jacket and head into the store earlier than Lola's used to.

I see her with several patrons. She's so distracted filling coffee orders, tea, and cashing everyone out that she doesn't notice me come in. I find a chair off to the side against a wall that's bigger and perfect for me, and I sit.

Making myself at home.

A few minutes later the front door opens. And what do you know, it's the neighbor with the twins. I see them come in and they're laughing and joking and having ice cream. Lola looks over, only having one customer left and she gives them a bright smile as she finishes their order before she steps out from behind the counter.

My eyebrows raise as I notice the emblem on their school jacket. They go to a very prestigious private school in the area and I frown. How the fuck can Lola afford that place for one kid much less two?

More things that again don't make sense.

If Dominic is demanding money from her, and she's got the kids almost full time, he's not paying child support and I doubt he's paying for the schooling. I start trying to piece it together as if it's a puzzle. Little book store, very nice house, two kids in private school. No child support. Her tip jar has never been super full.

How's she doing it?

The twins run up to her and almost knock her over with their boyish excitement and it takes a second to detangle herself.

"Thanks Frank." Lola says almost sheepishly to the man who is standing there with his hands in his pocket, sternly telling the boys to not bowl her over.

"Oh you know it's no trouble. Gotta fill up my retirement days somehow." He gives her a grandfatherly grin before she turns and reaches into the tip jar. She picks up every single dollar bill and then puts them together nicely before trying to hand them to him. He flushes and backs up a step. "Now Lola you *know* I won't take your money. We go through this almost every day I get the boys and I just don't know how many more times I need to tell you this before it get's through that thick skull of yours."

The boys have now gone to their usual chairs in the front of the picture window and I see them both start their homework. Lola breaks out into a huge smile.

"Nooo," Lola says teasingly, giggling at the older man. I see a spark enter her eye that fills me with humor it's so infectious. She begins walking backwards towards the storage door. "But I know something you'll *liikkeee*." She sings this next part and I get half hard at the way she says it, because *damn*.

Mama does something to me.

Lola turns and disappears into the storage closet for two seconds, coming back out with a big ass history book. Frank's eyes go wide, causing her to break out into an excited smile of her own.

"Lolita!" His tone sounds like he's slightly chastising her. *"You shouldn't have."* He takes it reverently, running his slightly knobby fingers over the face of the book.

She giggles and does a little hop. "Look inside, look inside!" And damn if my half erection doesn't turn into a full one at that.

She reaches forward and opens the book, pointing at something in the front. Frank's jaw drops and he raises his gaze to hers and they stare at each other for a minute before Frank's chest puffs out and he leans in, pulling her in for a big hug.

"Thank you. Oh my goodness you silly, stubborn girl. You must have paid a fortune for this!"

I see Lola melt, literally *melt* into this man's hug, and they sway there for a few seconds before she reaches up and wipes a tear out of her eye before she pulls back.

"Well, it's the least I can do. You treat us so well, Frank." They turn, making their way slowly to the front.

It's then she finally sees me in the corner. I stay silent, but give her a slow smile that lets her know I saw it all.

She blinks in surprise. *"Hi."* Her cadence is slightly throaty, causing my body to respond.

As I stare, letting her husky voice scratch over my nerve endings, she stands there for a second looking rather discombobulated. I'm sure she wasn't expecting me until our usual time.

"Hi." I say back with emphasis, that one word hangs between us, so loaded.

Her eyes cut away from mine to look to the side, and my eyes follow hers, seeing where she's put the massive flower arrangement I sent her.

I didn't sign it with my name, I had it delivered anonymously. But something tells me she knows it's me. Her eyes flick back to mine before lowering to the book she let me buy off her on the small table next to my now empty cup of coffee.

Yeah Lola, I am quite aware the main character leaves the woman roses when he's walking all inside her house, like a creeper. I'm not much better, but at least you're going to get a bouquet instead of singular flowers each time.

She watches quietly as Frank says goodbye to the boys before heading out.

"I'll be waiting for you to make it into the house tonight, Lola." He calls, and just for a second, his eyes meet mine. He stares hard at my face, before turning and walking out the door. Without him saying a word, I just know he saw me sneaking around Lola's backyard. I keep my expression cool and collected.

There's so much silent messaging being thrown around the room today. I can't wait to see what happens when Dominic gets here.

Lola claps her hands once. *"Okay!* Since there are no patrons-"

My eyebrow lifts as I tilt my head. *Because what the hell am I then, Lolita?*

"-do either of you have anything I can help with before your dad comes and gets you. I know he's not much help with homework..." She trails off, shooting me a little embarrassed glance.

The quiet one lifts his head. "I do."

"Tucker, lets see babe." She tilts her head curiously and places a hand on the table as she leans down next to him.

"It's this math problem, I don't understand it." He says, turning his paper towards her.

She bends down over him and my God, I see the top swell of her cleavage as her shirt gapes open slightly, revealing just the very edge of black lace. Pain erupts in my head at how hard I grit my teeth. Because her flesh is slightly spilling over the material and I just *know* her breasts slap against her ribcage when she's being fucked hard. I can almost hear it. My heart begins to race.

Goddamn it.

I torture myself with the mental image for a minute, my eyes flickering between her face and her cleavage for a bit. The whole watching her being a mom thing is killing me. Literally killing me.

She looks over at the other twin, who is putting his homework away and pulling out a book. "Tatum, you good sweetheart?"

"Of course mami." He says this quietly as he looks over at his twin who stiffens at his answer.

My lips tighten as I lose my erection. The quiet one is struggling, obviously not confident like his brother. I don't like it.

She spends another minute making sure Tucker does his problem, and not only does it but understands it, before she straightens back up and turns to me.

"Coffee?" She asks simply.

I smile, getting up with my cup to follow her to the counter. I toss my used cup into the trash next to her while she works to pour me a cup. She doesn't even ask me how I want my coffee this time. Her energy is different, slightly more subdued, and she's quiet.

"How was your day today?" I keep my voice measured, with no hint that I know anything about what happened the night before.

"It was a day." She gets a little smile on her face and then her eyes flicker momentarily to the roses set off to the side on the counter and she places the top on my cup. "How about yours?" She gives me a little up and down look. "You don't look like you had a hard day today. That's good huh?"

"I had some downtime today. Got some reading done. I had a very late night last night."

I see her nod a couple times and then just blink at me without attempting to keep the conversation going.

I'm trying to work my way in here, Loli. Talk to me baby. I tilt my head, waiting a few seconds in silence. Fine. I'll keep talking to *you* then.

"How was your night? Do anything interesting with the boys?"

Her lips purse and her eyes tighten slightly. "My night was fine, thanks for asking." She says this so monotone that the hairs on my arms stand up and I fight hard to not crush the coffee cup in my grip. I look over at the roses, grasping for a change of subject to get her mind off it.

"The flowers are pretty. Do you like roses?"

There it is. Her face loses that anxious pinch and she smiles warmly, a flush enters her face and her mouth relaxes. *"I love them.* I've never been given flowers before, much less ones that look like *that."*

I smile and hum, because even though she doesn't know it was me, I did that. *I* put that look on her face. But just as suddenly as her body relaxed, her eyes nail themselves on the picture window behind me and then her entire demeanor changes. I don't even have to look behind me to know Dominic is here.

"Dad!"

Just like I don't have to look to know that the greeting came from Tatum, not Tucker. But seeing as Lola was already heading to the storage room, coming out quickly with the boys lunchboxes and headed around the counter, I turn my body, crossing my legs at the ankle, and brace my hands on the counter behind me.

If that man knew what he was occupying space with currently, what I could do to him. He would think twice about being within five thousand feet of me, much less fifty.

What's interesting is Tatum doesn't try to throw his arms around Dominic this time. He just stands there next to him, and stares at his brother who is taking his time putting his stuff into his backpack.

"We don't have all day!" Dominic barks at the boy, causing his shoulders to hunch up.

The fact that he didn't even have a hello for Tucker lights my ass on fire.

Tucker throws his brother a dirty look before he walks over to his mom and just leans against her, already defeated. Doesn't even open his arms and wrap them around her. He just leans against her as if he's got the weight of the world on his shoulders. Lola's shoulders slowly hunch as she puts her fingers in his hair and just hangs onto him for a second.

Dominic's eyes suddenly flick to me and he tilts his head. *"Ey!"* He says sharply, his eyes pierce into mine, catching me blatantly staring at the whole fucked up situation. And I couldn't care less.

I raise my eyebrow but keep what I really want to say swallowed down. Because fuck if I'm going to open my mouth and make the shit worse for the boys who have to go home with him.

"Yes?" I reply, so damn proud of myself.

His eyes narrow at me as he gives me a full body assessment. *Yeah, I'm bigger than you Dominic, and much scarier.*

"Are you going to *buy* anything, or are you just going to stare like a freak?"

Hearing Lola chastise him quietly I give him a slow smile, my nose twitches and I feel my eyes narrow. "I think it's touching, watching a mother having a moment with her little boy. I wish I had kids of my own."

He doesn't even know it's a threat. But I do.

Dominic grunts and gives Lola and Tucker a filthy look that only Lola can see, as Tucker is still pressed into her belly for all he's worth. "Yeah well, you be careful who you have kids with. If she's anything like this one, she'll make them *weak ass punk ass little shits.*"

I feel my soul leave my fucking body, but then it thankfully gets put firmly back in place as several women suddenly enter the store, forcing Dominic and Tatum to shuffle to the side to give them room as they're blocking the entry way. Lola bends down to whisper something into Tucker's ear, and he nods before pulling away.

The boy's absolute look of dejection wrecks me, and I feel myself shaking I'm so angry. It's settled into my gut almost like an ice block.

This man needs his ass beat into the ground, and then some.

Dominic turns to leave the shop, leaving the boys inside. Lola greets the women, telling them to make themselves at home, before she pulls both of her sons over to the side. She squats down, making herself slightly smaller than them, and takes a hand each into hers.

She shakes her head almost encouragingly, whispering something furtively at them. I'm proud of her that she can be a glimmer of hope and strength in this moment for them. Someone strong that they can look up to because, though it's bad, it *could* be worse; they could have two parents who fly off at the handle at each other in front of them.

Tatum looks at Tucker, saying something to him that I can't discern over the women's chatter.

Both the boys nod and she gives them each a lingering kiss on their cheeks. Rubbing her hands down their arms before she opens the door, making sure they get into their dads car safely before she returns back into the store.

At this point, I'm behind the counter making myself another cup of coffee because I slammed the last one in my anger and attempt to keep my hands to myself. Lola doesn't even seem to mind because she's walking stiffly behind the counter, barely sparing me a glance as she slips into the storage room and closes the door.

I cast a quick look around the shop, seeing the few women are pre-occupied looking at merchandise before I slip in behind her. Shutting the door quietly.

I frown. She's on her knees with her arms around her torso, rocking. Little gasping sounds are leaving her making my heart ache.

"Lolita." I say softly, sharply, disregarding the use of her nickname.

Not having heard I came in behind her, she turns with a gasp and falls flat on her ass on the shiny tile with a shocked look on her face. I don't even think to hesitate. I reach down grabbing her by her arms, and haul her up and into me hard. I crush her to me, not giving her space to think, react, or much less breathe.

Wrapping an arm around her waist, I hook my finger in a belt loop in her jeans and place my other hand around her head, pressing her into my chest.

"You are not a bad mother, okay? *Do not* let that fucker break your spirit. You're too lovely, Lola." I whisper to her.

Even though I'm trying to comfort her, my body can't help but respond to her. At the feel of her pressing into me my heart pounds so hard that I know she has to be able to feel it beneath her cheek.

My skin heats up as we touch. My dick swells at the feel of her soft breasts against my abdomen, forcing me to move my hips back slightly to keep her from feeling it. She doesn't deserve to feel propositioned right this second.

She needs comfort.

Feeling her sag against me I tighten my arms even harder around her, holding her up. Her weight is nothing to me, but I feel her quickly stiffen and try to right herself.

Though I'd love nothing more than to keep her in my arms, I get it's a sudden, awkward situation. So, I let her pull back reluctantly. She blinks hard and scrubs her face of her tears and then the mask slips on. I recognize it because I've got one of my own, you see.

"Thank you, I needed to hear that..." Her voice is professional, resigned. I wonder if she also needs to be touched as badly as I do.

"Anytime," I say gruffly, "do you need me to cash out your customers so you can have a couple of minutes to yourself?"

I didn't mean to throw her off guard, but she recoils her head back and scrunches her face up. *"What?"* She gives me a once over that would be comical if the situation we were embroiled in wasn't so fucked up. *"No."*

I give her my own once over and then stand to the side, letting her exit first.

We split. I head back into the main part of the store, snatching up my abandoned coffee and then sitting back in my seat. But I don't pick my book up. I watch. There's almost no trace of her inner turmoil as she works to cash the women out. One of them holds a book up, the same book I bought off Lola. Then she loudly references her blog.

The women get really excited and rowdy for a second. They all laugh and Lola, my girl, places her hands over her face in embarrassment as they squeal and cackle. Then I hear something about a gun scene that's got my brow furrowing.

My eyes snap to the book.

What the fuck kind of shit are these women reading?

Intending to do a deep dive, I pick the book up and splay it open, quickly getting lost. Before I know it all the women are gone, leaving just the two of us alone. I stay quiet as Lola works to lock up the store, and she takes a minute to breathe before turning to face me and walking over to where I'm sitting in one of the two plush seats flanking a round table with a tall tiffany lamp.

"I am so, *so* sorry you had to see that, Hudson."

I look over at her and take a sip of my coffee. I give an appreciative gasp at the flavor before I pin her almost colorless eyes with a stare. She's obviously very affected by me, because her nipples harden visibly through her top. My eyes raise back to hers.

"That's unfortunate, because I'm not. I'm happy I could be there to hold you."

She blinks. As we stare I observe that the look we share is not *uncomfortable...* but it's not exactly comfortable either. It's charged. Multi-layered.

There's embarrassment, sexual tension, secrecy, openness. Curiosity, longing, desire, and the hot feeling you get when you're caught witnessing something about someone else that you know you aren't supposed to... and you know they don't want you to see.

"Have you eaten?" I ask. Lola shakes her head no and to break our stare for a moment, I pull up my phone. "You like lasagna?"

Yeah, I fuck around like that. I try to hide my grin but it's hard.

Her brow furrows and her lips part as her eyes become wide. I stare at her, not giving her an inch of a clue as to my little field trip to her house last night. I'm cool with letting her think it's a coincidence.

"I dooo..."

"Good, because there's an Italian restaurant by me that has the *best* pasta dishes."

"O-Okay." Her response is shaky and I can tell there's a whirlwind of emotions shifting through her. Her eyes slide to the flowers again and I smile, turning to my phone. "But in the meantime, how about a pizza. Do you have a favorite?"

"Uhm, you don't have to. I can eat when I get home."

"Nonsense. What's your favorite pizza?" I studiously stare at my phone, scrolling through the options, because if I have to crowd her back in the break room and lock her in with me to get her to spend time with me then that's plan B. But I'd rather us go with plan A.

"Hudson I'm kind of strapped for cash right now-" The embarrassment is back on her face and she's fidgeting.

"But I didn't ask you to pay, now did I?"

"Hudson-"

"I'm partial to supreme and meat lovers."

"*Hudson!*"

"*Lola.*"

My eyes meet hers and Goddamn it, I don't want to hit her with a stern stare after what we shared in the storage room and how that asshole treated her today, *and yesterday,* but if she fucking thinks she's wiggling out of my grasp this soon then she's got another thing coming.

As fucked up as it is, this is my in, and I'm taking it.

"Fine. Meatlovers." She sits back with a huff before getting up and walking to the register.

"Thanks so much for your cooperation, beautiful."

She throws me a look over her shoulder and begins to clean and straighten up behind the counter. I order us a pizza and some vodka and juice through a delivery service and sit back with my book, flickering through again.

A few minutes later I feel a blanket being thrown on me interrupting my book and I look up, startled, but she's folding herself into an interesting position on the stuffed chair next to me under her own blanket, holding a cup of tea, and cracks open a book of her own. I watch her read for a second in the soft glow of the lamp before turning back to my book.

We read like this in silence for almost an hour before there's a knock at the front door. Lola goes to move but I'm up first, unlocking the door and then tipping the delivery person. I grab the box, and the bags and place them down on the round table in between us.

"Time to eat."

She looks over curiously, and licks her lips at the sight of the cheesy melty goodness. I want to see a piece of cheese hit her chin so bad I can taste it.

"Did you eat today?" I take a napkin and take a slice of pizza and hand it to her. She looks at me and twists her lips.

"Yeah, I had tortilla soup. It was so good too. It came with the flowers I got today. Seems I've got a secret admirer." She sits back in her chair and takes a small bite of pizza, her eyes twinkle at me from her semi lit spot next to me and I chuckle.

This is incredibly romantic. Very pink tab worthy. I wonder if she thinks so?

"I feel like we should pink tab this experience. What do you say?" My eyes roam her face slowly.

She giggles again and then blushes. *"Hudson,"* she hesitates, looking down at her pizza. "Did you...Did you get me those flowers earlier today?"

"Yes I did." All she's got to do is ask.

She looks back up, and something passes between us I can't explain. Something I've never felt before.

"They're really beautiful," she whispers. "Thank you."

"You're welcome. They're to remind you to not forget to bloom." An interesting expression crosses her face forcing me to dig deeper, unable to help myself. "Lola, tell me about yourself. Have you always wanted to own a bookstore?"

She blinks before letting out a little scoff and glancing away. "Well, it's going to sound crazy. But I always wanted to have a little place I sell *wine* and books. It's always been my dream. I guess I only got half of it. Dominic made everything difficult, as you've seen."

'Hmmm. I don't think that's crazy at all." I wet my lips and tilt my head, regarding her intently. "I don't presume know your business, but If that man hurts you, if you feel *scared*... all you need to do is tell me."

She rolls her lips and we engage in yet another staring contest, except this time neither one of us blinks.

"Thanks but...I don't think there's anything you can do about Dominic-"

"You'd be surprised the things I'm capable of."

Lolita's eyebrow raises, however she stays silent, slowly nods her head and then finishes her pizza quietly. Sadly she's a neat eater.

We read for a while, and though it's not my cup of tea if I *were* a reader, I'm finding this book is quite interesting. When I get to the part where the man that the woman main character took home is trying to take advantage of her, and the male main character breaks in and saves the day, I damn near jump up cheering.

But then the gun thing happens, making my breath freeze in my lungs.

I glance up sharply at Lolita, seeing her peeking at me through her bangs with an embarrassed, yet slightly amused expression.

Would she like this?

I continue to stare at her for a moment. I'd personally never do anything like that to her pussy. I haven't even been in it yet and I know it's too precious to even risk playing around like that.

She gives me a little silent chuckle and shakes her head, putting her attention back on her book.

Now, I get it's a controversial scene. But that's it.

"I'm not impressed." I say, keeping my eye on the book. I'm about to fuck with her in a major way. Get ready Lolita. "If you intend to run a woman through, you gotta be a little smoother than this guy."

I almost hear her neck crack as she swings her eyes back to me. Unbothered, I stay looking at the book and flip a page. Reading just a tad more, I give a little grunt, a tiny shake of my head, and take a sip of my vodka drink as I read a little more.

My vodka I mixed with coffee by the way, not juice. The sweet stuff was for Lola.

Seeing the rest of the scene I frown. "My God." I say in an admonishing tone.

She decides to speak up on my prior comment. *"What the hell do you mean you're not impressed?"*

A give her a little chuckle and make her wait a second. "Exactly what I said. I'm not impressed." My tone is so non-chalant it's almost bored sounding.

"Oh." She scoffs. "So you can do sooo much better then, is what you're saying?" I look over at her, seeing she's giving me a playful look. I want to throw her to her knees and make her ride my face until she can't think straight.

"Hmm." I hum, teasing myself with how she might taste on my tongue. "I can." Her nipples become visibly erect through her top and I look back down at the book because I am so tempted it's not funny. "It's just not a decent way to go about consensual non-consent. If that's even what this is. I'm not really sure." I flip another page, still hearing silence. "And I'm *definitely* not impressed about making a woman think you're going to shoot her *there*." I tsk and turn another page. "There's other ways to go about instilling fear that'll drive desire that's much more effective."

I can hear her breathing become labored. In turn my dick stirs, reminding me of my above average size. I decide to make it worst and twist the knife, since I've plunged it in. I love watching her face turn pink.

"And I gotta say, if you're going to have a large dick, make her beg for it. *This boy*, I tell ya. What this woman needs is a *man*." I turn another page and read slowly. I tighten my lips and click my tongue. "This is definitely *not* how I'd fuck you." And with that, I look over and gift her my eyes since she's been silent for so long.

She's bright red, her knees are drawn to her chest, and her knuckles are pressed to her lips. We're back to the uncomfortable silence.

"Wait..." Lola's brows furrow as she sucks in a sharp, surprised breath. *"Who said I was going to let you fuck me?"* She says in an incredulous tone. She gives me a fast up and down look before her head recoils a bit and we engage in yet another staring contest.

I chuckle at her and flip another page, turning back to the book. I've read all I needed to read, to be honest. I snap the book shut and lean forward to take a swig of vodka. Snagging another slice of pizza because I'm not driving home with a buzz, I take a bite and swallow. Feeling my nose twitch as I regard her.

"I say." I watch as those words sink nice and deep.

Lola shakily drowns the rest of her drink.

Leaning forward, I promptly pour her a little more, ignoring the indignant glare she shoots me. It's quiet again, and I find myself beginning to weigh how much uncomfortable silence versus comfortable silence happens between us.

"And how would you fuck me?" She shoots me a little assessing look.

I meet it with a pointed look of my own, taking a second to admire her bravery with her question. As we stare at each other I feel a muscle tick in my jaw with the effort I'm extending to keep control over myself. It takes a second, but finally, I find the self restraint needed to speak to her in a civilized manner.

"Rough, and with no mercy. You need to be broken in."

Her eyes widen, and the sight fills me with so much pleasure I harden to my fullest extent.

"E-Excuse me?" She stammers, her face is bright red. *"Broken in?"*

I grunt and go back to my book. "You asked."

"Hudson I am a woman. Why would you ever tell a woman, *especially one you just met*, that you'd fuck her with no mercy?" I'm proud of her, she didn't stammer once.

Smiling nice and slow, my eyes roam her face.

"Oh I'm sorry. *Did I offend you?* I just thought I was answering your question. I mean...you did ask me rather boldly, so don't even bother trying to be coy. I sussed you out in just the first couple of times meeting you." She raises her eyebrows and glares at me, setting my blood even more on fire for her. "Why would a woman *ever* challenge a man...especially one she doesn't know?"

We stare at each, again, other for a few solid seconds while I wait for her to figure it out.

"Me?" Her eyes are truly ignorant as they meet mine. "I've been nothing but respectful and genuine towards you." She tightens her lips and shakes her head. "No freaking way, *Hudson*. I didn't challenge you! When did I challenge *you?*"

Her expression is angry and it's telling me that she prides herself on conducting herself in a certain way.

"Look at your tone." I say quietly, tilting my head and giving her a little grin, letting her no I mean no harm.

"My tone?"

"Hmm-hmm. Your tone."

She leans way over the plush arm of her chair, narrowing her eyes. "I didn't. Fucking. *Challenge you.*"

And this is what I mean by being broken in. She needs her fucking *Goddamn* feisty, prissy ass torn up real good a time or two to check that attitude.

Speaking of checking attitudes, I reign mine in right quick because this is really only our first couple of meetings. I tilt my head and sink deeper into my chair, giving her a slow look down her body, lingering on her breasts and her hips.

"You didn't?"

"No!" She places her book down and leans into me, staring at me with narrowed eyes, proving my point.

"So you don't call that hand shake you gave me the first time we met not trying to assert your dominance?" I see when it clicks, she physically recoils back in her chair but I dig in a little further, taunting her. "Sweetheart *you live in your masculine.* The way you subconsciously tried to prove you were stronger than me, the fact you are a business owner, single mother, a minority," I scoff, looking back at my book. "You're living in your masculine energy. And If I'd have my way, I'd fuck it out of you *tonight* if you'd let me. Women who operate in their masculine energy *can't* be treated the same way as women who operate in their feminine are."

I hear her jaw drop more than see it. *"I am not having sex with you tonight."*

"Not tonight." I agree.

"Nor tomorrow."

"I wasn't expecting tomorrow either." This makes her eyebrow go up.

"But you *do* expect it."

"Correct." I relish the disbelieving look she gives me and make it worse. "I expect you to eventually give it to me. I also *want it*. Would like it even better if you'd let me take it."

Her mouth drops open. "You don't even *know me*, Hudson."

Thank God. Lola's given me what I wanted to know so I don't have to ask her and potentially offend her. She doesn't just give her body to men.

"I know enough."

"Hudson," she leans forward. "You saw my ex. Trust me, you don't want to be involved with me. You don't want none of that."

I lean forward even more. We're not close enough to be in each other's space but it's close enough. I busy myself rolling up the sleeve of my long sleeve plaid. Her eyes flick down, catching the start of the big ass rattlesnake I have tattooed on my arm.

"Do you honestly think I'm scared of your ex, Lola?"

"I think you should be, if you're not."

I let my own mask slip momentarily and treat her to a slow smile. "Lola... you realize lion's are scared of snakes, correct?" I ask, feeling the blood begin to rush in my veins at the prospect of being able to lash out and strike her ex down.

And yes, I am well aware I just compared myself to a snake but it is what it is. Lola is aware too. Most men wouldn't do that, and now those damn thoughts are fucking back. There's a reason I have this snake tattooed on my arm, I love brands.

"Snakes are sneaky," she whispers.

I nod. "And their grip is strong, and their strike is fast, and their venom is deadly poisonous. I think you've got it wrong Lolita, it's him who should be afraid of *me*. Not the other way around, and I need you to understand that right off the bat." I check my watch, standing up. "It's late, we should go. I'll follow you home."

She gets up, folding up her blanket and grabbing mine from me.

"I can get home by myself, I'm okay."

I follow her to the back but stay behind at the counter while she takes the blankets into the storage unit and then comes back out. I've placed all five origami folded one hundred dollar bills in her tip jar. She doesn't notice it as she walks back out from behind the counter, seeing as she emptied it already.

I snag her waist as she goes to walk past me and I turn her, placing her hips against the counter. She inhales rapidly as she looks at me through her bangs. Her eyes flicker between mine and I give us a second to enjoy this attraction between us before I bend down towards her.

Her hand comes up to my jaw and the other one comes up to my chest, and she attempts to push me slightly away from her. Seeing it's halfhearted, I narrow my eyes before snatching her hand up in mine. My body fills with pleasure at the sight of her nipples hardening before I bend, slowly covering her lips with mine to swallow her little squeal of surprise.

Fuck her lips taste better than I expected.

Picking her up, I place her harshly on the counter top, pressing in between her spread legs, aware that I'm being rougher than normal. I'm kissing her so hard that she's arched back, her breasts are pressing into my chest and I fuck this woman's mouth with everything I've got. Because let me tell you, her lips feel exactly the way I fantasize, but her taste is better.

Making me feral. Breaking something that's been dormant inside of me.

Picking her hand back up, I place it on my chest and hold it there. "Touch me." I growl against her lips, tilting my head and kissing her deeper, stroking the tip of her tongue with mine as her palms explore my chest slowly, leisurely. As she smooths over my chest my skin breaks out in goosebumps at the feel of her enjoying me.

I work to kiss her even deeper.

Lola tastes like life. Refreshing. Like the first sip of water after you've been knocked out cold all night and you wake up parched. She tastes like the first bit of shade you get after you've been working out in the sun half the day and are dying for relief.

"Hudson," she whispers against my lips, but I cut the sound off quickly.

I don't want her words right now, I need more of her taste.

I'm licking into her. Exploring her mouth curiously. Sucking her tongue, biting her bottom lip, rubbing my tongue across the smoothness of her mouth and I groan deep in my chest, letting her know just how desired she is. How desperate she makes me. My hands are clutching her to me by her waist, and I drag one to her hip and tighten. Hauling her hard against me.

Lola whimpers before bringing her leg up to wrap around my hip and I grind heavily into her, making her moan.

"Baby," The endearment just rolls off my tongue. "You feel so good against me." I praise her.

Lola's arms loop around my neck. We're somehow kissing deeper, trying to sink into each other. We're rocking, clutching one another so desperately that I know I'm not in this alone. I'm not the only one fucked up over whatever this is that's happening so quickly between us.

I fist my hand in the strap of her bra at her upper shoulder blades, hanging on tight as I work to press even harder into her. I'm teaching her just how demanding I'm going to be when the time comes for us, and I'm pleased that she's meeting me step for step just as passionately.

She whimpers against me, causing me to rip my lips away from hers with an audible smack. We stare at each other, breathing hard. Her eyes are wide and her lips are red and swollen. A spark of vulnerability enters her eyes once more, forcing me to lift her head back up with a finger under her chin when her gaze falls down.

"I'm not going to fuck you, because you've been drinking and we agreed that tonight isn't the night for it. However, I'm going to follow you home because I need to make sure you're safe, and I'll see you here tomorrow. Same time?" My tone leaves no room for discussion.

Lola swallows hard. "Okay but...you can't come in my house."

I smile at her, brushing a thumb over her cheek. "I won't come in unless you invite me, or you need me." This appeases her.

We lock up the shop, and I make sure she makes it into her car before walking to my truck and we make the drive to her house. I pull into the driveway and watch as she lowers her garage door before meandering slowly to my truck. As the garage door lowers, I see a door that obviously leads into the house, but she doesn't seem to like to use it for some reason.

Opening my truck door, I ignore the truck's beeping and step out, meeting her before she even makes it down the drive to where I'm parked. The wind ruffles her bangs around her face adoringly and I reach up, brushing them off her forehead for just a second. Just so I can see her face in all its entirety. I rest my hand lightly on the top of her head holding them out the way, because I just need to see her.

And fuck if she isn't the most adorable creature I've ever laid eyes on. My God.

Lola sucks in a quick breath before giving me a little shy giggle. I grin back, seeing her flush. I love that she likes my smile.

"Thank you for tonight. I really needed to unwind."

I nod and give her a little hum. "I needed it too. So, same time tomorrow?" My hand drifts down, letting her bangs fall back into place and I cup the nape of her neck in my warm palm, squeezing lightly. Her eyes flutter closed and she sways into me.

"Hmm-hmm."

I chuckle again, giving her a little more pressure. Bending down I press my lips lightly against hers, feeling her tighten with shock as she wasn't expecting it. Cognizant her neighbor is more than likely watching I kiss her chastely, not like how it was earlier. Just soft kisses meant to let her know I'm still with her.

We pull back after a minute and then she steps away. My fists clench, wanting to reach forward and snatch her back to me.

I can't stand it, it's the opposite of what I want.

I walk her to her front door but I stay a step down, in case she feels threatened, and then she's gone. Lola disappears into the house, and immediately lights start flickering all over.

Understanding she does this when the boys aren't around hits me and I turn, making my way to the truck and getting in. Though I'd like to stay and watch the back of her house again, I really need to get home to my horses because I've been neglecting them lately and that's not fair to them.

I wonder if Lola rides? And I'm not just talking about horses either.

The next day we repeat. We eat, have a drink, read, and then I fuck her mouth like I want to fuck her body. I rib her about the book, letting her know just how different I would be and I drink in her laughs in between kisses. Because I think she thinks I'm not serious, but I can't wait to show her just how serious I am. If she lets me.

I begin to wonder, what the fuck is my next step if she doesn't let me. She's got the twins so it's not like I can chain her up to the boiler in my basement and leave the kids with their fuck up of a daddy.

No, can't do that.

As if to reinforce that she won't let me in any more than I already am, she declines my invitation for Sunday. Explaining she's got girl stuff to do. I really try not to push, because I don't want her to think I'm latching on too hard and not capable of giving her space. I don't want her to see me like she sees Dominic. I can be overbearing but I'm not abusive. So I let Sunday slide.

But my ass is not happy, let me tell you that.

I spend Sunday morning with my horses and Clayton, and we take the time to catch up. He thinks it's cute I found interest in a 'book keeper.'

I drive back to Lola's place after Clayton leaves, determined to see what she's doing. I won't have it. She's coming along whether she likes it or not, and if it has to be *unwillingly*, then I'll cross that bridge when I get there.

One things for certain, now that I've got her in my sights, she's about to be taken over.

5

BURIED

LOLA

I ROLL AROUND IN bed miserably Sunday afternoon. I do not need a fling, nor do I need a full blown relationship. The last relationship I got into fucked me and my boys lives up for eternity. Eighteen years I have to suffer through co-parenting with a narcissistic asshole.

The rest of my life I have to deal with this man just on the basis he's my son's father.

Oh God, the thought makes me *nauseated*.

I'll never be rid of this man. It makes me sick to think about a lifetime of misery. Because whereas I might not necessarily ever see him or talk to him if I don't want to after the boys are grown off living their own lives, I still have to deal with how he makes them feel. How his presence and actions affect them.

And what if we have grandkids?

I scream inside my head. It's never ever going to end! I'll have to co-grandparent with Satan's brother.

I bite back a sob, hating that my thoughts go there. I hate it. I want to be like the rest of the people in their mid twenties. I should be carefree, freshly out of college and enjoying the rigors of getting to know a new career, a new schedule, navigating a new adult life. But I made a mistake getting involved with him when I was eighteen that I can't run from.

The boys are my life, and I don't know how the hell to stay present with them, and to be there for them the way they need. But by God I'm giving it my all, dealing with shit I should not be having to deal with. Because I love *them*.

I wish I had my mom. I wish I had girlfriends to vent to.

I lay in bed naked, just lamenting and bemoaning my miserable fucking life. I couldn't even be bothered to put clothes on after my morning shower. It sucked to cancel on Hudson but I can't get involved with him. Dominic is making my life a living hell, my brother's life a living hell, and now I'm just supposed to keep what?

Supplying him with men to leech off for the rest of forever?

No. He can just keep sucking me dry and I pray I can make it until the boys are adults before I collapse, a drained shell of myself.

Because that's what I am. Just a shell. *Shellita* if you will. That could be my new nickname. I am a husk of myself. And I feel dead. I'm a dead person walking around, only come to life when I have the boys.

I sniff and reach for my phone. The desire to text Hudson that I'm sorry for bailing on him is strong, but I never got his number. The hurt look that crossed his face when I called off our plans on Sunday, after we had such a blissful two evenings in a row together haunts me. I'm such a freaking coward. I told him I couldn't meet with him today because of "girl stuff."

What the fuck is "*girl stuff?*" What a shitty excuse. All I've done is cry all day. I make myself climb out of bed and pull on a pair of sweats. I need to get outside for some fresh air because I can't allow myself to bed rot for too long, it's not good for my mental health.

With the midday sun beckoning my attention I head down to the kitchen to grab my bottle of wine out of the fridge, a pack of chips and dip, and go out to my patio and curl up under a blanket. I sit for a bit, just staring off into the woods. It's quiet. Peaceful.

But not peaceful enough to settle my soul. At least when the boys are around they're loud, so loud I can't hear my own thoughts.

I hate these thoughts that I can't be normal.

That I can't be free enough to even think about trying to move on, or even think about a future ahead of me without the boys. All I feel I can look forward to is pain and misery, and isn't that something. I have a super famous and successful brother, my own house that's paid for, a business, two wonderful beautiful kids, and I can't enjoy it.

Dante should create an eighth circle of hell he calls 'Lolita' and then toss everyone in who was unfortunate enough to luck out and be given a life where they 'sort of' get everything they want, but then *don't*.

Maybe we can keep each other company. Be a boon of understanding and compassion to one another. Because God knows I don't like complaining, it feels too self-gratuitous.

I pull out my phone and text my brother Skee.

> Skee, you busy? -Lola

He's on it immediately, I see the little dots show up. I smile, feeling considered.

> Hey Lola, I just got back from the studio, we're on break until tomorrow. Malfunction on set we gotta straighten up before we go back to filming. You good?-Skee

> Can you facetime?-Lola

The call comes through, shocking me. I can't remember the last time we facetimed, it had to be early May. He's usually too busy. I give him a smile as his face appears on the screen. And I can tell I'm on his video feed in his massive kitchen. He's moving around, looking like he's putting together a sandwich.

"Aww, you don't have Tiffany doing that for you?" I tease him, referencing his chef.

Yes, my brother has a chef. What I wouldn't give sometimes to have someone cook for me, even if it's just once a week to give me a break. One of the hardest parts about being an adult that no one prepares you for? You have to figure out what to eat every day for the rest of your life. Ugh.

Skee puts his face in the video and gives me a smile. "Stop it Lo'. You could be living here having a private chef too but you decided you were too good for the high life, remember that?"

"Whatever." I wince, because he's not exactly wrong. *"Fuck you."*

"Fuck you, *wench*."

We don't mean it. It's our thing, and it's all out of love. We spend a minute getting the brotherly sister vitriol out of the way before I get serious.

"Skee, has Dominic contacted you lately?"

"No, not yet. But you know how things work, speak of the devil and he will come."

I bite my lip. "Well, it's just he's been asking me for a lot of money lately and I'm starting to...to...." I can't say it. I'm not a beggar.

He braces his hands on the countertop and gifts me with his full undivided attention. "Lolita, how much do you have left baby girl?"

I twist my lips. "About twenty grand."

He chokes on his sandwich. And it's a funny thing, to see your brother, who has gone up on award stages, accepting Oscars and Emmys, and has even been the subject of a documentary himself, in a pair of sweats choking on a sandwich. It's priceless. He finally catches his breath.

"Lolita! What the hell, why didn't you tell me mami?"

I fight back tears, because he only calls me 'mami' when he's really serious. His big brotherly tone is stabbing me right in the heart and I feel guilty. So guilty that I've inadvertently dragged him into this drama that is my life with Dominic.

He doesn't deserve that.

"I just, I'm trying to do this on my own. So you don't always have to bail me out. But I'm struggling Skee. If you give me any more money then it's just going to get worse. At least this way I can tell him you cut me off. It gives you the option to cut him off too. We'll be okay."

"No. You'll lose them, Lolita! We can do this for another ten years, *it's okay.*"

I let out another sob, drawing my knees to my chest and burying my face in them, sobbing.

"Oh mami." His tone makes it worse. "Baby girl I'll deal with him like I always do when he gets ahold of me ok? Don't worry about me in this scenario."

I'm choking on my tears, hyperventilating I'm so upset. And he talks me through it thankfully.

I get off the phone with him a half an hour later and then go back into my house, to get dressed and grab my grocery list. I try to do the grocery shopping during the weekend when the boys are gone because it gives me something to do to keep from rotting away in the house.

I picked a dark blue simple linen dress that hangs to my mid thigh, and some black stockings that have velvet hearts on them, and black Rothy points. My favorite shoes.

I wish the hearts in my stockings were broken, like how mine feels all the time. I leave my hair down and take a painkiller because I feel like I might be trying to get a headache I'm so stressed, and I make my way to the grocery story slowly with the windows down so I can enjoy the crisp air.

Twenty minutes later I'm at the mega grocery store and I take a second to park. Walking inside I sling my big black bag into the cart I stand there for a second, clicking the baby seat belt in the strap in case anyone tries to steal it, they'll have a entire cart to drag around first. I'm busy pushing my hair to the side and across my front when someone behind me clears their throat.

I blush, looking behind my shoulder and hurrying. "Oh, excuse me. I'm sorry." I say apologetically at the young man behind me.

Jesus, I can't even go grocery shopping without feeling rushed.

I pull over to the side so the man can get his cart and I reach into the bag, grabbing out my list and my pen, and begin to wheel my way through the aisles. I pick all off brand products, and put back a pack of chicken in favor of a cheaper one that's sixteen cents less because every little bit counts.

I buy lemon juice and sugar because making lemonade is cheaper than buying it premade and I love to have the boys help, and sometimes I surprise them by getting strawberries to put in there. I idle in the beef section, really debating on treating myself to a steak, but when I pick up a ribeye I blanch at the price, hurriedly putting it back.

Instead selecting the cheapest pack of steak bites that I can find, and then head over to the seafood department.

"Hi there, what can I get for you?" The older man behind the counter greets me with a smile.

"May I have six pieces of shrimp please?" I kindly ask the man behind the seafood case.

"You don't want a half of pound? *Or a pound?*" I feel myself flush at his questions.

"N-No thank you...just six pieces-" I cut off as a voice rises over mine.

"Well *well*, I didn't know grocery shopping fell under the realm of 'girl things'." I hear from behind me.

My half blush turns into a full blush as Hudson's deep timber penetrates my brain.

Ohhh my God. I moan in my head. I take a deep breath and try to turn calmly to face him.

"Hudson... what are you doing here? This isn't exactly your neck of the woods."

I'm so fucking thankful I don't usually look like shit when I leave the house because oh my God I do not want him to see me looking rough. I tuck a lock of hair behind my ear and give him a small smile. My mouth waters as my eyes roam greedily. He's in some relaxed clothes, a pair of jeans, belt, boots, and a long sleeved sweater, and I can see the outline of his chest and ab muscles through the material. His brown hair is styled just so and my fingers itch to sink into it.

Like I did a couple times this weekend.

"I shop here sometimes when I'm in the area." Hudson responds simply and I nod stupidly not responding, because I obviously don't know how to act when I see people in places I'm not used to interacting with them at. I'm saved by the worker.

"Here you go ma'am. Here's your six pieces of shrimp."

I turn to grab my little baggie of shrimp and my eyes meet Hudson's rather awkwardly, what an embarrassing fucking moment to be caught in. "Thank you," I half whisper at the worker.

I begin to push my cart, and Hudson follows besides me with his own cart, and I sneak a look inside, seeing an incredibly expensive bottle of whiskey and that's it. I sneak a look up at him from beneath my lashes.

"It's good to see you..."

"Hmm-hmm. Likewise." He gives me a lingering look that makes my heart beat faster.

I try not to wince, because technically we were supposed to be having dinner tonight. We make our way down the pasta aisle and I'm just grabbing based off habit, trying to not let my trembling fingers show. But I clumsily drop a box of spaghetti, and then when I lean down to grab it, I smack my head hard on the handle of the cart stunning myself.

Placing a hand to my forehead I moan, suck in a sharp breath and close my eyes against the pain and embarrassment. Because who cracks their head the way I just did in front of the sexiest man alive? Me. That's who.

"Ohmigod, owww!"

The words come out garbled, and I realize I'm still on my haunches holding my head because oh man... I might have a concussion.

"Aw shit, sweetheart." Hudson breathes.

He kneels down to one knee beside me and he's so big that he still is taller than me at this angle.

Placing his hand over mine he tugs it away and then pushes my bangs back. I struggle against him momentarily because I already detest my forehead, and now its probably got a knot on it making it look even more unattractive.

"Stop it," he admonishes, not letting me scooch away, "be still and let me see."

He tightens a hand on my shoulder, making me still for his inspection and he pushes my bangs back, making me blush harder. He looks for a second then his eyes lower to meet mine and he chucks me under my chin.

"You're okay sweetie. You've probably got more of a hurt pride than a hurt head I'd expect."

In an unexpected move he wraps his arms around my shoulder. Palming my head, he pulls me into his chest and drops a kiss onto the throbbing spot on my temple that's probably going to swell like a golf ball, knowing my luck.

I scrunch my nose at him as he stands up fluidly, pulling me after him, and I'm struck by how graceful he is. You can tell he takes good care of his physical health. Blinking slowly, I try to remember the last time I ran a mile. Probably high school?

"Yeah, I..." I reach up and try to smooth my bangs down. "I'm not normally this clumsy."

Liar.

Hudson bends down and grabs my box of spaghetti off the tile, placing it in my cart before turning and grabbing his whiskey and placing it there, too. Discarding his cart off to the side, he wraps his arm around my shoulder once more and presses gently, forcing me to start walking.

Okay...I guess we're shopping together now.

I stop in the middle of the aisle and flick him a nervous look. "Don't you have anything else to get?" I question.

I have one more thing to get, but I don't want him to go down the feminine product aisle with me. How much more embarrassing could this shopping trip get? Hudson looks down at me with a smirk, making my heart skip a beat.

"Nope. Just the whiskey baby girl."

I melt, and I know he can see it because his eyes flick down and stay trained on my breasts for a few good seconds, letting me know he's blatantly ogling my nipples poking through my thin dress. His eyes meet mine again.

"You know, we could have had a *great* time at dinner."

I swallow hard, because if dinner is what I think he's alluding to, he doesn't mean food.

"Again I'm sorry. I just had s-stuff."

"M'kay...let's do the stuff then." He's pressing into my back again, and ironically we're heading towards the side of the store where the feminine products are.

I nervously run a hand down my hair and I feel hot, like I'm about to break out into a sweat. I pick up the pace and rush into the aisle, ripping a box of tampons off the shelves.

I'm distracted trying to maneuver the now heavy cart, damn near twisting my ankle trying to hightail it out of the aisle, when I see him staring rather hard at the couple of vibrators that are offered there. It hurries me up to try and flee.

I make it out of the aisle and am booking it faster than I've walked in a minute when he suddenly appears besides me, his long legs enabling him to catch up to me quickly. He gives my shoulder a bump with his as he leans over and tosses a pack of magnum condoms into the cart where it lands right on top of a bag of sweet potatoes.

My jaw drops.

"Hudson!" I gasp. I lean forward and toss a few things on top to cover it. "I know you're not putting condoms you plan on using on other people *in my cart!*" I admonish as my inner inappropriate sassy bitch, without my permission might I add, comes out.

His eyes flick up and down my face before his settles into an amused expression. He grins nice and slow, making the skin crinkle in the corner of his eyes just a little. I'm suddenly reminded we have an age gap, though I'm not sure how much.

"Oh baby," He chuckles as he wraps his arm back around my shoulder and leans down into my ear and I feel my face turn bright red at his next words. "Those are all for you and you know it. The fact that you would think I'd consider sticking my cock in another woman after I got you in my sights is quite insulting."

We resume walking. He keeps his mouth pressed intimately to the side of my head. To any regular shopper, we probably look cute walking side by side with me tucked under his arm, but I know the truth. His breath ruffles my hair and makes me shiver, which turns into a full on shudder when he begins to speak quietly against me.

"And when I'm able, I'm going to punish you *so good* for that fucking nasty mouth of yours that you won't be able to sit right for days afterwards. And if you keep saying shit like *that*, I'll start when we get in the parking lot. *Now say sorry.*"

My breath hitches and I feel him press one more kiss to my temple before pulling his head away and smoothing his hand down my hair. I'm biting my lip so hard I physically can't say anything, and before I know it we're in line, behind several people. My fingers are gripping the cart so hard my knuckles are turning white and my eyes flicker everywhere, seeing just how public this is.

But we feel like we're in our own little world.

"No." I whine, giving him a defiant look over my shoulder.

Hudson chuckles and steps behind me making my spine straighten with unease. I stand there fidgeting, running my fingers along the cart handle as I feel his eyes boring into the back of my head. I won't do it. I won't give him the satisfaction.

My mouth flies open on a gasp as I feel his hand smack my left ass cheek roughly forcing me to career forward on a sharp yelp before jerking to a sudden stop. I look down, breathing hard, seeing Hudson has wrapped his hand around the handle, keeping me from flying into the woman in front of me.

He pulls me back to him, trapping me between his body and the cart. He sneaks an arm around my waist, placing his hand almost on top of my pussy pressing me into him hard. He bends, places his mouth to my ear and softly caresses my hair away.

This is so inappropriate.

"Say it." He growls. *Growls.*

My poor panties.

"Fuck, Hudson! Owww." I put my hand over the spot where he smacked me, casting a quick look around to make sure no one is paying attention. "I'm sorry. *There.* You happy now?"

"No. *Not anywhere close, actually."*

I frown, trying to think of a response when suddenly I see we're at the belt, cutting off our conversation. Hudson walks up front and starts loading everything together, not separating our items.

"Wait," I flap my hands, tying to whisper and get his attention quietly. "Hudson, I can't buy your stuff! *I'm sorry."*

My eyes widen at the almost offended look he gives me and then he turns, making pleasantries with the woman cashier. I go on ahead and debate how bad it would be if I just fall over in a faint in the middle of the floor at the little sly look she gives me at ringing up the extra large condoms.

I can't risk it.

Instead I busy myself watching Hudson take the bags and start loading them in the cart, his arms are so strong, his thick muscles bunch as he works to load the cart back up.

Seeing everything's rung up, I push the cart hard against his hip, trying to give him a clue to move the fuck out of my way so I can pay. But Hudson puts a hand down and wraps it around the cart, effectively holding me still. He's nodding, telling the lady he would in fact like to donate to whatever charitable cause she's talking about. And before I can even get out a squeak of protest, he's swiping his card and paying for almost four hundred and fifty dollars worth of groceries, liquor, tampons, and condoms.

I want to crawl back in my grave and take a nap, honestly.

I roll my lips as he pulls the cart behind him and then waits for me to catch up to him and we exit the store together. "I have money Hudson, at the house, I'll grab some and pay you back if you'll just follow me home? I'm only like fifteen minutes from here. I'm sorry I was trying to tell you-" Hudson shakes his head and puts a finger to my lips.

"I see you have a hard fucking head, girl. Don't know how to let someone treat you right huh?" Hudson wraps his arm around my shoulder again and I realize for the first time how perfect I fit there. "I don't want money, but I'll tell you what I do want."

"Anything!" It's out before I even realize I say it and I roll my lips again, my eyes widening at the surprised but pleased look on his face. Hudson breaks out into such a sexy grin that I feel a bang between my legs. Ramping up that simmering desire that's never far, where he's concerned.

"I want you to have a quick drink with me. I'll follow you home and we'll sit in the driveway and talk for a second." We stop at my car and I let up the hatchback, and without even asking Hudson starts loading the groceries.

"Oh..."

But I don't like it. I'm not even going to lie and say I do because this feels like a trap for some reason. I pause there as I put the last bag in my trunk and I look up at him nervously.

"Hudson you've spent a lot of money on me...you know you don't have to right? I don't expect you to at all."

I don't know what I'm trying to get across. The fact that I don't want this man to feel like I'm using him? Or I don't want him to get the wrong idea that just because he spends a lot of money on me that I'll spread my legs for him.

"I'm not going to fuck you because you buy me stuff."

"Well that's a shame because..."

His eyes rake up and down my body so thoroughly that I actually look down at myself too like an idiot to make sure I still have clothes on, because the assessment he just gave me made me feel naked.

"You'd have me by the balls missy." A hard glint enters his eyes that causes my nipples to tighten and my core to clench. "I'd give you just about every fucking red cent and asset I own if that's what I thought it took to get you to open up to me like that."

I fold my arms and treat him to a grin, calling his bluff and teasing him. "Oh yeah?"

He folds his arms, mirroring my stance and leans against my SUV. *"Yeah.* How much you think you're worth?"

My eyes narrow. All I know is, we had better be fucking playing around. He can't think I'm serious.

"Five million dollars."

We stare at each other silently, and I'm ashamed to say that for the tiniest second, I must be subconsciously considering it. Because I told him the exact amount that was basically stolen from me by Satan's brother.

I'm completely unprepared when Hudson's eyes darken as he steps into me, pressing my hips into my vehicle. He molds his entire body into mine, and my eyes go wide at the size of the bulge against my belly. He hooks a finger under my chin and makes me look up at him and he leans down, getting real good and comfortable at looking into my eyes.

He's so close our breath is mingling.

"If you're serious, I would need your body carte blanche, I want to fuck you bare, and I want to be able to do anything and everything I want to you. And I mean *everything*, Loli. If I say jump, then you had better ask how high."

My heart skips a beat at his words but the nickname? *Loli?* I melt because aw, that's cute.

Ignoring the bang in my pussy I fight like hell for a nonchalant attitude. I bite my lip and give him a teasing look. *"Sounds like a lot of work."*

"I'm not afraid of hard work, especially in the bedroom." He treats me to a devilish smile if I ever saw one. "And oh baby, keeping this body satisfied will be a *full time job.* I can tell you're a greedy little thing underneath that timid exterior."

My lips part. *"Greedy?"* Now it's my turn to throw him an offended look. "Your sex radar must be broken because I don't even like sex like that." I smack my hand over my mouth in horror at letting that slip.

Why can't I just shut *the fuck up* sometimes?

I meant it though. Because that has to be the reason I can't orgasm like a regular person. And to be honest, sex wasn't good with Dominic.

Hudson's eyes narrows in a sly look. "Oh no baby, nothing's broken over here. You're fucking fiendin' for it. I can tell. I just need you to let me in there one good time."

My mouth drops.

So." He licks his lips, making me wet mine in response. I bite back a moan feeling my clit pulse. *"Deal* or no deal?"

My breath catches and I press a hand to my mouth, trying to contain my giggling. He gives me a chuckle and tilts his head, his eyes never leaving mine even though I'm comically falling apart pinned between him and my vehicle.

"Oh Hudson!" I gasp.

Taking my hand from my mouth and placing it on his chest I push against him hard. He steps back a foot and folds his arms.

"You're so funny!" I gasp between giggles. "Construction workers don't make that much money, but thanks for humoring me and making me laugh. It's *really* been a day!"

Something flashes in his eyes at the same time a muscle ticks in his jaw. I briefly wonder if I might have offended him when he taps his left hand against his right bicep, momentarily distracting me with his buff arms.

"I would have paid it, you know." He says quietly. His eyes rake down my body, making me shiver. "I would have paid much more than that, actually."

My brows furrow. "Pffftt." I scoff and wave a hand at him dismissively. "Well I'm *flattered*...but I think I'll just have the drink. You know, *not* like a prostitute."

He nods. "I'll follow you home. Act like you got someone following you and don't blow through any lights." Hudson chastises me, making me smile because he reminds me of Frank a little bit.

"You bet." I call after him, seeing him begin to walk up to a big ass expensive looking truck parked next to mine. He stands there, waiting for me to get in the car and I start my vehicle, seeing him climb in.

Twenty minutes later I'm in the passenger seat in his truck in my driveway.

He'd asked to bring my groceries in but fuck that, I've only known him like a week or two so I know better than that. I decline politely, and then proceed to get absolutely fucked up on the smoothest, richest bottle of whiskey I've ever tasted. And we're laughing, like truly laughing at *everything*.

The banter between the two of us is so easy. He teases me at how clean the outside of my house is, calling me a secret serial killer, which made me snort because I'd never hurt a fly. I in turn called him bougie, because why's a construction worker driving a truck that cost almost one hundred thousand dollars, and drinking eighty dollar whisky?

It makes no sense. Maybe he's irresponsible? I don't need another money sucking leech. I ignore these thoughts though, because whatever this thing is between us isn't going anywhere so at the end of the day what he's got going on in his life doesn't concern me.

"So," I look over at him, sipping more whiskey out of the bottle cap. "Why Loli? You don't like to call me Lola?"

He gets this grin on his face as his eyes zero in on my lips then lower, his touch grazes over my breasts then the center of my legs. He's not shy at all about letting me know how badly he wants to fuck me, and I find his boldness and confidence sexy.

"Because, I want to lick you up like a lollipop."

I roll my lips together and suppress a high pitched laugh.

"And you say *I'm* the fiend?" I tease. "Well, how do you know I'm not a serial killer then? I could take you inside... lure you in with the promise of a special taste of my candy, and then *off* you." I continue to joke.

"Hmm. I bet your candy is addicting too." He chuckles, pouring me another shot.

I notice that he hasn't drank much. So he does show restraint there at least which is good. I hiccup, holding a hand to my lips as he shoots me an amused stare and suppresses a laugh.

"You're either really responsible, which is admirable." I hiccup again, causing us both to break out in laughter. "Or you're trying to get me so drunk I let you in my pants. *For freee!*" I titter, laughing so hard I have my hand on my chest and my head thrown back.

"No," Hudson says rather harshly, giving me a look, "I'd never fuck you while you're this drunk. It's just good to see you have some abandon."

I give a little laugh, busying myself turning the vents off to get the heat off me, and look straight ahead into my garage door.

"Boy, you are a smooth talker aren't you? Almost like something straight out of a smut book." I look back at him, sipping a little more of the whiskey. "Are you going to start finishing my sentences next?"

Hudson throws me a sexy smile and then reaches over to place his hand on my thigh.

We both stare at my lap for a second while my muscles tense. Our laughter is decidedly dissipated, and for a second, there's no sound but our breathing. The second I relax he slips slightly under my dress to curl his hand around my thigh and then reaches even higher, making my dress ride up my legs.

My breath sounds loud between us as I shudder at his touch, feeling my pussy clench and become heavy and swollen with need. Bold, he doesn't stop until his broad hand finds the thicker fleshier part of my inner thigh, the fatty part I hate about my legs.

But he settles when he finds it and grips me firmly, the warmth of his hand seeps through my tights and makes me shiver with want. I fight to keep from clenching my legs together, but between the feel of his hand, and the whiskey, my pussy is throbbing miserably.

I blink when the thought hits me this man really never asks for anything, he just does. That's such a fucking turn on.

"Those men are fake, I'm afraid I am really, *really* real. Loli." The tone in his voice pulls my gaze from my lap, forcing me to meet his eyes, and in their depths there's something there that I can't recognize. "I don't want to just finish your sentences, I want to keep the book. If you catch my drift." He says, tilting his head.

I completely shatter inside and my legs tighten involuntarily trapping his hand between them.

I'm stuck, my breasts are heaving with tempered emotion and I can't do anything but whimper as he leans forward to capture my lips with his. He takes his sweet time exploring me.

This kiss isn't exactly gentle, but it's not rough either like how it was over the weekend. This kiss feels more possessive.

My hands wrap around his wrists trapped between my leg and I hang on tight. He squeezes me even firmer before sliding his hand just slightly further up my legs, and I break our kiss with a shuddering gasp when I feel his finger brush my panties against my clit.

He's breathing just as hard and I'm wondering why he's not taking it any further when he grins at me.

"You better be thanking every thing holy we have an audience right now. I was about to bury my head between your legs until you didn't know your own name."

It takes a second to process but when it finally does I lean my head over and look past him, seeing Franks curtains rustle.

"Oh God." I moan, leaning my head against the headrest and struggling to pull my dress back down. "That man is so freaking nosy. But I love him though." I say hurriedly, throwing Hudson a rather serious look.

I don't want him thinking bad of Frank. He's the closest thing I've got to a father.

Hudson gives me one last squeeze before removing his hand making me immediately miss his touch. I wish I were different. I wish I could invite him in, have what I think might be some awesome mind blowing sex before I kick him out.

"I'm sorry, it's been fun but I have to go crawl back into my lovely dirt now." I open his truck door and pause when he holds me fast by my wrist.

"Wait! What do you mean?"

Tipsy, my words spill out before I can stop them. "Oh you know, my home in my lovely little graveyard. Because I'm dead. Buried under a wealth of regret disguised as rotten dirt."

He tilts his head and we just stare at each other for several heart stopping seconds.

"You're not *dead,* Lolita. I see a woman who is very much alive."

"Do you?" I breathe. "Because I don't feel like it. He's killed me."

Hudson picks up my hand and kisses the back of it. "He hasn't killed you, not by a long shot."

His eyes meet mine as he slips the tip of my forefinger inside his mouth and then bites down hard, making me whimper and try and pull away. But he holds me fast.

This man's eye contact is insane.

"O-Ow." I gasp weakly, feeling my core heat up almost unbearably with his actions. At how rough he's being with me.

"Do you need me to pull you out of that dirt, then?" His breath washes over my fingers.

I feel every nibble zip straight to my clit, his teeth are currently lighting up every nerve inside my body making me hot and slick between my legs. I squeeze my thighs tight, trying my hardest to cope.

"What?" I sigh, completely distracted by this hold he has on me.

His mouth leaves my fingers to trail up to kiss the inside of my palm where he plants a wet kiss there, stunning me.

"I *said,"* he licks a trail to my wrist and nibbles at the skin there making me let out a moan. He ignores me, nipping at my flesh. "Do you want me to pull you out of that dirt."

My eyes fly open and widen. Is that even possible? My heart starts hammering. "I-I...I don't know if you can."

"Oh sweetie. There's so much I can do that you don't know about. Didn't I already tell you that?" He leans forward fast, burying his face in my neck and sucking at my ticklish spot.

I let out a little squeal and wiggle in my seat at how hot his words just got me. Does Hudson even realize how tightly I'm strung? So tight, that if he nibbles any harder I might break. He pulls his lips away but replaces them with the fingers of his other hand. They wrap around the warm nape of my neck and I feel the blunt tip of his nails dig in just slightly, keeping me in place for him as he meets my eyes once more.

Our faces are so close our breath mingles, and his hand sits almost deathly still against my pussy, like a threat. My pulse beats heavily in my neck, and I fight the dizzying feeling slowly taking over me. I'm sure as hell I'm going to faint dead away in his truck. Oh my God. I whimper, unable to unlock my vocal cords to speak.

"I want to touch you." He says quietly, keeping his eyes on mine. "I need to know what you taste like."

The words hang in the air between us, and I'm suddenly afraid that when I get up I'm going to leave a little wet spot behind on his seat. The thought causes my cheeks to flush bright red.

"*Hudson,* I-I have to go inside before Frank shoots out your window." I know I shouldn't use the man as an excuse but I'm really not lying. I wouldn't put it past him to do something like that.

Hudson lets my neck go, heaves a rough sigh, and then sits back, giving my wrist one last stroke with his thumb.

He carries all my groceries to my porch and then patiently watches while I take them into the foyer. Stepping back outside I close the couple of feet between us, wrapping my arms around him. He rocks me for a quick second before giving me a gentle kiss goodnight.

"Just so you know," he whispers against my lips, "you're worth so much more than five million dollars. You're *priceless* to me."

His admission makes my knees shake and it takes everything in me to keep from collapsing to my porch. I rub my hand along his jaw, feeling his soft beard.

"Por favor, it means a lot to me that you said that. Get home safe." I step back with a smile, closing the door behind me.

Once I get into the safety of my house, and put up my groceries, I cry the rest of my night away and get ready for the week ahead. Because I know Hudson's coming. And as badly as I'd like to see where this might go between the two of us, I can't. He doesn't deserve what's happening to Skee, or to me. It's not fair.

None of it is.

I drown myself later in the longest shower of my life, trying to put some life back into me. But it doesn't work, because I'm so close to dying I can feel it like a tangible thing. Like all I have is a couple more breaths left in me before they can tip me over into my grave.

Stubbornly, I keep my head under the water. Because If I die, maybe I have a chance at being born again into something better.

More me.

6

RATTLESNAKE
MARKINGS

HUDSON

MONDAY AFTERNOON I'M OFF work earlier in the day and headed up to Lola's shop with purpose. I couldn't think about work, as I was too distracted thinking about the weekend with Lolita, especially last night. Her comments about being dead has brought my world off it's axis, and I just won't rest until I can do something to change that.

I'm lost in thought pushing my way through the door, about to demand she let me take her out to eat for dinner this Wednesday since she canceled on me yesterday, when I pause at the eerie quietness of the shop. My eyes flicker around seeing no sign of her.

However after a second, the silence is broken in an alarming way that's got my eyes narrowing.

"I would never come into your place of business and cause a scene like this."

To say the hairs on the back of my neck stand up is an understatement. Not only do they stand up on my neck and my arms, my heart skips a beat before anger fills me and I feel my body flush hot and my muscles begin to tighten. Because that's my *Loli's* voice I hear, muffled.

My eyes flicker quickly around the store, seeing no patrons, but the perimeter of the storage room door behind the register is lit, letting me know where she is.

In a split second decision, I turn the 'open' sign to 'closed' and begin to walk to the front, wondering what's going on. And if I thought I was angry *before*, I become straight irate when I hear a man's voice in there with her. Clipped, deep, and obviously threatening.

I pause on the other side of the register, inwardly debating the risks at crossing a boundary when I still don't have all the information.

So I wait.

"You have no fucking respect for me, never have Dominic! I'm not giving you any more money! *I don't have any more!*" She's shouting, her English cutting off into Spanish.

My head recoils in disgust. Because what the fuck does an able bodied man look like asking a woman for money?

"Stop fucking *lying*, I know you're loaded!"

"No my brother is loaded. Not me! Now I've told you before, if it doesn't have to do with the kids, then we have no reason to talk!" Her voice is quieter, strained, like she's just barely keeping herself from yelling again.

He's in her place of business, not caring if she could lose customers over this? Not caring about her reputation with her customers?

"Dominic, get the hell out of my face!" I hear her yell and I'm moving before I even know what's up.

I vault the counter and within two seconds I'm at the door, hearing a massive crash and a scream that's quickly cut off.

I rip the door damn near off its hinges and stride through just in time to see Dominic has her pushed up against a shelf. Books are currently spilling out onto the floor from a knocked over box, and he's in the middle of snatching her head back by her hair.

But what really takes the cake for me, is his other hand is on her *throat*. And his eyes.

They're dead eyes if I ever saw them.

Lola's staring back at him in a panic, trying to suck in air. Busy trying to scratch and claw at his hand around her throat.

Around my girl's throat.

Anger is replaced by something much sicker. It fills up every empty space in my body until in this moment there's nothing but me, this man, and the ominous feeling of numbness informing me that the part of me that I keep so carefully hidden is front and center without my permission.

How I know it's a sickness? I can't even see Lola in this moment. She's faded away momentarily, letting me know my sanity is temporarily gone.

Hearing me enter the room, Dominic's head snaps to me and his eyes narrow, but I'm already on him without thinking. I calmly slap my own hand around *his* throat, locking down hard. He chokes in earnest, and his eyes bug as I mercilessly crush his windpipe, stunning him and causing him to let her go immediately.

His hands fly up to wrap around my wrists but he can't dislodge me, I'm too strong. I feel my face twitch as I tighten my grip even harder, informing him he's fucked with the wrong one today.

He gags as I meet his eyes with mine, and then they widen ever so slightly.

I don't say a word, I just begin to walk him backwards, pushing him towards the opposite wall. And, for good measure, I knock the back of his head into the concrete wall behind him.

I don't say a word. There's no need to.

I stare into Dominic's eyes and let him see my particular brand of crazy. The eyes that hide sick thoughts I don't dare let anyone know are there because I'm quite aware of what society thinks about people like me.

However for Dominic, I let the veil lift momentarily. My nostrils flare as the scent of the man's fear shines through, and a hot sensation travels up my spine in response.

And goddamnit... it's so inappropriate... but it makes my dick hard.

I ignore his jerking as he begins to truly feel the effect of the lack of oxygen and I reach onto my hip for my switchblade.

Letting the blade out, I don't even fuck with him like I want to. I don't hold it in front of him so he can see it, or tease him with it, none of that. No, I mean business with this one. Because he just had his fingers all over *my girl* like he had a right to. Was trying to drape his dominance over her like he deserved the honor, *the privilege*.

Lola and how I feel about her isn't a joke, and Dominic doesn't deserve to even think I'm playing around *at all*. So, though it'd give me sick pleasure to play with him the way a cat might play with a mouse, we're bypassing the bullshit and cutting straight to the point.

Literally and figuratively.

I turn his head with my grip, place the tip of the knife to the skin behind his ear, and I begin to cut as I speak to him softly. I keep my tone purposefully low so Lola doesn't hear.

"She's *mine*. And if you ever pull the shit you did just now ever again, her boys will be mine too. You feel me?"

My eyes flick to him momentarily and I stare for a second, letting him know how serious I am. I don't tell him he's already done for. I prefer to let him think he's got a tiny glimmer of hope. Give myself something to look forward to when I hunt him down later and take it from him.

He groans, struggling against me, but I tighten my grip even more, cutting off his air supply completely. I'm relentless, letting him know he's marked. I relish the blood dripping down his neck as I make the cuts slowly, deep, so he can *feel* it.

Retracting the blade, I lean in. "Get out." I whisper, letting his neck go.

I watch disgusted as he slumps to the floor on a hoarse whine, and begins to hack nasty coughs as he struggles to breathe.

Holding his hand to his throat, Dominic crawls a few feet away from me before stumbling to his feet and clumsily making his way out the door, loudly gasping for breath. He holds his hand to the spot behind his ear, and I don't even look at Lola as I follow behind him slowly, watching him make his way out the store.

I stride to the door after him and lock the door, and hightail it back behind the register area. I busy myself for a second, washing his blood off my fingers from where it dripped on me.

Toweling off my hands, desperately trying to get a grip on my control, I walk into the storage area where I find Lola slumped on the floor over the spilled box of books, crying. The adrenaline's gone, leaving her with a rush of emotions.

Anger, hurt, fear, and I'm sure embarrassment at having me see her-*them*-like I did.

Her hands are shaking as she tries to put the books back in the box.

"I-I'm s-s-sorry." Her head remains bowed, and her hand lifts to scrub the back of it on her face.

My eyes soften as she takes a second to try and smooth out her bangs.

"No Lolita," I say softly. I take literally one second to debate how she feels about me now, seeing what I just did to her ex.

Some might say it's a gross overreaction, but if you've never seen the object of your desire in an unfair power struggle with someone who wants to hurt them, you won't understand. If you've never seen the person you have *feelings* for be put in a situation where someone who *thinks* they have power abuse it, and lord it over them, then maybe my response might not make sense to you.

If you can say that you can observe the helpless look on their face, see the terror in their eyes as they understand that they're the weaker sex, and are in fact nothing but prey to someone who has nothing but bad intentions towards them. If you can see that and NOT react...

Fuck you, stop reading my story, and go to hell.

My need to comfort her overrides any need for propriety.

Approaching Lola quietly, I bend down, grasping her under her arms and hauling her up at the same time I turn my body to sit on the big stack of two boxes next to her. Without thinking, I drape her over my lap and cradle her close, nestling her head into my neck and I rock us slowly.

My heart tugs as her tears begin to soak into my shirt.

"How long, Lolita?" I dare to ask because so far I've been trying to let her come to me with this, but not after what just happened. I'm in too deep. "How long has he been doing this to you?"

She doesn't speak for a minute and I don't push, because the way she's crying is quite concerning.

It's the cry of a woman who's been forced to keep her emotions in way too long.

The cry of a woman who hasn't known what it's like to be comforted, to have someone see to her emotional needs. And I don't know if you know what that sounds like, but you don't want to. I promise us both the visit I pay Dominic is going to be oh so rich in pain it'd make Jeff Bezos blush.

"Since the separation about three years ago. He was ch-cheating on me. When I found out and filed for d-divorce, he started acting like this when he realized I wasn't going to take him back."

Lolita's a sobbing, shuddering mess.

It's rough, strained, and takes a while, but she gets it out. And goddammit that sick part of my brain decides to make an entrance and let me know how pleased I'd be, because if this is how she cries when she's overwhelmed with sadness, what's she going to be like when she's overwhelmed with pleasure.

And I'm concentrating on her, I really am, but this part of me that needs her the way I do is demanding to be fed. I work like hell to shut that shit down quickly.

"You don't have anyone in your life who can help?" I need answers. Like right *now* now.

"My parents are d-dead." The crying gets worse for a second, but I hold her through it patiently. "My brother's done more than enough. I can't keep asking him for h-help. He already helps me keep the store so I can continue to have my own b-business and be able to keep full time custody of the kids. I mean I know he's got money, but this is ridiculous for *anyone* to have to go through."

I trail my hand down her arm and take her hand, threading our fingers together.

"Thank you." She whispers.

Have you ever had anyone whisper anything to you with reverence? It's life changing.

As her tears dry up, she stiffens as reality hits. I just ran her ex off in the most fucked up way imaginable that she witnessed, and she's a crying mess in my lap. And though I'm not even hard, I know she can feel me through my jeans. I tighten my arm around her shoulders and my hand on hers. She looks down with a slightly shocked expression as if she just now realizes I'm holding it.

I flex my fingers around hers and contemplate how petite her features are. My hands swallow hers, easily. I turn her hand in mine, inspecting her nails. They're medium length, almond shaped, natural with clear polish. I rub my thumb on the soft skin of her finger, deciding I'm buying her a gold ring.

No. Not that kind of gold ring, but one that she can look down and smile when she sees it.

I fight back a grin because my obvious staring distracts her from the fucked up situation, and her little look of embarrassment is honestly the most adorable thing I've ever seen. Our eyes meet for half a second before she stiffens again and looks at the clock.

"Ohhh my Goduh!" Lola struggles anew this time, for a different reason. *"The store!"* She bites out quickly.

Lola goes to move and then lets out a pained yelp, pressing her face into my chest harder. "My earring is caught on your shirt!" She gasps, and I let her hand go so she can wiggle her fingers in between us and sort it out.

"Because God is trying to get your attention. Tell you to slow down." I say sternly, casting an assessing look down at her. "The store will be fine. Surely you can close early one day?" After the tussle with her ex, she needs to take care of herself.

Irritated, I fight like hell not to go after Dominic and take care of *him*.

As she frees herself from the snag on my shirt, she pulls away but I place my hand on her arm and still her once again. This woman is going to learn how to be still if it kills me.

"Well..." Lolita's eyes rise up to look at the clock on the wall and grimaces. She doesn't like not working. I like it and don't like it at the same time.

"Have dinner with me tonight?" My eyes search hers. I try to console myself at the disappointment I feel at the look in her eyes. I need this woman badly. I ache without her.

"Hudson, I *sh-shouldn't.*" She wiggles in my lap, but I don't let her up. The feeling of her plump ass and fleshy thighs against me is too good.

"Why not?" I arch an eyebrow and interrupt whatever she's about to say next. "No, tell me the truth. Why won't you have dinner with me?"

She stares at me, and I meet it boldly, enjoying the sudden labored breaths between us. My eyes trail down her face, her neck, until I get to her breasts and I feel myself stiffen at seeing her nipples poking through the fabric. They're thick and fleshy as they distend, making my mouth water.

God I am in trouble. So much trouble.

Can she sense how roughly I'd fuck her? Would that turn her on? I've never wanted to fuck a woman so hard it hurts her, but with this one... the desire is there. I have to admit it to myself so I can begin to get a handle on it.

She wiggles again, bringing me back to the present and interestingly enough we're still staring at each other. But she isn't answering my question.

"Is it because of what I just did baby? Because he deserved that, plain and simple."

Her eyes flicker away from mine but shortly come back, still silent.

"Are you scared of *me*, or what I just did?" I'm grasping at straws here.

"What you just did."

Her answer is immediate, and I gleam that if I give her short multiple choice answers to choose from, this helps her when she's overwhelmed. Which clearly I'm overwhelming her.

But baby you don't know the half of it.

I tilt my head and shift us a bit. "I would never do that to you." Not really, not in that context. *Do not lie to her Hudson, damn.* "I mean I might do *a version of it-*"

In a surprising turn of events that catch me off guard, I feel a rush of warmth against my thighs, right under her vagina and her cheeks flood, the color rising high on her face.

My God.

My nostrils flare. I inhale so hard that my chest turns to stone and she's wiggling again. "Let me take you to dinner."

I don't even know how I got the words out honestly, because I'm over here busy thinking what she liked about what I did. Was it the throat grabbing, the choking, the cutting? One look into her doe eyes, wide open with submission and I'm *fucked*. All the blood rushes south, and I am the most turned on I've ever been in my life.

I literally half nut on myself, like a damn teenager.

I feel my cum seep out of me and I endure it silently, pressing the back of my head into this shelf behind me, feeling my dick jerk and throb. A muscle in my jaw ticks and her eyes catch it before sliding back to mine.

"Okay, your place or mine?" She whispers.

Her eyes flicker back and forth between mine and she sucks her bottom lip in between her teeth. Worrying it. My dick jerks again as I raise a hand and tug it back out with my thumb, smoothing over the plump flesh. I wasn't expecting that. The urge to say my place is so viscous that it terrifies me, but I need to see hers. I need to see how she lives, her sanctuary.

"Yours." I force myself not to say it too quickly, because if I appear too eager, she might take it away.

"What are you thinking?"

"Is this a trick question?" I grin at her.

"I don't do trick questions. I meant what would you like to eat."

And goddamn it why do my eyes go straight to the center of her legs? They had one job, to stay on her face. *Fuck.*

Lola lets out a little sound that lets me know we're on the same page. She wants my mouth down there.

"I'm a hard man, Lola." I raise my eyes back to hers, communicating just how serious I am.

"I know. You come in after hours and make me stay late all the time, and do extra work for you. I know you aren't easy." She breathes this last part.

I put my hand to her mouth and insert a finger in between her lips.

"Open." I order, my tone stern.

Obediently, she parts her lips and I pull back on either side of her top lip, unashamedly exposing and inspecting her canines, and she lets me.

Narrowing my eyes I just let her have me as I am. "The first time I fuck you, you have my permission to bite as hard as you need to baby girl." My eyes leave her teeth for a second to pin hers and it's amazing.

Her breath soughs out of her lungs, seeping over my fingers and don't you know it, her fucking tongue slicks over the tip of one of them?

My control snaps and I growl, bending down to bite her nipple through the material of her top, hard, so she can feel it through the layer of her sweater dress and her bra. I commit her surprised yelp to memory and I don't even ask. I pull her back over my arm, and bend her left knee up and and back, and slide my fingers down her silky leg under her dress until I get to her panties.

Nudging it aside, I begin to agitate her clit with the rough pad of my thumb.

"God baby girl, you feel like velvet. Pull your breast out for me." I'm just telling her what to do. Not even asking.

Lola trembles against me and her nipples become even harder. "W-wait.." Her eyes widen and her breathing becomes labored.

I pull my head back and give myself room to untie her sweater dress and pull the two halves apart, exposing her purple lacy bra. I ignore her small hand grasping my wrist and I yank the cup of her left breast down and exposing her big breasts and fleshy red brown nipples.

"Shit," I moan, resting my head on her shoulder. My fingers go back to her opening and I thrust a finger inside her warmth, imagining her on my cock. "Baby girl I'm going to destroy this pussy."

The wet sound of me playing in her pussy fills the room and with no hesitation I bend down and take her bare nipple between my teeth, rolling and tugging up on it, lashing at it with my tongue. I thrust another finger high and hard inside her, spreading her out.

"You're so fucking *tight.*"

She lets out a sharp yelp, flinching before moaning, and it's a low beautiful sound. I wrap my lips around the tight peak and suck hard, feeling her wetness glide over my fingers in response. Perfect. I use the coating and shove three of them inside her to the knuckle at my palm with no warning, causing her to try to close her legs around my hand.

Her hoarse, shocked sound fills me with excitement that's quickly turning into bone aching need. I pull away from her flesh just long enough to compliment her.

"Fuck your nipples are delicious. You know that baby?"

I go back to her nipple, tugging with my teeth and beating my fingers into her roughly with no mercy. I'm not warning her with any of this. If I'm giving her everything I've got with no filter, then so is she. God she is a joy to touch.

I twist my fingers inside of her curiously, trying to map out the shape of her pussy. Every woman's shaped a little different on the inside, and I need to know her from the inside out more than I need my next breath. I press even harder, trying to see if I can reach the back of her. My fingers brush against her cervix, making her jerk against me, and I feel myself tighten up and growl against her breast.

I flick my tongue against her nipple and circle that spongy, tender spot again. Then again, hearing her whimper.

Aw *fuck,* those sick thoughts are back. I shudder as I break out into a sweat.

No, Hudson. Down.

I beat back the fucking thing inside me that I'm pretty sure is a demon at this point. Because the fact I'm thinking about trying to get through her cervix is fucked up. I know it is. I groan miserably, forcing myself to be soft.

"Hudson, *please...*" she cuts off with a mumble and a whimper as her head falls back, exposing more of her pretty throat.

Nibbling just a bit harder, I decide right then and there her breasts are my most favorite part of her body....I think.

"Uhhnnnnn." She complains, dropping her head completely behind her she begins to shake and I keep the pace, not letting her up.

And you know what I love? I love she doesn't come quickly. She makes me work for it and that shit is exciting with a capital 'E'.

I spend a long time teasing her, drawing out her orgasm. And because she makes me work for it, I'm going to give it to her how *I* want her to have it. So, just when she thinks she's going to be blessed with one, I take it away and watch patiently she becomes limper and more pliant in my arms.

"Please Hudson."

I swear to God if she says my name like that one more time I'm going to throw her to the floor and flip her dress up.

I force myself away from my thoughts, and busy myself with her breasts. I smack on and off her nipple, giving her rough nibbles, soft sucks, licking her slightly wrinkled areola with my tongue before I tighten my teeth on her again. They're drawn up tightly with her excitement.

Amazingly, her areola are oval, not round, which is really going to give me a lot to think about on my drives to and from work.

"Hmm" I hum. "Please *what,* Lola? Use your words with me."

"I want to...*to come.*" She pants as she stares up at me. Her doe eyes are big and wide, hesitant as they meet mine. "Hudson make me come?"

"Oh baby, you don't have to ask me, I want you. All night long. And I'm going to fuck you *like I hate you."* I growl at her.

Ooohh she really liked that. I did too, because hate sex is amazing. And the sex Lola and I are going to have is going to feel that explosive every time. I already know it.

I curl my fingers and find a spot that has her flinching and raising her head to look at me in disbelief. Her eyes are watering and her face is slightly damp, wisps of her bangs are sticking to her face in places and her plump pink mouth is moist. It hits me then that I haven't even kissed her today.

I raise my head up from her nipple, letting it go with an audible smack.

"What's the matter baby?"

Her hands had come up to wrap around my forearm, and they tighten, tugging at my skin.

Lola lets out a little whimper that's got my dick seriously aching. She twists her hands slightly, giving me more pressure but I continue on, giving her hard pumps and hitting that spot I know she's trying to get me away from. Because with every thrust, I feel more of her cum dripping out of her. And it's soaking through the back of her dress, seeping through and saturating my pants.

It's a lot too, letting me know how needy she is.

Her other leg works to pull back and I give her room, letting her bend her pretty knees back as far as she needs to because I'm not letting up on that spot, no matter how hard she's pushing against my arm.

The sound of me beating against her is honestly the sexiest noise I think I've heard ever. The sound of her pussy is divine. I look down and tilt my head at the sight of her fat pussy encased in her purple panties. The only part of her that's visible to me is one of her pussy lips, and I stare at it miserably. I imagine her clit and I lick my lips, knowing when I get a chance to wrap them around it, I will have also tied her wrists and her ankles back because I'm going to be eating for a long, long, long, long time.

And I need her to let me, because all I can think about is sucking on her until she's unconscious. Goddamn.

Her hands tighten harder, beginning to push slightly. I raise my head and find her eyes.

"Your little hands wrapped around my arm is not going to make me stop, beautiful. You're just not strong enough. And when I get to sink my fat dick inside this pussy, I'm not going easy on you because it's *just plump enough* that there should be no complaining from your end. I want to hear you scream until your throat suffers. And I need you to get that out of your system *first* before I tear your throat up." I thrust deeper, twisting my knuckles into her outer sex, stimulating every inch I can.

"Ayyyyy! Me lo estas dando tan bien." You're giving it to me so good.

I swear my heart stops beating.

Lola throws her head back on a tortured wail that has me grunting my own orgasm as my dick empties out the rest of my cum into my briefs. I shudder, partly with my own release, and partly with the knowledge of why my words affected her so much.

This woman harbors fantasies about being taken against her will. I would be willing to bet every fucking asset and red cent I own that I am one hundred percent right.

I stay right there, stilling my fingers high and hard inside her, bending back down to pluck at her nipple with my mouth. Letting her know that I'll let her up when I damn well please. But right now, I'm getting a small high off feeling her throb around my fingers, and I won't let her take that away from me just yet.

No, this shit is too perfect to let go right this second.

I need a minute to think about the fact I hit the jackpot, because what the fuck are the chances I managed to do that in both my professional and my love life?

Wait...

I still, settling my teeth around her nipple and feeling my breath shoot out hot though my nose. *Love?* I'm certainly infatuated, but love? Oh I definitely have a shit ton to think about.

Lola whimpers and I feel little tremors rack her body. She's still super sensitive, and despite me still obviously playing with her body, I won't let her come again. No. She's going to beg me for the next one, but I want her hungry for it first. I'm going to tease her and make her pay for making me feel the way I do for her.

"I'm sorry baby, but we might have to skip dinner. We're a mess and I need a change of clothes."

Yeah, more like a second alone to figure out what the fuck is happening with my heart.

I pull my fingers out slowly, and as if to reinforce my words, more cum sloshes out of her, and I feel a slight warmth again as it seeps through the material of my jeans. I stick her fingers in my mouth quickly and suck her scent off me. She tastes like sex, and pussy.

It's pure, tangy and fruity with a touch of her natural musk, and coats the back of my throat just right.

I have never seen a woman turn as red as Lola just did. Ever. She jackknifes up and looks down between her legs, seeing the back of her dress plastered to my thighs. We're soaked. Her mouth drops open on a gasp and she turns to look at me.

"My jacket only goes to my hips." she explains.

Her voice is small, embarrassed. I look at my watch. I just got here two hours ago and half an hour of that was spent on fucking her ex up. That means I've been playing with her for almost an hour and a half straight. One orgasm in an hour and a half. I know her body must be tender and overstimulated. I assess her quickly, seeing she's still slightly panting.

She's got goosebumps on her arms and her nipples are still hard. I smile.

"You'll be ok. I'll walk behind you to make sure no one sees." I help her up, keeping my hand on her arm as she sways slightly while she works to get her bearings.

She gives me a little smile and reaches up to her hair, taking the bun out. I stare, fascinated, as the dark locks begin to fall. She's got long, shiny hair almost past her waist. My throat goes dry and I swallow thickly.

I rewrap and tie her dress, ignoring her shy smile.

We spend a second trading our phone numbers and she laughs as I call it. Making sure she didn't give me a bum number which she thinks it's funny but I don't. I give her a smile anyway and follow her to her car, making sure her soaked dress is out of view. My jacket is long enough that it covers my own soaked jeans, but the cold air seeps through, making the fabric chafe my flesh uncomfortably.

I turn her before she gets in the car and she raises one thick eyebrow at me. "Get home safe." I bend down and place my lips to her forehead in a lingering kiss before stepping back and waiting until she gets in and pulls off.

I look at the sun beginning to go down, the streetlights pop on. I turn on a country music station on when I hop into the truck and crack my windows. Pulling on my shades, I disappear into my thoughts and take off into the evening, right behind her.

Because I have a change of pants in my truck.

7

10:30PM

LOLA

OH MY GOD.

Oh my God what the hell was that? I wail inside my head as I drive.

Keeping my eyes on the road I go way over the speed limit, hightailing it to my house like a bat out of hell. Not even waiting for Frank's usual greeting. I change into a fresh pair of clothes before hurrying back out to my car.

Pulling out my phone I work to type furiously, trying to find the nearest sex store in my GPS. Because after the experience I just had, I need something inside me.

I need more than a little vibrator tonight. I just have to. Or I might die. It might seem dramatic but I haven't had sex, or anything inside me in about three years. So I currently feel like I'm being doused with gasoline and set on fire.

It wasn't enough.

This man has unlocked something inside of me and I need fulfillment, *now.*

"Lolita!"

I stop for a second and groan. Frank.

I plaster on a smile and turn quickly, because I was such a mess and didn't want to see him, I hurried into the house before he could do our usual greeting.

"HI FRANK!" I call out, inching to the garage backwards to let him know I'm hurrying.

"Are you ok?" His mouth tightens before lowering into a frown. His gray eyes flick up and down my body fast, checking my body language, trying to see what's up. I quicken my inching my way to the driveway, praying that for once he'll release me from his talons.

"Yes, I just have somewhere to go. I'll be back in about an hour okay?"

"Ok, I'll be watching."

"Thank you Frank."

Getting in the car I throw the car into gear and and back up out the driveway. I'm following my phone to the nearest sex store when I get a call on my cell. I look at my phone, seeing it's Hudson.

My brow arches as I hit answer. Feeling the wind flick my hair I roll up the window so there's no feedback into the phone. However, I can't speak to save my life.

"Baby." His deep voice causes my pussy to pulsate. "You're not at home. What are you doing?"

"Oh," I giggle, sounding too breathless for my liking. "I had to run back out for an errand."

"Hmmm." He hums into the phone. "Well, since you're out, why don't you let me come on by for dinner like we planned. I assume you changed since you went home?"

I think dinner is now a code word for sex.

God he sounds so sexy. I bite back a little whimper at his delicious sounding voice. He sounds rough, a little gravely. Like a man. Maybe the kind of man Frank likes to talk about?

Hearing that he's obviously driving as well, I decide to tease him. Which sucks because I want some dick, which is why I'm going to the fucking sex store to begin with.

"How are you supposed to come over if I'm not even home?" I laugh, making the turn into the parking lot.

I open the door and hurriedly make my way into the store with its blacked out windows. I switch to my ear pods and put my phone in my purse.

"Well, you *are* going home after you run your errand aren't you?"

I let out a little laugh, waving at the woman behind the cashier who asks me if I need some help. "No," I mouth to her.

"I am. But I'm afraid I haven't cooked anything."

He pauses for a second, reinforcing my thought that dinner is also code for sex in his mind as well. However he pivots. "I can have something delivered to your place. We can have a glass of wine, talk."

I roll my eyes and chuckle into the phone. "Uh huh. *Sure.* I know what that's code for."

He laughs back into the phone, and my God I flood my panties worse than I ever have in my entire life. Seriously suffering, I find the back wall with the dildos and my mouth drops open at the sheer size of some of these things.

"Honey, I don't need to speak in code with you. If I want to fuck you, I'll just say it. Why? Do you think you need something inside of you tonight? Should I offer you my dick after our meal? What's that pussy need now?"

Whoa. I let out a disbelieving laugh and inch my way to the middle of the wall to find the more appropriate sized dildos. My eyes peruse, trying to find one that I think might look like his. He's breathing harder.

"It's around eight inches, *real thick*, about six inches in circumference...am I convincing you?"

I burst out laughing because *get real.*

"Now wait a minute, aren't you in *construction*. Do I need to break out my tape measure to show you what eight inches really looks like? Better yet, what buildings have *you* erected? So I can stay out of them."

Hudson's laugh is husky, deep, sexual. "Ahhhh shit." He pauses, chuckling further before letting out a hum. "I don't think you'll be schooling me in anything sweetheart. But you should be glad you didn't say that to my face. It's actually a bit over nine inches, but I was just being modest because women tend to run from men when we tell them we're a lot bigger than average...and they definitely like to run from the dick in the bedroom. And I can tell your ass is a runner. So I just thought I'd throw you some numbers to play around with. You know, trying to help you out here."

"Well *I* tend to think that men like to overexaggerate their size. You know you don't have to. I'm sure I could take it just fine."

"Oh I'm going to make sure you take it just fine. Don't you worry about that. If you walk a little to the right that's probably a good place to start."

My heart skips a beat, my head snaps to the side and I suck in a sharp breath that I know is audible through the phone. My eyes flicker around, seeing no one but the clerk in the store. I snatch the nearest dildo my fingers can reach and run to the register. I'm not asking him if he followed me. I refuse.

"Is that all you want ma'am?"

I nod my head, praying she stays quiet. The woman flicks her eyes to the little assortment of flavored lube next to us in the cardboard box on the counter.

"We have cherry flavored, banana, this one is good for making warmth, stimulation of your clit-"

I promptly hang up on Hudson and then die on the spot.

A thousand of them.

Little deaths, spread out nice and slow. I cover my face with my hand, feeling dizzy.

"Oh my God I had a man on the phone." It comes out strained.

The cashier gives me a little grin. "Well next time bring him in with you. We've got stuff for lovers."

I break out into a nervous sweat seeing Hudson calling again. I answer it.

"I'm so sorry, I think we must have gotten disconnected."

"What an interesting word to be disconnected on." He pauses, letting it marinate.

And marinate it does. Fuck. Yep. He heard the woman say 'clit'. I start sweating heavier.

"Lola, want to tell me where you are?"

No because you already know where I am.

The cashier saves me, sort of. "That'll be one hundred and sixteen dollars."

"Whaaattt!" I almost screech. "Why so much?" I go to dig the toy back out of the box to investigate.

"Well," the clerk says with a cheeky wink. "You got the *big dildo* with the veins and ridges."

I almost break my finger trying to hang up on Hudson again. "Keep the change." I say, throwing the woman a hundred and fifty dollars and run out the door as fast as I can and fling myself into my car, not caring about my boobs bouncing or how I look, if he see's me looking crazy, or any of that because I just have to get out of here. This day is going to kill me and all I can think about is making it home in one piece so that I can finally be rid of this nightmare.

But Hudson's calling again, requiring my attention. I faff my shirt and fight the feeling of needing to faint before answering, swallowing the nerves back hard. "Y-yes, I'm so sorry my phone reception is not-"

"Your titties bouncing are amazing. You know that baby? Do you have *any* idea of fucking incredible of a view you just treated me to?"

My heart draws to a complete stop at his words and the raw desire in his voice.

"O-Oh." I say stupidly.

"Hmmm. I'm leaving teeth marks on you next time." He roughly grunts a sexually stimulating sound deep in his throat. "So, can I see?"

"M-My tits?" I stammer.

"Uh-uh. Whatever sex toy you just bought yourself, my greedy girl."

All the blood drains from my face and my car swerves hard enough to cause me to break out into a sweat. It's happening. I'm going to pass out while driving, go figure. Because the sexiest man on the face of the earth heard the woman talk about clits, and stimulation, and dildos, and veins, and *extra big*. And he's talking about leaving teeth marks on my boobs.

A tear slips out of my eye at the thought. It might kill me. "No. *Uh-uh.*"

"Oh come on, it'll be like show and tell."

I bust out laughing, and can't stop. It's like my body is determined to get a release out of me one way or another and here I am. Instead of passing out and crashing, I'm going to die of laughter *first.*

"Well, it doesn't matter anyway, because when you get home you're handing it over."

I see lights flash in my review mirror and my jaw drops. He actually did it. He followed me to the sex store. But wait, what did he just say?

My brow furrows. "Huh? Say what?"

"Oh, cute. You suddenly forgot to speak English now? You heard what I said."

The audacity! "I'm not giving you *shit-*" My mouth falls open as I hear the click of the phone disconnecting.

I say a string of curse words in Spanish, and then pull into my driveway. Not even waiting for the garage door to go up to park in the garage like I usually do. I grab my black bag and race to the front door, ignoring Hudson, who just parked behind my vehicle with his impressive, big ass truck.

I hurry, trying to haul ass up my front steps. But before I can reach the doorknob I'm snatched up by Hudson, who suddenly materialized behind me and snatched the bag from my hand.

"Give it to me." He growls.

"No!" I snap, trying to yank it out of his hands but he's not relenting. Why I won't give in and just let him fuck me is a mystery.

We're having a small stand off on the steps of my porch, and I have exactly three seconds to stare into his green eyes before we're interrupted.

"Lola, who is this man?"

We both turn in unison. Hudson is able to fix his face a hell of a lot faster than I am. However I'm incapable of speech. Somewhere in the middle of dying of embarrassment, and being *sick* from embarrassment. The only reason I'm even still standing is because Hudson is holding me up.

"How are you doing sir? My name is Hudson." Hudson puts on all the charm for Frank. But Frank just stands there in the glow of his porch light, giving Hudson a slow once over.

"Well *Hudson*, I want you out by ten thirty. Do you hear?"

Hudson bites back a slight chuckle and then inclines his head in a respectful manner. But my jaw gapes.

"You were *just* asking me if I was a pansexual, and now I have a man over and you're telling him to leave by *ten thirty?"*

Frank just arches an eyebrow at me, staying silent.

Hudson throws me a frown and gives me a little once over. "Do you mean asexual?"

Irate, I snatch my bag out from Hudson's grip who was kind enough to give it to me. Probably to keep from alerting Frank to him being an ass. I grab it to my chest and then turn to stomp like a child up my front door and jam the key in, letting myself in.

I hear Hudson close behind say *"Yes sir."* Causing my blood pressure to spike and making me slam the door on him because I hear Frank yell back, "You be careful Hudson, she's *a spicy one.*"

I scowl because right now it's not funny.

I'm irritated, turned on, pissed off, and embarrassed that I couldn't just come home and fuck my new dildo that I paid too much money for. Hudson of course stops the door with his foot before coming inside. Uncaring that it's rude, I'm headed up my stairs before I even think.

"Fine, you can sit in the foyer. *I'm going to my room!"*

I'm literally operating on feeling at this point before I feel my ankle snatched and then I'm falling into the stairs and being drug down them and back into the foyer.

"NO!" I yell the word and twist to my belly with one hand on the floor, and the other still gripping my black bag.

He begins to drag me down the foyer. With a grunt, I reach up and grab the iron railings of my stairwell. Feeling my resistance he pulls hard, stretching my body midair, parallel to the floor.

Honestly this whole thing might be comical if I weren't so fucking turned on I was in pain.

"Give me the motherfucking toy, *Lolita!"*

"NO!" I scream. "You can't make meeee!"

The next thing I know he heaves so hard my fingers lose their painful purchase and I fall to the ground with a dull thudding sound.

In an attempt to catch myself I drop the bag and land on my hands, trying to crawl fast for it. He sticks out a long leg and kicks it with his boot and it goes flying a few feet away bouncing off the front door.

"You like it wild huh?" His deep voice is smooth as he teases me.

I turn my head and start cussing him out in Spanish at the top of my lungs. I claw at the floor, trying to hand walk my way once again to my bag. It's the stupidest thing I've ever done in my life. But surprisingly, he lets me almost make it. However, when I reach out a hand for it, he yanks me back.

But he doesn't let my ankles go, so I'm forced to hold myself up by my hands or fall face first into the hardwood.

We repeat this several times. Me, just hand walking to my bag, before then being drug back almost all the way to my kitchen. I'm breathing hard, and my arms are shaking, my muscles are on fire.

Utterly exhausted, I collapse onto my chest, putting my head to the side with my hot cheek against the cold hardwood.

Hudson stands there, remaining silent. The only noise is the gentle ticking of the clock hanging on the wall. It's weird *and* comforting at the same time.

His thumbs begin to smooth rhythmically across my ankles, and we stay this way for a bit before it hits me that I'm soaking through my leggings and he can probably see. God, what is *with* this man always seeing me in my worse states?

"Okay Hudson. *You win.*" I let out a defeated whimper.

I sigh when he chuckles, and lowers my legs gently to the floor.

"Good girl." I hear him praise as I huff and puff rather unladylike against the floor.

His hard boots walk past me and damn it everything's tired from my arms to my legs. "That's a *real* good girl."

Though I'm tired, I feel something spark to life inside of me.

Staying silent, I roll over onto my back and pull my knees up, planting my feet on the floor. My chest is heaving as I hear the crinkle of the bag and I close my eyes against the sight because I know he's pulled it out and my face is absolutely on fire.

He disappears for a second into the powder room and I hear running water. He's washing the toy, meaning he's about to let me use it. Pure relief fills me, making me even weaker. I keep my eyes closed because well, I'm still embarrassed.

I hear his steps come closer and then a weight on my stomach. I open my eyes in surprise. There's the dildo, just sitting on my tummy. My eyes rise to watch him as he lowers to his haunches right between my legs which he spreads.

"Is that what you want?"

My breathing becomes ragged as we stare each other down. Silently I nod.

"Well you lucked out Lola, you didn't get one near as big as me. So, I'll allow you to use it."

My heart stops and then I say the most fucked up thing imaginable. Because I am a grown ass woman. But I don't say that.

"Thank you, Hudson." Is what I hear come out of my mouth. Dammit.

"You're welcome." Hudson says this with a smile and then he's reaching into his boot, grabbing that knife from earlier.

The blood drains from my face, and I'm seriously worried about my physical health at this point. He reaches between my legs and grasps the material and ever so slowly cuts the fabric between my legs down the middle, then spreads my knees.

I'm shaking so hard I can see the dildo quivering, but he reaches deeper in between the torn fabric. His knuckles are hard against the lips of my pussy as he slides two fingers inside grasps my panties, ignoring my nerves.

"Ayyy, H-Huudsoonn." I whine, bringing shaky hands to my face I moan miserably.

He continues to ignore me, and I feel the coldness of the steel blade replace his fingers, caressing my lips down there gently. His breathing hitches, becoming noticeably harsher before his wrist jerks. The fabric tears with a audible ripping sound, and then the warm air of my house caresses my naked flesh along with his hot gaze.

"Jesus," He raises an eyebrow. "You *do* have a beauty mark there. Shiitttt." He groans.

God his voice is so sexy, I feel my juices trickle out of me and run down my ass cheeks.

I can tell he sees it because his eyes narrow. He refuses to look away, just staring unashamedly. Taking me in. And for one heart stopping moment I think he's going to bend down and lick me, but he doesn't. His green eyes land on mine and I freeze.

"Pick it up and put it in your pussy."

"Hudson-"

"I won't ask again."

I lift shaky hands to the toy and grasp it, sliding it down my mound and through my wetness over my clit a couple times, getting it wet before I bend my knees back deeper and put the broad tip to my vagina. I turn away from him because this is way too intimate. I can smell my arousal.

And if I can smell it, then I know he can.

I feel his hand wrap around my wrist and then he's pushing, forcing me to arch my back for him, making me feel oh so full.

Too full.

Suddenly his words come to me, about how I didn't get one near big as him.

I tense. Stopping us before the toy gets too far in. I need a second to adjust. I pull it out slightly, fucking myself with the tip. My lips quiver as I tilt my head, seeing his eyes tight on mine. And right as I'm busy getting lost into his eyes, he gets lost pushing the damn thing several inches into me without warning.

My muscles protest being split apart but still he pushes firmly. He hits a spot inside of me that makes me flinch with pleasure, and I tilt my head back on a silent scream, I'm so shocked.

My back arches violently as he rears over me on his knees. I startle as he puts a broad hand between my breasts and pushes me back down to the floor while his other hand presses it even further inside me.

"Come on pretty thing, you got this." He says. "You have to, because this is *easy right now.* And I'm not going to take it easy on you when I fuck you. So you need to show me that you can handle this. Be a good girl and show me, Lola. Open that pussy up."

"I haven't had anything inside me for *so long.*" I whine softly, working to bend my knees back.

I heave out a soughing breath and then look down between us, seeing my lips spread wide around the toy, and my clit protruding slightly. I let out another frustrated whimper.

"This pretty pussy's been empty, huh?" He says quietly, meeting my eyes. His stare is so hot it takes my breath away.

He removes his hand from my chest and then grabs my clit between his thumb and forefinger, pinching it.

"Oh God." I whimper. I'm shuddering, rolling my hips into him.

In and out he treats me to steady, measured thrusts. Rolling and tugging at my clit the entire time. My body is broken out into a full on sweat and his words do nothing to help settle me, only keeping me on the precipice.

I'm gasping, my toes are curling in my shoes when suddenly his eyes leave my pussy to meet mine in a hard look. My mouth drops open, feeling his fingers flick harshly against my swollen, oversensitive clit. One, twice.

I clench my teeth and throw my head back on a strained wail. Suddenly orgasming on the dildo, on his hand, on my floor, on myself.

It's everywhere.

He takes advantage of my orgasm and thrusts it just a bit deeper making my eyebrows furrow and my head hits the floor with a thump. He stops pushing when it's just a little over halfway in he begins to thrust hard, making me slide in my wetness slightly.

This entire time he's completely silent. Just giving me what I said I needed. But there's nothing in this for him, I don't think. Feelings of shame intermix with these feelings of acute pleasure.

I begin to withdraw inside my head and I turn my face from him and attempt to close my legs.

"Look at me."

I turn my head back, seeing his eyes roam over my face slowly.

"You take your pleasure now, *while you can*. Do you understand me? Because when I get a hold of you the first time's going to be a hard ride. I'm just warning you now."

And I don't exactly know why but that broke something inside me. My body heats up, because I feel like he's letting me know something crucial, but not making me fully informed at the same time.

"No." I say, because I want more.

My hips are jerking with the dildo and we're rocking into each other perfectly attuned, I hiss as it slides slightly deeper and I reach over, grabbing the leg of my side table and I grip hard, needing to feel grounded.

I'm not prepared when he reaches out his hand and snatches my nipple between two fingers, rolling and tugging as he begins to beat the dildo in and out of me. The wet, sucking sounds are my undoing.

"Nooooo!" I scream, twitching and arching, trying to buck him off.

I'm too sensitive, and it's the same nipple he was just abusing earlier with his mouth. His fingers tighten and I twist my body trying to get away.

"These pretty girls are the secret to getting you off I see." He growls. He rips down my top, exposing my breast, and then leans to suck me into his hot mouth. "Fuck you're delicious. This is my favorite part of your body." He nips at my distended nipple, causing me to jerk in pleasure and for my vision to waver.

I become super hot and unbearably sensitive all over. "Oh god please." I plead. "Dios! Por favor, NO!"

I feel manic, overstimulated, and this orgasm I'm about to have is scary. My feet become hot and I'm desperately trying to work to get my shoes off, I'm thrashing on the floor trying to help myself have relief. Thankfully, I get one off somehow and then kick at my wall, trying to slide away from him.

"HUDSON!"

I'm screaming for mercy but Hudson's head raises just slightly, tugging up at my nipple and then meets my eyes, sucking my nipple over and over again through his teeth.

Suck, nibble, suck, nibble.

My heart bangs uncomfortably as my second orgasm washes over me in painful waves. I'm thrashing my head, feeling my hair swinging everywhere, all over my face, down my breasts. He takes pity on me and pulls the dildo out, letting it fall to the side with a thudding sound.

I'm shivering, shaking against him as he continues to work my nipple. Making these little grunts and hums that's letting me know that he's really enjoying himself. I am too, ironically. With every harsh suck, I feel a corresponding bang in my pussy.

This man just taught me something new about myself. He was right.

He releases my nipple with a little popping sound and I look down, seeing it's elongated and red. It's a little softened due to my two orgasms and how much he's sucked on it and my eyes go wide. Seeing there's a slight indentation of his teeth on the tender nub of my nipple, and the sight is almost enough to throw me into another orgasm.

I get half a second of warning before his hands come down and spread my lips down there for his inspection. I'm shocked speechless as I feel him open my vulva wide. To make matters worse his thumbs come up and pull on the hood of my clit, exposing me completely to him.

He's really in there looking. His head tilts but he doesn't say a word.

I'm shaking, my nerves getting the better of me. I've never been this vulnerable to anyone before.

Just then the doorbell rings and I shriek, feeling my heart pound. Hudson throws me an amused grin and rises up from his crouch fluidly. Grasping me by my ankle once more, he drags me along side him as he walks to the front.

To say I'm scared is an understatement.

I'm trying to unlock my throat to say something, *anything* to Hudson. I don't want who's at the door to see me like this. But then he drags me to where I'm against the side wall so that when he opens the door, it's against me. Hiding me from the line of sight from whoever's outside.

This motherfucker.

My eyes narrow. I peek up along the length of the door and I see Hudson's side profile. He's relaxed, smiling all thirty two freaking pearly whites at the delivery person as if he wasn't just ripping me apart and then taking time to inspect his work in the middle of my damn hallway floor.

"Hey man, here's your tip. Thanks for delivering. Be safe."

Be safe.

I scoff. Trying to raise up off the floor, I sort of make it to my elbow, but then Hudson reaches down and then grabs my ankle again and then he's dragging me slowly. Up the stairs. Without a word to me.

Neanderthal.

He finds the double door entry to the masters and opens it, dragging me the entire way. I let him, because I'm really at a loss as to what to say at this point.

He puts the food down on my nightstand and then lets go of my ankle when we're safely inside my bedroom. I just lay there silent and unmoving. Hudson chuckles and then bends down, picking me up in his arms bridal style, covering my lips with his.

And holy shit this *kiss*. This kiss is life changing.

This was the, 'I'm going to break you off, but then treat you like a princess right after,' kiss that we all read about in these smut books we like so much. This is the, 'I can do whatever I want to your body, but you're still my Queen,' kiss that I've only ever dreamed about receiving.

You get the point.

I whimper, sinking my hand into his brown hair and I tilt my head, letting him in deeper. The way his beard is scratching my face is so sexy, and then I'm suddenly struck by the odd fact that this man is fully clothed. Making me aware I'm in my cut up leggings, and my panties are hanging awkwardly off my body, I'm only in one shoe, and currently smeared in my own cum.

But holy shit. This is the kiss of all kisses. And he didn't even fuck me. Not really.

When he's done taking my mouth, he places me on my bed and then goes to one knee, takes my other shoe off, then pulls off the rest of my clothes carefully. I don't mean to be funny, but I cross my arms over my nipples because this man just doesn't realize how sensitive they are and I'm nervous.

He catches the movement and looks up, giving me a soft, knowing smile. I'm aware we're not speaking, but I just don't know what to say. What do you say after something like what we just shared? Hell... *I* don't know.

He rises, bending down to give me another kiss before turning to the nightstand. He likes kissing me I notice. The realization fills me with pleasure I don't think I've ever felt before.

"Uhm," I'm attempting to speak but my mind won't stop racing. Vulnerable, I reach over and pull my fleece blanket that I keep folded over the bottom of my bed and spread it out, curling it up under my chin. *"S-So...what did you order?"*

Hudson, who was busy pulling the food out of the bag, takes a second to check his watch. "Chili dogs. And we have forty minutes to eat before Frank comes a-knocking."

I let out a laugh, pleased that he ordered a dish so hearty for the fall, and something that I know is going to knock me plain out after he leaves. I take the one that he offers me.

"Come on, I don't think the man will come over here and actually knock on the door." I take a bite, moaning at the flavor. "Do you?"

Hudson scoffs, taking a bite of his own chili dog before sitting down in the chair next to my bed. It's then I notice the absence of my purse. "I absolutely do. I recognize that's a real man. What do you want to bet he's over here at ten twenty five just to make sure I have my ass in the foyer?"

I laugh proper now, because I've seen Frank's curtains fluttering enough that I know he's always watching. It makes me feel warm and fuzzy. Albeit it's a bit much sometimes.

"I haven't felt looked after since my mom passed. I know he can be a bit rough around the edges, but Frank's been a Godsend to me and my boys."

Hudson nods. "Hmm-hmm. So, if the man gives me a curfew, I'll respect that. For now anyways. What do you keep looking at baby, are you alright?" He looks around him curiously.

"Oh, its just, I never leave my purse downstairs. I always keep it up here with me, in that chair where you are sitting, when I'm at home."

Hudson nods at me. "Smart girl." He praises me with a wink.

I give him a shy smile and bite into my chili dog again. We eat in silence for a second while I look any and everywhere except at him. Because who the hell knows what he's thinking about. Probably about the fact he just made me walk on my hands in my foyer, begging for my toy.

I know *I'm* thinking about the fact I let him do that.

The sudden image of me struggling against him while I was latched onto the the stair rail, and he was holding me midair just letting me hang there before I fell, hits me hard. Hard enough that I hurriedly swallow my last bite and get up from the bed with the blanket wrapped around me to go to my dresser. I feel too naked.

I clear my throat as I rummage around, finding a tank top and another pair of leggings. I don't bother with a bra, seeing as he's leaving and I'm just going to hop in the shower anyways. I maneuver my way into my bathroom, trailing the blanket behind me and close the door to shimmy into my clothes.

I look at my nipple curiously, seeing his teeth marks are gone. It makes me sad. I catch my reflection in the mirror and see I'm pouting but Hudson calling to me takes me away from my musing.

"That doesn't even make any sense, Lola." I hear him call before he lets out a deep, amused chuckle. "I know what you look like, gorgeous, you don't need to hide."

And though he's right, it makes sense to *me* to dress in my bathroom. I'm too vulnerable with this man. I literally let him do shit to me that I never let Dominic do, and the thought gives me pause. Because if I let Hudson do this to me, then what else will I let him do? I need a little bit to think about that, because I already have one crazy man in my life. I don't need another one.

And though Hudson doesn't strike me as crazy, I just met him so what would I know, really.

I come back out into the bedroom with my hair brushed back into a high bun and something else hits me... he's in a new pair of jeans. But he didn't have time to drive home to Bainbridge Island to change clothes then come back here. I blink. Those doubtful thoughts begin to creep in.

He gathers the trash before jerking his head to my door. We make our way down the stairs where I see the mess we left in the hallway and groan in embarrassment. There's a puddle of my excitement on the floor, the dildo is cast off to the side, and the little decorative items I had on my table are knocked over haphazardly.

"I'll get that." I say, but Hudson's already bending down, picking up the dildo and then shoving it into the fast food bag with the trash. My jaw drops. *"Hey!"* I say angrily. "Give me my-"

"This was a one and done beautiful, the next cock you have inside you will be mine. And if you don't scream loud enough after I shove it in the first time then I'm going to know you've disobeyed me and been stretching yourself out anyways after I told you not to." He pins me with a stare.

I sway on my feet, slap my hand to my mouth, and blush the hardest I know I've ever done in life.

Averting my gaze, I bite my lip and stay silent.

Walking to my little laundry area off the kitchen, I grab a wet mop and come back around the corner and busy myself spraying the floor and begin to mop, erasing the evidence of our reckless moment of abandon.

He fixes the table, and I notice he's curiously looking around the downstairs area of my house. We stay quiet. It's as if we're both re-playing the last hour of time, trying to figure out our next move. God knows I don't know mine. I don't know this man.

What's my next move?

Hudson clears his throat and then turns to me. "I have a big project I'm working on tomorrow so I don't think I'll make it by the store in time to catch you before closing, and I know you've got the boys. This is your weekend with them right?"

Propping the mop against the wall I look at him, thinking it's eerie that he's paid enough attention to already gleam my schedule. But then I'm also thinking *of course* he can't come see me now. He's already gotten what he wanted from me. I squeeze my eyes shut as shame fills me.

"Yeah." My tone is irritated as I mentally berate myself.

Stupid stupid stupid. Letting a stranger come to your house and shove a dildo in you after you let him drag you around like a ragdoll-and up the fucking stairs at that. Who even DOES that?

Hudson interrupts my thoughts.

"Well I was thinking. I have horses. *Three* of them, and I was wondering if you would like to bring Tate and Tuck to my place this weekend and take them for a ride."

My lips part with shock, and my brows furrow because I'm again not understanding something. Eighty dollar whiskey, hundred thousand dollar truck, all the hundred dollar bills he's left me, and now he's telling me he's got three horses?

What the fuck is going on? Isn't he a construction worker? I frown, feeling really, *really* confused.

"I've been coming home late the last couple weeks, and I'm sure they'd love to have some attention from someone other than my neighbor's teenage daughter."

My eyes bore into his and to say I'm speechless is an understatement. "W-Well, they've never gone horseback riding before. I'll ask them and if they want to," *of course they'll want to,* "then I'll let you know."

Hudson nods before looking at his watch. He quickly walks up to me, bending down to treat me to a possessive kiss if I've ever felt one. He grabs my hand, treating me to a sexy grin before hauling me behind him to the front door.

"Lock up, sweet thing. I hope you sleep well tonight. You deserve it." And with one last smacking kiss that honestly I'm standing up on my tip toes to keep from ending, he opens the door. To Frank's face.

I let out a disbelieving giggle, looking up at Hudson who's already walking through the threshold, holding his hand out to Frank and giving him a friendly clap on his shoulder. Frank steps aside to let him pass, then he leans against the railing of my porch, staring after Hudson who's climbed into his truck.

Which starts almost silently, surprising me.

Aren't trucks supposed to be *loud?*

Frank continues to stare as he pulls off and his red lights disappear down the road slowly, making his way to the stop sign in the distance. His truck crawls to a stop, and then just sits. Frank looks at me.

"Now *that's* a man. Watch this."

He leaves me without another word, heading down my porch steps and then to his own house, where he disappears silently and closes the door.

I'm pursing my lips, wondering what I should be looking for but then I see Frank's curtains rustle and then I see him, staring out the window towards the entrance of the cul de sac. Where Hudson is still stalling. I hear my phone ping from its place in my purse on the foyer table.

I reach for it and see a text from Hudson.

Go inside baby. -Hudson

Feeling slow, I hurriedly close my front door, then rush to my own living room window, where I can ironically still see Frank standing at his own living room window, still watching. After a second, Hudson turns his blinker light on, and then pulls off. Disappearing down the street.

My phone rings, making me jump anxiously. I answer it without seeing who it is.

"I guess you aren't no pansexual, *huh?*" Then the line goes dead.

I almost die laughing, because Frank is hilarious. After a minute my laughter goes quiet and then I think on it for a second, because Frank is right. Hudson is a man. A man's man.

Inspired, I fly up the stairs to my bedroom, breaking open my computer to begin a new blog for my bookstore. They're going to get three this month, apparently. And I couldn't be happier to surprise them.

Because God knows, I was.

8

Staighten Up

Hudson

Man, women will get a wax and automatically think their pussy goes in your mouth.-Clay

I pause from my spot on the terrain, watching my men in their diggers grading the plot of land for the Tech development company and let out a chuckle before typing out my response, because he can be so ignorant sometimes.

But it does.-Hud

And just like that, I'm back with Lola how we were last night, when I was holding her pussy apart, letting my eyes drink in her nakedness. The thought makes me absolutely weak. Feeling my chest tighten, I look back up, giving my people another once over before I turn my back on them and pull up her number to text her. My hard hat helps shade my phone from the glare of the sun.

Hey baby. Good morning. How're you doing? Have you had a chance to ask the boys yet if they want to come over and see the horses? -Hudson

I'm so hopeful, because I want her to see my place. What I've accomplished for myself and what I'm so proud of. I want to show her Champ, Beauty, and Nay Nay. See how they get along. Is she scared of big animals? It's eight o'clock, and I'm not sure if she's up yet, what her schedule with the boys looks like after they come back from their dads.

She answers me fifteen minutes later.

> Hi there, good morning.-Lola

She sends me a smiley face emoji. I grin, she's so expressive.

An employee walks up to me. "Grading's finally done sir, and we can start setting the foundation." I give him my thanks and keep my eyes on the little bubbles letting me know Lola is still writing.

> Their father takes them to school after his weekends, so I won't see them until they get to the shop. I'll ask them then, and then I'll let you know. But honestly, you can probably plan on it. I don't see any planet on which they'll say no to an adventure. -Lola

> What about you? Are you the same way? -Hudson

> What way? I thought you're working so how're you texting me? Don't you have like a big machine to drive or a jackhammer to man? -Lola

I burst out laughing, because she thinks I'm a construction worker. I just never specified what exactly it was I did in construction. And I've got a jackhammer alright, she'll find that out soon.

> I'm watching the guys move the equipment to the trailers so we can begin foundation work. You didn't answer my question though, are you up for adventures as well? -Hudson

I snap her a picture of my men loading the equipment in the trailers against the backdrop of the graded land showing her the awesomeness and scale of it all. I wonder if she's going to catch *H. Montgomery Construction* on the side of the trailer? She does.

> Hudson. Is your last name Montgomery?-Lola

> It is. -Hudson

There's no response for long enough for me to begin to feel nervous. I stare at my phone for a bit, making my way to my truck and debating on whether or not I should call her when I finally see the little bubbles pop back up.

> Hudson I'm sorry, I don't think I can get involved with you. It's been fun, refreshing even, but this isn't going to work. Thanks for all you've done. It's been so wonderful to get a glimpse into what I think a true connection should be like with someone and for that I'm forever grateful but I think it's best we part ways. Please take care of yourself, you can come in for a free cup of coffee whenever you want.-Lola

Because that's just unacceptable, I pick up my phone and then call my right hand man Tyler. He answers on the third ring. I can hear him breathing hard, as he was helping to load all the equipment.

"What's up Hud, you good? You're normally out here helping us with the equipment," he says.

I can hear Tyler slam his own truck door, before the roar of his engine in the background. He's got a loud truck, not like mine.

"Yeah listen, I need you to take over the rest of the day." I hit the gas hard, gunning it away from the job site and through the open gates of the wire fence. "I'm sorry but something urgent just came up."

I look at the clock, it's eight thirty, she should be on her way to the shop right now, getting it ready for the day. I have about an hour before I make it to her, about a little over an hour before the shop opens. It's perfect timing and I feel like the Gods have thrown me a win. A muscle ticks in my jaw when I realize this woman's truly going to make me work for it.

If she knew how hard I worked, she wouldn't be making me. I can guarantee you that. Because I'm about to ride her ass so hard she isn't going to know what hit her.

"Yeah boss, you don't even have to apologize. All's good over here. I can't even remember the last time you had a day off. Take care. We got this. See you tomorrow."

I hang up the phone, and make it to Lola's shop in record time. Her door is still locked, but I can see her through the window, she's dusting.

Fucking cleaning. Like any other normal morning. As if she didn't just rip my heart out and stomp all over it. My lips tighten.

I begin banging on the door, not fucking around. I'm *pissed*. Madder than I've been at a woman in a minute. Lola drops the towel, looking over with a concerned look on her face and the next thing I know the door is being ripped open. She stares up at me in shock.

"Hud-"

I don't even let her get my name out right before I'm on her, I snatch her to me and then walk her backwards enough to slam the door back shut and I lock it. I don't care if her store is open a few minutes later. She's going to get what I've got for her.

I'm so hard I'm in pain. As my mouth ravages hers I'm aware that she's pushing at me, trying to get enough room to speak, but in my humble opinion she's already said enough this morning.

I bend, putting my hands under her ass and hauling her to me. Thankfully she let's me without too much of a fuss. She moans, wrapping her legs around my waist.

This whole thing is so unexpected, but you have to learn to work with what you've got, right?

I carry us through the store and into the storage room, kicking the door closed with a grunt. I put her down, watching her stumble back from me in shock with the back of her hand against her lips, placing her hips against the wooden table on the far side of the door. She's panting, her eyes are wild with an angry glint to them, and she's breathing hard.

"Hudson what the fuck!?"

"Tell me to my face." I grit out, my lip is curled and my eyes are flashing just as dangerously at hers.

I struggle to tighten the reins on my self control, because I am suddenly hit with the awareness that this woman's got power over me that no one else has ever had. *Ever.*

"Well, it's not going to work!"

Lola crosses her arms and tilts her head, looking at me with an obvious defiance that if we weren't in her shop she would be in real trouble over. There's something in her eyes that's a challenge, trying to force me to break in *her* time and not mine. Her tone is wide open in its innocence, letting me know she really meant the gauntlet she just threw down.

No she didn't dare to say it.

My blood pressure rises, and I feel a muscle in my jaw tick as she did it. She pressed the button I'd thought no one had access to. The spot inside me that could give a damn about self control. And what's more, her lips were in a slight pout too as *she did it*. Like a child who purposefully stares you in the eye and touches the hot burner on the stove right after you tell them not to do it or they'll get burned. What the fuck.

"It's not going to work, huh?" I parrot back.

Seeing her doe eyes feign innocence, I feel my control snap. She'd unknowingly been fucking eating at me for the last two weeks. Just small nips and bites at my sanity, flaying my ass down to the white meat, and that was the last nibble I needed to truly break.

"How the hell are you going to be able to deal with a fuck up and her ex who is *bound* to start hounding you for money as soon as you involve yourself with me?"

Lola's nostrils flare and I take a step closer, fighting with everything in me to not pounce on her because I know it's not going to be pretty. I'm too upset to be gentle. She's slapping her palm into the side of her hand as she addresses me, and the sound begins to reverberate in my skull, making everything ten times worse.

"Lola-" I try to warn her, but she's gone. Lost in her verbal assault.

"Sure, *it'll be fun for a second* getting your dick wet and all. But the moment shit hits the fan are you going to be able to handle it? *Want* to handle it? *Will you even think I'm worth it?"* She yells, and her anger makes me snap.

Clicking my tongue I snatch her by her wrist and pick her up roughly with a grunt.

Ignoring her startled yelp, I slam her hips rather hard on the table behind her causing her to cry out in shock. It's like music to my ears because the shit that just came out of her mouth shocked me *too*, and fair is only fair.

"*Worth it?*" I growl, ignoring her eyes widening. "I knew you were feisty, but baby, your audacity is going to get you fucked in a way I'm not sure I'm comfortable with. The nerve of you to ask a *man* that. How fucking *dare* you question if I think you're worth it?"

Shoving my way in between her legs I reach behind to my hip, unclipping my switchblade and click the button, exposing the razor sharp knife. I hold it up in front of us. Showing her she best not fuck with me too much, because I may play about a lot of things, but her alluding to the fact that she's worried about if I think she's worth it, especially as bad as I've wanted this with her, is no joke to me.

"Rule number one, Lolita," My voice is hard. "You don't *ever* let a man *even think* they dictate your worth. Not even me, sweetheart. *I see I've got a lot to teach you.*" Which was too much, the last part. I slipped, and it pisses me off even further, and because I'm pissed, my anger's getting taken out on her pussy.

Plain and simple.

Lol makes a scoffing, disbelieving noise in her throat inflaming my already heightened irritation. The thickened air around us crackles with sexual tension that I can tell affects her deeply. Just a deep as it affects me, I hope.

"Look at me." I get in her face and when she turns away, I grab her jaw and yank her back roughly. *"I said look at me."*

Her nostrils flare as her eyes meet mine.

"I'm about to stretch this pussy out."

"Oh please don't fucking *flatter* yourself." She snarls at me, any closer she might bite me.

I'm tempted to lean in and let her but I'm not sure how rough she gets when she's angry and I have a sudden vision of her ripping out my jugular with her teeth, and then letting me bleed out in the floor.

I give her a little laugh. "You're about to get it harder just for that comment. Keep talking, I'll *gladly* take away your ability to walk. Want to keep pushing me?"

The sight of her plump, dark pink lips parting, and the small gasp of fear she lets out makes my blood boil, and I feel my cock thicken even harder. And for just a moment, I debate doing this to her. I wanted our first time to be slower, so I had time to soften her up and not be so shocked at how brutal I can be.

But honestly, it's either her pussy or her mouth, and since she has the boys later in the day, I decide to be kind and not tear her throat up the way I really, *really* want to.

Would even argue I *need* too, but, that'll be for another time.

I keep my eyes on hers, the anger, sexual tension, and frustration makes the room almost unbearably hot causing a trickle of sweat to lick down my spine. Eyeing her, I see Lola's face and neck has broken out into a fine sheen of sweat which makes the heat on my own body raise to uncomfortable levels and I fight like hell to keep my clothes on. I want to rub my entire body alongside hers, make us smell like each other. Scenting her, because I'm not letting her go.

She's fucking crazy for even thinking that I would.

My lip curls with displeasure. "Rule number two. You best think twice before you try to break up with me over text."

It was never made official but yeah... *there's an us to break up, baby.*

Her eyes go wide as saucers as I put the blade between my teeth, shoving her dress up her legs. Exposing her pretty dark skin to my eyes. Man she's fucking gorgeous. My hands grasps her ankles in a not so gentle clasp, bending her knees back to place the soles of her feet on the table, and scoot her little black lace covered pussy to the edge. Taking the blade from between my teeth, I keep my head down as I talk to her.

"When's the last time you've been fucked?"

Her embarrassed sound is cute.

"Answer me."

"Four years ago."

"Okay, so this is going to hurt a little more than normal, I'm afraid. I'll take it a little easy on you." I meet her eyes and time stops as I relish in her shocked look. "I can't believe you're making me fuck you in your storage room, woman. Is this what you wanted... huh?" She stays silent, her eyes flickering between mine. "You wanted me to come over here and fuck you...*prove to you that you're mine?*" We stare at each other quietly for a second, and I see it. The truth in her eyes. What she really wanted. I narrow my eyes and lean into her until our faces are only an inch away. *"I'll fucking pull you out into your store and fuck you for all your customers to see if you piss me off at work again like you did this morning trying to test me. You want that too?"*

That thing inside me has lost his mind, but I don't care. We're standing on business, crazy and all. Lola's brow arches but she stays silent.

"Yeah, *I thought so.*" Taking the knife quickly I put the dull edge of the blade against her thigh, slide it into her panties and jerk my wrist hard. Causing her to squeal in shock.

"Hudson!" She looks at me furiously. "What is with you cutting off my panties-"

"Oh!" I grit with a humorless scoff. "So, you *can* speak. Even if it's only to give me some attitude. Huh, Lolita?"

"I'm not giving-"

"*Hush*, you've said *enough.*"

Her mouth slams shut but the fire in her eyes finishes what she was going to say. Keeping her gaze I take the knife and put it to her forearm, sliding it down slowly until the blade wedges between her bangle and her wrist. I feel my eyes narrow just as I slam it down into the table, driving it deep into the wood, keeping her trapped for me.

I see the effect of my action immediately. She doesn't say a word-smart- but her eyes dilate somehow even more, and her cheeks flush darker. Betraying her desire.

In a way, I'm happy seeing all good signs. Because this is tame. So tame, comparatively.

I pick up my leg, bracing my boot on the table, and snag my secondary blade from the sheath at my ankle. Turning it in my hands quickly, I rip through both the strap of her dress and her bra, repeating the movement with the other side. I yank down her dress, exposing the center of her bra and slice through that too. I tear it all off, leaving her exposed for me.

And I groan, seeing perfection.

She's trembling, understandably, but one glance at her perfect little pussy and the moisture there tells me all I need to know.

I secure her other hand to the table the same way. Blade through her bangle, into the table, and step back. Licking my lips hungrily. Her own lips are quivering, her beautiful breasts are heaving, but I'm not worried about any of that right now.

"Tell me no." I test, flicking my eyes back to her. "Say it." My dick twitches.

"N-"

I interrupt her. "There'll be time for softness later." I assure her.

Unbuckling my belt, I reach in, pulling out my cock. Shit it's *swollen* and throbbing to the point I almost feel dizzy. I fist it angrily, pumping once down to the tip, feeling my precum leak out. I don't even need to look, I've been feeling it dripping this entire time I've been at her.

It's *her* reaction I need to see.

Her eyes go wide and I admit, the sight pleases me so much more than I know it should, seeing her suddenly yank against the knives keeping her still for me. I thank all that is holy that I am a knife carrying man. I didn't put the blade facing her skin so she's fine there, but the effect is the same.

The color goes even darker on her cheeks and the fact that she's scared, scared of my cock, fills me with so much pleasure I could almost nut all over the floor in front of her.

Almost.

I step into her and lean in, giving her a smacking kiss before I tilt my head deeper, making her part her mouth for my tongue as I swirl the tip of my cock against her clit. Giving her pleasure before I tear her apart. Because I'm not a monster. Not really. I feel her shaking as I manipulate that little bud between her legs, and she feels so damn good against my skin.

So velvety.

"I'm going to fuck you hard, because you made me do this." I whisper against her lips. "You deserve to be eaten out for a while. Have your nipples sucked, kissed for a bit... not fucked like a whore. Yet here we are. So, I'm not going to go easy on you. Because you and that feisty little mouth need to learn what you're dealing with."

And with that I slam all my body weight into my hips, smacking through the clasp of the tightest pussy I've ever in my life had the pleasure of being inside. Sinking my cock mercilessly in her until it stops about halfway she's clenched so tight. And in a surprising turn of events, Lola tosses her head back and lets out a growl to cope.

Not a scream. Not a wail. A *growl*. Followed by a whimper, and it's the fucking sexiest thing that I've ever heard.

We struggle against each other momentarily, because she's pushed up on her feet to try and move her hips away from me. So for a minute, it's utter chaos. I snatch her hips, slam her back on the table and press harder while she's yelling something at me in Spanish I can't discern.

"Oww," She complains. "Oh my God, *owww...*" She sobs, great heaving breaths sounding like she's about to have a panic attack.

I still us both and press the side of my head into hers, pressing my chest hard into her breasts, letting her know I mean business even if I am giving her a second to adjust to me.

"Be quiet." I murmur quietly. She shuts up immediately, but her breasts continue heaving against me while we're engaging in a viscous battle of wills. I relish the ragged breaths escaping her mouth, washing over my neck. "I love the way your cunt feels, beautiful. I'm not going to stop until I'm pressed all the way into the back of your pussy. So, I need you to take a breath for me because I need to go deeper."

Lola inhales a ragged breath and the feel of her fleshy nipples against me is enough to drive me insane.

"Come on," I say to her, catching her eye. They're tear filled and beautiful. *"Deeper."*

Her plump lips part as she takes what is hopefully a calming breath. I interrupt her before she says anything.

"*Yes.* You can take it deeper baby."

I sink my hips a little more into her, hearing her trap a small sound bravely in her throat. I grind my pelvis against her outer sex, and her eyebrows furrow as she tilts her head back to look at me. Yet she stays silent. We're staring into each other's eyes as something raw and intimate passes between us.

I contemplate her quietly as I see her face flush with a mist of sweat, and my own body responds in kind, heating up to what feels to be the exact temperature of her core that is currently melting around my thick dick.

"Do you like me inside you?" I whisper against her lips, rubbing my mouth against hers softly.

"Y-Yes. *Very much.*" She gasps.

"You're going to understand that I mean what I say." We pause like this just for a second before I pull my hips back with effort, as her vagina is sucked around me so tightly I can hardly disengage.

Ignoring her small whimper, I begin a hard, slapping rhythm. Finally earning a scream from her. Making a shiver race down my spine and causing the hair to stand up on my arms.

It's a rich throaty scream. And the fact that I know I earned that in all its glory makes me hotter than even the time I cashed my first million dollar check.

The scream that came out of her mouth was otherworldly. I commit it to memory, knowing the sound of it is what is going to fuel my days and comfort me through sleepless nights. I meet her cries with a grunt of my own, but for the most part, I fuck into her body silently, my breath harsh between us.

This woman feels like a storm rolling through the sky getting ready to pour down on me. But in order to feel the rain, I have to deal with the thunder and crackling of lightening that comes before the inevitable, torrential downpour. Fire hot electricity simmers between us, letting me know we're close.

With every thrust into her, I feel myself brushing against her cervix.

The thought that I'm so close to her womb drives my desire to unparalleled heights. I tighten my hands on her hips even more and clench my jaw, every rough smack into her body pulling a guttural grunt out of me that's got my throat tight.

I feel a tiny fission of sadness race through me, catching me off guard.

It hits me just now just how much I've missed sex, and having intimacy with another person. And though I am elated that my body is finally getting some relief, it comes with another blast of emotion that I wasn't prepared for. I slow just a tad, as disappointment and irritation with myself begins to take over, and I decide right then and there that neither one of us is finishing. Not this time.

My eyes leave hers and go lower.

Her big breasts are bouncing, and for a second, I'm even more saddened that I anchored her to the table the way I did because I'd like to know how she would touch me. Like to be able to bend down and take a straining peak into my mouth and taste her. Pleasure her like this while I'm spreading her tight pussy out.

Next time, I promise myself. Next time we'll have a do over. Do it the way it was meant to be done. But as much as I'm irritated with myself, I'm irritated with her even *more*. Because she made me slip up. Forced my mask to fall for the first time since I slid the fucker on.

The power this woman has over me is quite horrific, and causes my anger to surge even hotter.

"You thought you were just going to break up with me, huh?" I grit into her ear, feeling her clench around me in response. "You thought you were going to get away from me? Talk to me. Now!"

"Noooo!" She wails, laying her head against my shoulder.

"Yeah you did. You thought you were going to get away without letting me-" I growl, feeling her gush over my dick, "in-" *thrust,* "here-" *thrust.*

"I'm sorry! H-Hudson-I'm sorry!" she shouts, straining against the knives.

"I don't play games with my feelings Lolita, surely you aren't surprised." I raise a hand to her breast and roll her nipple in between my fingers.

It's plumpness makes me drive my hips faster, just a little deeper. She flinches, her wetness suddenly running over my cock in a hot, slippery mess making our sex sounds even wetter. Echoing poignantly around the room.

"No, wait! Not there!" She gasps.

"Yes *there.*" I stress. If I can't touch this woman's nipples, I'll go put a bullet in my brain to take me out of my misery. *"You like it,"* I say quietly, "don't tell me you don't. You're dripping onto the floor."

She nods, making my heart skip.

Her eyes are wide, but I still continue rolling her nipple in my fingers. I figured she liked it despite being sensitive, but damn, baby girl is creating a mess between us.

Knowing she takes a while to come, I keep this short because I'm not letting her orgasm right now.

"Look down." I order. When she complies I pull all the way out slowly, and we watch together as a string of our excitement connects us via a thin string. "I warned you that I would fuck you rough and with no mercy. *Even our first time.* Look how excited you are baby. I'm so fucking happy that I can do this to you, make you feel like this."

I raise my head and catch her eye before I ram back in hard on a sharp guttural grunt.

She tosses her head back and lets out a sound that sounds so tortured it makes me pause for a beat, and then suddenly I'm hissing as she clasps so hard on my cock it makes me tighten. My body breaks out in a sweat, and I feel my balls draw up as my body feels she's about to succumb to her orgasm.

My lip curls, and I bite back a snarl.

"Nope. *No, Lola.*" I chastise, sliding out of her reluctantly right as her pussy starts grasping and sucking me in earnest. Her head flies back down and she catches my gaze in shock. "Absolutely not. Your hard headed ass doesn't deserve to come right now. You're going to learn to not play with me."

I'm still upset, and I think the only thing that's going to cool me off is to try and fuck this anger out of my system. It might take all night.

"Hudson!" She screeches at me.

Her thick brows furrow and her eyes flash angrily at me, the fact that I'm denying her. *Us.* And if I weren't also denying myself, I'd keep messing with her, make it worse.

She sucks in a deep breath and begins yelling at me in Spanish so loud I'm momentarily stunned at her viciousness. I chuckle at her, unconcerned, and pull my pants back up, zip my fly and buckle my belt. The whole time she's still yelling, not even pausing to take a breath. This lets me know when I do fuck her face, I don't need to worry about silly things like stopping every few seconds to make sure she can breathe. Because Lola is proving her breath control is insane.

Thirty seconds she's been constantly yelling without drawing a breath. It makes me insanely happy.

"If you keep it up, I'm going to turn you around and make your ass even tanner than it already is. I'm done being tested today. You've pushed me hard enough. Reign it in, now!"

Lola settles down almost immediately, her eyes flicking to my belt. Now that I'm straightened up, I walk back to her and take the knife away from one bracelet, bracing myself for what I know is coming, and I am ready. I want it. Want to feel her fighting against me.

The pain that radiates through my face as her palm connects with my cheek is as hot as the words she just spoke to me, but I take it, my head barely moving.

I'm proud of her, honestly. She trusts me enough to slap me and doesn't worry I'll hit her like her dickhead of an ex. I smile at her and wet my lips, letting her know all is well. I want to thank her for throwing the beast a bone, something to chew on and satisfy me until I can really get her alone and play properly.

"You're going to pay for that later missy. Straighten yourself up."

With a grunt I snatch the other knife up.

Retracting the blade I step back and fold my arms. Lola's shaking, pulling her dress to herself. I'm happy all I did was cut the straps, but her bra is ruined. She begins to pull it on and tuck the straps in and she looks like she's wearing a strapless dress now, with no bra. And though it delights me, she won't be walking around her shop and her customers like that.

"Give me your key so I can go to your house really quick and grab you another change of bra and panties." I lean over and grab an apron I see hanging on a rack.

Dismissing her defiant, infuriated stare I put it over her head and then lean down, giving her a sweet kiss. Thankful she let me because the way I just fucked her then denied her, she would have been more than warranted to slap me twice.

While she's rooting through her purse I bring out my phone and pull up my app, downloading duo lingo.

"Oh by the way," I say to her, clicking the button twice to pay for it. "You've got maybe a good three to four weeks to get out all the bad language and bullshit you want to say to me in Spanish. And once I understand what you're saying there too, it's going to really be a fun time for you, ain't it baby?"

Holding the phone up I click the button and hear it prompt me to say 'hello' in Spanish. Lolita's mouth drops open and I chuckle.

"*Hmm-hmm.*" I give her a truly wicked smile, take her keys and turn, making my way to the door.

I know it's fucked up and wrong on so many levels, but I make a spare key to her house while I'm out.

9

YES NO

LOLA

IT's A LOT.

It's *a lot* a lot. The way my head is whirling, the way my heart is pounding, and the way my vagina is, well, suffering. It's all a lot. So much so, that I don't even think twice when Hudson asks me for my keys to my house to get me a change of undies and just leaves.

I have *never* given anyone a key to my house, other than Frank one time. But I made him give it back. *Skee* doesn't even have one. What the fuck was I thinking?

And what the fuck? He cut my clothes off me in the middle of the morning in my shop. A public place!

My eyes flit to the clock on the wall and I see I have about fifty minutes before the shop officially opens and I just know he won't make it in time. He's probably going to be nosy, rifling through my intimates drawer, looking in my bedside table, my laundry basket. I let out a choked sound as the blood drains out of my face, and I feel faint once again for probably the hundredth time since I've met this man.

I think I have period underwear in my hamper needing to be washed. At the unpleasant thought, I groan, grabbing my phone to text him.

YOU HAD BETTER NOT EVEN THINK ABOUT GOING THROUGH MY DIRTY LAUNDRY HAMPER HUDSON! I'LL KILL YOU!-Lola

I know that was very dramatic of me, but I'll die a million deaths if this man sees my period undies.

Once I'm sure I have a handle on how badly my legs are shaking, I take a deep breath and hop off the counter and immediately bend at the waist.

This man just rearranged my insides I think. Dominic's the only dick I've ever had, and the dildo that Hudson used on me last night was the biggest thing I've ever had in me until just now. And I have no clue what's going to go down between the two of us, but if this man lets me measure his dick I'm going to be doing so happily. Because in my head, we've got some lies to reveal.

"Six inches in circumference my ass." I mumble under my breath.

I stalk out of the storage room and begin to start the tea, coffee, and lemonade for the beverage section of the store. Anxiously looking at the clock. Hearing my phone ping, I answer it, seeing it's Frank. I smile because Frank's always on, no matter what.

"Yes Frank, I know he's there." I beat him to the punch, already knowing what's up.

"Okay. He said he's grabbing you some clothes. Is that true?"

I hear Hudson grumbling in the background. Frank's amazing.

"Yes Frank. It's true." I let out a little hilarious laugh of my own because let's be honest, the shit's hilarious.

"Well okay, if you say so." It sounds like he turns his head away from the phone. "You can go ahead and go on in now. I'll be out here waiting, don't take too long snooping now."

"Thank you, sir. Much appreciated." I hear Hudson chuckle fade as he no doubt walks into my house.

He's such a respectful gentleman. Sort of. My flesh burns between my legs reminding me of how *not* gentlemanly he just was.

"Frank, *were you blocking him from going in?"* I just gotta know.

"Well yes." He says sternly. "Don't nobody *need* to be in your house, Lola. If you would have let me keep that key a couple years ago we wouldn't be having this problem. Now I gotta wait for this doodad, *who I don't know,* go in there and get for you you what *I* could have done. And now, you got people in your house. See how that happens?"

I shake my head, starting the tea machine. "Frank, what the hell is a *doodad?*"

"It's just an *any old body,* Lola!" He pauses a second and then I hear Frank ask Hudson to show him what he's got in the bag.

Feeling my heart bang uncomfortably I snap. "Frank no! You don't have to see, I trust him!" I all but screech into my phone.

"Oh hell okay, you don't have to scream Lola, I'm not deaf yet. Hey Hudson, you want a hog head cheese sandwich?"

And to my utter and sickening shock, Hudson says yes, the sound of his sexy voice keeping me on the phone the whole time as I work. It's quite funny listening to them chit chat back and forth. Hudson's telling him about his construction company, and Frank is telling him about his time in the war, and how Hudson should be grateful Frank served. Because now men like Hudson get to be able to go after their dreams and become successful.

Feeling a smile break over my face I literally hear Frank release Hudson from his proverbial eagle talons, and in my head I can hear his screech as he flies through the sky.

"Lola I'm going to let you go, I'll be there at four with the boys. Do you want me to bring them to my house for dinner tonight so you can have some time with your new man? I don't mind."

The offer makes me pause, because Frank has *never* offered to bring the boys to his home after school before.

Don't get me wrong, Frank obviously loves the boys. He's done things with them, including coming to every school function. But the man has never offered to keep them for dinner after school. From what I understand, that's his sacred time. He eats his dinner in front of a picture of his wife and talks to her about his day.

It's the sweetest, most heartbreaking thing I've ever heard of.

"Does..." My voice catches and I clear my throat. "Does that mean you like him, Frank?"

Frank takes a pause of his own. "Well, we're going to just wait and see, okay Lola? I don't want to say just yet because it's too soon to form an opinion. We gotta be patient with these things."

Why do old people talk this way? I giggle into the phone.

"Okay Frank. I get it." And because Hudson and I have a lot to talk about, mainly about how we just had sex with no condom in my storage room, I accept. "Actually, that would be great. We won't need long. I'll come get them when Hudson and I are done talking later tonight, okay?"

"Okay Lolita, I'll feed them some bologna sandwiches. I know they won't appreciate my head cheese so I'm not even going to waste it on them."

I laugh. "I'll order them a pizza Frank, just open the door and take the box."

"Ok then. Love you, Lola."

My heart stops and my eyes fill up with tears. *Oh my God, he's never said he's loved me before.*

"I love you too, Frank." I choke out, completely undone for the day.

I hang up the phone, take my ear buds out, and make my way back into the storage room where I'm still sniffling when Hudson comes through the door. I know I don't imagine his eyes softening.

"Are you okay?" His concern touches me even more, his green eyes assess me as he walks up. "Loli... I wouldn't have left if-"

I shake my head, ignoring my heart skipping a beat at his nickname for me. "Frank said he *loves* me." I blubber, looking like an idiot. I walk forward and snatch my clothes from him. "Th-*thank y-you.*"

I turn my back to him and I dump the clothes out on the wood table I was so romantically *knifed* to, seeing not only did he bring me my favorite pair of undies, he brought me another dress. I keep my back to him and begin to pull my undies on under my tattered dress, before taking the ruined dress off and putting on the new one.

"You're welcome." His voice is confident, sure. Not like how I feel at all. I don't feel sure about anything. I'm too scared to. "Lola what can I-"

"We need to talk. Later at my house, after I get off work. Frank is keeping the kids for a bit so we can have time together." I say this rapidly, shoving my ruined dress in the bag and then putting everything to the side next to my purse.

I yank my hair out of my bun and shake it out. Needing its protection from this intimidating man's gaze.

He pushes off his shoulder and walks into me, lifting my chin up so I can meet his eye. "I'm not sorry for how I took you. You need to learn to not play with me, and my emotions. I won't play with yours, so don't play with mine. I'm a grown man, and I *know* what I want." His fingers tighten on my chin, letting me know he's dead serious. "And if you ever, and I mean *ever* insinuate you aren't worthy to me again, *Lola,* I will make sure you regret it wholeheartedly. There are just some things I won't tolerate."

It's straight out of one of my smut books, I swear.

Rolling my lips, I shiver at the intensity in his eyes and dammit all to hell if the shit doesn't turn me on. He threads his fingers into the hair at the back of my head as I lift on my toes, meeting him halfway for a kiss that's so sexually charged, lewd, and full of promise that a whimper escapes my mouth at the sheer rawness of it.

Another thing he's introduced me to; a way of kissing that'd like to burn your flesh from your bones, leaving me completely eviscerated.

The doorbell to the shop rings, making us pull away slightly. Our foreheads touch, and we spend a minute just breathing into each other's space. I move first, heading through the door and back behind the counter, my mask back in place as I smile widely at the patron who just entered. But it's Hudson who has my attention.

He's moving behind me, making himself a cup of coffee before walking into the main part of the room where he settles down into a chair with a book I didn't see him snag. I blink and my eyes flicker for a second, feeling unsure. *He's just going to sit there?*

And do what?

For the next eight hours I find out. He chats with the patrons who come in and won't leave him alone. He takes a few phone calls about his job. He orders us lunch, and we eat together at the counter standing up while I show him my website. He tries to ask me questions about my family and my brother that I attempt to evade, successfully managing to not disclose even his name.

And he's just *there...* the entire time until I close.

He walks me to my SUV, climbs in the back of his truck, and follows me when I detour to a drugstore to buy a contraceptive pill. He doesn't say a word, just letting me do my thing as I walk through the aisles slowly. He shops as well. Buying condoms, lube, a bottle of water, and a huge bag of peanut m&ms.

I peek up through my bangs at him, seeing he's paused with a contemplative look on his face.

"You or the boys allergic?" He asks gruffly, holding up the chocolates.

I shake my head no. My eyes go wide, but I stay silent while he purchases everything. Not even seeming the least bit phased at the obviously teasing look the very young clerk gives us.

Back in my vehicle I almost kill myself trying to open the package. I'm taking it *now*, not when I get home.

"Here. Don't hurt yourself, let me help you." Hudson says gently.

He pulls out the knife that seems to become his third arm and opens the package with it, popping out the little pill and placing it on my tongue.

I stay quiet at the tiny flash of hunger that flits across his face before he quickly hides it. Wonder what that's about.

I don't bother to ask as I suck the pill down along with half the bottle of water, wiping my mouth with the back of my hand. I feel instantly better. Taking a deep breath I nod at him, letting him close my door. He follows close behind me and we make it to my house in a record ten minutes, barely giving me any time to pull it together emotionally. I park in the garage, coming out the garage to go through the front as usual because Frank will kill me if I don't give him my daily greeting when I get home.

What I wouldn't give sometimes to just be able to walk into my house. But I love Frank, and know that he takes pride in watching out for me.

In a stroke of luck Frank actually stays in the house. But I see him in the curtains looking. Always alert. He gives me a thumbs up, letting me know all is well, and when Hudson catches his eye he puts a finger to his watch and gives him a pointed look.

Curfew is at ten-thirty. Yes, Frank, we know.

Hudson and I look at each other and chuckle. It's not a ten-thirty kind of night, the boys bed times is eight thirty, after all. I start sweating.

"Uhm, Hudson?" I say quietly as we make our way in the door.

"Yeah baby?" He sounds relieved and I feel bad, because I'm aware I've been shut down, but I've been so caught up in my own feelings that I couldn't help it.

We're standing in the foyer, facing each other, and I am just *shaking*.

I can't make myself look at Hudson as he moves to close the front door behind us.

He clears his throat, looking at me expectantly but I'm lost in my head trying to figure out my next move. What do I say? What am I supposed to do now that we're here? I can't stop my mind from reeling, and I can tell...*just tell* that I'm about to break off into a full blown panic.

I raise my gaze, looking into his eyes for just a second before breaking away, not able to hold his eye contact yet. Biting my lip, I can't help my fingers tremble nervously as I struggle to take off my jacket.

In my clumsiness my purse hits the floor. I bend down trying to grab it, but Hudson is there, lifting me back up with his hands under my arms, hauling me to him. Pressing me hard into his thick, muscular chest. His arms sneak under my thick jacket, looping all the way around, and he just holds me. Rocks me gently side to side while I shake.

But for some reason, the tears won't fall. I'm just shaking, and my eyes are flickering all over my hallway unseeingly because I don't know where to look.

"Shhh..." Hudson soothes, holding me to him even tighter while he rocks me side to side. God, he's *so warm*. Hudson feels nostalgic. Soothing. I bury my nose in his neck and inhale, and damn if he's not doing the same thing to me.

His nose buries deep in the vulnerable flesh right at my pulse, nuzzling me. His breath washes over my skin and suddenly I feel that shift I've heard other people talk about. The unexplainable one. There's a tie between us that feels tangible; like if I wanted to reach out and touch it, I could grasp it between my fingertips.

He pulls my head back gently but keeps my body pressed to his and he pushes my bangs back, which feels like the most vulnerable thing he's done to me so far, ironically.

"I'm not on the pill." I manage to gasp. My throat feels so tight I can barely talk.

"It's okay. It's okay, Lolita." His broad palm strokes my forehead, smoothing my bangs back again and again. And we're just rocking while he's stroking me.

My heart cracks.

This man's going to break me, and it's not going to feel like Dominic. I already know. His green eyes are staring into my soul and I can't look away. I feel the blood rushing hotly in my ears as something new floods me. My eyes widen, seeing Hudson's not letting me free. The tears well up in my eyes, and his face becomes momentarily blurry through the sheen of my tears before I blink and they spill over, betraying just how internally damaged I am.

I let out a shuddering breath, unable to keep my emotions inside.

"You're going to hurt me. Oh my Goddd."

My face contorts and I just let it out, my tears finally break free. I'm aware I'm a blubbering mess but I can't stop, and he wont let me look away. Taking a hand and gripping my chin, making me face him head on. I can't hide from him.

Could I ever?

He's shaking his head, and dammit if I don't see something I've never seen before in another person's eyes flash before it's gone. Being replaced by something warmer, softer. He's melting from the inside out and I can tell.

"No. No, Lola. I'm not." His breath washes over me we're so close the intimacy sears me. I feel it in my very psyche.

"Yesss." I sob, aware I am like a child at this point. *"Yes you are."*

"No-"

"Yes-"

"No-"

"Y-Yesss!"

We go on and on like that for who knows how long, trying to convince each other. And the whole time I'm staring into his eyes, just astounded how patient he is. I've never had anyone be patient with me, and it's painful because as humans we're so into instant gratification and I've never been this way unless put under duress. I always take my time with everything and everyone.

Until today, when I let this man fuck me the way I've always wanted to be.

And it hits me. He's giving me what I need. *Effortlessly.* I don't have to ask. Even now all day he hasn't left my side knowing I'm out of sorts, he stayed with me.

"Don't you have some big company to run?" I whisper up at him, finally breaking the "no" "yes" battle we've been embroiled in for at least fifteen minutes.

"Yes." It makes me smile, because he's been saying no for so long now. His eyes lower to my teeth and his smile breaks free, and I see his lip twitch just a little, as if he's holding back.

"Hudson why did you fuck me like that?" I can't believe I asked it, to be honest.

"Because," his voice is level, low, he's so patient. "It's what you need. It's what I need. You need to know you're chosen. I chose you, baby."

My eyes widen and the urge to spill every deep dark secret is there. Because this man. This sexy, intimidating, hunk of a man is rocking me in his arms, indulging me in my breakdown and helping me through my trauma, without question. Without probing. He's making himself available to me.

I take a deep breath and place my forehead to Hudson's chest, feeling his lips lower to the top of my head, something else that knocks me askew at the intimacy of it all. I curl my fingers into his shirt.

"Would you like to meet my boys?"

I feel Hudson's chest swell ever so slightly. "I'd love to."

Was that relief I heard in his voice? I look up, aware my bangs are sticking every which way. We stare at each other and then he's smoothing them down, making me smile as he puts me back in order.

"Okay then, let's go."

We walk over to Frank's house side by side. His arms around me and then we get to Frank's front door where we knock and I'm so nervous because I've never introduced my boys to anyone ever before.

Franks opens the door and the house smells like old people which makes me smile because that's how it should be and I smile the biggest smile at seeing my boys sitting in front of the television on the floor, with what looks to be thirty year old coloring book paper in front of them.

"Mami!" They both jump up and throw themselves at me so hard I topple backwards and Hudson is helping to steady me.

"Como estas mi amors!" I greet them, just so happy to see them after them being gone all weekend. I try to look them over but they've got me in a vice grip.

"Now boys, how many times do I have to tell you that you need to be careful around your mother? *She's short!*" Frank scolds them.

Leave it to Frank to be sweet and mean at the same time. Ignoring Frank, they treat me to the biggest squeezes I think I've ever felt from them, to the point I let out an involuntary gasping moan because they're literally squeezing the air out of me.

We all break into laughter and the boys step away seeing Hudson behind me, waiting patiently.

"Hey you're the guy from the bookstore!" Tatum says in a loud voice but Tucker just looks for a second, turning around and then going back to the coloring stuff where he begins to clean up.

"Tuck, you want to come say hi?" I ask him, but he keeps his back to me. I throw an apologetic look at Hudson before looking at Frank in concern.

Frank tightens his lips and for a minute we just silently communicate. Tucker has been getting worse after his weekends with his dad. I seem to lose my ability to even talk, and Frank comes up to me and puts a hand to my shoulder, trying to give me comfort. I blink the tears away and walk over to their discarded backpacks on the couch. I'm shaking because I know what I'm going to find.

I pull out their lunchboxes and look inside and see Tatum's is full, and Tuckers is empty. I can't help it, I burst out into tears. It's just too much.

"What is going on?" I wail, turning around to face Tatum and Tucker, both their eyes are wide, but for some reason, Tatum's is fearful. Tucker just looks...dead. Like how I feel. I'm dying because my little boy's suffering and I don't know how to help.

Frank and Hudson come closer and I'm begging, pleading for something, any explanation.

"You can tell me, Tuck! Baby *It's mommy you can tell me.*"

Tucker turns away and stares at the door as Frank steps over to me and presses my head into his chest.

"There there." He shushes me, patting my back.

"I just need someone to tell me what to do. *What do I do.*" I moan into his chest, just crying. Who cries like this?

"Hey kiddos, do you guys have a baseball? We can go play outside for a little bit?" Hudson springs into gear pulling the little boy's backpacks from me and then trading a look with Frank, who's stroking my hair.

"You can stay later, it's fine. I'll be on the lookout." Frank says to him, and if I weren't so distraught, I'd think it was funny. But it's not.

Hudson, Tucker, and Tatum leave and I spend half an hour crying onto Frank's chest, telling him how scared I am. How Dominic's energy is slowly taking over. When my tears dissipate, Frank pulls me to a room in his house and ushers me inside, turning the lights on.

My mouth drops. There's five gun safes, and three tall cabinets that are filled with rifles, handguns, I think there's a couple AK 47s in there too. And there's a very suspicious box hanging out in the corner I try not to inspect too closely.

My jaw drops, because I'm sure what that black box is is incredibly *illegal,* and to think I've been living next to it for so many years has got me messed up in the head.

Frank gives me a look. "You are going to learn how to protect yourself do you hear me? And if for any reason you need one of these, the code is six twelve nine. There's no safety, you come get what you need and you blow that fuckers head clean off you hear me Lolita?"

I nod, still stunned.

"We'll start at the gun range next week on Saturday morning, bright and early."

I nod because well, when Frank tells you to do something, you do it. And if you don't, you're a fool.

I leave the house feeling better about potentially being able to defend myself, and I hear the boys laughing in the back so I head between our two houses just standing there, watching Hudson play catch with them.

My jaw drops, because I've never seen the boys play catch before, their dad never wanted to. And for a second, I see some happiness enter my boy Tucker.

And in turn, some happiness enters me too. But it's not enough, I'm still numb. I'm afraid of what will happen if I become any number.

10

WHAT I AM

HUDSON

"WHAT DID YOU SAY you were doing?"

Clayton's voice irks me sometimes, because he *knows* what I'm doing. He's just trying to fill the empty lulls in our conversation because he doesn't like to shut up. So I ignore him.

"Did you find it yet?"

"Yes!" His voice is triumphant. "His address is nine-four-two Westfell drive about twenty three minutes away from where you are now."

"And his family members?"

"From what it looks like he has one grandparent who will still talk to him. He's estranged from his parents, who are also estranged from their extended family, but from what I can tell it's because they're off living a decent life in Texas. The others are in gangs, presumably in drug activity. Dominic's family doesn't have much to do with him at all. And there's very little social media presence, probably due to the criminal stuff the family looks to be involved in. However, there's a few pictures that Lolita used to post of them all but that stopped around the time the kids were three. He has a very weird, fucked up family."

I grunt, still staring through my binoculars at Dominic Patrick, who is currently in the middle of a gangbang at a mansion. Attempting to fuck this sleezy, diseased looking bitch in some living room with about eight other people. He's currently holding a stack of money, flinging it in the air while the woman sucks on a cock that, honestly, I'd cut off if it were mine.

Be better off without one the shit's so puny.

No one's using protection and it's disgusting to watch so much fluid slinging everywhere but it is what it is.

I pause, thinking about how I didn't use protection with Lola earlier this morning. I lower my binoculars, seeing all that I needed to see, and reach into my bag grabbing a tracking device. Taking a second, I check it, before I slowly round my way to where his vehicle is. I shimmy under the carriage, attach it somewhere discreetly, then head back to my truck about half a mile away

Thankfully this mansion isn't too far from my place so getting home won't be a problem. I'm so looking forward to the nut I'm about to give myself thinking about being buried deep inside Lola this morning.

"So what's the plan?"

"The plan is I'm going to watch him for a little bit. I need to figure out a way to get his abuse of Tucker handled somehow."

I get into my truck silently and pull out my phone. I text Lola, really hating to do this but after what I just saw, it needs to be done.

> *Hey babe, please don't be upset. I just need to know when's the last time you had an STD check?* -Hudson

She said the separation and divorce were within the last three years so I'm just trying to cover bases here after what I just saw, because she can't know about this. It'd break her heart. That's what he's using her money for? Hookers?

> *Hudson I promise I'm clean. I had my last STD check around the time I last had sex with*

Satan's brother, about three and a half years ago.-Lola

My eyebrows fly off my face at her nickname for him.

Is Satan's brother Dominic? -Hudson

Yes. -Lola

Do you have a nickname for me?-Hudson

I chuckle because Satan's brother is funny, she's so freaking nutty I love it.

You have not earned a bad nickname yet.-L ola

She's so disrespectful. I laugh, and forget that Clayton's on the phone.

"Jesus man, that's some laugh. When am I going to meet her?"

I sigh a deep soughing breath. "Perhaps this weekend, You can come by for a bit on Saturday around noon. She's going shooting with her neighbor, then the next weekend I'm bringing her and the boys over for a couple days."

"Nice. Okay I'll be on by. Listen, here we go. *Are you ready?*"

"Well, like a pretty little thing always tells me; if you stay ready, you don't have to *get* ready." I grin, thinking about Lola.

'He's got about two hundred and twelve thousand dollars. He owns the house at the address I sent you, and he owns the car he's driving. That's it."

I grunt. I wonder how much of that is Lola's?

"Your girl only has nineteen thousand in her account, I looked it up because I knew that was coming next."

My heart stops as a hot flush of anger rolls through me.

"But it's strange," he continues, not noticing my pause, "because she *used* to have a lot of money. I did a deep dive. She's been hemorrhaging money the last seven years. Ready for this? She had *five million dollars* in inheritance money from her parents, and that includes their life insurance money. She *was* sitting real cushy."

My lips tighten.

"And what's also interesting, is that her house is paid for. Completely, and has been paid off since she was seventeen. *And* she inherited the house from her parents. It's the only asset she's got that's paid off aside from her car. *Eevvvery* now and then she gets a small amount of money dumped into her checking account from an LLC. and it's been helping her stay afloat but that's it. There are large withdrawals of money throughout the years and guess where they are deposited?"

"Satan's brother's account."

Clay pauses. "What?"

"Nevermind. Thanks for that Clayton, I appreciate you."

I click the line shut, truly hoping Dominic is enjoying himself because playtime is almost over. I turn up the radio and chill out for the short drive to my ranch.

As I pull in I park my truck next to the horse stables and head on inside, needing to feel my horses soothing presence.

I go straight to Champ's stall, let myself in, and chuckle at his snicker and the way he turns his head to look at me. I grab a brush, even though I can tell Hannah's already done it, and begin the long soothing strokes I know he likes.

"Hey buddy, thanks for being so patient with me these last couple weeks." I talk to him, hearing Nay Nay let out the loudest neigh yet, vying for attention. "You too missy." I holler over at Nay Nay, shooting her a wry grin.

What is with the girls in my life and their mouths? I chuckle, thinking about Lola. I cannot wait for the boys to come. The horses will love it as much as I think the boys will. They need to be interacted with a little more.

As I brush down Champ's coat, I let myself get lost in my thoughts. I can't remember the last time I sank my dick into anyone, much less someone I feel this way about. And it's only been two weeks. How is it possible to feel like this about someone in two weeks?

It was more than just our bodies uniting. I feel like my soul merged with hers. That's the thing I can't seem to be able to verbalize.

The entire day I was just seeped in her so deep I couldn't even leave her side. I *needed* to be near her. There's also no way I would have fucked her like that and then left her. What kind of asshole would that have made me? And her boys... the way they grab onto her is more than just mother and son love, there's something going on there that's sinister, and there's nothing you can tell me to convince me otherwise.

That man is doing something to those boys they don't want to talk about. There's most definitely deep seated fear in Tucker, especially. But what I'm trying to figure out is, why one over the other? Tatum seems outgoing, and unless you know what to look for you won't see it. But I see it. That's a boy that's protecting his twin.

I'd be willing to bet money that Tatum is protecting Tucker from his dad, using his charm as a buffer somehow.

Only problem is, it's not *working*. And seeing Lola break down after looking in those kids lunch boxes has got me seriously considering how much longer I can hold myself back. But I need to sus them all out more. Need to figure out how they all tick in order to get this to work. And that's including Frank.

I'm so thankful that the man is how he is, but my God, he's going to fuck around and become a casualty if he doesn't lay off a little bit. I don't want the man hurt.

I move on to Nay Nay, because Beauty is being a good girl, and think about my property and how I want to go about doing this. The timing needs to be perfect. The *alibis* need to be perfect. I don't want Lola getting sucked into this at all, and I need the boys completely gone to make this work. There's too many variables that can go wrong, especially with them around.

So I pray.

I pray that that fuck up of a man can behave himself just a little bit longer so I can do this right. In the meantime, I also need to think about how to seduce this woman I'm falling so madly in love with.

Lola broke something inside of me in her foyer. I'll never forget the way she looked when she expressed I was going to hurt her. Like it's a done deal. I didn't care if I had to stand there for five years just rocking her, eventually something would have clicked. I'm not going to hurt you.

No baby, quite the opposite. I'm going to *save* you. But I need you to give me some time, honey. Good things come to those that wait.

I move on to brushing Beauty and suddenly that growl is back, echoing in my head. Causing me to harden with such a swiftness that it scares me to be this fucked up and aroused over a woman. You know how they say people who play sports shouldn't fuck before a game because they need their strength?

Yeah, Lolita's sapping my strength already and I've only been in her maybe fifteen minutes today. I don't even want to think about when I really get a chance to get in there the way I want to. Because she took it almost too well.

God she took my fat cock like a *good girl*.

I let out a little grunt, stomping my foot into the floor, willing the hot, heavy feeling down. I tell the horses goodnight and make my way into my house, setting the alarm and going straight into the the shower in my bedroom. Before I discard my clothes I grab out her pretty pink panties I stole from her hamper and hold them to my nose, letting out a rough groan at her smell. I pull them away and run my fingers along the crotch, seeing the slight period stain there at the edge, taunting me.

Goddamn I need a taste.

I step under the spray, letting it hit my back, unwilling to take her from me just yet. I fist my erection and squeeze roughly, pumping hard. I look down and see a string of precum trailing from the tip of my dick and I shudder, imagining burying my face in between her legs.

Jesus, she's just saturating me from the inside out.

Feeling pained, I let myself go wild with images of myself fucking her the way I need to. I think about how I want to take her next, knowing it'll need to be on the safety of my property.

I remember the night before, how I held her legs up and made her crawl her way to the toy she purchased. The desperate look on her face. The way she smells...*holy fuck*. The way she sounds when she's angry, which might be my biggest turn on, her attitude. If only she knew that was barely the tip of the iceberg of the things I want to do with her.

Fuck. I want to make her *feel*. Because she makes me feel.

My hands press and rub her panties to the side of my face where she lashed out and hit me this morning, and I shudder. Letting my imagination go even more wild. In my mind, Lola's slapping me, scratching me. I'm making her do all the filthy, fucked up shit I know I truly crave but probably won't be able to experience. At least, not right away.

Because If I ever get a chance to fuck her the way I want to fuck her, I won't be able to feel her hitting me. I'll have to tie her beautiful hands up so she can't.

But God knows I want to feel her rip into me, deep into the very recesses of my soul and even deeper if possible.

The feel of her slap tortures me.

So, In my head, she's slapping me. Just like she did this morning. Except this time she's under me and slapping me because I'm forcing her to take it. I'm overstimulating those nipples I've found she doesn't like touched too much *but baby, you're getting over that.* I'm ripping her clothes off and she's resisting me, with a touch of fear in her eyes. Not because she's truly scared of me, but because she's terrified at what I'm going to do.

How I'm going to do it.

I told Lola I was nothing like that main character in that book and I meant that. What I am is much more sick.

I press her panties to my lips and groan, wishing she was in front of me. Here in the shower.

Baby girl I need you kicking and clawing and screaming underneath me. Wild for it. *Scared for it.* And when I snatch you back by your hair and ram my dick inside you, I need to see that moment of surrender. I need you to lay everything down for me. Your heart, your emotions, your fear.

But most of all your *will.*

I need it all gone, so I can fill you up the way you're meant to be. Because I can't hurt you if you aren't you. I meant what I said when we were rocking in the foyer love, I won't hurt you. Because at the end of this all, *you won't be you.*

You'll be *Hudson's.*

And if I have to brand my fucking name into your skin as a physical reminder, then I will. So, enjoy being Lolita, because Lolita's almost dead. I'm going to kill what you once were, and give you a new you, sweet thing. You can be sure of it like you're sure of your next breath, while you've got it.

I grit my teeth and bear the sharp hot feeling of my cum spurting out of my cock at the memory of the way you were breathing earlier, taking my dick. I take the feeling of my orgasmic death like a man. Inwardly I rejoice, because although the sound of your ragged breaths as you were about to come makes me weak, I just know your last exhale is going to be even more perfect.

The very thought sends chills down my spine.

I get into bed and stare at the glowing fireplace with the memory of Lola's taste on my tongue. The feel of her silky skin under my hands, the way her neck arched just right under me as I pleasured her. The sound she makes when I'm playing with her thick nipples between my fingers and lips.

Heaving a deep sigh I roll my head to the side, looking over at the empty pillow next to me in bed, I can't help but imagine us laying together, wrapped around each other. Would she like to sleep with me against her? Enjoy my skin touching hers the way I like hers on mine?

I torture myself to sleep, my final thoughts of that growl when her tight body accepted all of me into her. I wonder if she will eventually grow to accept all of me, all the stuff on the inside I hide. I pray she will.

She will...because she just has to.

That weekend I call family social services when I see through the tracking device that Dominic's car was out in the early hours of the morning when he was supposed to have the boys, thinking I'd found my chance. But no. Apparently, he'd left the kids with his elderly grandmother for the night. according to Lolita. Who's sounding increasingly more and more frustrated.

Frustrated, I begin to track his every move, trying to learn him and his patterns. The man is a sneaky little fuck, as abusers are. But people like him tend to make a wrong move somewhere a long the way. They always do.

II

WHO I AM

DOMINIC

WHO THE FUCK DECIDED that parenting had to be so stringent? Why do they need clean stuff? It's not necessary. All this prissy shit leads to nothing but weakness. Then you got little gay kids running around wondering why they like boys. Men aren't men anymore and I firmly believe it's because their moms are fucking pushover cunts. Creating pushover cunts with *penises.*

It's a shame.

I slam the dryer shut, striding out of the bathroom that doubles as a laundry room, and throw the bundled fitted sheet to Tucker Fucker.

"Here," I grunt. "Make the bed."

"But what about the-the top sheet?" Tucker Fucker says to me.

God his voice is so *annoying.*

He keeps his gaze averted and I am so thankful because he knows it's the quickest way to piss me off.

Fucking scum. I sneer at him, bending down and putting my hands on my knees and staring him in the eye, seeing he's shivering with fear.

"Stop. Talking. To. Me." I say curtly, bending up out of my crouch, Ignoring the hurt look in his eye, I bump into him as I walk past their room. Tatum stands off to the side, hanging his back pack on the wall. Staring. Always staring at me. I curl my lip at him. "And what the hell do you think *you're* looking at, pendejo?"

Tatum narrows his eyes at me, as he turns to face Tucker Fucker. But his eyes keep mine.

He's annoying as hell too, but when he looks at me like that. It reminds me of a young me. Something I can't stand to think about. Shit, at least he's *got* a fucking brother. But no matter, I enjoy seeing them at odds and love to encourage it. It reminds me of me and my brother, and it gives me the most serene feeling of nostalgia.

They both can kick rocks and get knocked off.

Grabbing a beer from the fridge I kick it closed and head back down the hallway, past their room and to my bedroom. Kicking that door shut too. Not caring that they're holed up in their room, alone.

Good riddance.

I don't even want them here. I only have them because it hurts *her*. And anything I can do to hurt her, even if it means inconveniencing myself with these two whiny dumb fucks I don't even want, is worth knowing she's at home, miserable.

I sniff, irritated. Because I guess I can't say that anymore can I because she's not at home being miserable. She's spreading her legs for that piece of shit who thinks he's hot shit.

I rip off my shirt, the material catches on my ear, tugging at my skin and causing the half healed mark behind my ear to protest painfully. I hiss, putting my hand there and pressing. As if she called my name, I raise my eyes to the picture of me and that bitch hanging up on my wall. I keep it there as a reminder that better things are yet to come.

Walking to the wall, I take a swig of my beer and narrow my eyes at the sight of a nineteen year old Lolita in her pink dress with spaghetti straps.

She was pregnant in this picture, but neither one of us knew it at the time. I thought I had me something good. Perky nineteen year old, loaded, wealthy, and dumb enough for me to afford the lifestyle my brother was making for himself.

A lifestyle that my family said I wasn't smart enough for so they shunned me.

I take another deep swallow and head to my closet, reaching into my shoebox and grabbing the manila folder out the top and opening it. Perusing slowly as it's a lot of figures to look at, I take my time walking back to the picture flipping through page after page. With each paragraph my grin get's bigger and bigger.

I raise my head, staring into her eyes.

"Oh chica, the best is yet to come indeed." I slap the folder shut and then pull out my phone.

Lolita, the washing machine just broke and I need about four grand for another one. Tucker's already complaining that I couldn't clean their top sheet. -Dominic

I wait for a second, seeing the text bubbles. She sends me five grand, along with a text that says that's all she can give me for another month. She's so *stupid,* just like Tucker Fucker. I cackle, sitting on the edge of my bed, and pulling up another number.

Here's five more grand to go with the other thirty I sent. I only owe you twenty more and then we're good to go right?-D

It only takes about a minute, but the reply comes through.

Yea. How about you send it all at once instead of acting like my service is a layaway plan.

He signs off with a symbol. Not even a name. Which is fine with me. My eyes raise to look at the picture once more. Seeing her smiling, clueless.

I'm not done with you. I think, ignoring Tatum knocking on my door, asking for dinner. *Not by a long shot you stupid, hard headed*

cunt. And when I'm done, I'll show everyone that they're wrong about me.

I *am* smart, a lot smarter than any of them give me credit for. And then they'll see who I am, in time. I don't need their drug connections. I'm above them. They'll see soon enough.

And then they'll be sorry.

12

TORN UP

HUDSON

WEDNESDAY EVENING I OPEN up her blog and there it is in black and white. My heart swells too big for my chest, and I just know she's going to need to take a day off after I get my hands on her. Because she wrote this shit on purpose. Subliminal messaging at its finest. Don't ask me how I know it but I do.

And I'm absolutely fucking her *up* tonight, no questions asked.

I put my eyes to the screen and begin to read. The first sentence alone has me letting out a grunt and causing my dick to jerk because Lolita's been holding back on me I see.

> Now, while I love a good face pounding scene, and while I myself can hang with the best of them, there's something about being pushed into the dirt, and a belt yanked around the main characters neck that gives me pause for just a second.
>
> We need to contemplate this rationally ladies. Can we discuss this?
>
> What is it about a man taking control that's so sexy? You know how we are ladies... we act coy, like we don't like it.
>
> "We don't want it," we say. "We want to be treated like a lady," we say.
>
> We hang tight to our feminine propriety like a badge of honor. But then we walk around reading these books that have these

men absolutely rearranging the main characters lady parts, and we throw money at the books every single time. Every time.

So what I want to know is, friends... can we be *real* with ourselves about our innermost desires?

And not only can we be real about them. Can we let ourselves dare to experience it, even if it's for just a moment? What's it going to hurt if you let him pound your mouth till your throat is raw? So what you gotta suck on a halls for a few days?

Isn't it worth it for the way he runs you through and gives your kitty cat what she needs afterwards?

I pause, chuckling. Because *what the fuck* Lolita.

And let's get *real* real here.

We read books about men with wings, flying and screwing their love interest in the air, or orcas with monster cocks that shouldn't even be able to fit into a human beings body, but we love it because it suspends the reality of time and space.

What I'm trying to tell you is ladies, your men don't need wings or big green cocks to satisfy you. Let him tear that mouth up one good time. *Just once,* and I promise you, he'll give you anything you want afterwards.

Start your breathing lessons now so you aren't panicking when he goes down your throat. Practice with a banana, learn to fight your gag reflexes.

Do the work and train yourself ahead of time so you can blow your man's mind. Isn't it worth it for him to tell you stfuattcltg-gya?"

What the hell is that?

I pull the acronym up through google and seeing the results I'm quickly up. Headed for my truck, done for the day. I pull out my phone, uncaring of any plans she's got this weekend.

She will not tell me no, not after what I just read and the way she's got my dick aching. Feeling like a steel rod in my pants.

She answers on the second ring. Good girl.

"Hello."

I feel precum leak out the tip before a deep throb makes my thigh muscle tense hard. Fuck

"Lo', I'll be at your shop at seven. Close up and put a sign out that you're closed for a few hours tomorrow. I'm picking you up to go to my house. Also, you're coming over this weekend with the boys."

Lolita's response is immediate.

"But Hudson! *I can't just open the shop late like that-* "

"Bye baby."

I disconnect the call, because she heard what I told her to do. And unless those plans involve me, and my house where I know I can give us what we both need without neighbors interference, then they don't involve her either.

I head into the store at six fifty eight on the dot and see she's finishing up with two customers.

I flip the store sign to closed, because she didn't listen to me, and head straight past the register into the storage room to grab her purse and her jacket. I bring it back out and then place it to the side, ignoring her side eyeing me. I notice the two customers watching me with interest as well, but I ignore them as I proceed to do her closing down chores for her.

Lolita's absolutely bristling, but I couldn't make myself care even if a gun was held to my head. This shit is too serious to me.

I pour myself a cup of coffee and then dump the pot, washing it quickly and then replacing it listening to her talk with her customers. I'm sweeping her floor by the time she gets to her last customer, and this one. Jesus. My irritation ramps up to dangerous levels.

This one won't stop talking. She's holding onto her books and chit chatting with Lola about an old blog of hers, and hasn't stopped to *breathe,* much less put her things on the counter for Lola to ring up.

I clear my throat, trying to make someone get a clue but no, they're still chatting. I dump the trash, replace the broom, and then head around the counter.

"Hi there." I interrupt her, flashing the woman my brightest smile. She stumbles across her words for a second then finally stops talking, she's clearly affected. "Congratulations ma'am, you are the last customer for today! You know what that means right?" Both Lola and the lady look at me with something akin to shock and curiosity. "Your merchandise is on the house."

I put my arm around the woman's shoulders and turn her. I keep my tone light and cheery and begin to march her straight to the front of the store. I ignore Lolita's jaw dropping in pure shock and that thing inside me grins wickedly. Yeah baby, *it's like that.*

"*Ohh,* I didn't know! Is this every day?" The customer asks curiously.

"It's for today only ma'am, congratulations again and have a goodnight!" I close the door and turn.

My heart is pounding, and blood is roaring in my ears making me feel off kilter. Lola is standing at the counter looking like a deer in headlights and it's perfect. *So perfect.* She's confused, scared, unsure. It all feeds this fucked up swirling tornado of lust that currently got me by the balls, gripping on and leading me straight to her.

"You-" She's gasping for air, almost like she can't breathe. *"You had no right to interfere you maldito psicopata!"*

Thanks to learning some choice words through online, I gleam she called me a fucking psycho. So, we can add anger to the emotions running through her, and honestly, it's the cherry on top of the cake for me. Because I'm a little angry too, to be honest. I keep my expression the same and head back to the back of the store.

I can't say anything really, because she does make me feel psychotic.

As I round the counter, she starts backing up until she bounces off the wall behind her.

"You mad at me baby?" I ask, slowing my steps purposefully, making her wait for it.

"Yes! That was a *fifty dollar book she had*!" Her hands ball up and I can see she's trembling.

Ohhh she's *mad* mad. A spark of defiance enters her eye and here we go.

The seriousness of the moment hits her finally, and she tilts her head, taking a step forward.

"No."

I feel myself twitch at the way she curls her lips to say that one word, baring her canines and I just know, I gotta get the blow job out the way *first,* so that I have time to recover and chill out on the way home before I truly get to tear into her. Because if she doesn't learn anything else in life ever about me... it's that she'll never again shape her mouth to say "no" to me in quite the way she just did.

I tilt my own head looking her up and down. I don't chuckle. I don't smile or grin. Or give her any smoke and mirrors to make her feel safe. She's not safe right now, and she knows it as well as I do.

"I read your blog." I say in a matter of fact tone.

And then it clicks for her, what's going on.

I narrow my eyes, watching the blood rush to her face as she tries to step back before bouncing off the wall again. There's a tense few seconds of time where we stare at each other. The sexual tension is the room is thick, and I feel my chest swell, my jaw tightens, and my cock throbs in response.

I take a slow step forward. Heel to toe.

Her eyes flicker down, watching me place my foot slowly on the ground. Her eyes raise back to mine and in a brave move she launches herself at the counter to vault it but I'm too fast. I calmly snatch her up by her arm and her hair, ignoring her shrieking and shove her to her knees behind the counter.

Ignoring the rough grunt she makes, I focus on keeping myself from blowing my load in my pants at the way her knees and palms sounded as they slapped the tile.

I begin to drag her like that. Making her crawl and shuffle to the storage room where I walk us inside and close the door.

Game over baby.

"Hudsoooonnnnn!"

She's full on screaming, stroking my desire even higher. But I keep one hand on her hair, ignoring her clawing at my legs and hips. With some amusement I see she's struggling, slipping on her knees. Her tights make her grapple for purchase on the floor. I manage to get my buckle open one handed, and honestly the metallic clink of my belt coming loose makes me even more hot for some reason. I look down into her beautiful face.

"You did not tell me you could suck dick the way you allude to in that blog. You been holding out on me, which I don't appreciate. And what you don't realize is..." I get my pants pushed down a bit and pull out my cock. "Blow jobs are a treat to me. And after the shit I just read, you're the fucking perfect dopamine hit I need." I pull her to me and make her rub her face against my cock.

I grind my feet into the floor a little bit, just hearing her whimper. Her tongue licks out between her lips, making me feel momentarily frozen with the sensation. My heart feels like it's beating out of my chest.

"Can't you see what you're doing to me baby?" I grit harshly, groaning against the wet feel of her hot tongue lapping up my skin.

I feel wetness along with the moist smoothness of her lips rubbing against my shaft. She presses her lips halfway down my dick and then nibbles the skin there, forcing me to let out a sound that takes me back a bit. I attempt to steady and center myself.

"I'm getting ready to fuck your face. *Hard.*" I warn her.

She doesn't acknowledge me. Busy putting trembling hands to my hips, I grip her scalp even tighter smearing her lips against me. Fuck I want my scent on her. Those sick thoughts come back again and I growl deep in my throat, beating them back. My eyes narrow at her, seeing she's playing with me right now.

But that's okay, because I'm going to get her back as soon as we're on my property. I'm going to make her pay dearly for teasing me.

"Cough. Get it out the way." I command.

She complies. I am absolutely dying on the inside. I snatch her face up and bend down slightly, getting a good look at her face. "I know you well enough by now from watching you to know when you'll need a break, when you can't take it anymore. Open your mouth."

Lola stares up at me and the longing in her face has me weak, because she looks almost enraptured. My world is tilted off kilter, seeing just how much she likes this, *likes me.*

"Obey me."

Obediently she opens her mouth and sticks her tongue out a little and I thrust two fingers against her tongue. Slowly for a second, and I'm pleased as I feel myself get to the back of it and then I see her eyes well up with tears but she doesn't cough. Doesn't jerk or gag. I slide my fingers a bit deeper and a tear slips out of her eye, but that's her only reaction.

I'm currently pressing into the spot past her throat that should be making her react, and she's not. Other than that singular tear. I feel my eyebrow twitch.

"You been practicing for me, baby?" I say.

Lola nods.

"*Hmmm* I like that. Ready to get tore up baby?" I whisper, holding her eye contact.

She nods again slightly and I pull my fingers out and guide her straight to the tip of my dick.

I feel every muscle in my body lock up. I'm afraid if I don't, then I'm going to blow apart to never be put back together again. Lola's lips part just enough to slide my tip in, but then she's sheathing her teeth and clamping down into a tight grip that has my skin pebbling up with goosebumps.

Fuck, she finally has her mouth around me. I may not survive this.

A trickle of trepidation crawls up my spine and forces me to grapple with my sanity. She's got way too much power over me, and it makes me tighten my fingers on her head. But then suddenly the flat of her tongue strokes hot and slow up the head of my cock, agitating my sensitive flesh, and swirling in the little hole there. Effectively erasing the worry as if it was never there to begin with.

"Aw fuck." I gasp.

I grunt and feel myself break out into a sweat. We stay like that for a second, and she slides deeper. Her cheeks are hollowed and I feel myself being sucked into the wet cavern of her mouth. The sides of her cheeks are rubbing against me, the ridges at the roof of her mouth offer so much stimulation, and her tongue has me pressed mercilessly upwards it. And the *heat*.

Fuck her mouth is so hot.

I begin to suck the air through gritted teeth because she hasn't done much and already it's the best I've had. I let her take control for now, and once I'm ready I'll take over, but right now, this is all Lola.

She keeps herself clamped on me, and then I'm sliding deeper to the back of her throat. I feel her shift slightly, my first clue, when suddenly she makes a small sound and then I'm down her throat. All the way down.

Small puffs of air are popping against my pelvis and I'm dying.

The growl that leaves me is unholy because I've never been all the way inside anyone's mouth before. My hands slide into her hair. All ten fingers encase her from the top of her head to the nape of her neck as I cradle her for a minute. I keep her pressed against me for a second while I work to get my bearings.

I look down, seeing her staring up at me through her bangs. Her mascara is running, making her wispy bangs stick to her face in places, which is the hottest thing I've ever seen in my life.

"Are you ready baby? I'm about to be rough." I spread my legs slightly and bend my knees, preparing. "Your pussy's going to get it rougher tonight, though." It's supposed to be comforting.

She winks at me, and then I pull back and begin to just straight fuck her mouth. The little gluck sound she makes as I pound in and out has me weak. I'm well aware her hands have gone up the back of my shirt and her nails are sinking into my back.

My own fingertips tighten against her scalp in response and I'm pounding, seeing her lips start to swell and she's making these little sounds that are driving me crazy. The dull thudding sound as my body meets her mouth is going to be in my dreams for a long long time. My lips are tightening, my chest is tightening, and I feel that tingle start in my balls and make its way down my shaft. She lets out a whimper and I pull all the way out, hearing her gasp for breath and then I'm back in and suddenly something happens.

She turns her face, making me enter her mouth at a new angle and she doesn't have her teeth sheathed. My entire body jerks and breaks out in a sweat when I feel her canines slide down my cock at this new angle, tugging and catching on the flared mushroom head of my dick. My chest seizes up, then I feel a tear run down my own face at the feeling.

"Fuccckkkkiiinnnggg Goooddd." I roar, completely shocked.

I fall to my knee but she lowers with me, and my hips are fucking into her face still. We're struggling. Both struggling to cope because my God, this is the dirtiest, messiest blow job I've ever had in my life.

And I can't go back, I won't.

"I'm fucking you so good when we get home baby. *God I hope you can take it*, t-take my dick. Because I'm not going to go easy on you. But it's okay, because you can stay on your back the entire time if you want, love." I'm slamming her face into me roughly, probably too rough.

I ease up just a little bit as to not harm her. She reaches up with her hand and then grabs my balls, tugging down and the move shocks me so badly my orgasm hits me by surprise. I slam into her mouth one more time and then hold her there, just pouring myself down her throat.

"Such a fucking good girl baby." I'm rubbing my hand down her temple and her face reverently and she's just sucking, sucking my cum down. I go to pull back and thankfully manage the decency to go slow.

I plop out of her mouth wetly, catching her before she topples over onto the floor.

We're both gasping, and I pull her to me, just holding her to me for a second. I bring my head down and find her lips, cradling her head in my hands. She's still on her knees, leaning on one hip and I spend a second kissing her, licking into her mouth, tasting my scent on her. I feel changed. Brand new.

Because God damn. What we just shared was unreal.

"You like my cum?" I ask her gruffly. My fingers fist in her hair, not letting her retreat.

"Hmm-hmm, very much," she breathes.

"Good, because there's plenty more where that came from. Next time I'm not pouring it down your throat, I want to watch you suck it off my cock."

Lowering my lips to hers I kiss her for a long time, I can't help it. If this is all I could ever do to her I'd be okay, honestly. Her mouth is heaven, so easy to get lost in. And the way she kisses me back, as if the answers could be found within my lips, well, it makes a man feel like a king.

She's busy nibbling on my lip when I realize she's not going to let me go, so, I push up to my feet and pick her up bridal style, grabbing her purse and jacket.

We make our way out the store and she keeps her lips pressed into my jaw, giving me just enough space to get her into the passenger side of my vehicle. We don't say a word, we don't need to. Climbing in the drivers side I pull off, stopping to get her a vanilla ice cream cone first on the way home.

We share a laugh, and I like that. Like that I can do what I just did to her and she's not turned off or scared. I hope that trend continues. And based on the reaction tonight, I believe it will.

I turn on a playlist that I know she'd like and I hold her hand the entire way there. I might have to buy a truck that has no middle console so I can hold her to me while I'm driving. The thought makes me smile, and we drive off into the sunset, heading to my property.

13

STFUATTDLAGG

LOLA

I'M SHAKING THE ENTIRE way to Hudson's house, nervous in part because I've never been before. My heart pounds, and to say this is the most alive I've ever felt is an understatement. I can't *believe* he fucked my mouth like that, and what's worst, I might have had a weak orgasm just servicing him.

My jaw *hurts*.

All I could think was if he fucks my mouth like that, what's it going to be like when we're really in bed, entwined around each other. I mean, he had his dick in me before yes, but that was like shock and awe.

I want the real thing, from beginning to end. We've already got the foreplay thing down, now I want it all. From start to finish.

I look over at him, catching his eye. My pussy is clenching, I'm hot, throbbing, and everything in me wanted to beg him to fuck me on the floor of my storage room, but he wanted to go to his house. Which to me is kind of wild, because my house is closer by at least half an hour. But I relented, because I want to see his place and the horses he cherishes so badly I can taste it.

I look over at him, suddenly nervous now that he's going to deny me.

"I don't want you to tease me. If you aren't going to take care of me then don't-"

Hudson snatches my hand up and presses it to his mouth. His breath washes over my fingers and I just melt. He knows it too, because he's smiling against the back of my hand, almost like he's got his own little inside joke.

"You do not have to worry about that at all Lola, I got you baby."

Warmth flushes me because I just know he does. When he was fucking me the first time when he denied me, I almost came. And what's more, it was the quickest I've ever achieved orgasm. To me, seems kind of excessive to drive an hour to only be fucked for half an hour, but it's okay because again, I get to see his house which is exciting in itself, and the horses.

I look at him. "Am I going to get to meet Nay Nay?" I giggle, and he throws me a look.

"Not tonight," he chuckles back.

His mouth moves back up to my fingers to nibble on my knuckles, making me feel warm just about everywhere.

"What?" I gasp, turning a little in my seat to face him. "Why not? We're only going to be...you know...for just a bit, and it's still early why can't I see them?"

This draws another laugh out of him which makes me blush, confused.

But suddenly my attention is diverted. We've turned a deep bend in the blacktop, and I see a glowing, ginormous house in the distance, partially blocked by trees. It takes a second, but when I can get my eyes unglued from the house in the distance, I feel we're slowing down to turn the truck onto another blacktop road.

He maneuvers us in between two huge stone pillars topped with tall gas lanterns that are about five feet in length affording an impressive display of the entrance to what looks to be a rather long blacktop drive. Arched over the blacktop driveway is a cast iron sign that says H. Montgomery. The drive is lined with mature trees and I get chills.

This is his property?

I peek a look at him, fucking *floored*. And I hate to admit this, but the sheer intimidating size of the place has got me cooling off a little. I tug my hand from his, shakily pushing my wispy bangs behind my ear, and begin fidgeting. He reaches back over to take my hand in warm, comforting grip.

But it's no matter. Despite the gesture, I'm shaking harder and harder the closer we get to his home.

Suddenly it hits me, how brutal he was just a little bit ago, and the way he fucked me the first time, as if he just wanted me to *feel* it, give me a taste to let me know what he was working with. Him dragging me in my house. He just takes what he wants, unapologetically.

Its disconcerting to see that this man's tastes might be the perfect fit to mine.

I frown, not one hundred percent trusting it. Then, my thoughts shift, and it hits me that I'm with a man with *wealth*. Someone who had the type of lifestyle that you can only get with hard work, taking life by the bullhorns and show you're stronger than everyone else. The best.

It's killing me.

I slide my eyes back to him, and as if he senses my struggle, he stops the truck in the middle of the road leading to the driveway. He's silently staring at me, his green eyes flick over my face before narrowing. Then drifts lower taking in my breasts, belly, hips, my hands.

"You're panting." He says this quietly.

I'm astounded by the fact he just stopped his truck in the middle of the drive to check in with me, make sure I'm okay.

I nod in a rapid movement, and I *feel* the pants, hot and moist through my nose.

And that's not the only response I got going on either. My breasts are heaving with trepidation. I'm hot and wet between my legs, my body is confused, at war with my mind and heart. I haven't had sex with anyone since Dominic, been empty for years. Now all of sudden I find myself completely taken over by this insanely charismatic, beautiful man and my body doesn't know how to respond.

I've *never* been this attracted to anyone before and the feeling is terrifying. The fact he can hurt me is *terrifying*. The fact I know this man has the power to yank me out of my rotten dirt and then shove me back in if he wanted to, *terrifies* me.

Do you understand what I'm saying?

I'm so immersed in fight or flight that I can't help my lips parting. My inner sassy bitch betrays me. To my utter and complete horror, the weak Lola... the one I try to hide from Dominic... leaps out to make her appearance.

"I'm scared." It comes out before I even realize it and I slap my hand over my mouth, turning away from him slightly.

What the fuck Lolita!

I squeeze my eyes shut, more embarrassed than I've ever been in my entire life. But what shocks me out of it is his response.

"Then your instinct is a good one."

I keep my hand over my mouth as I turn my face slowly to look at him with wide eyes.

Hudson turns his gaze back ahead of him and as I'm still staring at him in shock, his truck starts moving, ramping up my heart beat. He's telling me I need to be scared and then slowly bringing me to the place where the object of my fear is about to be manifested?

Hudson suddenly hits the gas and the truck starts flying up the drive. My heart leaves my body because what the fuck is this man doing?

He brings us to a screeching halt, however, the screeching doesn't stop. Because it's coming from *me*.

It tapers off into just regular panicked heaving pants. I'm shivering, broken out into a full on mist of sweat and I can feel my nipples are pulled tight against the material of my bra.

"I'll tell you what I want." Hudson's completely ignoring my screaming.

He's talking. *He's talking.*

I turn my head with difficulty to look over at him, seeing his big mansion in the background through his drivers side window and it's *just* homey enough looking to give me a tiny bit of comfort.

"I'd like to come to an agreement."

"Uh huh." I pant.

"Aww baby. Calm your pretty self *dowwnn.* " Hudson gives me a smile, flicking his eyes to look at my mouth, then back up to my eyes again making me flush even harder than I already am. I must look a mess, because I know I sound it.

Well this is different. I feel my heart rate start to come back to normal. I nod, because I can do agreements.

"I'll give you something you want first, *if* you give me what I want. But you gotta tell me what it is you want first. If I agree to give it to you, then you have to give me what I want."

"I-I d-dont think that's quite how agreements work-"

He pins me with a look. I say fine, because what can he do to me? He already ravaged my throat.

"I would like to see the horses."

Hudson lets out a slow smile that lets me know he already expected that and my eyes are wide, because I feel like I just dove head first into a trap. The truck starts moving, driving past his house. A few hundred feet later we're at some *really* nice stables. I climb out of the truck, casting a look around. Fighting fresh feelings of inadequacy.

"Jesus, these horses live nice!" The horses live in a nicer home than I do.

Hudson puts his arms around me and leads me through the door that leads into the building and I'm struck back by the cleanest, comfiest stables I've ever seen in my life. Which is none, I've never seen any except for in movies.

"*Wowww.*" I breathe.

I just stand there for a second, knowing I have the goofiest look on my face because Hudson's paused to now look at me with interest with his own smile breaking over his face. He chuckles, the dark sound reminding me that I still have my end of the bargain to fulfill.

"You have ten minutes." He says, stepping aside and giving me space.

My eyes flicker, seeing a tan horse, a black, horse, and a white horse with big blotchy black spots like a cow.

Suddenly the white one lets out a bay that has me taking a step back it scares me so bad.

"OH!" I shout, covering my mouth.

I look at Hudson who's chuckling at me, shaking his head. "Silly girl." He says, winking at me.

It's enough to settle me.

Feeling my heart rate slow I walk in deeper, taking in the cleanliness of the space. Hudson's hung these cute wooden plaques over each horse's stall that has their names burnt into the wood. He's got a retro red full sized refrigerator in nice utility area in a far corner with a huge iron wood burning stove that has a chimney that lets out of the twenty foot ceiling, showing me he spends a lot of time in here with them.

The horses stalls are huge, only taking up one side of the stables, the other side looks more like a work shop.

I look over at him and throw him an appreciative smile, seeing his eyes are sparkling as he watches me observe the space and I can really tell these horses are something he truly loves.

And though he hasn't said it, if he treats animals like this that he loves, how would he treat a woman?

How would he treat me?

I make my way to the white horse. "So you're Nay Nay, huh? Ohhh your daddy has told me *so* many good things about you." I greet, holding my hand out to her nose. She nudges my palm gently and I coo at the soft velvety texture of her muzzle. "Oh my gosh, you are bonita, mi amor." I whisper, placing my forehead against hers.

We're silent for a second before I hear another snicker. Looking over at the noise I see the tan one. He stamps his foot and snickers again.

"You must be Champ!" I say with a bright smile.

I go to Champ and then to Beauty who is so incredibly gentle, giving them kisses and rubs. I'm so relaxed that I get lost for a second, forgetting about Hudson in the background.

Looking over at him I flush, seeing he's staring at me with a hungry expression on his face. He's hauled himself onto a stainless steel table with his boot propped up, just patiently waiting. Giving me what I wanted. I glance away from him as my tummy breaks full out in butterflies.

But he doesn't let me hide. He whistles loudly, bringing my attention back to him.

"Playtime's over." he says.

What a thing to say because honestly... why would you say that to someone you're about to make love to?

"Goodness, *someone's* impatient." I respond with an eye roll.

Turning and making my way to the front of the barn I go out into the late evening sky, seeing the sun is almost set. The breeze ruffles my bangs, carrying the unmistakable scent of fall and I feel my body break out in goosebumps.

Hudson comes up behind me and presses his front into my back, lowering his lips to my ear. The action makes my nipples hard and I wrap my arms around my chest, protecting them.

"Time for what I want." Hudson says quietly. "You going to give me what I want, baby? Hm?"

He places his lips to the side of my neck and I moan at the incredible, romantic feeling that I wasn't expecting. I'm freefalling, lost in the feel of his lips on my skin when I tense, also feeling a tugging. He slides off my jacket, dropping it to the ground.

When he goes to raise his hands to lift the hem of my shirt, I clamp my arms around myself again.

"Hudson we're *outside.*" I hiss at him but in a rough movement he jerks my arms down and I feel my breasts jiggle.

I inhale raggedly, feeling something different between us.

That nervous feeling is back, beginning to take over. My desire is currently at war with what I know to be proper, and I can't let him see too much, let him know I like this as much as I do. But Hudson and I seem like fire and gasoline, inevitable things happen when we touch each other.

But if he blows me apart he'll see my secrets, see that I have things I want that I don't know he'll accept. And selfishly, though I have to hide it, I want this man to accept me.

More than I think I've ever wanted anything.

He begins to raise my shirt up once more but I refuse to cooperate. We struggle against each other for a second and then the next thing I know, I'm being walked forward then shoved into the front of his truck, stunned.

"Hudson." I yell, turning to look behind me.

I go to step to the side but he's right there with me, not allowing me any breathing room, much less space. My pussy clenches hard, making me miserable. I place my hands against his broad chest, pushing him with all my strength but he's unmovable. In turn he's tugging at *me* hard, with a stern look in his eyes letting me know he's through fucking around.

Distracted, I gasp as I hear my shirt tear.

When am I going to learn this man cares nothing about my clothes?

I look at him in shock and I'm perfectly aware I'm soaking, dripping down my legs again. Because this is our thing, this is what we do. I turn to run as the need to flee hits me hard but in a move I didn't see coming, Hudson tackles me to the ground and we're rolling.

The damp, dewy smell of the earth fills my lungs as my face rubs against the ground. His grass is so soft and plush it almost feels like a pillow. His grunts fill my ears as I'm trying to get my bearings, and as I'm struggling for purchase I feel a lightning bug hit my face. Grounding me.

I raise my head, gasping, and see his property is lit with hundreds of them. And I'm struck by the odd thought that any other time this would be romantic. But he's busy rumbling above me, determined to ravish me in his front yard.

His chest is tight against my back as he just plays with me.

He's playing with me, because if Hudson really wanted to truly hurt me, I know he could.

I *know* he could truly hurt me if he really wanted to, but if you've never rolled around on the ground with a man who is also trying to tear your clothes off outside in the front yard, you won't understand the sudden desperation that comes over a person when this is happening to them.

The memory of him talking to me in the bookstore as he was reading my annotated book hits me.

'This is not how I would fuck you.' He'd said. And he meant it.

But I can't let him think I like this. Can I? *Am I supposed to?*

My emotions swell bigger, and that desperation fills me once more forcing me to I haul my arm back and slap him with everything I've got. Which is a lot because his entire head turns to the side and snaps back to look at me with this crazed expression in his face. And it's then I fear I might have taken the night just a smidge too far.

Which actually makes me fill up with true, genuine fear.

Fear real enough that I roll back to my belly and begin to army crawl across the lawn. Currently so terrified that I can't even stand up on my own two feet. I'm breathing way too hard. Short, panicked sounds are coming out of me but I can't stop, won't stop.

I probably sound like a cow.

Hudson grabs my ankle before yanking my shoes off.

"Come here, baby." He makes a displeased sound as I attempt to crawl away again. "I said *come here!*" His voice is hoarse with desire. Stern.

I whimper as his fingers grasp the waistband of my skirt, ripping it down my body so hard I get drug back a few feet with the movement as he bares me from the waist down.

The cold air immediately sweeps over my naked flesh, and I just know if this man gets his mouth on my nipples, I'm done for. Because that's truly what he wants. The part of my body that he knows is overwhelming. The part he says is his favorite.

He's toying with me, not saying a word. I'm just being drug around and worked over while my clothes are being torn off, and it's the most exhilarating experience I've ever had.

Hudson flips me, catching my wrist before I can deliver another smack. But jokes on him because while he's preoccupied with my hands, I get my left foot in between us and I push with all my might. However, now the jokes on me because the action sends *me* flying up the lawn, not him.

He snatches my ankle on a deep chuckle, yanks me back to him, and then rolls us so he's on bottom. I'm discombobulated enough that he has time to jerk his pants down, and then impale me on a hard thrust that has me screaming. I jerk hard and then grit my teeth, cutting off my scream with a hoarse moan as he spreads me apart mercilessly.

He goes to roll his hips up into me, but I rear up on my feet and push up a little, seeing as he's built so broad I can hardly touch the ground when I'm on top of him. I struggle hard against him, because his cock really is thick. Something about us just full on fighting against each other in his front yard because he couldn't wait until we are inside the house, has got me so excited that I don't know what to do with the feeling other than scream.

"*Yes!*" I scream, throwing my head to the sky.

He laces our hands together and then presses them to his chest, holding me so tight I can't move. I take advantage of the sudden stillness and let my eyes flicker around as I pulse around him, gasping.

There's lightning bugs everywhere, and I decide then and there that this *is* romantic after all.

It's the most romantic thing that's ever happened to me before in my life. I press the soles of my feet harder into the ground, thankful to be on this side of earth. My fingers fill with dewy grass and crunchy leaves that are falling that's so fresh. And because of how rough we rolled all over the ground, I know that its taste is wet, grounding me even more as the lingering earthy flavor settles deep on my tongue.

Now that I'm out of my grave, clawing my way up through the dirt that's been slowly rotting me, I see this side of the ground is so *pretty*.

"Oh God Hudson. It feels so *gooooddd*." I'm full on wailing.

Not even caring he's running his hands over my breasts, stimulating my nipples even more. I don't care because I'm *alive!* He gives them a gentle pinch and tug over my shirt before his hands encase my hips.

"Scream all you want baby. There's no one here to hear you but me." He says, putting his hands to my hips. "Ride me. Show me how much you want this," he snarls, grinding upwards so deep I swear I can feel it in my throat and it's amazing.

We're still struggling against each other, but this time it's to find our pleasure, not run from it. He's snatches me to him while I bounce on him. It's painful. It's exhilarating.

And it feels enough like my dirty fantasies to have me squirting on him.

We roll again when he manages to get my shirt and bra pulled up, making me buck in earnest under him. I balk when I feel the weight of my breasts lose the support of my bra, and this somehow makes me feel even *more* sensitive. Like the weight is stretching my nerves out pulling them even tauter than they already are.

"No! No Hudson they're too sensitive!" I'm wailing trying to get away, but he just holds my wrists hard to the ground with his hands and grinds his big dick all the way inside me, making my feet bob in the air with the force of it. Bending, he sucks my bare nipple in a harsh, warm, tight clasp. And for a second, time stops. Literally stops as the wetness of his mouth sears me.

I still completely, letting out a shuddering exhale as our breathing stops, our movement stops, my heart stops.

It's just him. Pinning me to the ground by his cock and his lips around my nipple for a few, time suspending seconds and all I do is *feel*. I feel his teeth close softly around me before nibbling, and my heart skips a beat before deciding to gallop away in my chest. I let out a desperate whine, praying that I don't splinter to pieces underneath him, not prepared for when he tugs on my nipple harshly.

I break. Absolutely shattering apart underneath him.

I feel my orgasm attack me viciously, without mercy. My mouth opens and I clench hard on him, but he's got me spread so wide that I'm just throbbing and sucking down his length as my body fights him. My inner thighs are being chafed by his jeans, but I can't stop wiggling, moving.

I'm suddenly aware I'm screaming.

He's pulled his hips back and he's fucking me *hard*. His clothing rustles loudly as he works his body into mine. The wet sound of him slapping against me has me clawing at his jacket, gripping and holding on tight. Now that he's let my hands go, he bends my knees back, folding me in half so he can get as deep as possible. He swivels his hips and grinds hard into me at every downward thrust, causing me to yelp harshly.

God this man can *fuck*. If I thought the blow job earlier was a killer, then this is the murder.

I'm whimpering, shivering. This man took my body and completely owned every second. He's barely panting above me as he leans down into my face forcing me to meet his eyes.

"What *I* want, is this body, *all fucking night long*. All night long, Lolita. Until I decide I'm done. Which I'm thinking won't be till the sun comes up, *if you're lucky*."

My eyes widen.

"And because you won't be still like a good girl, I'm tying your legs back."

My lips part on a weak whimper and he looks down between us, seeing me squirt on him. It's embarrassing, but it's happening and I can't stop it. He looks up at me with a wicked smile, and I notice his eyes are now a dark stormy green.

My lips part at the sight, and though I'm laying in the grass, covered in sweat, cum, grass, and dirt. This is the most alive I've ever felt.

Hudson picks me up, and I'm once again struck by the fact that he's strong. Like *really* strong. I get he's a big man but I have curves that should at least throw him off balance, and he still picks me up like I weigh nothing. I shiver hard. Still gasping for air because of how thoroughly he just ran me through.

As I rest my head on his shoulder I see a few lightning bugs crawl on my discarded clothes, still lying on a heap in the grass. I have the weird feeling he's carrying me away from my old life where I felt buried. It's symbolic.

He pauses at the door and I want to ask him to let me look at the outside for a second, because his home is truly beautiful, but I'm aware I *am* completely naked, and it's chilly.

I burrow into his warmth while he hunts for his keys. Bracing me against a thick leg that he's hiked up. Setting his foot on a rung of what looks to be a tall leaning decorative ladder by the front door that houses lanterns, matches, plants with long curving vines, and other knickknacks. I look above me and see a beautiful lighting fixture, and to my left and right I see more singular hanging lighting features in between ceiling fans.

His property is so big that the main level porch extends all the way around.

My heart starts beating faster at the knowledge that this man is *successful*. And it really does something to me that a man that can afford a stable that looks more expensive than my house, has a property big enough to house a million lightning bugs, and a home that...lets be honest, is ridiculous for one person to live in wants *me*.

And the fact that he could fuck me in the front yard and not have to worry about neighbors hearing me screaming or seeing...well. The shit makes me feel like Helen of Troy. *Conquered.*

We're in the house and I'm taken aback by how pure and fresh it smells. I tighten my fingers in his shirt, swiveling this way and that way trying to see everything I can because he's not stopping for me to look at anything. As we head up the stairs, I peek down at myself and see that I'm filthy and it causes my mouth to tighten because I'm always put together.

Hudson seems to keep getting me in situations where I'm a disgusting mess, my clothes are either in tatters, or gone, and I'm always covered in something. He seems to like it.

I peek up at him. His beard makes him look so worldly, manly, and I see in our interactions he's shed his long sleeved flannel allowing me to get a slightly better look at his snake tattoo on his arm than I did the other day.

It hits me then that, I've never seen him without his clothes on. Every interaction has been him completely focused on me. And I want to see him. Need to see this man's body.

Hudson looks down at me suddenly with an arched eyebrow.

"Are you okay?"

Am I okay? No. And I know that he heard my breathing become more ragged because I'm wondering what he looks like completely naked. I don't have to wait long though because in what feels like two seconds we're journeying down a long impressive hallway upstairs.

There's even an enormous iron structure of a horse reared on it's back legs at the end of the hallway that goes from floor to ceiling and it's backlit.

"Wow." I whisper, because it's seriously impressive.

He turns me to face the glass iron double doors of what I presume to be his master bedroom. Doors that are way bigger than mine at home.

"Open them."

I look at him, seeing he never really *asks*.

"Eres tan exigente, senor."

"What?"

I smile at him. "You're so demanding, sir."

He looks down at me and really gets comfortable looking in my eyes.

"I'm demanding because I have the right to be. If you let me take you through these doors into my bedroom, there's no turning back Lolita. You've only seen just the tip of how it will be between us. Once I get you in here, I'm closing these doors, washing you up, and then I'm going to collar you and tie your legs back so I can finally have my own release. I'm meaning to take what you agreed to let me have."

My eyes widen and I suck in a deep breath. *Holy shit* this man's the real deal.

"Uh huh." I exhale the word. But I can't inhale, the air is gone. I'm dying, waiting for him to give me my next breath.

He leans forward, pressing his lips to mine. "I need a yes. Just one word." He seals his lips over mine, giving me a kiss that's just enough to give me some life so I can speak what he needs to hear.

"Yes."

And just like that, I turn the knobs into his doors. Keeping his eyes on mine he pushes them open with his foot where I break our eye contact curiously seeing we're in the most succulent bedroom I've ever been in in my life. I am a sucker for beautiful houses, and this one does not disappoint. I can't believe I'm in here to be honest.

I take it all in greedily, because he's striding to the bathroom that's on the far side of the room but oh my gosh. It's amazing, and I can't believe my first introduction to his house is by him carrying me in covered in *yuck*. I turn irritated eyes to him and narrow them.

"You are not a gentleman, *Hudson!*" I emphasis his name and I see him smile, his chest tightens as if to hold back his laughter.

"I never claimed to be one, baby girl. I thought you would have understood that when I told you I wasn't impressed by your book."

My mouth drops. *"Well I liked my book!"*

"Oh, I could tell. Some of those tabbed spots are about to get you in a world of trouble Ma'am."

I blush so hard I feel it in my feet. "Hudson." I wait until he looks at me. "Will you give me a tour of the house before you...before we...." Is it possible that you can die from being too embarrassed?

He carries me into the biggest bathroom I've ever seen, aside from my brothers, and see he's got a deep soaker tub in the wall to wall, ceiling to floor glassed in shower. That's neat.

"Before we do *what*, Lolita?"

I throw him a scowl as he places me gently on the vanity and in my horror I see what I mess I really am.

There's grass, leaves, dirt stuck everywhere. All over my back, it's all in my hair, smudged in my skin. I actually look like I crawled out of the ground I always say I'm buried in. He yanks off his long sleeved plaid shirt and I am riveted. My gaze is pulled back to where he stands in front of me, getting my first true look at the naked skin of his arms.

That tattoo? *Deadly.* It looks vicious as it wraps itself all the way up his arm, and I see as he pulls off his t-shirt that it disappears behind his shoulder, wraps around the other side and the tail ends on his chest. What I thought was a cobra is actually a rattlesnake.

"Before we do.....*s-s-stuff*..." I'm aware I look and sound like an idiot.

I can't stop staring. The man is exquisite. Are you supposed to call a man that? Well he is. Hudson is just miles and miles of hard slabs of muscles. A *twelve pack*. His chest is broader than I even thought, and I swear I can make five of my hands fit on just one of his pecs.

The man doesn't miss shoulder day, I can tell. His shoulders and arms are absolutely ripped to shreds and his biceps, oh my God, there's not an ounce of fat on this man. He has a bulging vein that ropes up the side of his non tattooed arm, and swirls up to his shoulder.

The vein disappears before reappearing in his neck. He has a light down of hair on his chest and it tapers, disappearing into the v of his abdomen. He is easily the most attractive man I've ever seen in my life. I hear myself make a choking noise. I think I'm drooling.

I am.

He reaches forward with a finger to swipe across my lips to where it has accumulated. And for the first time since I crawled my way up out of the ground, I want to sink back in it because he literally caught me drooling over him. How freaking embarrassed can one person get?

"Oh God." I moan.

I shut my eyes and let out a small sound and go to move, determined to walk what's probably a three day journey home. But I'm quickly pushed back on the vanity.

"Where are you going sweet thing? You trying to run from your end of our agreement?"

The way he says it lets me know I better sit my as still. My eyes rise to meet his green ones, and I do this weird thing where I'm shaking and nodding my head at the same time. I can't get ahold of my nervous system with him, everything's failing, my mind, my body, my sanity. It's all going away.

He lets out a chuckle. "I'll tell you what, let's get cleaned up, and I will show you around the house okay? That sound like a plan?"

I smile and nod, correctly this time. "Yes." I manage the word but what gets my heart pounding again is his eyes go straight to my teeth, before turning a stormy green.

I remember his words when he was looking in my mouth and told me I had his permission to bite him the first time. I run my tongue over one of my canines and that bulging vein in his neck gets bigger, as does the tent in his pants. I also remember the absolute feral look on his face after I slapped him. I tilt my head as it hits me, the realization of the power I have over this man.

I don't want to abuse it.

"I didn't bite you the first time." I whisper.

We stare at each other for a second and this look passes in his eyes that oh my gosh I want to stay there. I don't want just glimpses of it.

"I know." His chuckle fills the bathroom and he seems completely unconcerned that I keep my arm across my breasts. "There'll be other times."

I nod, thinking. "Do you like fucking me until I hit you?"

There it is! There's that glimpse again! Oh my God, *stay there!* Aaannddd it's gone. Dammit.

Hudson clears his throat and gives me another smile that I'm terrified has left a puddle underneath me on the vanity, and I tentatively smile back, encouraging whatever keeps flashing in his eyes to come back to me because I like it.

He finishes picking out the leaves and grass out of my hair and he takes me into the shower, shucking off the rest of his clothes and putting it neatly away in a nearby hamper. It makes me smile and then my brows furrow again.

"Hudson, what am I going to wear? My clothes are dirty, and out in the yard."

He ignores my question and backs me up under the spray. I moan, tilting my head back.

I find myself drifting under the heat of the water, temporarily suspended in my own world for a second. The water helps me elevate even more, sucking me into my own personal space of time that lets me know I'm still alive. And with Hudson here with me, nothing in me wants to put my head under the water to suffocate and make myself smaller.

No, Hudson makes me want to stay on this side of the earth, with my boys, the grass, the lightning bugs.

I open my eyes at the feel of his hands in my hair and his lips pressing into the center of my neck. Letting my own hands explore, I run them up his arms, pressing my thumb into that vein that's teasing me. And I make the decision right then and there to sink my teeth into it when I'm able.

I bet that evasive thing that flashes in his eyes will come to me then.

I smile, plotting. My hands roam greedily, and Jesus his chest is so hard it makes my fingers tremble to think this is what's been powering into me.

His hands leave my neck, and a second later I smell the most delicious scent. It's masculine, deep, dark. It's his shampoo, he works it into my hair steadily. I peek down at his still erection, still hard between us, and it hits me then he didn't orgasm with me earlier in the yard. He was just busy claiming me, not getting his own.

Putting my hand between us I grab it hesitantly, still unsure what he likes and what makes him turned on. Though I thought my blow job a couple hours ago was stellar, we're still trying to learn each other. I explore more, not able to wrap my fingers around his penis and touch.

He's got a very thick prominent vein there, and I bet it's the same vein in his arm, in his neck...

I raise my hands and return the favor with shampooing his hair because I bet he doesn't get the treat very often. I know I don't. His eyes drift shut, he leans into me, bracing a hand against the wall besides my head and I hear a slight rumble in the center of his chest that tips my mouth up at the corner with a self-satisfied smile.

"God that feels good, baby." He says quietly, catching my eyes with his.

We stare at each other for long seconds before I flex my fingers digging my nails in slightly, watching his eyes drift back shut and a look of bliss passes across his features. He loves having his scalp massaged. But tell me what man doesn't?

"I'm glad you like it." I say softly.

He rinses out the shampoo out of my hair, and his, and then he's putting in conditioner. Really working it in too, which is nice because I have thick hair, which is part of the reason it takes me so long in the shower.

But Hudson doesn't seem to mind. Doesn't vocalize he cares that we've been in here longer than what I know a lot of people usually do when they shower.

"Hudson you don't have to stay, I can finish." I say quietly, watching him lather up a towel as I wind my hair into a bun at the top of my head. He gives me another laugh and then reaches forward, surprising me with soaping me first, and not himself. I blink at him and step away. *"Hudson."*

He reaches and grabs me by my upper arm and pulls me back where I was, beginning to soap me up. Rolling my eyes and blinking, I'm struggling with waves of inadequacy. He quietly lathers my front and then his eyes catch mine, and he's silently communicating something to me. Something I'm ashamed to say I don't understand because I've been underground for so long I don't know what all these little looks mean.

"You won't have anything to wear until I'm done with you. I'll show you my house naked, because I want to watch your ass bouncing as you walk."

It's simple, shocking, but blunt. And I appreciate that about Hudson.

I feel something grow in my chest for him, something I respect. So far, this man has sugarcoated nothing for me. He hasn't attempted to placate me with meaningless words or actions. He just shows up and handles what needs to be handled. As the realization that this man is as steady as a mountain fills me up, it causes the hard compact dirt surrounding me to loosen just a little bit more.

And I just know that if I wanted to sit in this shower for five hours straight, he'd be right there with me.

I lean forward and press my mouth to his neck and press right over that vein, feeling him pulse under my lips. I have this desperate burning desire that I can't explain take over me, and I part my lips on a whimper, latching onto his neck with my teeth hard.

Then bite down even harder until I pierce his skin slightly and taste copper. I suck, wanting his force to fill me up. I'm not prepared at the absolute feral growl that leaves his chest and then he's banding his arms around me, pressing me so hard into him it's almost painful. God his skin tastes so good. It's clean, slightly salty.

I've never pegged myself as a biter before, but because I might not get a chance to do this again, I tighten my teeth even harder, hearing his deep exclamation of breath and a whimper.

This man whimpers. For *me.*

I moan, tugging at him, at his hair, trying to get closer, sink deeper. I get it's crazy but he's letting me so it's gotta be okay, right? I bring up my leg to wrap around his hip and he hauls me up on a grunt that I'm ashamed to say has me squirt on him, however I *unashamedly* grind myself on his cock, trying to rub my scent into him. I can't let go of his neck, I won't. He can't make me.

I feel his hands tighten hard on my ass.

"You're going to get this tour you want because you asked for it, but I'm going to bring you back up here and make you pay for what you're doing to me."

His words send a thrill through me.

"And if you think because we walk out those doors, that what I said before we came into my bedroom doesn't stand, you've got another thing coming. I'll fuck you anywhere. You're not safe *anywhere. So let the fuck go.*"

I release my grip and pout. I guess he can make me. He pushes me back under the spray and in his eyes I see it. I swear I see it and it's killing me that as soon as I see it it's gone. His lips drop to mine and he kisses my pout away as the conditioner runs off my hair down the drain and then he walks us out, grabbing a towel and drying me off briskly. I go to tie it around me but he snatches it away and then tosses it into the hamper. Lola 0, Hudson 1.

I scrunch my nose at him as he stops by the dresser and pulls out a pair of briefs and pull them on.

"Heeyyy!" I scrunch my face up even more. "That's not fair. Why do *you* get to cover yourself?"

He throws me a wry look. "Because it's *heavy.* I need support."

My eyes widen and I twist my lips and look away cause *damn.* Okay.

He ushers me out of the room and back into the hallway, leaving the doors open. "Explore away."

I can't help but throw him a bright smile before turning on my heel and taking off in excitement. I feel like a kid in a candy store. And by the sound of his chuckle, seems like I can buy whatever I want.

14

THE SUN'S UP

HUDSON

THE REASON, AND I mean the only reason, she's not flat on her back in my bed right now is because I desperately need to get a handle on myself before I fuck her so hard I hurt her. No matter the desires and fantasies I have I don't want to traumatize her, or take it too far between us at the start of this relationship.

No, I need a shot of whiskey to calm myself down, slow me down enough to take the edge off.

But I'm hopeful.

The fact that she let me fuck her the way I did, in my front yard no less, leads me to believe that Lola's got some deeper layers to explore. And I can't wait to peel those layers back and see exactly what I'm working with. So I'll push a little. Just a little every time we're together like this, to see how much she'll let me do to her.

She didn't flinch when I told her I was going to collar her and tie her legs back, and I wonder if she's done that before. Or if she's read enough of those smutty books to see if she'd like to have it done to her. She told me that she's not been with anyone other than Dominic and I believe her.

So has the fucker tied her up before? I'm going to rip his skin from his body.

Ignoring the misery from denying myself my orgasm in the front yard, I put my emotions to the back of my mind focusing as I walk closely behind her, watching her beautiful ass cheeks bouncing. I'm busy looking at the beauty mark on her left one when she starts peeking into every bedroom, all six of them up here, and then the laundry room which she's so impressed by it makes me laugh.

We pad downstairs and she is just absolutely overjoyed at ransacking through the place. It makes me happy she seems to like my home so much.

There's a library and study to the right of the stairs. Just past that, down the main hallway, is a powder room, and then a small guest bedroom that could dub as anything, really. I usually put Clayton in there when he gets too drunk to leave. I tried to drag him up to the second floor one time, and his dumbass fell down the stairs, resulting in an all night hospital trip. So I usually just put him in there.

This hallway dumps into a media room at the end which really gets her excited. She hurries back up the hallway and around the stairs to the other side, where there's a formal sitting room with plush seating, a priceless work of art, lamps, and a sideboard that holds all the knick-knacks from my travels with my parents.

Down the hall past the formal room is the dining room that has a large gas fireplace that takes up half the height of the wall. I put a twelve seater table with white barrel style chairs atop a beautiful rug in there, even though I never have any company other than Clayton. I did it just to fill the room up; however, now that I have Lola and the boys, I may need to figure out different chairs for the table because boys are messy.

By the way she meets my eyes, I know she's thinking the same thing, which makes me smile.

Past the dining room is the informal lounge that spills out into a humongous kitchen that has an eight burner stove with a griddle, ovens in the wall, and a big double door stainless steel refrigerator that was topped to look like the cabinets. To the right of that is another cabinet door, a faux one, that if you open it leads to the secondary hidden kitchen and butler pantry. I keep all my appliances there and stuff that makes a regular kitchen look messy.

I'm busy taking the shot of whiskey I pray takes the edge off when I see she's throwing me a look. Her confusion amuses me as I see she's trying to figure out why there's no refrigerator, or any appliances other than the stove and ovens in the wall.

She tilts her head to look up at me and I can see her arm is back over her heavy breasts which amuses me to no end.

"So...so where's all your *stuff?*"

I smile at her. "This is all there is to see. Except through those doors."

Lola turns and raises an eyebrow, turning to look at me in challenge. She makes the decision for herself and proceeds to open the door and peek her head in.

"Are you satisfied? Have you seen everything you need to see?"

In other words, can I finally get my turn now baby? You're really taking your time, eating this up. But that's ok because I'm about to take my time, eating you up. She nods.

"You're very clean..." Her eyes still flicking around, trying to see into the other lounge. Stepping forward, I grab her hand and begin to pull her, because even I have patience that runs out.

"Nooooooo."

The word is long and drawn out. Desperate and almost manic sounding. God it makes me so fucking happy.

"Yeessss. Yessss, baby girl.*"*

I wince as she tightens hard on my dick, throwing her head back on a desperate, strangled scream that she's trapped in her throat. I've been fucking her for over half the night and she's tired. I know she's tired, and I still won't relent. I just want to see if I can fuck her all night.

If her body can physically take it.

Lola's face and chest are flushed and she's sweating, trembling, clearly spent.

My hips piston against hers, and I hear the chains that connect her collar to the bands around her knees that are keeping her wide open for me rattle. She's whimpering, her head is slowly shaking side to side.

"Hudson." She tries, but it won't work.

"Uh huh Lolita. *We agreed.*"

Goddd her pussy feels amazing. I groan, swiveling my hips harder, making her wiggle under me.

"B-but-"

"Don't you dare go back on your agreement with me."

"But-"

I have a tight control on my breathing, on the cadence and force of my thrusts, ensuring I can keep this pace for a good amount of time to come. I wet my lips and tilt my head, regarding her for just a moment.

"No. I gave you what you wanted. *Twice* actually. But when it's time for what *I want,* you're ready to give up? No. *I said no.*" I lower my head and take her nipple in a harsh suck in between my lips and I latch on hard. Warning her not to fuck with me. "You can plead and beg all you want to. For tonight, the answer is *no.*"

The headboard has been banging so hard for so long into the wall that I'm going to have to check and make sure there's not a dent in it.

I might have to buy a different bed, one I can anchor to the wall. I'm not fucking her with everything I've got yet, I won't do that tonight.

But I'm fucking her hard enough to scratch this fucking itch I need scratched. It's barely enough to give me relief, but it does the job. Sort of.

Lola lets out a keening noise that almost makes my heart stop before a series of sexually distressed sobs leave her, and I grunt in response feeling her clamp down hard on my dick. She grits her teeth and seizes up, and I see her pretty mouth relax for a second before puckering into a pout. Her fingers leave my back and slide over my chest, desperately rubbing and clutching onto me.

She feels so good against me, better than I ever imagined. More than I could ever dream to want.

"Lolaaa," I groan reeling in her response to me. "I've been waiting a long time for this."

My heart bangs in my chest, and from the way Lola's tightening her fingers against me, I know she can feel it. However, her eyes narrow at me in a challenge that I'm all too ready to meet if she wants to keep testing me.

"Yeah all five or six times, huh? *Poor baby...*" Her gray eyes widen in faux concern that's got my blood boiling. "You must have been *suffering.*" She teases me with her sassy mouth.

"Yeah all five or six times." I give her five or six rough smacking thrusts, ignoring her jaw clenching as she tries to cope. I put my lips to hers. "Baby it might only be five or six times I've been in your shop, but I wanted to fuck your from the moment I laid eyes on you, and now I've got you right where I want you. Right where you belong."

I swivel my hips on a deep thrust and hold my pelvis hard against her, making us moan into each others mouth. I tilt my head, licking into her mouth, kissing her deeper. Sucking hard on her bottom lip and biting down, causing her to whimper.

I groan again at the feel of her fluttering around my length before clenching down hard around me, but I keep on, not letting her body fight me.

"While you were standing there... acting like you needed more coffee?" She whispers, her eyes still holding mine.

I begin my rhythm from before, slapping even heavier against her, seeing her face pinch as she arches slightly.

"No baby, while I almost got run over in the street after I saw you in the window." I lean into her and lick the salty flesh of her neck. "I just knew I had to get my hands on you. You were so lucky I didn't haul you over the counter and take what I wanted."

Her body immediately flushes hotter around me, and I feel a stream of wetness erupt over my dick at my words. I keep fucking her through it, deciding I like talking to her while we're having sex.

"I knew I had a bad man standing in front of me." Her voice is breathless and I tilt my head as I work to wipe her hair out of her eyes. "Just talking to me about random *nonsense.*"

I lean forward and press a kiss to her cheek, chuckling. "Well this bad man was busy trying to figure out if you had a beauty mark on your pussy, what your nipples looked like, if you would let me suck your clit until you passed out, and if you liked big dicks or not." I press just a little deeper, into that spot that I know shocks her, reveling in her small breathy sound. "And I especially wanted to know if you'd let me tear your cunt up all night. Which is why we're here at *my* house and not yours. I couldn't risk anyone hearing you scream."

"Oh someone's arrogant." She narrows her eyes at me. "You just knew you were going to make me scream, huh? What would you have done if I were a quiet bitch?"

I narrow my eyes back, slowing my thrusts but making them much harder, causing her eyes to go wide.

"Then I would have made you a loud bitch, and your poor back would be suffering until it happened. *I promise you that.*"

It's been fun, but talking is over.

I reach up towards her face and snatch away the pillows around her, getting rid of anything soft or comforting before I reach further and curl both my hands around the headboard and grip hard. She knows it's coming, and her eyes widen with something akin to fear and she makes a little choking sound before whispering.

"No, no, no, Hudson! *No.*"

Something I've learned tonight; she does *not* like me curling my hands around this headboard. I get too deep, apparently. But that's what I want, and what she agreed to give me.

I ignore her, raising up on my toes in a deep squat and begin to truly fuck into her helpless body. I'm pounding into her so hard the skin on my pelvis is stinging with the force of it. She throws her head back in a hoarse scream that tapers off into what sounds almost like a laugh, but it's just my girl being overwhelmed.

By this thick dick that's hers. And hers alone.

After a couple of very rough minutes, she suddenly seizes up again and turns her head fast to the side and sneezes into her arm. I pause, waiting, because I'm not a monster. But my fingers flex impatiently, and my erection jerks inside of her even more so. I look down at her, making sure she's okay.

Her brows furrow and she sneezes again, and again.

I raise my eyebrows, lower back to my knees, flickering my eyes over her face. I've heard of this but never experienced it. I give her a second to breathe before I pull out halfway slowly, preparing to begin again but then tense as she clenches around me on another sneeze. I bite back an amused smile.

"Are you good baby?" My voice is deep, hoarse. I'll wait a *second*.

I really don't care about her nervous system being fried, she's going to give me what she owes me. But I'm flattered to have done this to her, honestly.

She nods tightly against her arm. *"Are you going to let me up now-"*

I begin pounding again, battering my dick against her tender pussy and work at keeping my smile hidden. But I want to let my joy free. She's a twitching, shuddering, sneezing mess underneath me and I couldn't be happier.

"What's the matter, sweet thing?" I say to her in a sympathetic voice. "Your body betraying you?"

She shoots me a filthy look that has my balls drawing up and I smack through her swollen muscles, grinding my hips into her on a deep hip thrust that's got my lip curling and a snarl ripping from my chest. Her eyes roll into the back of her head, she tries tilting her hips to the left for relief, and I see her momentarily stop breathing before I feel it.

It's like my dick got sucked into a vacuum, then clamped down on in the harshest grip I've ever been treated to, before it's bathed in liquid fire. My heart stutters and then simultaneously she's screaming at the top of her lungs.

Her nails slash down my chest and I look down, seeing her cum slicking up her mound, pooling in the crease of her abdomen and down her navel.

God it's so sexy.

The fierceness of her orgasm, and the sight of her juices slicking everywhere does me in. I orgasm myself, and it runs up the length of my shaft and pools between the two of us where it leaks out. And if I weren't locked inside her body already, my cum would be figurative glue that seals us together.

My chest is heaving with exertion.. Lola's taken a lot out of me tonight, which is only fair. But I'm irritated, because if she could have just controlled herself and not orgasmed the way she did, then I would have been alright.

I could have fucked her all night straight without a break, but she didn't let me.

I yank myself out of her silently, ignoring her small cry and her dripping off me and turn towards the door. "I'll be right back." I call over my shoulder.

Hearing her let out a moan, I pad into the kitchen. Still breathing hard, I grab her a glass of water, and I pour myself a cup of coffee. Sucking it down as I head back to my bedroom. Her eyes are hooded and she's laying there still splayed open via the collar and leg chains. She's trying to fall asleep, and that's something I ain't having.

I clear my throat hard, seeing her eyelashes flutter as her eyes open once more. Veering into the bathroom, I take a hand towel, wetting it with warm water and humming a light, unconcerned tune.

Reaching into the linen closet, I grab a bath towel and double fold it before walking back to the bed. Leaning over, I take care to wipe her face carefully, and her neck and chest before I swipe the towel through the lips of her vulva, collecting all the sticky mess we made.

"Hudson?" Lola's voice is small. I acknowledge her with a hum as I work to shove the folded bath towel under her hips, and over the wet spot we made. *"Hudsooonnn."* The whine she emits makes me look up at her and throw her a kind smile.

"Yes baby?" I maneuver myself in between her legs and lower my head to her.

She doesn't respond to me, aside from a shuddering moan as I suck her clit into my mouth. I settle in for a while to play with her pussy, because whether I can be inside her or not is *not* determined by dick. So, we're still going to be at this for the rest of the night. Baby girl's not off the hook that easy.

She already has acknowledged I'm a hard man, now we're working on truly accepting that fact.

A bit later, I release her from the collar. She's too weak to run, and her muscles are so loose and languid at this point I can maneuver her just about however I want.

I don't hear anything else from her until almost three hours later, when the first rays of sun turn the window pane gray and she's desperately trying to let me know.

"The suns up, the suns up, the suns up." Lola's chanting, but I'm growling against her neck and thrusting nice and slow. Losing myself in her like I've wanted since the moment I laid eyes on her.

Dragging my cock through her swollen tissues. Thinking about the bite she gave me, marking my neck.

Making me hers.

"Go on ahead and be quiet, Lolita." I say quietly, relishing her small sound as she bites her lip and turns her head away. "I'm taking care of something right now, and I'll not have you interrupting me."

Truth is, I really don't care when the sun's up, I'll stop when I'm ready.

I've waited for her for so long, a singular night of fucking feels like a tease. It takes a bit for me, because I'm trying to figure something out about her. I'm holding her head still in between my hands, treating her to slow smacking thrusts that's got my back burning, looking deep into her eyes that are filled with tears when I *finally* see it.

The question in her eyes that she's asking herself if I lied to her about honoring our agreement. The hint that I might be taking it too far and that she isn't verbalizing it to me, but yet letting me do what I want to her does it for me. I smack one more time into her body with a rough grunt.

I refuse to break eye contact as I feel myself sinking deeply into her.

"Who do you belong to?" My eyes stay on hers.

Lola's lips tremble adoringly as she blinks nice and slow before answering. "*You*, Hudson. I belong to you." She lets out a trembling breath and it's enough to have me surrendering to my own little death.

I nod as my cock swells uncomfortably.

I orgasm hard, groaning her name. Deep inside my girl, circling and massaging it in. My lips lower to hers, drinking in her whimpers.

"You're damn right you do. *Well done.*" I whisper against her mouth. "Excessive lovemaking looks good on you Lola."

And it does...it really does.

15

HUDSON'S

LOLA

"FRANK!"

I wake up with a start, yelling out the old man's name. It literally sounds like how when Catherine O'Hara's character in "Home Alone" yelled out Kevin's name when she finally realized hours later that she left her son well, alone.

I don't know what we were thinking. It's late Thursday morning, my responsibility and common sense just flew out the window last night along with my abandon and I feel myself literally about to have a heart attack as my fingers grapple against the nightstand trying to find my cell.

I moan, seeing I have about forty missed calls from Frank and I'm suddenly scared I might have given *him* a heart attack with his worry.

The bookstore! I groan again.

My head falls back into the bed and I can't bring myself to care that I can't make it in time to open my shop. I was still trying even though Hudson told me I was going to be late. I feel like I've been ran over by a train. And when you feel like how I do right now, well, nothing else matters, to be honest. But I know I need to make it matter, because I have to at least get to the shop by the time the Frank gets there with the kids.

I don't even say anything to Hudson, I'm scared if I look at him. It's going to sentence me to another two hours of sex. And I at least need *one* of those hours to get to my shop.

I hit the button to call Frank who answer's on the first ring.

"You with that man?"

Damn, I can't even get a hello. Just straight to the point.

"Ye-"

"The next time you pull this shit and do not call me and let me know you won't be home, I'm going to beat your ass into the ground in your front yard and I won't even warn you. *You hear me Lolita?"*

I groan, putting my hand to my head and taking a deep breath because I kinda already know what it feels like to get beat down in a front yard and I don't want a repeat of that this soon. *"Yes sir. "*

Frank grunts and then hangs up on me.

I hear a deep low chuckling and close my eyes against Hudson's bright green gaze. I'm not ready to face him just yet, not after what he subjected me to all throughout the night. I didn't even know it was possible for a person to fuck the way he did, despite all the books I've read.

I should have been way more prepared than I mentally was.

"Good morning, beautiful."

The rasp in his voice makes my pussy clench, already trained to react to the sexy sound of his voice. I stubbornly keep my eyes closed. How do you look at the person who made it their business to turn you inside out for hours? I don't know, so my eyes will stay shut for now.

"I don't know what to do." I whisper. "You've ruined my clothes-*again*. I don't have anything clean to wear." I'm suddenly being dragged into him and just that simple movement has me whimpering. Why this man thought it was a good idea to fuck me all night on a weekday the way he did is beyond me.

Why I *let him* is beyond me.

Hudson raises up on an elbow and bends down, giving me a lingering kiss. I rip my mouth away and tighten my lips, my eyes finally open, and glare at him furiously.

"Can I at least brush my teeth?" I crinkle my nose at him. I mean I haven't had any water or anything and he wants to tongue kiss me? Yuck.

Hudson laughs, leaning further down to press a wet kiss right in the center of my neck and my flesh breaks out in goosebumps because damn, how unexpected. I raise a hand and place it over the wet spot he just left, willing the tickle sensation to go away.

"Come on sexy, let's get your teeth brushed. There's a store around here we can stop at and buy you an outfit."

"Okay but in the meantime can you please stop fucking up my clothes? Clothes are expensive."

He pauses in the middle of putting his pants on and gives me a look that has me blinking, making me avert my face from him. It's like he wanted to say something, but doesn't. I pause, getting my first good look at his bare torso. While he was fucking me all night I think my eyes were crossed for most of it and I couldn't pay attention.

This man gave me ten orgasms, when I struggle with one. It's a goddamn miracle.

We get to the shop and Frank comes a bit later with the boys. The twins do their usual bowl me over move and while they're busy attacking me, he walks up to Hudson, looking like he's going to attack *him*. Frank stares at him for a second before Hudson opens his mouth.

"I'm sorry, sir-"

"I don't want to hear it. *You should have called me.*"

"With all due respect sir, I don't have your number."

Frank doesn't miss a beat. He keeps Hudson's eyes and he points an arm at me. "*She* does. Use your fucking brain next time. You know, the one in the *right* head."

My mouth forms an "o" shape and I let out a little "oh" sound, and turn my face away. Because Frank just let us know he knew what we were doing. And even though I'm a grown woman, he's throwing a gauntlet down of his own.

"It won't happen again, Mr. Jackson. I promise you." Dare I say, Hudson looks a little sheepish.

"I don't care what *needs* y'all are trying to fulfill. Do you know what kind of person her ex is? *She needs watching over!*" Frank steps into Hudson's space, still staring at him and I wonder if Frank remembers he's seventy-one years old.

"Yes sir, I'm aware."

"Okay then, *act like it.* Let me know what's going on. I need to know these things. Next time you pull some shit like this Hudson I swear 'fore God and the United States of America I will make you pay."

Hudson, God bless his soul, takes it in stride.

"Yes, sir."

Frank turns to me and his face softens just the tiniest bit before he clears his throat. "He take care of you?"

If the floor could open up and swallow me whole, I'd be forever and ever grateful.

I feel my face redden with the worst blush I've ever blushed before at what this man just insinuated. How deep is it possible to entrench yourself into someone else's personal business before you cross a line? I honestly don't know the answer to that, and apparently neither does Frank.

"Yes sir." I choke out. Shock just colors my tone, with the thirty-year old crayons that my boys were coloring with the other day, as a matter of fact.

Hudson has the sense to erase his wicked smile he was giving me from behind Frank's back before Frank turns around and catches him. He walks to the front door and lets himself out, without a word for any of us. Frank likes dramatic entrances and exits I've learned.

"Ohh myy Gooood." I moan, placing my head in my hand and looking away from Hudson.

"You'll be alright baby. It's just sex, he was married for a long time so I'm sure he remembers how it is," Hudson chuckles, turning to go to the twins who have now started their homework.

He sits for the next two hours and helps them with their homework, patiently. Doesn't raise his voice once. He even orders dinner to the shop so we don't have to eat late, and we eat together for the first time, there in my little bookstore. It's peaceful, homey.

Perfect.

And it's now I finally realize we didn't use a condom.

Goddamn it.

I don't care what no one says, having the right man dick you down right is life changing. Hudson is life changing.

It's all I can think about as I'm attempting to keep a neutral expression on my face as he drives the boys and I to his home on Friday night. He enticed me with lots of popcorn, wine, movie time with the boys, and of course the horse ride.

Tomorrow we're supposed to go somewhere but I can't remember what he said. Some sort of monster truck show. I'm not sure. But it sounded like something the boys would like and though I can't afford it, I offered to pay for our tickets. But he told me he already bought them. Which was lucky for him that I said yes because like he does everything else, this man just seems to take what he wants.

What if I would have said no?

I tried to give him cash but he's one unrelenting man, I tell you. So, I swallow my pride and let him. Because Tucker was extra reserved after his Wednesday visit with his dad and I just know some fresh air, a horse ride, and whatever this monster truck thing is will make him feel better.

I trust Hudson. I know I haven't known him long but something about him feels safe. I hesitate to say it feels like home, because so far the only thing that's made me feel like home is the tight, stressful, chaotic feeling of always being on edge. And I haven't been out of it long enough to know what feels like home yet.

What I do know is, I'll be damned if I tangle myself up the way I did with Dominic, so I have a gyno appointment in three weeks so I can get on birth control. Sex with this man is too good to give up so we're going to have to be diligent with the condoms I know I saw him buy. I already bought a couple of plan B pills I have stashed in my purse.

And I know... I know. You're not supposed to use it as contraceptive, but I'm not getting pregnant.

Fuck that. The sex is amazing, he seems like a good guy, but so did Dominic at first and now look at me. I'm a mess. So I'm going to be a semi responsible mess since I can't control my lady bits and this man wants to act like he doesn't know what a condom is when we're deep in the moment.

This is not a slight against him I swear, because to be fair, neither do I.

I see in the rearview mirror that the boy's are holding their breath as we turn onto Hudson's property and roll under the sign that says his name. We're arriving at dusk, so the fireflies are out. I catch Hudson sneaking a look at me with the most handsome grin, and I can't help the smile that breaks out over my face at the memory of our *real* first time surrounded by thousands of fireflies.

"Wow." Tatum whispers, he's got his head stuck out of the window and is laughing in joy.

I see Tucker sitting there, and just staring at the window.

He looks pensive, and I hate the set of his brows that seems to just be more and more set in a permanent furrow. I put an arm back and rub his knee encouragingly. I don't want to make it a big deal but I want him to know I'm paying attention to him. I see Hudson catching the movement in the rearview mirror before his eyes flick back to the front. I feel my breath catch in my chest at how incredibly handsome he is.

My eyes stray down his face to where I know that vein is, currently hidden behind the collar of what I've found is his favorite outerwear, a plaid long sleeved shirt. His rough, sexy voice interrupts my ogling.

"Okay boys, what's our first stop? In the house for food, or to the stables for horses?"

He slows his truck before we get to the house and we suddenly see all the lights pop on in the property, and I know he timed it perfectly because he just seems that kind of man. The kind to just smoothly usher you into a magical world and you don't even realize he's doing it until he's already done it.

"I'd like to see the horses." Tucker states. Surprising me.

The truck speeds a little, we're driving past the house and I can hear as soon as the boys see the stables in the background.

"That's the nicest house I've ever seen!"

"That's what I thought, Tate!" I turn and laugh with Tatum wishing I can pull Tucker in to join in our joy.

We get out of the truck and then they run to the front, ahead of us. I glance shyly at Hudson through my lashes and feel butterflies in my stomach.

"Thanks so much for doing this. They're going to remember this for a long time." I say softly.

I place my hand on his chest when he puts an arm around my shoulders to pull me close and we walk like that for a minute, taking our time. I get the sense that though he's indulging my kids, he's also not ashamed to sneak his moments with me either, and I wonder what the night has in store for us.

I still haven't quite wrapped my head around the fact we're spending the night. The boys haven't seen me with a man since their father. What if they get up in the middle of the night and they want me and knock on the door, will he be angry? At the thought of the night coming up I begin to get nervous.

I hang back a little as Hudson unlocks the door to the stables and I hear none other than Nay Nay bay her hello.

"Okay boys." Hudson stops them with a hand on each of their shoulder. "I need you to listen and listen good. Horses are sensitive creatures. They pick up on energy. You need to be calm and don't spook them so we're going to walk in *calmly,* not running. We're going to walk up to each horse, let them smell you, and then I'll let you into Nay Nay's stall because she's the neediest and will want lots of love."

The boys nod their head solemnly and to say I'm floored is an understatement. Hudson just has that natural dad thing that is so sexy. I lick my lips, giving him a shaky smile as he has them step back for a second.

"Let's let mom walk in first okay? Always remember, ladies first."

If that doesn't seal the fucking deal, tell me what does?

I smile and walk in, leading the way to Nay Nay who literally starts stamping and blowing her nose at the sight of me. I give her a little kiss on her nose and then step back, letting Hudson do his thing with the boys.

They pet, talk, brush, and I'm so absolutely impressed at just...everything.

We stop at the truck to grab our fried chicken bucket meal we bought for dinner and then head into the house where Hudson gives them a tour, letting them run around excitedly. As I expected they absolutely lost their minds at the media room. I hear them yelling in there, excited by the popcorn machine and I'm busying myself putting the chicken that's gotten too soggy for my tastes in the air fryer to crisp back up, when Hudson sticks his head in the kitchen and gives me a little whistle.

"Hey, lets go upstairs and show the boys their room."

Closing the air fryer I wipe my fingers on a towel and then let him take me by the hand. Hudson threads his fingers through mine and tells the boys to head up the stairs.

"Wait! Grab your backpacks, don't be messy!" I admonish, making them straighten their shoes in the mudroom and grab their backpacks with their change of clothes before we head up.

They hurry ahead of us excitedly, flying up the stairs.

"First door on the right." Hudson calls, and I look at him with a raised eyebrow, seeing he's put the boys on the same side of the hallway as us but with two rooms in between theirs and ours.

He studiously ignores my look but I can tell by the grin he's trying to hide he put so much space between us so they don't hear when we're intimate.

Tatum bursts through the doors first and I also remember this is the biggest room, aside from the masters. It has its' own bathroom, and is attached to the second floor wrap around porch.

I pause as Hudson and I enter the room, completely taken aback. I arch a brow because this is not how I remember this room looking. Last I looked in here, there was a king sized bed and a singular dresser.

Now there's two queen sized beds with a nightstand in between them, two dressers with a flat screen TV mounted on the wall between them and underneath it a cool gaming system set up and two expensive looking gaming chairs. He didn't even tell me he was planning this. He just did it, without feeling the need to inform me, or even needing my input. To have that invisible burden be lifted, even just slightly, loosens my chest and makes that wall I keep erected crumble even more for this man. And seeing my kids excited, well, it makes this momma feel good.

"This is so cool!" Tatum exclaims, he throws his backpack on one bed then heads straight for the door that leads to the wrap around porch.

I hear Hudson call Tatum back real quick, and then start talking to both boys about staying away from the porch without permission but it's in the background, I'm headed to the closet.

Opening the door my brows raise, I didn't realize there was a walk-in closet in here. I turn on the light and step in and gasp.

Holy shit.

There's rows of boy shirts, pants, boots for the winter, sneakers, boots for riding, jackets, coats, shoes all lined up nice and neat. And there's double of everything. I'm standing there blinking, aware I've must have entered into the twilight zone. But in my daze something breaks through. In my peripheral I see something red standing off the floor and I turn. In the corner of the closet is a little retro fridge. Small.

I go to my knees on the thick carpet and I pull it open. There's juice boxes, small water bottles, and wouldn't you know it. Two lunch boxes tucked neatly side by side. Curiously I pull it out and see each of their names written on the front. Opening them up, my heart stops. In Tucker's lunch box there's little cut up turkey wraps and a bag of grapes and a Nutella cup, along with a note.

> Tuck, this is for you buddy. Eat whatever you want.
> Hudson

I hold my hand up to my mouth, just overwhelmed.

You know what the boys tell me they sleep on at their dads? A mattress. On the floor. And they share a three tiered plastic bin from a department store as a dresser.

I sniff, bringing my hand up to wipe my tears away but it doesn't matter. My heart feels broken. Because there's men out here who do stuff like *this*. And I fucked up and gave my son's a worthless piece of shit for a father. I want my sons to have *this*. Grow up with *this*. I see it's possible so why didn't I pick better?

I stare at the open lunch boxes, each of them have their own note, and I just shake and let the tears come.

"Lola?"

I startle, Hudson's deep voice breaking me out of my crying fit and I sniff again, trying to will my trembling fingers to cooperate and zip the bags back up. I can't look up at him. Not yet. I'm such an ugly crier.

"I'm so s-sorry. I'll be right there!"

Jesus how long have I been in here crying?

Hudson walks up to me and bends to a knee beside me, turning my head by my chin to face him. He stares in my eyes and pushes my bangs back in the way he knows makes me weak, and I feel two more tears escape my eyes. Without a word, he lowers his lips to mine, and gives me such a soul shattering kiss that I'm not even sure what my name is. Because it doesn't feel like Lola anymore.

Hudson's.

That's what it feels like.

16

LOOKING OUT FOR ME
TATUM

"MAMI LOOKS SO HAPPY." I whisper, trying to stay quiet.

I scoot a little closer to Tuck where we're huddled on the wrap around porch. He pulls further away, making me sad. My eyes prick. I miss my brother... doesn't he know how much I love him?

I'm sorry he's doing this to you Tuck. But I'm trying my hardest for you.

I hate daddy. But I have to act like I love him so he doesn't hurt Tuck more, or hurt mommy. And now there's Hudson. What if he says he'll hurt Hudson too?

My heart begins to pound hard, and I look at Tuck, seeing he's got no expression on his face. Not like before. Now, he never smiles anymore. I look down at my hands. I don't want to cry in front of him.

I want to talk to you about it Tuck but you won't talk to me anymore.

I'm doing my best Tuck.

We made a pact to not tell mom because he'll hurt her. But maybe...maybe we can talk now?

He won't look back at me but he just nods quietly. Tucker do you hate me? I'm just trying to protect you.

His eyes stay trained on mami and Hudson who are dancing on their balcony. Theirs didn't connect to the porch we are on.

"Come on, Hudson told us not to come out here." Tucker mutters quietly.

He turns to crawl his way back into the room, so not to get noticed by Hudson, but I stay out here making sure they're okay. Just like with Tucker, I'll always stay close.

Like that one time daddy didn't think I was watching and he was about to punch him.

I came around the corner just in time and when he saw me his fist dropped. I have to make sure to be close just in case mommy needs saving too. I can bust in the bedroom and push him over the balcony.

I look over my shoulder behind me. I wonder if the Angel mami says watches over me is back there? *Are angels real?* I'd like to think I'm being protected too.

I don't think I am. I can't be.

If I were truly protected, I wouldn't have a daddy who tries to hurt Tucker and mom because I love them. So that means daddy hates me too because he wants to hurt who I love.

I hate him.

Hudson leans down to kiss mommy and I feel my face scrunch up. Ew. Gag.

She laughs and then turns to walk back in the bedroom. But Hudson stays behind, watching her walk away quietly.

Okay Hudson, if you're out here, then I'm out here too. What are we waiting for?

I hunker down even more, ignoring the cold air on my bare feet.

I gasp as Hudson's head turns fast and his eyes meet mine. How can he see me? I'm huddled in the dark. My heart races as Hudson whistles at me and the hair on the back of my neck stands up.

He takes a finger and points silently to the door for me to go inside. I wet my lips nervously.

He knew I was here the whole time? It was me he was waiting for.

I scramble. Not even trying to hide like Tucker did. I close the door and leap into bed, seeing him asleep. Staring at the little horse night light against the wall it hits me.

I guess someone was watching out for me after all. I turn and face my brother, reaching my hand out to touch him. The only time he'll let me touch him anymore. The closest thing I have in this entire world. The other part of me.

I love you, Tuck.

17

PANTRY PLANTINGS
HUDSON

MY EYES OPEN AT the small knock on the bedroom door and I look over, still seeing Lola sleeping on her side. She's breathing evenly, and I don't want to disturb her. I took my time with her in the shower, fucking her nice and slow against the wall.

I wasn't going to sleep with her tonight, but after seeing her reaction to the boys room and their closet I needed that connection with her, and I believe she did too.

It took her a while to orgasm, partly because I was holding back, and partly because of those thoughts she was thinking as she was kneeling on her knees in the boys closet.

She didn't share them with me, but I know what she's thinking. Because that asshole put those fucked up thoughts in her head that she's not a good mom. She's thinking she picked a horrible father for her boys. And I don't like her thinking stuff like that.

So I treated her to a dance outside, not even bothering to mention the boys were watching. Then made sure to love her nice and long in her safe space, which so far I've found is the shower. I made sure the orgasm she had was so powerful she went completely limp in my arms, then I put her to bed.

I roll out of bed, pulling on a pair of pajama pants and open the door seeing Tucker. I give him a grin and kneel down to his level, putting a hand on his shoulder.

"Hey buddy," I flick my eyes down his face, trying to get a feel for what's going on with him. "You okay?"

Tucker flashes me a nervous look before his eyes lock on my rattlesnake tattoo.

"I can't sleep."

"Well your mom's asleep. See," I move a little so he can see Lola in the bed behind me. "But lucky for you, I know the perfect cure. Come with me." I stand up and hold my hand out to him. "You like warmed milk?"

Tucker nods and places his hand tentatively in mine. I take him downstairs and straight into the kitchen into the butler pantry and set him on the counter.

"Now, there's nothing like a cup of warmed, spiced milk. It's kind of like eggnog and Christmas. Do you like eggnog?" Yep, you best believe I'm making Christmas plans.

Tucker smiles and nods. "Yes, and mom makes the best chocolate chip cookies. We put out cookies and milk for Christmas every year. Last year mom put a little glass out for herself next to Santa's and when I asked her why, she said it was because she wanted to have a conversation to let Santa know she had something she wanted for Christmas. Do you know what she wanted? Did she tell you? I'd like to get her something but dad..." He cuts off.

I'm busy heating his milk for the frother, then I decide to add a little more because I want some too. Keeping my voice neutral I try to encourage him to keep talking.

"But dad what?" I lean over and grab some honey and cinnamon, letting him take his time.

"But dad... never takes us to get anything for her."

I sneak a look at him, seeing him staring between his legs at the floor. "Hmm. What are some things you'd like to get for your mom?"

This makes Tucker look up at me. I add his honey and cinnamon, and give him the cup and a spoon.

"Stir it how you like it." We're firmly on the road to confidence and self sufficiency. "I like to stir mine about fifteen times then it's perfect."

Tucker takes it and gives me a nod. "I'd like to give her flowers, there's this lotion she likes...and there's a perfume she always stops and sniffs when we're at the mall."

"The mall huh?" I take a deep drink and wink at him. Tucker gives me a tentative smile and takes a drink himself.

"How about this. Give me a couple weeks, and we'll go get your mom that perfume. You, me, and Tatum."

Tucker gives me a little look, and I can tell he's doubtful.

"You don't believe me?"

At me questioning him Tucker shoots a nervous look at the door and I widen my stance even more, I spread my legs, my arms, and I lean back into the counter behind me.

I won't hurt you Tuck.

"Do you know how much the perfume is?"

Tucker shakes his head.

"I'll tell you what. I'm not in the habit of making promises I don't keep. Why don't we make a pact to trust each other? I'd like to show you something, then give you something."

Tuckers eyes go wide.

"But what I'm about to show you has to be our little secret."

His gray eyes go wide. "Can I tell Tatum?"

"Yes." I smile.

"Can I tell mom."

"Of course."

This appeases him.

I turn, open a cabinet, and pull down a little flat box. I bring it to him and pull the lid off showing him five thousand dollars in one hundred dollar bills. It's running low because it's my stash for his moms tip jar.

"I want you to take two of those, put it in your backpack, and hold it until I see you, Tatum, and your mom again. The next time I see you, we'll take this money and go get her perfume. If I don't see you for whatever reason, I want you to take this money and get her perfume the next time you're at the mall. How's that sound bud?"

You're not going to have to do that Tuck, but it's the principle of the matter.

Tucker doesn't reach into the box. He just raises his eyes and looks at me. I'm so struck at how alike his and his moms eyes are. It's like staring into Lolita's. My heart cracks, and I feel so much love for this little guy that I can't do anything but stand there, holding this damn box that I feel like could make or break this thing between him and I.

Does he know he's wrapping himself around the very parts of me that make me who I am? Embedding himself into the fabric of my soul, so that no matter what happens for the rest of my life, this boy will mean everything to me. Forever.

As I stand there waiting, hoping that Tuck can find it in his heart to let me in, he reaches into the box and takes two hundred dollar bills. And even though he's taking from me, he's actually giving me something himself. Tucker's taken a seed and reached into my heart, planting himself deep. Right next to where his mother is. And fuck it do you know it almost kills me to keep my tears from falling?

I heave a deep breath and replace the box.

"Thank you Hudson." His voice sounds a little stronger, a bit more sure.

"You're welcome."

"I'm ready to go to bed now. Thanks for the milk."

I smile, because the way he says milk without pronouncing the 'k' is adorable.

I walk him to his room and make sure he climbs into bed, next to Tatum, and then tuck them both in a little tighter.

"Goodnight bud." I whisper, leaning down to ruffle his hair.

This time, I don't go back to Lolita, I pull on a heavy jacket and go to the stables and take Champ for a ride. I need to think, and some fresh air.

I get up early the next morning, wanting to give Lola a break from always having to be in mom mode. I look over, seeing she's on her back deep asleep with her arms thrown above her head, and her hair mussed. The covers slipped down, showing me that one of her breasts slipped out of her nightgown in the middle of the night. She hadn't wanted to go to bed nude, just in case the kids barged in.

I smile, enjoying having these intimate moments with her.

Leaning over I give her a kiss on her nipple before pulling her nightgown straight, and then the covers back up. Seeing her sleeping peacefully, I pull her hair out of her face and kiss her cheek before rolling out of bed quietly.

Brushing my teeth and washing my face, I look over and see her dirty clothes in the dirty clothes hamper and smile. I look forward to seeing more of her things pop up around the house, and the boy's things as well. Returning back into the bedroom, I slip on my sweatpants and a simple white T-shirt before heading down the hallway.

I knock on the kids door before sticking my head in and see them scrawled all over the bed tangled around each other. Pushing the door open I lean against the doorframe and cross my arms and legs.

"Hey boys, wake up." I call out quietly, turning on the dimmed light feature in the room.

Tatum stirs first, stretching so hard he grazes Tucker in the face with his fist, effectively waking him up. I walk into their room, bend down, and grab a foot each, shaking them.

"Hudson..." Tucker yawns, "What are you doing?" He asks, the words coming out garbled.

"Hey you two," I say quietly, "let's get up and surprise your mom with breakfast in bed!" I chuckle, seeing both boy's eyes pop open as they sit up excitedly.

"Breakfast in bed!? Do we get to eat in bed, too?" Tatum asks, running to the bathroom before I get a chance to answer.

Tucker swings his legs out from under the covers and turns to look at me. "I don't know how to cook." He says softly.

His expression turns sad, and it makes my heart tug for him. I reach forward and pause, seeing him flinch away, hunching his shoulders in as he rolls his lips and flickers his eyes nervously.

The action makes me bite the inside of my cheek harshly; because that fucker did this to him, made him scared to let another person be affectionate with him. Keeping my cadence level, I talk to him slowly, daring to reach forward even slower, running my hand down his curls before squeezing his shoulder lightly.

"Well we all gotta learn, and I don't mind teaching you. Say, what do you guys like to eat for breakfast?"

Tucker furrows his brow. "Pancakes, sausage, bacon, and eggs." His eyes flits back to mine. "B-but if it's too much-"

"No, it's not too much Tuck. But what about some fruit? Do you like strawberries on your pancakes?"

"Ohhh..." Tucker says, his shy smile showing me a missing tooth that's starting to grow back. "Tate and I love strawberries. Mom puts them in our lemonade sometimes and it tastes really good!"

I smile back, looking over to see Tatum walking out of the bathroom. "You wash your face?"

"Yes."

"Brush your teeth?" I raise my eyebrow inquisitively.

He comes up to me and then smiles brightly, pointing at his mouth.

"Good boy!" I praise. "Your turn!" I say to Tucker. He gets up and then heads to the closet. "Hey," I call out, "Leave your pajamas on, it's part of the fun. We're probably going to get messy anyways, so just wash your face and brush your teeth so we can get started."

Tatum starts to make the bed so I go to Tucker's side and help, seeing Tucker standing still in the doorway of the bathroom unsure. I look up at him, seeing he's hesitant.

"We're going to wait right here for you bud, we'll all go down to the kitchen together."

This appeases him, and he disappears into the bathroom, the door clicking shut softly behind him. Despite our late night talk, something about him this morning feels off to me.

We make the bed then wait. And wait.

I look over at Tatum, who's got a funny expression on his face.

"What's the matter?" I frown, *"Hey,* does it always take your brother this long to brush his teeth in the morning?"

"No," Tatum says quietly. He glances at me before looking away. "I think he might be sad."

My brow furrows as I push off the bed and then knock on the bathroom door. "Tuck, you okay little guy?" It's so quiet, but I barely hear a sniff. Biting my cheek I crack the bathroom door. "Hey, can I come in?"

"Yeah..." Tuck says.

He's sitting on the lid of the toilet and wiping his tears off his cheek with the sleeve of his pajama top. His face is red and he's looking down at the floor, not meeting my eye. I look back at Tatum.

"Hey Tatum, go downstairs and put a show on in the media room. We'll be down in a second, okay?"

Tatum nods, leaving obediently, but I can tell by his walk that he's reluctant to leave me with Tucker.

Walking into the bathroom, I sit on the edge of the bathtub and lean forward to place my hand on his back. Tucker looks at me before quickly looking down again. I'm worried about him. First he gets up in the middle of the night, and now he's waking up sad? I'm going to have to talk to Lola about trying a better counseling practice out my way so Tucker can have someone better to talk to then the places she's tried. I'll pay for it.

"What's wrong bud? Want to talk about it?" I ask, keeping my voice low.

Tucker's eyes well up with tears before he blinks them away and then sniffs again. He's silent for so long, but I don't repeat my question. He heard me just fine, he just needs a minute to think about things. Just like his momma.

Tucker takes a deep breath and then looks at me. "My dad doesn't love me."

My heart literally collapses to a stop in my chest. I feel my lips tighten, then my chest tightens to the point of pain. I work to keep my hand from trembling on his back as his words processes. This little boy should never have been made to even feel like those words could come out of his mouth.

"Tucker, I'm so sorry you feel like that," I say slowly. "I-"

"You treat me better." Tucker interrupts me.

I sit for a minute because Goddamn, I don't know what to say. It's not often I'm rendered speechless. What do you say to a boy who is eight years old, at such a tender developmental age in his life where every little word and interaction counts?

Leaning forward I take his hand in mine, squeezing his little fingers tight in my palm. "Tucker, sometimes in life, people don't always treat us the way they should. But the universe always has a way of giving us what we need. And if I can help with this thing between you and your dad in *any* way, you just tell me, and I will. Okay buddy? You can always talk to me, *and your mom.*" I say softly.

Tucker looks up at me, before leaning his head into my chest, just like he did his mom that day that his dad went to pick him up. Like all his fight was gone.

Maybe it is, but I'm going to give it back.

I wrap my arms around him and pull him into my lap, pressing my lips to the top of his head and just hang on tight until his little tremors leave and he pulls away, giving me an embarrassed look.

"I want to brush my teeth now." He says simply, keeping his eyes averted.

Realizing I'm dismissed, I nod, and walk back into the bedroom. As the muted sounds of the sink turn on, I feel my mask fracture. My face twists with emotion, and I fist my hands hard, willing the tears not to fall. I take a deep shuddering breath that does nothing to calm me down, pressing a fist into my chest, right over my heart.

I am so fucking *angry*.

I don't even think angry is the word. It's been taking everything in me not to fuck the boy's dad up, and the closer I get to them, the more this feeling swells inside of me to the point where I'm not sure how much longer I'm going to be able to control myself.

I dig my nails into my palms hard and ride out this sick feeling that's come over me, and by the time he opens the door I'm almost back to normal. I put my hand on his shoulder and walk him out of the bedroom, seeing *his* mask slipped firmly back into place, as is mine.

We go downstairs and proceed to tear the kitchen up making every breakfast item we can think, and the chaos is enough to calm this storm inside of me for a while. And I pray it's enough for Tucker, too.

We walk into the room with three trays of food, but of course I carry the heaviest one. Lola's still asleep and the sunlight slants over her in the bed perfectly. She's shifted again further down the bed, and I instruct the boys to set the trays down on the bench at the end, so we can wake her up.

"Shh." I say, putting a finger to my lips and motioning for them to crawl on the bed with me. The boys trade a devilish glance before smiling conspiratorially, crawling on the bed with me. I approach from the side, and the boys approach from her feet.

Pulling her bangs back I give them a nod as I bend down to kiss her forehead.

"Mamiiiii! *Wake up!*" The boys begin to jump up and down on their knees, bouncing the bed. "Wake up, *wake up*, you have to get up!"

Lola's eyes fly open on a gasp, and she clutches the blanket to her hard before her eyes meet mine. I give her a grin.

"Wake up beautiful, the boys have a surprise for you!"

She relaxes instantly before laughing. "Oh my Gosh you guys! You scared *meee!*" She giggles, putting her hands to her face and rubbing.

She suddenly stretches so hard I hear her spine crack before the boys pounce on her, and she welcomes them with open arms. Not wanting to miss any of this, I crawl in with them. They snuggle in on either side of Lola, and I grunt as Tuckers elbow digs into my chest as he works to squeeze his way between the two of us.

"Mom we made you breakfast!" Tatum says, burying his face into her arm and then looking up at her. Lola looks down at him and then over at Tucker, who's winding around her other arm. But I see he's burying into her neck.

"Oh you diiiddd?" Lola looks over at me and gives me wide eyes. *They did?* She mouths, giving me a 'what the hell' look.

I chuckle and shrug my shoulder. "Yes, I promised them we could eat breakfast in bed, so here, sit up you three!" I maneuver them all, and once they are sitting up against the pillows I place everyone's trays in their lap.

Lola's eyes goes wide as she sees the food. I loaded her tray up with enough for me too so I could eat sitting across from her.

"You made pancakes?" Lolita says in a hushed tone, picking up her knife and fork to cut a slice which she drizzles in syrup, and holds out to me first. I lean forward, winking at her as I take the food off her fork. She brushes bright red making me chuckle deeply.

"And eggs-" Tatum says excitedly.

"-And sausage-" Tucker interjects.

"*-and bacon.*" I finish, chuckling seeing them tearing into their food smearing syrup on their mouths. "They did such a good job cooking, you should be proud!" I gush, seeing the boys smile through their mouthfuls of food. *"So,* here's the plan; when we're done eating we're going to load the dishwasher, wipe the counters, and then shower before leaving to the monster jam show. We gotta get there early so we can buy headphones." I tell Lola absentmindedly.

My dick hardens, seeing her put a piece of sausage in her mouth with her fingers before licking it off. She makes a little pleased moaning sound that does nothing to make my erection better. I clear my throat, working hard to beat it down.

"We can't wait!' Tatum says, leaning over his mom to share a look with Tucker who smiles at him.

"What was that?" I ask curiously, my eyes pings between the two of them.

"Oh, well..." Tucker starts. "We just think...." He pauses, giving Tatum another look. Who's smiling so hard his face looks like it'll break in half.

Lolita turns her head side to side between the two of them. *"Oh no!"* She whispers almost to herself, giving me wide eyes.

"WE WANT OUR OWN MONSTER TRUCKS!" Tatum yells, throwing his arms in the air so hard his tray rattles, forcing Lola to grab it quickly.

"You want one of your own, *huh?*" I say as I shove another bite of pancakes into my mouth.

I'm going to have to work this off somehow, maybe Lola will let me fuck her an extra hour tonight.

"Yeah, so it can go *vroom vroom!"* Tatum says, returning to his food.

"What about you, Tate? You want one to make go *vroom vroom* too?" I tease, glancing over at Tucker who's got a little half grin on his face. He's trying to hide it but his lips are twisted, giving him a comical look.

A sparkle is in his eye that I've never seen before.

"Yeah, that'd be fun." He says quietly, looking up at me before glancing at his mom.

She gives him a little kiss on his head, and when she turns back to her food he keeps staring at her, like he can't bear to look away.

My chest tightens because deep down I know why. I just wish it didn't have to be this way. We finish our breakfast and we listen to the boys talk to each other about their friends at school, and how they can't wait to tell them about the monster show.

I work my hand under the blanket and find Lola's foot, who jerks when I dig my thumb into the sole hard, pressing a sensitive nerve there getting her attention. She flushes bright red, raising her eyes to look at me. I give her another wink and turn my attention back to the boys.

Whatever happens, we're going to learn to have a good balance of intimacy *and* family time.

I'll see to that.

18

MI QUERIDO
LOLA

> So you letting some man fuck you around my boys now huh? -Dominic

> You fucking slut. -Dominic

> You're kidding me right? They told me all about the room he set up for them. And his horses. He thinks he's better than me huh? Well, I'm not going to let some dick take my place. And YOU better not either. Tell him to leave my sons alone, and stop buying them shit. Fucking bitch.-Dominic

> He won't always be there. -Dominic

THE TEXTS COME EVERY half hour or so.

I'm upset yes, but I just ignore them, because words can't hurt me and all of that. I'm ringing out my customers on Thursday evening a week later, waiting for Frank to drop off the boys after their Wednesday visit with their dad, and have been getting hateful texts all day.

Between their weekend visit with him, and then this Wednesday, I'm worried he's going to retaliate against the kids and have been trying to not rock the boat. I've even kept it from Hudson, because I see the look in his eyes when Dominic gets the kids, and seeing the two men stand off silently is not getting any easier to endure.

And today is Dominic's day. So that means another uncomfortable stand off.

I put my phone in the storage room because I need to concentrate on my patrons, and not my phone lighting up with something new every fifteen minutes. Hudson's back there, and I hear a box bang loudly as it drops on the floor.

He's helping to unload a book order. And I feel bad, because doesn't he have a business of his own to run? I'm handing my last patron her receipt, when the storage door flies open and Hudson steps through the threshold. Holding my phone, looking murderous.

My eyes go wide. *Fuck!*

Wait, why's he holding my phone again?

"Lolita, come here please." His face is stony as he looks at me, letting me know it's bad.

My irritation doesn't matter, not when he's got that tone of voice. I groan and make my way into the storage room, hurrying more when he reaches out a hand and yanks me inside, making me hustle.

"Okay, God. Why do you have my phone?" I snap at him, momentarily unconcerned with his anger.

"No," He grits. *"Not okay. Look!"*

He turns my phone and shows me the screen, his green eyes are flashing and his jaw is clenching hard. He's fuming mad. Like *livid*. I take the phone, reading the text open on the screen and groan. Because Dominic really knows how to be an asshole.

> You still having problems orgasming? I bet he can't hit it the way I did. You had the best dick and still couldn't cum, broken ass cunt. -Do minic

> *Should I tell him how hard I had to fuck you*
> *to make you cum? I'm sure he won't like you*
> *then.-Dominic*

Hudson is standing in front of me, rubbing a hand down his face where he rubs his lips hard and lets out a harsh groan. He's shaking his head slightly, and the tension has got his body rigid in a way that terrifies me a bit.

I'm talking before I'm thinking. "You can't be here when he picks them up."

I cannot have them fighting in front of the boys, and from how the last confrontation went, someone's going to prison and I'm not entirely sure that person is Dominic. I've never seen anyone cut another person quite the way Hudson did, and I'm still waiting to pay for it. Hudson's head recoils, and he looks me up and down with an expression like he think's I'm crazy.

"Hudson you two are too *alike-*" I cut my sentence off when I see his posture immediately change and I wince.

Wrong fucking thing to say-wwrrrooonnggg. Don't ever ever ever say that again, Lolita. I mentally chastise myself as his lip curls and he folds his arms, giving me a hard look.

"I am nothing like that man. *Nothing.*"

Whew. But something flashes in his eyes to let me know that even though I shouldn't have verbalized it the way I did, I'm not entirely incorrect. Hudson is about the most pissed off I've seen him yet.

The features in his face are so tight that I know if Dominic dared to walk in the shop right this second he'd be a dead man.

"Carino," I step into him, pressing myself into his front, place my hand on his chest and bat my eyelashes at him. Praying that my softness can make him melt a little. "That is not what I meant. Lo siento, mi querido."

He relaxes instantly and I breathe a sign of relief.

"Please?" I say softly, rubbing my hand in soothing circles. *"Please for me?* No fighting, I don't want him to hurt...to do anything to the boys."* I have tears in my eyes, begging him to please just stand down so my babies won't be threatened.

He gives me a hard look, and just stares. His chest is rising and falling slightly harder than usual, and I can see the wheels turning inside his head.

"For you Lolita... I'll behave. And for the boys." Hudson unfolds his arms and grasps mine, pulling me firmly against him.

I breathe a sigh of relief. *Thank you God.*

I nod at him and continue to rub my hand on his chest. Raising up on my tiptoes, I press my lips against his and we kiss softly. I'm moaning, trying not to let the kiss turn sexual because every time we do, he cuts a piece of my clothing off and we're still at the shop.

Unconcerned with me trying to be restrained, he deepens it purposefully. Tugging and sucking at my lips and tongue. I'm wet before I realize it so I pull back hastily, and turn to walk away. Hudson leans forward and slaps me on my ass, causing me to squeal.

"And if you need it harder, you just let me know." His voice is raspy, letting me know he means it.

I feel the blush enter my face and stay. "Okay." I choke out, knowing there's other things I wish I could let him know, but I don't want him to judge me. And God, if I ask him for what I need, what will he think of me?

Will he want me still?

We head out into the main shop just in time to see Frank come in with the boys from school.

"Mami!" They yell, racing each other to bowl me down.

I actually fall this time, I think they've grown at least three inches and I know in no time at all they'll be taller than I am.

"Boys!" I hear both Frank and Hudson sternly correct them, but I'm on the floor laughing and just having a great time with my little guys.

Because I love their laughter, and want to hear it as often as I can. And as long as they don't break anything, a little rolling on the floor action never hurt anyone.

I see Hudson trying to fight back his own laughter, and the sight is enough to send me in another fit of giggles. Because after all the vitriol I've been subjected to from those nasty texts today, I needed this from the men in my life who love me.

My laughter immediately dissipates.

Love?

I glance up at Hudson through my lashes. Does this man love me? Can't be, we've only known each other just a few weeks. I know he lusts after me... even likes me, which is more than I could say for my last relationship. But *love?*

Nah.

"Come on you two, let her up." Hudson admonishes as he helps me up off the floor.

I stand up and wipe my hands down my dress and give Frank a huff.

"Now Frank, you know I care about you-" Frank cuts me off with a little wave and a scoff, tugging at his jacket. "So we have a little surprise for you. Come over here and see, Hudson and I want to show you what we've been working on." I throw Hudson a little smile and lead Frank to a column of shelves in the wall.

I see him frown, seeing the little *'Frank's History Corner'* plaque Hudson hung up this morning, then his eyes roam down and widen. He breaks out into a bright smile.

"Lolita! Are you serious?" He throws me a little look as he tentatively steps forward and gets a closer look.

Seeing dozens of books on various wars, presidents, and biographies about soldiers and even a massive photo book depicting dogs who've served.

Hudson wraps his arm around my waist and tugs me into him. I look up at him and scrunch my nose playfully, seeing Frank's grabbed a book and sat down in a cushy chair to read.

He didn't even say thank you, but you know, the man has never sat down one time in the six years I've had my shop. So that honestly was thank you enough.

He's still here when Dominic comes to get the kids, and he looks over the rim of his reading glasses curiously as I walk out of the storage room with the boys lunchboxes.

"Here you go." I sing cheerfully, trying to keep my playful mood.

Last thing on Earth I want is Frank having a up and front row seat to this man's assholery during pick up.

Dominic, who was looking down and saying something to Tatum, glances up sharply at my tone, and I work hard to keep a little smile on my face as I zip up

"I hope you two have a good visit, and remember that I love you so much." I say to the boys, ruffling their hair.

"Lolita, did you get my texts?"

I ignore him. "And I want you to be extra good, and I'll treat you all to a movie tomorrow night."

"Lolita, did you get my texts."

"And *you,*" I bend down and get into Tuckers eyelevel. "You've been doing such a good job on your homework! I'm so proud of you baby. Do you know your newest report card had all A's?"

I give him a little excited squeal and pull him in for a big hug. And as I look over my babies shoulder, I let my eyes show my displeasure with Dominic. But I give him a wink.

He gets an evil look on his face and takes a step forward. "I asked if you-"

"*She* didn't get them," Hudson steps into my back and puts his hand over my hair nice and slow. "But *I* did. And I dare you to walk a step closer."

Boldly, he reaches out and pulls the boys in for a hug himself, and then lets them go with a little ruffle to their hair.

"Bye boys, be good for him, eh?" Something passes between Tucker and him that I can't discern, and then Dominic looks up at him with pure evil on his face which Hudson meets with a raised eyebrow, keeping his hand steady on my waist. Too steady.

I pull out my phone and then send a text of my own. Dominic's phone dings and then he pulls it out and looks at my text.

> Hey, I know you've been having a hard time. I'm sorry I couldn't give you money the last time you asked for it so here's three thousand dollars, I'm sorry I couldn't give you the full amount you asked for but next time don't threaten me please, just ask nicely. -Lolita.

And with that I send him three grand through a money sharing app and take a screenshot for proof. I'm racking up a defense to take him for full custody. Dominic's face goes beat red and he turns around.

"*Come on.*" He barks at the boys.

They give me one last hug then hurry out of the store after their father. I walk up to the window and look out, seeing them get into the car before pulling off.

"Boy, I'm so proud of you Hudson. You've got great self control! You're better than me, son." Frank says from his seat. "Couldn't be me. At all." He rises then tucks the book under his arm, heading towards the door. He shakes hands with Hudson before leaving, and it's just then I realize he left without buying the book. That man.

I blow out a deep breath, ruffling my bangs. "Thank you." I say softly, leaning into Hudson's arms as he pulls me close.

"Anytime." He says just as softly, but from how tight his body is I can tell he exercised an immense amount of self control. "Come on, lets get you closed up!" He walks me to my register with his arm around my shoulder, and begins to help me close down.

An hour and a half later he's pulling up at the side of his house, right as the property lights turn on.

"Hey baby, do you mind taking this inside and putting it in the oven to keep hot, so that I can take care of the horses before Clayton and his sister Amanda come over?"

"Sure babe." I take the thick plastic bag that houses the catered fettuccini alfredo dinner he picked up on the way in, and jump out the truck, hearing a rumble close by.

"What's that?" I ask curiously, meeting him around the front of the truck seeing he's digging around his pocket, fishing for his keys.

"Oh, that's Haley. Must be your lucky night, you get to meet her. I didn't tell her to come take care of the horses tonight, but I've been gone so much I guess she's been sneaking over here even when I don't ask her to. What you want to bet she's got some carrots, or celery or somethin' for them?" He throws me a panty melting smile, holding out the keys for me to take.

"Those aren't your house keys, Hudson." I say, pulling my hand back patiently, hearing the four wheeler get closer.

A second later a tall, lanky girl with blonde hair appears from behind Hudson, and she flashes us a bright smile as she takes off her helmet.

"Hi!' She says excitedly as she climbs off. "You must be Lola! *Ohhh* I've heard so much about you!"

And to my utter shock she steps right into me and wraps me in a big hug. She's so tall that her chin rests on the top of my head. I let out a little peal of laughter because she's so friendly it's refreshing, and she steps back, showing me two rows of teal bands on her braces.

"Hi Haley, it's so nice to meet you!" It must be all the time with the horses that's got her so friendly.

She really is like a breath of fresh air. I eye her curiously in her ripped skinny jeans, black tank top, and button down that's open. She's got a leather necklace on, and a matching leather band around her wrist.

"Oh my Goosshh, what do you guys have?" She says, trying to peer into the bag.

I open it up and show her the container with clear lid fogged over with condensation. "It's alfredo dinner night! You want to join us?" I hurriedly close my mouth and then throw an apologetic look at Hudson. I didn't mean to just invite company over to his house. Dominic always made me feel like shit for inviting anyone over especially without talking to him first and I wince, feeling those inadequate feelings take over. "Sorry Hudson. Uhm... I didn't mean to-"

"Nonsense!" He smiles. "Haley you're more than welcome, come here kid. You're just going to ignore me now that Lola's here now, huh? I see how it is." Hudson good naturedly leans into Haley and

affectionately pats her on the shoulder. "Isn't it about time to get your braces off?"

My eyes widen. Picking up that he really pays attention to other people, and is free enough to let them know that he cares.

"Yup, two more months! I'm so ready! Ugh I think I'm going to die of happiness when they finally come off!" She laughs and then reaches to grab the basket attached to her four wheeler. "I'm going to give them their treats."

"Alright, thank you Haley. I'll be right there so it'll get done earlier and we can hopefully be done by the time Clayton and Amanda get here."

"Oooh, Amanda's coming?" Her face brightens even more, if that's possible. "Yay! She's so fun!"

"Yes." Hudson laughs. "Now go on, I'll meet you in there."

When Haley turns away to walk towards the stables with her basket, he turns back to me then puts a hand around my nape, pulling me in for a harsh, surprising kiss. I let out a soft sound as he tilts his head and kisses me even deeper in response, pulling me harder into him. That dull thudding between my legs that feel like it's always there begin to ramp up.

He pulls away with a smack and I'm panting, blinking.

"What was that for?" I ask incredulously, feeling a hot shiver race up my spine.

"Because I'm excited to host with you, baby girl." He leans back in and kisses me again. Speaking against my lips. "Put the food in the warmer, go take a quick shower, and change into something more comfortable." I look down, seeing he's pressed the keys into my hand. "That's for you. Two keys for the house, one for my truck, and one for the stables."

My eyebrows almost fly off my face. He's giving me a key to his house? No... not the house. His entire *kingdom*. I'm so shocked I don't know what to say.

"Hurry up Lolita." Hudson says with a little more roughness to his voice than usual.

He turns and begins to walk to the stables.

"Hudson wait, I don't have any clothes to change into!" All I've brought with me is a pair of pajama's I've already learned I'll never wear, and a change of clothes for tomorrow.

"Yeah you do, I bought you some. Look in the closet."

With that news I race to the door, letting myself in the house and hurrying to put the food in the warmer before booking it upstairs. I make my way into the closet and turn the light on and stand there, stunned.

Oh my God.

He filled up his entire half of the closet with nothing but clothes for *me*. Dozens of blouses, pants, dresses, lots of boatneck garments letting me know it's his favorite thing to see me wear. And when I look into a drawer curiously, I see a ton of strapless bras reinforcing that fact, and even more underwear. Folded in perfect little squares, letting me know he plans to cut them off often. Because no woman needs what looks to be around four hundred pairs of underwear.

I look over and see a couple pairs of fancy riding boots, and I balk.

As much as I enjoy petting the horses there's no way I'm riding one. I'll kiss their noses and love them without getting on them. They're too big, and what's my five foot two self look like getting on one of those things? No.

I hurriedly find a very chic looking but comfortable maroon tank, pants, and oversized sweater and jump in the shower, setting my alarm to make sure I only take fifteen minutes. I'm busy brushing my hair into a bun at the top of my head, when Hudson walks into the bathroom and strides to stand behind me purposefully.

He pulls off his shirt in one smooth movement and then reaches around me, pulling me to him hard and looping his arms over my stomach, leaning into to kiss my neck.

"You smell amazing." He says softly into my ear. His gritty rumble scratches along my nerve endings and pulls my nipples tight against the material. "I had a feeling you were going to like this set. Your ass looks amazing in this, by the way.

I let out a giggle. "Oh yeah?" I hold his eyes in the mirror. "So you bought me a thousand pairs of underwear because you thought I'd look amazing in them too, so you wanted to see a different pair every day?"

Hudson gives me a laugh. "Oh no baby, I just didn't want to hear that smart mouth complain any more about me cutting them off you."

See. What'd I say?

I click my tongue and give him a little headshake. "Boy you really are something *else,* you know that? So audacious. How do you even know I'm going to even be with you long enough to even wear them all?"

Uh oh. I back pedal at the look in his eyes. Feeling him grip a firm hand full of my ass I let out a little squeal.

"You're not going anywhere, missy."

"Okay I didn't *mean* it, Hudson, *Goddamn.*"

The pure possessiveness in his eyes is everything I've ever dreamed of seeing when a man looks at me.

He puts his lips to my ear. "And because you even let that come out of your mouth, you can expect for me to *shut it up for you later.* You're going to learn to watch what you say to me."

I feel my knees buckle, and my heart begins pounding out of my chest as he lets me go, stepping into the shower himself, quickly beginning to wash up robotically as if he didn't just make me almost collapse to the floor with his words. I stand there the entire time he's washing, ogling him. I don't even realize I'm doing it until he steps out, and gets a knowing look on his face. The grin he gives me would like to kill me.

"Baby," He arches a brow at me. "Can you grab me something to wear?"

I nod stupidly. "Yeah uhm..." Fuck, that rattlesnake tattoo is so sexy I can't think straight. And the way he towels himself, there's so *much* of him to dry. "What would you like me to grab for you?" I say breathlessly.

"Briefs, jeans, and a thin, long sleeved shirt please."

I throw him a smile and then leave, coming back quickly with his things. "Here you go."

I lean in to give his shoulder a kiss before I hightail it out of there and to the kitchen. I'm busy making and dressing the salad when I hear a bunch of noise through the front door, and I wipe my hands down my sweater in a nervous motion.

It's been so long since I've hosted anything I don't know if I know how to anymore.

I see Haley first. She walks into the kitchen and comes straight to the sink and starts washing her hands. Behind her comes a plumper, beautiful, brown haired woman with a round face. And she's so drop dead gorgeous my jaw drops.

"Oh you must be Lolita!" She squeals in a high voice and does this little shuffle to me like she just can't wait to get to me so she's gotta stomp the energy out first. Oh my gosh it makes me feel so safe.

I get a wide smile and forget myself.

"Ohhh que bueno conocerte! ¡Tú debes ser Amanda, eres tan bonita y hueles tan hermoso!"

As if we're in some movie we come together on a squeal and a laugh and hug each other as if we've known each other for years.

"*III* do not know what you just said, but you did say something is beautiful, and oh my goodness you are so freaking pretty! Lola look at this *bodyyy!*" She pulls back and gives me a once over.

Just then Hudson walks in the room pushing a hand through his hair, followed by a tall, almost French looking gentleman who's wearing cowboy boots, a white cowboy hat, and a plaid button up long sleeved shirt.

I bite back a laugh because it fits him, oddly enough.

"Lola," Hudson's eyes are bright as he walks past me to reach in the cabinet behind me pulling out bowls and plates. "This is Clayton."

"Hiii!" I shake Clayton's hand when he offers it to me. "It's so nice to meet you, I've heard so much about you."

"All good things I hope."

"*Yess!*" I laugh smiling even brighter.

"Wow, Hudson wasn't kidding, you are gorgeous Ma'am."

I blush a little and busy myself getting out silverware for everyone. I look to the side and see Hudson has already brought out two bottles of wine and starts uncorking them.

"Who want's red?"

Amanda throws me a look. "Do you like tequila?"

I give her my own sassy look in return. "Are you kidding? I'm *mexican* baby, all you need to say is 'margarita' and if you make it a *frozen lime*, then I'm down for anything." I giggle at her.

Hudson throws me an amused glance as he takes a sip of whiskey.

"Okay then me, too! Let's make plans to go out sometime!"

I throw her a shy smile and as we all work together to set the table, I relax into the insane comfortability of everyone's presence. They feel like I've known them forever. And by the end of the night, when they're all gone and Hudson's ramming his cock into the back of my throat, punishing me for my words earlier, I don't even wince.

Because he's comfortable and safe to me, too.

19

A NAME FOR EACH

HUDSON

IT'S LOLITA'S WEEKEND AND we all spend Friday night together at my place. While she's cooking, I have the boys come to the stables and help me put grain out for the horses, and they help me brush them. Tucker has really taken to Beauty, which is fun to see. We spend the night watching movies in the media room and drinking hot cocoa.

We stay up entirely too late because we all fall asleep in the lounge. Thank God for plush reclining couches that can double as beds.

Morning comes and I get up, seeing Lola is making breakfast for everyone. She's making sausage biscuits and gravy which is my favorite, and we eat at the table while I tell Lola I have a surprise for her. I bought her a massage and facial package at a nearby spa in town, and the look of wonder on her face has got me seriously penciling in spa days, trips, romantic ferry rides, and anything else I can think of to splurge on her.

"But wait, what about the boys?"

I smile at her and eat another bite, winking at Tucker and Tatum, who are watching me with interest.

"We got our own boy stuff to get into while mom's do mom things." I keep it simple, because I don't want the three of them to know what I've been planning.

She looks nervous, and she pulls me to the side later to ask me if I know what it's like to be left alone with two eight year old boys.

I appease her, tell her I used to be an eight year old boy. I kiss her senseless, tell her not to worry, and to track their watches if she's super nervous.

I won't hurt them, I promise.

Thank God for those watches and GPS devices because honestly, Lola probably wouldn't have let me take them without it. She double checked with them to make sure they were okay with coming with me. She had this particular conversation with them in the library, where I wasn't supposed to hear. It touched me that she considers their feelings in these situations.

The three of us see her off to her SUV and wave at her as she heads down the driveway to hopefully destress.

I walk the boys to my shed, who are curious little things. Their eyes go wide at the thirty foot trailer and they look at each other, sharing a smile.

I spend time loading the trailer onto the back of the hitch of my truck. Biting back a grin as the boys follow my every movement intently.

"Hudson, what are we doing?" Tucker asks hesitantly.

Being the more cautious twin, he stands back slightly more than his brother who is almost right on top of me, watching me attach it and lock it down.

"*We,*" I say with emphasis looking up at him and wagging my eyebrows, "are going on a *field trip.*"

Tatum's eyes go wide with excitement, this little man seems down for anything, his brother, however, doesn't trust a thing. I'll work on that, diligently. Because though trusting your gut is such a precious skill to have, being able to discern when you're being too cautious and not able to take risks can end up costing you blessings and opportunity. And I want the little guy to thrive.

"Does mom know?" He asks tentatively.

"Yes." I pause. "Well, she knows where I'm taking you." I smile.

So incredibly excited that I get to be able to do this for them.

However, Lola doesn't know what I'm *getting*, because I'm surprising her, too. She's going to get a cherry on top. And the best part? I'm going to have the boys help me pick it out. Finishing my job, I double check everything is attached correctly and I walk to the side of the truck, opening up the front and the back.

"Get in." I instruct them, waiting until they clamber in the back. I close the door and climb in myself, listening to their oohs and aahs as they take in the leather seats and fancy interior. "Seat belts."

As I listen to the clicks, I reach over into the console and snag out two pairs of kid sized boy sunglasses and reach back, handing them out.

They say thank you, before promptly fighting over who gets what color. I lower my own sunglasses and lower the rear view mirror, getting them in a good view before I whistle, catching their attention. They stop bickering immediately and stare at me, riveted. I pin them with a hard stare and an even harder voice.

Letting them know I'm not fucking around.

"The way you handle getting these sunglasses is going to determine if we're going to get anything while we're out on our field trip." I give them a moment to sort it our for themselves.

They look at each other before nodding, and in an impressive move that I can only describe as their secret twin bond, they decide on what color and slide them on. I pull my rearview mirror back in place, and push up my shades. Smiling to myself as I pull the truck onto the long driveway and take my time. I roll down the windows, put on some fun music, and we sing our way down the highway headed to the tractor supply store.

The boy's eyes are wide as I pull into the back of the parking lot, needing to park sideways, requiring me to take up several spots.

"Let's go."

We hop out and make our way into the store hand in hand. Their eyes are wide as their heads swivel this way and that way trying to take it all in. The fluorescent lighting, the big machines, the rubber smell. I smile, because they have no clue. My heart begins to race with excitement and I struggle to contain my glee.

"May I help you sir?"

"Yes ma'am," I smile at the kind looking woman who walks up to me. She's wearing two inch heels and has a dark brown felt skirt that falls past her knees. "My name is Hudson Montgomery, I called a few days ago to make an appointment to pick up my order. I was told we'd have several colors to choose from, so we're here to select what we want."

She nods, picking up her tablet and typing for a few seconds. She looks up with a smile and bends down to look at the boys.

"You two are the luckiest young men in the world."

Tucker and Tatum look at each other and smile, showing a missing tooth each.

"We are?" They ask in unison, drawing out a chuckle from me.

She smiles. "Yes, the *most* luckiest! What's your names?"

"Tucker." His response is reserved.

"Tatum!" I wince, as he yelled it in his excitement.

The woman giggles and stands back up, pivoting swiftly in her heels. "Follow me boys, they're displayed in the back."

They look up at me and I nod at them and they spring into action, running behind our helper before falling into step on either side of her. They're quiet, and I can feel it's simmering energy like a tangible thing. It's like Christmas morning, when you wake up, not realizing you fell asleep drunk off cookies and warmed milk and you get out of bed, knowing it's time.

Knowing the object of everything you've waited for all year is just around the corner down the hallway under the Christmas tree, and it's time to finally open the wrapping.

My heart swells as we get closer and then suddenly there they are. Eight shiny brand spanking new ATV's lined up in a row just waiting for us. Lit up beautifully under the lights of the store.

The shock hits first and they pause for a second, shoulder to shoulder.

I inch a little to their right to see their faces. They stare, transfixed. Not sure where to look first because there's black, white, green, silver, red, blue, orange, and camouflage. Their chests puff out almost at the same time, and somehow their eyes get even bigger and they look at each other. Their faces almost breaking in half at the wide smile that suddenly overtakes them both and then there it is. What I've been looking for.

The feeling I've been waiting to top me giving my parent's five million dollars, come in the form of two boys just gifted their first ATV. Fuck, it's sweet and discombobulating at the same time.

My eyes water and I clear my throat.

"Pick a color." I call out, willing my heart to slow down just a second. I pull out my phone to give myself a minute and look at Lolita's picture on my screensaver and unfortunately for me, the tightness becomes worse. The boys swivel their heads now to look at me in disbelief. I glance up at them with a sly grin. "Well I know you can't think I just drove us an hour and a half to tease you with something you can't have now do you?"

They each get the same exact expression on their face, before turning to look at each other and I know. I just *know* by the look they give each other, though they didn't say a word, language passed between them that lets me know that fucking prick ass piece of sorry excuse for a '*daddy*' has done this to them before.

And if I thought I hated the man *before*, this feeling has morphed into something dangerous.

For Dominic, *not me*. Let's be clear.

Tatum moves first, not surprising me as he's the more outgoing one. He races to the orange one and steps onto the landing for your foot, hauling himself up. In spite of my happiness I look down, a bit concerned.

Tucker hasn't moved. He just stands there, his little eyes flickering back and forth. The woman throws me a little smile and nods encouragingly.

I step closer to him and kneel down on one knee, getting to eye level to him and put a hand on his back. "Hey little man, what's going on in that big brain of yours, huh?" I keep my voice steady and my tone soft.

His eyes stop flickering over the ATVs and then looks at me, and what I see in his eyes breaks my heart.

"Are you going to give it to me then take it away? Because if so I don't want it." He almost whispers this in a thin voice, and I see his chin tremble. He wants to want it so bad, but doesn't trust it.

"Tuck," I say, tilting my head at him. "I already bought it. It's yours. I promise."

"But what if-what if-"

I shake my head. "There's no what if, Tuck. If you want it, it's yours. No strings attached. We'll keep it in my shed because there's no room at your mom's place, but it's yours."

We stare at each other for a bit, and I let him take his time. He looks over and sees his brother making little revving noises with a look of abandon on his face.

"You know, I think you'll look super cool on the red one. They'll match your shades." I encourage. Tucker stares at me again.

Please trust me Tuck, I won't hurt you like he does. I yell it so loud in my head, hoping that the thought will somehow magically appear in whatever strange invisible twin channel he and his brother use to silently communicate. And as if the Gods decided to be kind and grant me a miracle, Tucker turns and heads to the red one. I share a look of my own with the woman.

"And can we get the white one as well?" I call to her, solidifying Lolita's ATV color.

She lets me know that I am ready to pull my truck up to the loading area and I give her my signature on her tablet.

I leave the boys to their excitement for a moment and stepping aside, I pull up my phone. My friend Stephen answers on the second ring.

"Hey Hud, what's up man?" Steven's voice rings through clear, and I can hear the going ons of the shop in the background.

"Hey Steve, can you fit me in, in about an hour? I have three little jobs for you. They shouldn't take long. I'll pay you extra for the convenience."

"Sure, what are you needing done?"

I motion to the boys to come to me and turn on my heel. Placing my free hand on Tucker's shoulder I squeeze gently and tell Steven what I need as me and the twins head out of the store and to my truck. Backing the trailer efficiently into the loading area, and waiting for the workers to load our purchase.

"We got one more stop, kiddos." I call back before making sure they're buckled in right and get their shades on.

Cracking the windows we pull off into the afternoon highway traffic towards Stevens' shop.

Three hours later after another pit stop at the mall where we get Lola the perfume Tucker told me about, we're halfway home. Looking in the rearview mirror, I see Tatum looking out the window with a goofy smile on his face, looking excited. But it's Tucker I'm curious about. Flickering my gaze to his reflection, I see him looking down at the key to his ATV attached to a thin chain around his neck.

The look he gave me when I slid the chain over his head made my chest puff out and my throat burn. And though I am not opposed to men crying, I was not about to make that moment about me.

The hug he gave me right after...yeah. I left the boys with Steve and had to go to the men's restroom for a second and let a tear or two fall. Because though he broke it in the ATV store with his reaction, the boy put my heart back together in that simple affectionate gesture watching his name get sprayed in big black letters, naming his ATV.

A name for each one, Tatum, Tucker, and Lolita.

I'm back! Oh Hudson, it was sooo lovely. Thank you so much. Dinner's in the oven.-Lola

I smile at her text, seeing it pop on the screen of my truck. Not even knowing what the meal is yet, my mouth waters at the thought of a home cooked dinner I didn't have to make. The sun sets as we cross the bridge and I see the boys in the back knocked out. Tatum's glasses are sliding off his face, making me smile even wider. Feeling this moment in time is so goddamn perfect I never want it to end.

I want the boys to be mine. So I need to take care of Dominic.

"Hey baby." I greet her through the truck window with a smile, seeing Lola come through the front doorway of the house as I pull up.

I roll my window up and climb out the truck, closing it softly so as to not disturb the sleeping boys in the backseat. My eyes roam greedily, her hair is down and wavy, and she's in a really pretty white dress that hugs her curves and flares out in a flowy pattern at her hips down to her mid calf.

But what really gets me excited is that she's in an apron that looks like it has a couple red stains on it. She walks right up to me in a pair of thin dark green flip flops and throws her arms around me. I bend, picking her up to slant my mouth against her in a deep kiss.

"Did they behave?" Lola mumbles quietly against my lips when I let her up enough to take a breath. I smile against her mouth.

"Like little boys should." I assure her.

I place her back on her feet and put my hand on her lower back intimately, pushing her towards the door of the trailer.

"Now, do you want me to wake them up for this or would you like to see what we got for you?"

"No, let's not wake them up, they hardly ever nap so they must have been really excited. Let's let them show me later, but you show me now?" Lola says with a determined smile on her face.

I bend forward again, giving her a little smacking kiss and I reach forward, opening the door to the trailer. She pushes her head forward and squints before her mouth drops open.

"Hudson you didn't." Lola breathes, putting a hand to her mouth.

Her light gray eyes are wide, and she's just staring in shock.

"I did. I really did."

Is this what pure unadulterated joy feels like?

I give her a chuckle, and pull the spare keys out of my pocket to show off her key first, attached to a book charm.

"This one is yours." I hand it to her and then hop in the trailer, reaching to the side to pull out the two ramps to set it up so I can begin to unload the ATVs. When I have it set up I take her wrist and pull her into the trailer with me. "Get on." I instruct her, watching her blink.

She turns a beautiful shade of red from her cheeks to the tips of her ears.

"Hudson, I'm in a *dress!* And I still have my apron on." She protests, but I hop on and pat my thigh, gesturing for her to get in front of me.

"Pull up your dress and come straddle your new toy woman!" I say playfully.

Reaching forward I drag her to me, watching as she pulls up her dress obediently, exposing miles of beautiful tan skin to my gaze before throwing a leg over in front of me and flashing a tiny sliver of black panties. My cock instantly jerks.

I start the ATV and maneuver out of the trailer carefully down the ramp. Giving the engine a little rev, I reach for her hands and place them on the handles, squeezing gently. She lets out a little giggle and we propel the few yards to my shed where I'm storing them and we park it. She has tears in her eyes seeing her name on the side.

"Hudson, I don't know what to say." She sniffs, bringing up the back of her hand to wipe an errant tear away.

"You don't have to say anything, Loli. It was my pleasure."

I take her hand and we head back to the trailer and grab the other two, with her riding in front of me each time. We walk back hand in hand. I grab Tucker from one side of the truck, and she grabs Tatum.

Staying silent, we carry them into the house and into the room they like to sleep in. Tucking them in carefully.

"We can wake them up in thirty minutes for dinner." Lola whispers as she pulls their door closed.

But I'm already on her. She lets out a surprised gasp as I snatch her to me and kiss her senselessly, pushing her against the wall and dragging the hem of her dress and the apron up.

"Wrap your legs around me baby." I instruct as I lift her. Pulling her panties to the side, I take my freed dick and line it up with her and looking into her eyes, I slowly but firmly press all the way in. "Shhhh." I console her ragged gasp, knowing how big I am, and knowing that she struggles at times depending on her mood. And because I didn't soften her up, and we're right outside the boys room, I don't ram into her the way I sometimes do.

No, this is a time for connection and sweetness.

I'll fuck her properly later when we're in bed and have the whole night to ourselves.

But I gotta say, the fact I'm fucking her with this apron on, and knowing she's still cooking has got me hot. So I place my hand over her mouth, and begin to thrust, making her bob up and down. Her wavy hair bounces and she clenches her thighs tight around me as I rock us. I grunt softly, feeling her breath warm and moist against my hand.

She's struggling to keep her sex sounds down, and I struggle myself momentarily, wanting to make her do that throaty scream I adore so much.

I fuck her steadily against the wall for several long minutes, feeling her dripping down my length. She's wetting my balls with her excitement and I grind our sexes a little harder, a little rougher this time, and she lets out a strangled moan against my palm. Making my heart race.

"That's it beautiful," I feel her sucking, throbbing at me, and pretty soon lewd sucking sounds fill the air around us. "You got this, come on."

I thrust her up the wall sharply and she sucks in five short, sharp breaths before she whimpers and flinches against me, slamming her knees hard against my ribcage before she breaks.

Her eyelashes flutter closed and she sounds like she's almost crying against my hand with the force of her orgasm. The tight, rhythmic throbbing of her around my dick has me falling over with her on a soft grunt, and I lean against her, placing my forehead against hers as I remove my hand from her mouth.

"Holy shit." Lola breathes, keeping her eyes closed as she attempts to calm her breathing.

I nod against her, jerking my dick inside her playfully, making her giggle. Keeping her wrapped around me I turn us, carrying her into the master bedroom where we clean up quickly and she hurries back to the main part of the house. Leaving her phone on the dresser.

I'm not trying to be nosy, but it keeps lighting up. I'm toweling off, having taken a quick shower. As I run a brush through my hair I pick it up, wondering what's going on that it won't stop buzzing.

You may call me a stalker, and even nosy at times, but never unnecessarily. I scroll through the notifications to see a text come in from someone named "Skee", and then another one. Then a text from Dominic, then a phone call. Then another text from "Skee."

I frown, picking it up and abandoning even putting a shirt on, I pick up her phone and journey down the hallway towards the kitchen. Seeing the boy's bedroom door still closed, I tap once before opening it and leaning in, switching on the dimmed lighting feature instead of the blaring overhead light.

"Hey you two." I call out softly. "Tate, Tuck, wake up, it's almost time for dinner."

I wait until they stir and open their eyes before I head back down the hallway, taking the stairs quickly as Lola's phone will not stop buzzing.

She's bending down into the oven, pulling out a mouthwatering lasagna when I round the corner barefoot, and bare chested. Making my way with purpose to her.

"Loli baby, your phone won't stop ringing. Dominic has tried to contact you, *and* someone named Skee."

I catch her sharp look at me before she throws the pot holders down and takes her phone from my hand, turning it to herself and using her facial recognition feature to open the screen.

"Thank you," she murmurs.

I wait there briefly, seeing the lasagna still bubbling, wondering if she's going to explain who this 'Skee' person is. However, I don't have to wait long because she surprises me and calls him first.

"Hey." She exhales hard as if she's already frustrated. "I'm sorry I didn't pick up, I wasn't by my phone."

My brow arches as I lean my hips against the island and fold my arms, wondering why she jumped immediately to apologize. Who the hell is Skee? I feel my nose twitch as irritation floods me, two men trying like hell to contact my woman at the same time will do that to you.

Lola pauses for a second as an irritated look of her own flashes across her face before she sighs, putting a hand up and rubbing her forehead.

"I'm sorry. I'll call him-" she cuts off, being interrupted. "Listen, I'm trying my best here. I know, I know you told me not to get involved with him but I can't do anything about that now, *eight years later.* No, I don't expect you to keep throwing money at the situation, Skee. I'm trying to navigate this the best I can!" She pauses again, pursuing her lips. "I *know* you're fucking busy, you haven't even called them to talk to them lately!"

Then her face flushes. "Dumbass." She grits through clenched teeth.

My brow lifts.

She gasps. *"Puta!"*

I know what the word means. I growl feeling a muscle tick in my jaw and I push off the counter to intervene but she turns quickly, snapping into the phone.

"I get it, Skee. My mistake. I don't know what to do, okay?" Lola puts a hand to her nape and squeezes hard. "I *know* he can blackmail you if you try to handle it-*Goddammit shut up for a second will you let me talk."*

Her frustration and anger seals the deal for me and I snap. Reaching forward, I pull the phone out of her hand and hold it up to my ear, causing her eyes to go wide.

"You need to fix your tone." I snap.

My eyes narrow and I jerk my head and arm out the way when Lolita's eyes go wide and she tries to grab for the phone.

"Hudson, *no!"* She whispers, her eyes are wide in alarm. "Give it back!"

"Who is this?" Skee's voice is deep, cultured.

Hoity-toity.

His voice sounds so familiar it bothers me. But that doesn't bother me the most, the way he curates his reply, however, does. It's way too careful and secretive for my liking. He pauses for a long second before orchestra noise in the background fades away, and he sounds like he enters in a very quiet space

"I'm sorry, *who is this?"* I say in a clipped tone.

I don't like seeing Lola freak out like this. Hearing her phone ping I look at her notifications and see Dominic, *again*.

"I'm not telling you that."

I raise an eyebrow at Lola, she's biting her lip and fidgeting. I hold out my arm and she walks into me, putting her hand on my chest.

"Lola may not know what to do but *I might*. What's going on with Dominic."

"He keeps calling me and threatening me for more money. I've given him almost a million dollars in the last year so he won't keep those kids from me but-" He stops, obviously catching himself saying too much.

"Why do you need to pay to see the boys?" I ask, confused. Really hoping it clicks soon because *damn*.

"He gives Lola a hard time, won't allow her to let me see them. But if I pay, he doesn't give her grief and I can get them when I want."

"I'm sorry, who are you?" I ask again.

"I'm her brother."

"Oh," I say, freshly irritated that I had to jump through hoops in order to get that info. "Well why couldn't you *just say that then?*"

Then my brow furrows as it hits me. *He's paid a million dollars in a year to see the boys.* My eyes slide to Lola. I tighten my lips because I'm about to make it worse.

"Because, we keep our lives separate except for the boys. I know it's not ideal, but it works better this way because of who I am."

I blink and turn my head to address Lolita. "You into some cartel drug shit?" I say plainly to her.

She recoils her head and throws me a rather offended look. You'd think she'd be used to my bluntness by now. But Skee jumps in, and he heaves a truly long suffering sigh if I ever heard one.

"No she's not in with *the fucking cartel*. Goddamn man. I work in Hollywood, *okay?* I'm a movie director. You know, with celebrities? Lola doesn't want to be a part of this life and I respect that. But Dominic knows, and he's using my status-our status, for money."

"Oh." I say simply. Hearing the phone ping again I glance at it, hearing the boys coming into the kitchen I pull away from Lola and whisper "I got this." Making my way through the sliding doors to the screened in outdoor patio.

"Hey," I say to Skee, clearing my throat. "We obviously don't know each other, and I don't know how much you know about me-"

"Lo's told me she's seeing you. She offered to bring you up to meet me but I turned her down. I'm sorry, I don't need another Dominic."

"I don't know how much you know about me," I continue, not liking being interrupted. "But I do not need your money, I have enough of my own. And I could care less about your status." I pause, my eyes perusing the background of my property as I debate my next words. "But this Dominic thing is worrisome. Are you aware of how badly this man treats your nephews?"

Skee pauses himself. "What do you mean?" He asks, his voice turns from slightly irritated to super serious.

"Well, the fact that he pits the boys against each other. Tucker seems to want nothing to do with him, the couple of interaction's I've witnessed between them is worrisome. He withholds affection, him and Tucker do not speak. And the way he looks at Lolita." I squeeze my eyes shut, wanting to hurt the man, but I have to stick to the plan so I don't get caught.

"No. I didn't know that. I barely get the boys and when I do, It's always around a time that I have work so I end up taking them to a premiere or something like that. I take what I can get but I don't have a lot of time to chit chat."

I grunt. Giving up, I put him on speaker and open her phone and pull up the notifications from Dominic.

"Hold up, he's texting non-stop blowing up her phone." I scroll through.

Call me. Now.-Dominic

Do you not see my venmo requests?-Dominic

Why aren't you answering the phone? You have my boys, you should always make yourself available when you have them.-Dominic

I'm outside your house, where are you?-Dominic

Skee is ignoring me.-Dominic

Bitch I'm fucking taking you to court for full custody since you want to be so nasty.-Dominic

That piece of shit man at your shop can't save you. He won't always be around.-Dominic

I need forty two hundred dollars tonight. Tonight Lolita.-Dominic

I read them all to him. Hating she has to be subjected to this. I screenshot it and send it all to my phone. I give Skee my phone number and make him text me so I have his information.

"I just googled you man, you do good for yourself." He says, surprising me.

"Thanks. So head's up, I'm getting ready to call him, and I need you to record our conversation."

Skee is silent, then blows out a breath. "Here we go. I knew this shit was going to come to a head at some point."

I make quick work of it and dial Dominic on three way. He answers on the second ring.

"You fucking bitch, don't you ever make me wait that long again-"

I interrupt him. "Dominic, you must like having to go to the hospital huh?" My voice is stern and I hear him cut off quickly, obviously not prepared to hear a man's voice on the other end of Lolita's line. "I suggest you make this your last phone call until you have to pick the boys up on Wednesday."

"Who is this?"

There's that question of the day. My nose twitches at how much of an idiot he is.

"You already know. You remember me. I put that mark behind your ear?" I pause for a few seconds, letting him remember. "You are done with this sick behavior towards Lola and the boys. Straighten up your attitude, and do not ask her for money anymore. How as a man, does it sit right with you to hold your hand out to a woman? The mother of your children? And then to her brother? I can't believe God wasted a dick on you. And by the way, if you retaliate against her *or the boys* because I called you, you better be prepared for the repercussions."

"Oh you mean she hasn't told you I fucked her last week when she gave me that money?" His voice is smug.

My chest tightens at the thought, even though I know it's a lie. Welcoming the cool fall breeze coming through the half open, screened in window, I let it calm the flush of anger that's erupted on my skin.

"Dominic, you *might* can play these games with someone else who isn't as aware as I am, but your manipulation isn't going to work on me. There's no way she fucked you."

"Yeah? Prove it."

"I don't need to prove it. I know what she tastes and smells like by herself, *and* with me all over her skin marking her. You haven't fucked her. I hope for your sake you know better than to cross that boundary, because what I said that day in the storage room still stands brother. You're really getting on my bad side."

"Uh huh, well if you know what's good for you then *you* can start paying me. I'll stay away from her if the price is right."

I chuckle because his audacity is quite idiotic.

"You're going to stay away from her regardless. I'm not giving you access to my money you worthless piece of shit. Lola is *mine*, she belongs to *me* and I don't appreciate you fucking with my things. So, if you continue to push me, you're in for a world of hurt."

I hang up on him and then block him, making a mental note to unblock him on Wednesday. My job is done, he knows there's another dick in the equation.

Skee grunts. *"Your things, huh?"*

"Yeah. But you don't need to worry your pretty little Hollywood head about that. Hang on." I say to Skee. I work quickly, dialing Clayton.

"Hello?" Clayton answers hesitantly, probably due to not knowing Lolita's number.

"It's me. I need a favor."

"Oh hey Hud. What's up man? You got a new number?"

"No." I snap, God he can irk sometimes. "I'm calling from Lolita's phone. Hey, I need you to install some cameras around Lolita's home and the surrounding area facing the backyard, I need the tech feed forwarded to her brother's phone."

"Okay I'm on it, what's her brother's name?"

Skee answers quickly. "Alejandro Perez."

I go silent and I can just hear Clayton's jaw drop through the phone. When the man said Hollywood I didn't realize he meant *elite* Hollywood. I know this man has at least two Oscars. No wonder Dominic was trying to milk them for money, and no wonder Lola preferred the quiet life. I would too.

Her brother's notoriety is literally infamous enough that even *I* knew about it. Not to mention he just directed a movie with my favorite actor. Goddamn it, now I *have* to keep him on my good side.

Clayton recovers quickly, slipping into professional mode making me proud, and thankful. "I'll have it in by the end of the day tomorrow." Clayton says in a professional clipped tone and I bite my cheek, already knowing I'm going to be hearing the shit tomorrow.

Maybe tonight, even.

Just then, a knock sounds on the glass and I turn, seeing Tucker wave at me. I throw him a smile, seeing Lola just beyond him at the island, plating up lasagna and putting salad into bowls. She bends down to give Tatum a kiss on the forehead as he's lingering close, keeping his arm around her waist. Those boys love her, their easy affection is a sight for sore eyes.

I finish my conversation quickly, hang up with the men, and then journey back into the kitchen, walking right up to Lolita, who looks worried.

"What happened?" She whispers, keeping her voice low.

I ignore the question, preferring to not talk about it in front of the boys.

"Thank you, for trusting me to handle that." I say to her, leaning in to kiss her lips and pull back swiftly, seeing we have an audience. Two pairs of eyes who don't miss much. Giving them a wink I lean back against the counter and pin them with a stare. "Your uncle is pretty cool. Do you two like going to his big movies when you see him?"

Lolita's jaw drops, I'm sure she's surprised how much information I was able to gleam from her brother in such a short amount of time. I turn my face from her, still focusing on the two boys in front of me. Her and I will have all night, but they only get about three more hours before bedtime.

We can talk while I'm inside her later in bed if we need to.

Tatum smiles a huge smile. "Yes! The parties are so fun Hudson! We got to go to one a while ago and we got to wear a very fancy suit!"

"Ohhh it sure does sound fancy. What about you Tucker, do you like wearing a suit to the parties?" I grin at him, wanting him to open up more, not just when he comes to get me in the middle of the night.

Tucker nods, seemingly more interested in the lasagna than the fancy party his brother is referring to. I know then that there's going to be one twin chasing the spotlight, and the other will want to be in the background. I reach forward and ruffle their dark curls affectionately.

"I'm going to grab a shirt to put on. Help your mom put the food on the table. Be right back." I bound back up the stairs and hurriedly pull on a dark blue t-shirt, keeping my feet bare.

We sit at the table and eat, and the boys tell me how excited they are to take their four wheelers out for a ride tomorrow.

"Hey Hudson, can I get a snake tattoo like what you have? It's badass!" Tatum says suddenly, causing Lola to choke on her food.

I push her lemonade to her, keeping my eyes focused on Tatum.

"Tatum that's a bad word, and you're too young to use it. Where'd you hear it?"

His eye's go wide. "My dad. H-He said I could use it."

My fingers wrap around Lolita, tightening enough to let her know to keep quiet while I handle this. Boys need a strong male to look up to, and to not always be disciplined by their mother.

"Now Tate, that's not a good word to use. Boys your age should not be using such language especially in front of your mother. It's disrespectful." I pin him with a hard stare. "You should apologize to her, and not let it happen again."

Tatum rolls his lips and looks at his mom, flushing with embarrassment. "Sorry mami, won't happen again. I promise."

Lola nods and gives him a little smile. "Thank you Tate, that means a lot to me. Um...and it's a no to that tattoo, but maybe we can talk about it when you're a little older, okay?"

"So," he says with his eyes brightening up. "So it's not a no?"

"Hey, what about me?" Tucker speaks up, sounding offended.

Lolita's eyes go wide. "Boys!" She chastises with her brow furrowed. *"Where's this coming from all of a sudden?"*

"Hudson!" Both boys damn near yell my name together. "Hudson's tattoo is so cool, and we want one! I want to be just like Hudson one day, he's so *cool!"* Tatum shouts, repeating himself in his excitement.

I just know I have a stupid grin on my face.

"Okay *okay,* calm down!" Lola giggles, leaning forward to pour me some more coffee, seeing it's getting low. I smile at her feeling considered. Heat blossoms in my chest. I wrap this little interaction close to me and imprint it on my memory, never wanting to forget it. I feel like we're a real family.

"Thanks guys," I say gruffly, "I'm so proud that you all look up to me like that. I'll order you some of those fake tattoos online *only if* your mom is okay with it."

Lola tilts her head down, trying to hide a smile, and I wonder if she feels the same way about tonight that I do. Something feels shifted between the four of us that I don't ever want to shift back.

As we continue to eat, we talk for a bit. They tell me about their friends at school, and we eat the most delicious lasagna I've ever had in my life. I throw Lola an appreciative glance and compliment her, placing my hand over hers and squeezing. I catch the boys notice the action, and they throw each other a little look and have a silent, twin conversation.

I just know they haven't seen their dad be tender with their mother like this, and I'm pleased to show them what treating a woman right looks like.

After dinner, I have the boys help me load the dishwasher and we settle in for a movie. They want to watch Pirates Of The Caribbean.

So, for a bit of fun, I give them a little Jack Sparrow Accent while I search for the movie on the big screen, making them laugh hilariously and try to copy me.

Tatum does well with accents, solidifying my instinct that he'll probably try and glom onto his uncle's success and pursue a career in Hollywood,. He sure has the personality.

I love both those boys even more for their differences, knowing that they'll bring a spark into my life regardless of being outgoing or more introspective.

I hope they love me just as much back.

20

PAPI

TUCKER

I TURN OVER AND look at Tatum, sleeping peacefully in bed next to me. Even though we have two beds, he always crawls in here after I go to sleep no matter if I want him in here with me or not.

He always waits till I go to sleep to fall asleep himself. I scrunch my nose, hating that he has to feel like that.

I think we're okay here though, Tate. But I love you for making sure I'm okay. I try to make sure you're okay too....but you don't need protecting the way I do. Dad loves you.

But he hates me.

My eyes sting with tears. I do my best not to cry. And the only time I can is in the middle of the night when everyone else is asleep and I know I'm safe to. I know for a fact I won't be hit me in the middle of the night because Dad's too drunk to care by then.

I don't know why he hates me...why he wants to hurt me. Only me.

It's not like I want him to hurt Tatum, but...*why me?* What did I do so wrong? I only wanted to feel like he loves me.

I look over at Tatum, feeling a tear slip out of my eye. I sniff and brush it away with the sleeve of my pajama top hard, making my skin sting.

Why can't dad love me the way he loves you? Are you the only one he loves? He doesn't love me...or mami...

Why does he hate me, Tate? Have you asked him? You haven't told me that you've asked him or that he's given you an answer. So why won't you help me find out what's wrong, Tate? *What did I do?*

Tate moves in his sleep, kicking his leg out from under the blanket. *Do you love dad? Do you like seeing him do this to me?*

I don't feel like you do...but I don't know. Because you smile at him, and try to touch him...and I just don't understand why you would do that when you see how much he doesn't like me.

Which is weird...because we look exactly alike, we even have the same voice. I'm just not as good at school work the way you are. But I've been working on that. I even think I might have all A's. Mom said I did.

I turn away from Tate, and pull my hand out of his. I always wake up hungry and find his hand in mine. I look back at him, feeling sad.

Why do you touch me like you like me? Why can't you see how hurt I am?

I'm not hungry tonight though. I'm never hungry when I'm at mami's, or Hudson's. No, Hudson put a refrigerator with special snacks in it. And I haven't had to touch it once because he always makes sure I'm full before I leave the table. He even treats me to my favorite dessert.

I get out of bed and head to the door, looking back at Tatum and seeing him sleep with his mouth open. I grab my ATV key from it's hook where it hangs on the wall next to the door. Hudson told me I can't sleep with it, he's worried about me being strangled in my sleep.

It makes me feel happy to know that he's worried about me, about things that might happen to me that haven't yet.

But Hudson... the key won't strangle me. There's something else much bigger and scarier than a key and a necklace.

My dad.

Can I tell *you* how he treats me? Or will he threaten to kill you too? Like he threatens to hurt mami if we tell.

I pad down the hallway and knock on Hudson's bedroom door, I'd like some milk. But I hope he won't be mad at me for doing this again. I just want to feel like I have a dad that loves me. And after the way Hudson treated me this weekend and the last time he was here, I don't think he'll be mad. I hope not.

Will he be?

Wringing my hands, I look over at the lit up iron horse that reminds me of Beauty and I think about sneaking out to her stall. I want to sleep with her. She's so gentle, the only thing I feel I can trust right now to not hurt me, or to disappear when I need them the most.

Not hearing anything, I wait another second then lower my head sadly, taking off my ATV necklace and turning to go back to bed. Pausing, I turn back when I hear footsteps on the floor, and it doesn't sound like mami's footsteps.

I fight to keep a smile off my face, I don't want to look too eager, just in case he's angry. I'm used to being disappointed, but it always hurts when you have your hopes up and you're slapped in the face anyways. Dad has done that enough. I don't think I'm going to call him dad anymore.

The door opens and I stay in the middle of the hallway, not wanting to get too close. Hudson appears in the doorway, running a hand through his hair and he gives me a grin, getting down on one knee. I like that he does that, it makes me feel safe.

"Hey buddy," Hudson reaches out a hand and I step into him, letting him touch my shoulder. He grips me firmly, making me feel like he's got me. "What's the matter? Can't sleep?"

I shake my head. "No, I'm sorry. I was hoping maybe we can have some warm milk again?" My eyes widen at his expression, not sure what's happening in his head. *"O-Or* I can go downstairs and get myself some... if that's okay? *I'll clean it up if I spill some, I swear!"* I try to make him understand I don't want to be a bother.

Hudson shakes his head. "No, buddy, don't worry about that. I was just thinking, why don't we warm up some milk, I'll pack us a thermos, and we can take Beauty for an early morning ride and watch the sun come up? What do you say?"

This time, I can't help the smile that breaks free. He's going to take me on a horse ride too? *Yes!*

"Thank you papi!" I whisper, throwing myself at him and snuggling deep.

Hudson won't hurt me...I just know it deep down. He's not like that bad man at all. He's so different, and he feels like what I should have as a daddy.

Hudson wraps his arms around me and pulls me so hard into him I lose my breath, but I just wrap my arms around his neck and squeeze him back as hard as I can because this is going to be our thing. I just know it.

I know he doesn't mind me squeezing him back like this.

He pats my back, the heavy broad feeling of his hand on my back just assures me that he won't let anything happen to me, and pulls me off his neck. He keeps his face turned away so I can't see him good like I'm trying to.

"Hey," Hudson sniffs and then stands up. "Give me a second to get dressed okay? Go downstairs put your shoes on, and meet me in the pantry. I'll make our milk and then we'll go to the stables and get Beauty ready."

I furrow my brow for a second, Hudson's eyes look wet. But he just gives me a wink and jerks his head for me to get going.

I nod and then try to hurry down the hallway quietly. I'm so excited that I feel like I could bounce off the walls.

A little bit later I'm grinning, sitting on top of Beauty, holding mine and Hudson's warmed milk that he put in two small thermoses. I take a sip of mine, smacking my lips because he makes it just right.

I don't know what he does to it, but even mami doesn't make warmed milk taste like this. Don't tell her that, though.

Hudson hoists himself onto Beauty behind me and takes the reins. Steering us out of the stable and into the night air. I feel him move my helmet slightly, making sure it's tight before his hand reaches in front of me.

"Can I have my thermos bud?"

I hand it to him, his fingers give mine a little squeeze. It feels good. Safe.

He takes it and I hear him take a deep swallow before he lets out a sigh. "Man, Tuck. I haven't had warmed milk in so long I forgot what it tastes like. Thank you for coming into my life and reminding me how much I like it."

I bite my lip...because he likes me too? As much as I like him? He's happy that I brought something to him?

"Milk is good." I say softly.

"Hmm-hmm. Hey, why don't you take the reins? I'll hold our thermos for a bit."

I turn to look at Hudson over my shoulder. He's arching an eyebrow at me and giving me a grin I call the Hudson grin. I grin back.

"Are you sure? What if I mess up? I don't know what I'm doing?"

"You won't mess up bud! Just try it, you might like it." Hudson's voice is low, and calming.

But I just don't know. Can I *really* trust him? What if I'm wrong about Hudson after all? I haven't seen him mad. What if I make him mad? I lose my grin as unease fills me. If I mess up and make Beauty hurt us somehow, or hurt Beauty, will he hate me like dad does?

"No. I-I don't think so. I'd rather not." I say slowly, clutching my thermos harder, wanting to ask him to take us back home.

"Buddy, what's going on in that big brain of yours? Talk to me."

"I just... what if make you mad?"

Hudson's quiet for a second, so long that I wish I could take my words back. Because now he knows that I think he can be mad. And if he knows I think he can be mad, then he might be mad. My bottom lip quivers.

What do I do? Tatum's not here. My heart begins to pound hard in my chest and I feel my eyes well up with tears.

Mami...

Hudson's hand lands on my shoulder and grips gently. Something about it's heaviness and warmth immediately makes me feel better.

"Hey Tuck, I want you to listen to me okay? I'm not going to be mad at you like however your dad is. I'm not saying that I won't *ever* be upset at you in the future though, but I promise, whatever you worry about with your dad, you won't have to worry about with me. Okay, little guy? I won't hurt you, you have my word on that. *I promise.*"

I'm quiet, thinking about his words.

"Do you want to talk about your dad, Tuck? I can see it's bothering you. I want you to know, that you can talk about it."

I shake my head. No I can't. "No. I don't want to." Because he'll hurt mami, and I can't risk that.

"Okay buddy, I'll respect that. But I'm here okay, whenever you're ready. Me and your mom both are. Hey, remember how we made a pact to trust each other?"

I turn again to look at him over my shoulder, feeling Beauty moving under us nice and steady. "Yeah..."

"Well, I trust you to take the reins and let Beauty take us wherever you want. If I see we're about to go somewhere that's unsafe, I'll take back over. Okay? That sound good?"

I debate for a second. Hudson trusts *me?* I swallow thickly, handing him the thermos before I lose my nerve.

"There you go, son. *I'm so proud of you.*"

I feel my heart soar. I've only ever heard my dad say that to Tatum. I feel a tear fall down my cheek and I wipe it away quickly before he can tell he made me cry.

"Now, flick the reins lightly, and take us where you want to go. We've got a lot of ground to cover so don't be shy."

And you know what? I won't be, not this morning. Because Hudson has his hand on my shoulder and he trusts me.

I wonder if I make him feel as safe as he makes me?

I hope so.

This feels good. I feel good. I want to feel like this forever.

But... I know this can't last forever. So, we spend the next hour exploring Hudson's property, and he lets me go wherever I want. Only taking the reins once when we saw a snake in the distance. He told me not to be scared, because even though snakes look scary, they're good for eating rats.

I look over my shoulder at Hudson again, thinking about his tattoo. I wish a snake would eat my dad so I don't have to worry about him anymore.

ALSO BY

S.K. PRESLEY

In You
Mounted(2026)

The Billionaire's Assurance Duet

The Pain We Nurture

The Pain We Allow

Unmasking Me Series:

Lola Unmasked pt. 1

Lola Unmasked pt. 2

Lola Unmasked pt. 3

THE KING DYNASTY SERIES:

THE HEIR

THE SPARE

THE REIGN (2026)

THANK YOU

FOR ALL MY READERS who have supported me along this way, thank you. For all the readers who have in turn become friends who are near and dear to my heart, thank you.

To the over decade and a half of experience I have endured in order to hopefully bring you all realistic characters, thank you for all the lessons.

To all the beautiful souls who endured sleepless nights with me, the various phone calls spent bantering with friends, all the "what if I did this?" questions, thank you for keeping me sane.

To all of you who have supported me through my debut novel The Pain We Nurture and stayed along for this crazy journey, I thank you.

To my betas and alphas, you are invaluable. Absolutely *priceless* to me.

Tia Fanning your conversation, knowledge, and your wit is even more stellar.

Tracy, the emails between us that are probably in the hundreds count. I love you, and I appreciate you. Your support was invaluable.

Jessica, Cheryl, and Ashli, ladies you've been a gem. Like, a beautiful sparkling emerald of a gem.

And to all my misfits, you're adored beyond measure.

Best,

S.K. Presley

www.ingramcontent.com/pod-product-compliance
Lightning Source LLC
Chambersburg PA
CBHW060359260626

47160CB00006B/2367